**The Soviet President's man is missing . . .**

In Moscow, two men are kidnapped. One is dead. One is missing.

In the Kremlin, there is deep fear. For the second man is Brezhnev's personal choice to represent the Soviet press at the Soviet-American summit meeting in Vienna.

In the Soviet government, there are shock waves. Unless the missing man is found, someone will have to inform the President of all the Soviets. It won't be you.

For you have just been given seven days to find the second man—dead or alive.

You or him.

*Berkley books by Edward Topol
and Fridrikh Neznansky*

**DEADLY GAMES**
**RED SQUARE**

# DEADLY GAMES

EDWARD TOPOL AND FRIDRIKH NEZNANSKY

BERKLEY BOOKS, NEW YORK

Translated from the Russian
*Zhurnalist dlya Brezhneva*

This Berkley book contains the revised
text of the original hardcover edition.
It has been completely reset in a typeface
designed for easy reading, and was printed
from new film.

DEADLY GAMES

A Berkley Book/published by arrangement with
Quartet Books

PRINTING HISTORY
Quartet Books edition published 1983
Berkley edition/August 1985

ISBN: 0-425-08021-8

A BERKLEY BOOK ® TM 757,375
Berkley Books are published by The Berkley Publishing Group,
200 Madison Avenue, New York, New York 10016.
The name "BERKLEY" and the stylized "B" with design
are trademarks belonging to Berkley Publishing Corporation.
PRINTED IN THE UNITED STATES OF AMERICA

# Part 1

*Moscow, Monday, June 4 1979, 09:15 hours*

"Shamrayev to the Chief Public Prosecutor's office!" boomed the intercom.

Kolya Baklanov fell silent. He had wandered into my office to tell me how he had spent his vacation. He raised his eyebrows in surprise, wondering what could be going on with the Chief Public Prosecutor and me.

I didn't know either. I pressed a button on the intercom and said, "I'll be there immediately."

"Igor Iosifovich," came the reply, "come as quick as you can. He has to go to the Central Committee on Staraya Square afterwards."

"All right, all right," I said, stuffing into my briefcase the bottle of *Chornye Glaza,* a Soviet wine which Baklanov had brought back from the south. God knows what the prosecutor wanted me for!

I locked the door to my office, told Baklanov what he could do with his sarcastic "Good luck!" and went to the elevator. On my right were the offices of other investigators, "specials" like Baklanov and myself. The safes behind those doors contained the details of scores of sensational crimes, any one of which would have provided the plot for a detective novel or caused a huge stir in the much-vaunted Western press. The affairs of every department of state pass through this building, giving the Public Prosecutor's office enormous power. It's not surprising that when the MVD and the KGB joined forces a few years ago to take the responsibility for carrying out investigations away from us, the Public Prosecutor made such a fuss that the whole affair reached the Politburo. After all, what would the Chief Public Prosecutor have become? A general without an army...

Now what could he want me for? I had just completed

work on a case involving the Ministries of Forestry, Inland Waterways and Railroads. The noose had been drawn very tight, since there was evidence linking two ministers and four railroad chiefs with illegal financial dealings involving hundreds of thousands of roubles. But being summoned to the Chief Prosecutor's office was a bad sign. I walked through the general office and into his reception room. Vera Petelina, his personal assistant, nodded urgently in the direction of the padded double doors which led to his office. I opened them and found myself in the Chief Prosecutor's modest room, which was quite small and not at all what you would have expected of someone in his position. All his deputies had enormous rooms, finished in walnut and fitted with soft furnishings, imported from abroad. But not the Prosecutor himself. No, he was modest. And the secret behind his "modesty" was quite simple. Immediately after the Revolution, in the 1920s, this very building had housed the Central Committee of the All-Union Communist Party—the Bolsheviks, and this tiny room had been the office of the future CPSU Secretary-General, Joseph Stalin. So today's Chief Public Prosecutor finds himself "modestly" sitting in Joseph Stalin's own office, and using the same desk.

The seventy-year-old Prosecutor raised his aging posterior out of the sacred relic of Stalin's armchair, fluffed up now with an extra cushion.

"Ah, Igor Iosifovich," he said, offering me his flabby hand. "Take a seat. You look the picture of health, and yet you're asking to take a vacation. Do sit down."

I am always amazed at how well informed he is. Sometimes he doesn't see his subordinates for months on end, yet he knows every little thing about us.

"Well, it *is* my turn to take a vacation, Roman Andreyevich," I replied. Realizing I was now on the defensive, I sat down in the chair next to his desk. "And there seems to be a trip available to Gelendzhik . . ."

"I'm afraid it won't work out," the Prosecutor replied sorrowfully. "But how do you like your new apartment?"

So he knew about that, too. After my divorce from Irina I had spent a couple of years moving from friend to friend, renting a room here and there. Nobody paid any attention to it. The authorities and the party committee don't approve of people getting divorced. But a month ago, by some miracle, I'd managed to get a co-operative apartment—really out in the sticks, beyond the Izmailovsky Park. No sooner had I moved in, it seemed, than the whole Public Prosecutor's Department was buzzing with the news: "Shamrayev's got a co-op!"

"Thank you, Roman Andreyevich," I replied cautiously. "The apartment is fine. It's a little ways from downtown, but that doesn't matter. It's habitable."

"I should say so! With the park next door, fresh air, mushrooms! What do you need to take a vacation for? Why waste your money?" His watery, bulbous eyes held me in their pale questioning gaze, as if he had summoned me here solely to convince me not to travel to Gelendzhik and spend all my money, seeing as how the marvelous Izmailovsky Park was spread out so invitingly beneath my balcony. "Or have you got more money than you know what to do with? You have just bought yourself an apartment, after all . . ."

I laughed. When you've got nothing to feel guilty about and you're as poor as a church mouse, you can afford to laugh, even in the face of a Chief Public Prosecutor.

"The local trade union committee's mutual benefit scheme provided the money, Roman Andreyevich," I replied. "You can check, if you like."

"My dear fellow, what do you mean?" he said, sitting back in his chair with a reproachful smile. But we understood each other and he finally adopted a more businesslike tone.

"No, Igor Iosifovich. Let's postpone your trip. There's no reason to blow the local trade union committee's money to the wind, either. You know the old expression: borrow other people's money, but give away your own. In any case, it's not right that a special investigator should be forced to buy a co-operative apartment miles from anywhere and waste two hours a day traveling back and forth. As if the city council couldn't provide you with a new state-owned apartment in the middle of town! I'll have a word with Promyslov. Now . . . Take this file away with you. It contains one body whose whereabouts are known, and another whose aren't.

That's all. It won't delay you very long. Only it *is* urgent..."

He handed me a gray file bearing the following inscription: *MVD USSR. Investigation No. SL–79–1542. Begun May 26 1979.* Today was June 4, so the case had been started nine days earlier. I knew that nothing good would come from this summons. There's nothing worse than taking over a case that someone else has already begun: It will be all messed up. Dirty marks will be everywhere: every lead will be broken, all the evidence jumbled, the witnesses picked clean for no purpose, the criminals put on their guard ...The Chief Public Prosecutor certainly knows how to screw you! And how gently he does it, even offering you an apartment in the center of town! And not even a co-operative one, but one belonging to the state—and costing practically nothing. So what kind of priceless corpse is this that the Prosecutor is talking about? Whose body is it? I hope not the son or daughter of some big government wheel who's been bumped off. In that case, it wouldn't be so much a question of an investigation as of making polite inquiries. Just try cross-examining Kosygin or Suslov! And if you go to see them, they'll soon tell you where to get off—and you'll have only yourself to blame. The whole game isn't worth it—it has to be you, a special investigator, who carries out the inquiries. They wouldn't entrust the case to anyone lower in the hierarchy. Can you imagine letting a simple investigator near any government corpse?

So there I was, holding this gray folder in my hands, not daring to open it. It could have been a landmine. "So whose body was it?" I asked.

"Just go ahead and open the folder, and don't worry," said the Prosecutor with a laugh, as if he could read my thoughts. "One of the bodies is a tramp, a drug addict from somewhere in the Caucasus. And the other one, the one that hasn't been found yet, well ... Do you read *Komsomolskaya Pravda?*"

"Well, yes..." I said, somewhat uncertainly.

"Have you ever come across the name of Belkin?"

"Yes, I have," I replied. In fact, this was one of the three or four journalists' names that I really do know. It was Vadim Belkin, I think. Yes, I'd read some of his articles about the deserts of Central Asia, the fishermen of the Tyulkino fleet, and the border police. He always chose gripping subjects from everyday life to write about. His style was simple, even conversational, but what he wrote was always absorbing, as if he hadn't been infected by the usual run of journalistic clichés. I looked at the Prosecutor and said, "Has he really been murdered?"

But there was no time for him to reply. Vera Petelina's voice suddenly interrupted our conversation. "Roman Andreyevich, it's the Kremlin on the line—Comrade Suslov."

The Prosecutor lifted the receiver off the red telephone, which sat by itself on a separate table. I got up to leave, so as not to disturb the conversation, but he motioned me to stay where I was. He had turned away from me slightly and I could see him in profile. Two stars indicating his marshal's rank were sewn onto the collar of his uniform, and they were pressing against the folds of his somewhat flabby neck. Yes, I thought, the former scourge of the Nuremburg trials is getting on now. This fat, tired old man was the one who ought to be gathering mushrooms in the Izmailovsky Park, but here he is, a marshal, sitting in Stalin's former office and rising to the occasion, as always.

"He's already dealing with it . . . Of course . . . The best we have available . . . The most energetic of our people . . . By the eleventh at the very latest, I understand . . . Of course, I'll keep an eye on it personally . . . Of course, alive if possible . . . No, I think we'll be able to manage without the KGB . . ."

I felt a sinking feeling in the pit of my stomach. Were they really discussing the case we had been discussing? If that were so, then everything the Prosecutor was saying referred to me. I thought hard. What was this all about—"the most energetic", "the best we have", and so on? What about Baklanov? He'd just come back from his vacation and had more experience than me . . .

Meanwhile the Prosecutor had hung up and turned to face me.

"Did you follow all that?"

"All what?" I said, pretending not to have heard, let alone to have understood anything.

He gave me a hard stare for a few seconds, as if making

up his mind and then endorsing his decision.

"Look, Igor Iosifovich," he said, "I know that this is a difficult case. But there is no choice. Andropov and Shcholokov are just biding their time. If I refuse to take it on, they'll say to the Central Committee, 'Look, here he is. He won't surrender responsibility for criminal investigation to us, but he refuses to take on the difficult ones.' So listen to what I have to say. In ten days' time, on June 15, Comrade Brezhnev will be flying to Vienna to meet Carter. He'll be accompanied by a press corps consisting of five of our best journalists. Leonid Ilyich confirmed the selection of participants himself long ago, and Belkin was his own personal choice. But two weeks ago Belkin disappeared at the Kursk railroad station in Moscow. He was meeting some dubious acquaintance of his, a drug addict from the Caucasus. The two of them were thrown into a car in the square right in front of the station and driven off somewhere. Two days later the drug addict's body was found underneath a bridge outside the city, with a broken skull. Meanwhile there was no trace of Belkin at all. Whether they've killed him or not, how are we supposed to tell Comrade Brezhnev that the journalist he chose personally to accompany him to Vienna has disappeared without a trace?"

So that was it, I thought. Belkin didn't matter. Nobody was concerned with him, even if he was a really talented journalist. He'd disappeared, and that was that. What was really getting the Prosecutor and all the others going was the question of how to tell Brezhnev. Here is Brezhnev on the eve of his momentous meeting with Carter, and someone is supposed to go up to him and say that they can't find his favorite journalist. "What do you mean, you can't find him?" Brezhnev would reply. "Where is he?" "We haven't the faintest idea, Leonid Ilyich" . . . No, it was absolutely certain that no one would risk saying such a thing to Brezhnev, especially just before his departure abroad. And yet, on the other hand, somebody would have to tell him, if . . .

"So, you see, Belkin has to be found, dead or alive. By the eleventh," said the Prosecutor, appearing to read my thoughts again. "Of course, it would be better if he were found alive," he continued, "but that doesn't depend on you. On the twelfth the journalists are due to be briefed by

Zamyatin and Suslov. Two days later they're due to have lunch with Leonid Ilyich himself, and on the fifteenth they fly to Vienna. Now there's no question of sending a corpse along to lunch on the fourteenth, as you can see. Which means that the latest time for finding out what has happened to him is Monday, June 11. You've got seven days at your disposal, just like God. If you can resurrect Belkin in that time, you'll have a chestful of medals, a place in the middle of Moscow, and you'll be promoted to the rank of senior juridicial counselor, despite your ... er ... youth."

I think that he had some impediment other than my age in mind, but he thought better of it at the last moment and used a different word. And if I didn't suspect myself of oversensitivity, I would say that I knew what he was driving at. He had in mind my Jewish patronymic, or, to be more exact, my half-Jewish origins. People might hurry over my patronymic, but there was no getting away from my Jewish background. Certain people have had their careers ended for less.

So Belkin might be my Waterloo, God damn him!

"But even so, Roman Andreyevich, I've just completed work on a very important case, and I'm really overdue for a vacation. And there's plenty of time for me to gain promotion to senior counselor ... when I get a bit older," I added with a certain air of defiance.

This attempt to get out of it was, of course, rather clumsy. The Prosecutor made a wry face. He leaned back in his chair and eyed me coldly from head to foot.

"Well, this is the position, Igor Iosifovich. The Central Committee has ordered us to find Belkin, dead or alive, by the eleventh. And I'm entrusting the case to you. If you feel that it is beyond your capabilities, then tell me so officially at 9 a.m. tomorrow, and I shall draw my own conclusions. And it's an interesting case, too. I've glanced through it myself. Drug addicts, journalists, and all that. The only thing is, you'll get pestered from above. But then who isn't? Do you think I'm spared myself? Now, why don't you just get on with it?"

He stood up and reached across the table to shake my hand. "And don't forget that you've got complete freedom of action in this affair, including the Petrovka. But then you know all this yourself. Consider yourself as working on behalf of the Central Committee and assume whatever powers you need. If you find Belkin alive, you'll be getting all of us out of an awkward situation, Zamyatin and Suslov included. Also . . . not that this really matters," he added with a smile, as if suddenly remembering something, "my grand-niece is head over heels in love with Belkin. He gave a couple of lectures at the Faculty of Journalism, or something, and they're all nuts about him. Not that it's of any importance, of course. They didn't have an affair, don't worry."

So that's what it's all about! Brezhnev, Suslov, *Komsomolskaya Pravda,* my foot! Rudenko's grand-niece is in love with him! To hell with all of you! A special investigator is to be used to find the Chief Prosecutor's grand-niece's boyfriend! They've certainly got enough people to do their bidding! And it wouldn't be so bad if these bosses were the only ones you had to serve; at least they hold important positions. But no! You're expected to serve their grand-nieces, too! I remembered a rather stunning, long-legged creature with a teenager's sultry looks. I wondered whether she fell for Belkin *before* he became Brezhnev's favorite journalist, or after.

I went back to my own office and hurled Belkin's file into the corner of the room. As it flew by the table, it took a paperweight with it. The crash echoed so loudly down the corridor that Baklanov looked out of the adjacent office.

"What's wrong? Want to go and have a beer?"

"Yes, let's go," I said angrily. "They can all go fuck themselves. Be their servant? I'd rather become a defense lawyer!"

"Be whose servant?" asked Baklanov curiously.

I looked him in the eye and replied with great emphasis, "The working people!"

If the walls of the Prosecutor's Department have ears (an assumption that cannot be dismissed)—so much the better. Let them hear! Meanwhile Baklanov and I went off to have a few brews.

*Secret*

To the Moscow Prosecutor
State Juridicial Counselor Second Class
Comrade Mikhail Grigoryevich Malkov

### SPECIAL REPORT

In accordance with Secret Instruction No. 24 dated August 5 1971, requiring that you be personally informed immediately of any cases of violent death occurring within the area of Greater Moscow, I have to inform you of the following:

On May 26 1979, at 6:15 a.m., an unidentified corpse was found by a track maintenance man at the foot of a railroad bridge, crossing the Moscow River in the area of Tsaritsyno Ponds about fifty yards from the Moscow River railroad station on the line to Kursk. The body is that of a young man aged between seventeen and twenty years and bears the marks of a violent death.

The corpse has visible injuries such as scratches and contusions, which were inflicted while the victim was still alive and which indicate a measure of self-defense on the victim's part. In the opinion of the forensic expert, death was the result of damage to the skull inflicted by a heavy object or by being hit against a heavy object. The most likely thing to have happened is that the victim was hurled onto the tracks from a moving train. No papers were found on the corpse. The word "Sultan" is tattooed on the back of his hand, and both forearms show the marks of injections from a hypodermic syringe.

A CID investigation team traveled to the spot where the corpse was found. The murder investigation has been transferred to the Moscow River Prosecutor's Department, in whose area the crime took place. The murder inquiry is being led by Investigator V. N. Pshenichny.

At the same time I have given instructions for the Head of the Second Section of the CID Third Department, Lieutenant-Colonel M. A. Svetlov, to take active measures to uncover the perpetrators of this crime.

CID Head
Mayor-General P. Minayev

Moscow, May 26 1979

It is a well-known fact that beer weakens the system and a bar relaxes the nerves. After our third pint of *Zhigulyovskoye*, Baklanov and I decided to view life philosophically. If I saw that the case wasn't worth it, then I would say so to the Prosecutor the first thing in the morning, and go away on leave. And there wouldn't be a thing the Chief Public Prosecutor could do about it. You don't find investigators like us growing on trees. If worst came to worst, I could become a defense lawyer. And if I came unglued, so what? Fishing out logs of wood in the River Pechora was no worse than looking for the grand-niece's boyfriend. Although the latter would be more interesting: you were looking for a living person, after all. Only what was the connection between him and the corpse of "Sultan"?

*Secret*

To CID Head
Major-General P. A. Minayev

OFFICIAL TELEGRAM

Concerning the discovery of an unidentified corpse on May 26 1979 near Moscow River railroad station, I have to report the following:

On May 26 at approximately 10:30 a.m. outside the liquor store in the village of Lenino-Dachnoye, a certain Aleksey Popov, a person who has been compulsorily dried out from alcohol in the past, sold a diamond necklace weighing one carat and worth 1,750 roubles to Citizen M. P. Korkoshko for 50 roubles. Drinking in the company of friends, Popov announced that earlier that day he had accidentally discovered a document case, containing jewelry, in bushes not far from Tsaritsyno Ponds.

A CID agent nicknamed "Carthorse" was present at this conversation. At a signal from him we arrested Popov. The impounded document case was found to contain diamonds, jewelry, rings, earrings, and pendants of great rarity. According to the preliminary estimates of experts, the valuables are worth no less than 100,000 roubles.

Since the document case was not found far from the spot where the corpse was discovered, I took steps to have the case dusted for fingerprints. This revealed prints from the right hand of the man whose body was discovered near the railroad platform on May 26. This would indicate that the document case belonged to the deceased, and was thrown from the train 850 yards from the spot where the body itself was ejected.

Head of Second Section
CID Third Department
Lieutenant-Colonel M. Svetlov

Moscow, May 27 1979

You need to know how to read the official documents that form part of a criminal investigation. The important thing about this telegram was not that jewelery had been discovered, nor even that it belonged to "Sultan", but that Lieutenant-Colonel Svetlov had taken the initiative himself, and, also, that his efforts and those of his agents had been successful. Nor had he lost any time in informing the head of Moscow CID of their success. This was the real reason for sending the telegram in the first place, I said to myself with a smile. After all, I knew Svetlov's character. He was clever, but he liked to boast.

I leafed through some of the other documents in the file. I came across something which had more to do with Belkin himself.

### REPORT OF EXAMINATION AND TRANSFER
### OF DOCUMENTS

May 28 1979, Moscow
... An examination of the incident book at the Kursk Station Militia Office in Moscow has revealed that on May 24 1979, at 12:56 hours, the duty officer, Captain Abushakhmin, was approached by a woman called Aina Silinya, born in 1962, an inhabitant of Riga, who was passing through Moscow. She reported that she had seen

four unknown criminals seize Yury Rybakov and Vadim Belkin at the taxi stand outside the Kursk railroad station and forcibly throw them into a car. In her account Silinya mentioned that she and her acquaintance, Yury Rybakov, had arrived in Moscow by train from Baku on May 24. On the platform they were met by Yury's friend, the journalist Vadim Belkin. When the three of them walked up to the taxi stand on the square in front of the station, they were unexpectedly approached by an old *Rafik* ambulance, the registration number of which she had no time to memorize. Four men got out (two of them were dressed in white overalls) and rushed at Rybakov and Belkin from behind, shouting out as follows to the people standing in line: "Comrades, help us capture these mental patients!" Drowning out the protests of Rybakov and Belkin, they pushed them into the ambulance. Then one of them, who was in his early fifties with metal teeth, grabbed Aina Silinya with one hand and tried to force her into the ambulance as well. She bit his arm and managed to escape. People standing in the line tried to help the so-called medical orderlies by stopping her, but the former, seeing a militiaman approaching, hurriedly got into the ambulance and drove off.

Having made her statement, witness A. Silinya returned to her place of residence, No. 5 Artilerius Prospect, Apartment 7, Riga.

Comrade Silinya's statement has been removed from militia files and appended to the series of documents relating to the murder of the unidentified individual, found near the Moscow River railroad station.

Investigator V. Pshenichny
Witnesses

TELEGRAM

To the Head of the Riga City Militia, Lieutenant-Colonel Robert Baron GIVEN URGENCY OF INVESTIGATION RE-QUEST YOU SEND TO MOSCOW IMMEDIATELY COMRADE AINA SILINYA RESIDING 5 ARTILERIUS PROSPECT APART-MENT 7 STOP HER APPEARANCE AT MOSCOW RIVER PROS-

ECUTOR'S OFFICE ESSENTIAL STOP INVESTIGATOR
PSHENICHNY
May 28 1979

FORENSIC ANALYSIS REPORT

Moscow, May 29 1979

At the request of Investigator Pshenichny, I, forensic
expert S. Fradkina, have carried out a biological analysis
of blood, saliva and urine samples from the unidentified
corpse found near the Moscow River railroad station.
Samples of tissue and part of the stomach of the deceased
were also analyzed.

Traces of chemical substances found in the blood and
urine prove that between five and ten hours before death
took place, the victim had injected himself with powerful
drugs—morphine and derivatives of the tranquilizer phenothiazine (whether with triftazinc, sanapax or aminazine
has not been determined).

Forensic Medical Section
Moscow City Health Department
Senior Scientific Officer
Sofia Fradkina, MD

NOTE: The general diagnostic picture (based on organic
changes occurring in the veins, brain, stomach and other
organs) is of an organism which has become inured to
drugs of the morphine type over a number of years. For
this reason the presence in the body of phenothiazine
derivatives, which are considered to be powerful drugs
used in psychopharmacology, is unusual, but biological
analysis is not able to explain the reason for this substi-
tution.

S. Fradkina

So "Sultan", who was probably Rybakov, was injecting himself with drugs. Nice company for one of the
country's best journalists: a drug addict and a jewel speculator! I wondered what part Belkin had played in this
business with the diamonds.

At this point, I came across something about Belkin himself. I turned up the following letter from the chief editor of *Komsomolskaya Pravda* on a sheet of personalized notepaper:

*Urgent, By Special Messenger*

To the Moscow City Prosecutor
Comrade M. G. Malkov
Copy to the Head of CPSU Central Committee
Ideological Section
Comrade L. M. Zamyatin

Dear Mikhail Grigoryevich,
    Yesterday and today, without any search warrant, V. Pshenichny, an investigator at the Moscow River Prosecutor's Office, conducted a series of illegal searches at the editorial offices of *Komsomolskaya Pravda* and at the apartment of our missing correspondent, V. Belkin.
    Without wishing to interfere in the operations of our investigative organs, I should like to make the point that any attempts to locate the whereabouts of the missing journalist at his place of work or at his home in an apartment block belonging to the Komsomol Central Committee, are in our opinion quite senseless. The searches which have been carried out compromise the reputation not merely of the newspaper's editorial staff, but also of the Prosecutor's Department entrusted to your care.
    Speaking on behalf of the entire editorial staff of *Komsomolskaya Pravda,* I beg you to transfer the responsibility for finding V. Belkin, a talented writer and one of the country's leading journalists, to an investigator who is both better qualified and politically more mature.
    At the same time I have to inform you that, as a special correspondent representing *Komsomolskaya Pravda,* V. Belkin has been included in the press corps which will report on the meeting between Comrade L. I. Brezhnev and President J. Carter, due to take place in Vienna from June 15 to June 18.

The disappearance of Vadim Belkin, and the absence of requisite action to discover his whereabouts, is a source of concern both to the editorial staff of our newspaper and to the CPSU Central Committee's Ideological Department.

Yours sincerely,
Chief Editor of *Komsomolskaya Pravda*
Member of the CPSU Central Committee's Central Auditing Commission
Deputy of the RSFSR Supreme Soviet
Lev Korneshov

To the Moscow City Prosecutor
State Juridical Counselor Second Class
M. G. Malkov

### REPORT

In connection with the complaint received from the chief editor of *Komsomolskaya Pravda*, Comrade L. Korneshov, I have to report the following:

On May 27 I assumed responsibility for investigating the death of an unidentified person. Thereafter I took action to ascertain that the victim was one Yu. A. Rybakov, aged seventeen years, who had been kidnapped at the Kursk Station in Moscow on May 24, together with *Komsomolskaya Pravda* correspondent V. Belkin. (The corpse was positively identified by A. Silinya, an inhabitant of Riga, who also witnessed the said kidnapping.)

Since the document case belonging to Yu. Rybakov was found to include diamond jewelry to the value of not less than 100,000 roubles, it became necessary to examine the nature of the contacts which Yu. Rybakov had with the abovementioned Belkin. In connection with this, and in the presence of witnesses (employees of *Komsomolskaya Pravda*, living in the same apartment block as Belkin), on May 31 I conducted a search of Belkin's home and removed for further examination certain of his personal effects and manuscripts connected with the case in hand. Among the former was one of the notebooks which V. Belkin had used during a recent assignment in the south. Marked *Tashkent-Baku No.1*, it contains information of crucial relevance to the investigation and is appended to the case-file. Apart from this, the search of Belkin's apartment also brought to light a number of books, proscribed by the censorship, including A. Solzhenitsyn's *Gulag Archipelago*, V. Voinovich's *Life and Adventures of Ivan Chonkin* and issue No. 3 of the journal *Kontinent*.

In an attempt to locate notebook No. 2 or any other jottings written subsequently by V. Belkin, on June 1 1979 I searched his room at the editorial offices of *Komsomolskaya Pravda*. This search revealed that his desk was nearly empty. All his manuscripts and notebooks had disappeared. Furthermore, I was informed by I. K. Tarasevich, a journalist who shares Belkin's office, and I. G. Uryvskaya, the office cleaner, that from the day Belkin disappeared until yesterday evening (May 31), the latter's desk had been filled with his papers and notebooks.

Thus it cannot be ruled out that documents of direct relevance to this investigation have been deliberately removed by a person or persons unknown.

At the same time, I would draw attention to the low level of professional discipline among Belkin's colleagues at *Komsomolskaya Pravda*. Despite the fact that his last visit to the editorial office took place on May 24, nobody at the office became worried by his absence for a whole week. And it was only as a result of the search conducted by me that the editor, Comrade Korneshov, grew aware that this employee of his, this "talented writer and one of the country's leading journalists", had disappeared at all.

In view of the fact that Comrade Belkin's name has been included in the press group due to accompany Comrade Brezhnev on his journey to Vienna, I consider that the process of discovering the whereabouts of Belkin and of the criminals who abducted him and Rybakov would be greatly accelerated by the formation of a special investigative team, including agents of the CID. For one investigator, in this case me, to coordinate everything would be extremely difficult, especially if it is borne in mind that at the present moment, apart from the case involving Rybakov and Belkin, I have eighteen investigations of various kinds on my hands—including five major embezzlements and three murders.

Investigator
Moscow River Prosecutor's Office
Legal Expert Second Class
V. Pshenichny
June 1 1979

The more I read about Pshenichny, the more I liked him! Not a mistake made, apart from one blunder—inviting neighbors who subsequently turned out to be work colleagues of Belkin's as witnesses to the search of his apartment. I can imagine this suburban investigator, overwhelmed with work, tired, getting on in years and paid a mere 165 roubles a month. Five embezzlements, three murders and another ten cases of lesser importance—my God! What a weird world we live in! It's a round-the-clock succession of embezzlers and speculators, conning ordinary citizens with the help of the Great God Economic Shortage. Everywhere you go you meet men worn out by overwork, routine and alcohol, who beat their wives to within an inch of death; fights and squabbles in communal apartments; the violence of thugs hanging out in the doorways of apartment blocks; the day-to-day boozed-up existence of a country in which 90 percent of criminal acts are committed by individuals under the influence of alcohol. Half a million criminal and civil actions are heard by the Moscow courts every year. There are tens of thousands of arrests, hundreds of thousands of people are held for questioning, and an unimaginable number of cases, perhaps a million, have been processed by People's Courts throughout the country in the past year. And all of it constitutes the exhausting daily routine of thousands of ordinary investigators such as Pshenichny. And he's clever, too. It goes without saying that a special team will have to be assembled to investigate the Belkin affair, and first in line for inclusion in the team will be Investigator

Pshenichny himself. And this despite the fact that the chief
editor of *Komsomolskaya Pravda* has lodged a complaint
against him and the case has been taken out of his hands.
Still, we'll make sure it works out for you, Pshenichny. I'll
take that responsibility on myself...

And the second member of the team should be Svetlov,
I think. He's a first-class detective with a trained nose for
these things. Of course, he's already a lieutenant-colonel
with a whole CID section at his command, a sleuth turned
administrator. He's become one of the bosses. All the same,
we'll have to have him with all his staff...

As all this was going through my mind, I opened a large
gray envelope attached to the file and extracted from it the
famous No. 1 notebook, marked *Tashkent-Baku, April–May
1979*, which, according to Pshenichny, contained "information of crucial relevance to the investigation." The writing had been rapidly scribbled and was difficult to follow.
In fact, in places it was downright indecipherable.

In addition to the notebook, the envelope contained forty-
eight numbered typewritten sheets, clipped together, which
had also been found by Pshenichny at Belkin's apartment.
Obviously Belkin had been transferring the contents of his
notebook to his *Colibri* typewriter.

I lit up a cigarette, settled back in my chair and began
to read.

VADIM BELKIN'S MANUSCRIPT
(opening pages)

I can't keep it to myself any longer. If I don't put down an
account of all the terrible things that have happened, I'll
have to go and drown myself in the Caspian. But if I display
the *whole* horror of events, then who will read it—or rather:
how will I succeed in concealing it from potential readers?
I will have to mix fact with fiction, and vice versa, so what
I am about to write must bear the label "adventure story"...

Chapter 1
A Coffin without a Corpse
In May 1979, I, Andrey Garin, special correspondent for
*Komsomolskaya Pravda,* the most popular youth newspaper

in the Soviet Union, happened to be flying home from Tashkent to Baku. To be perfectly honest, my assignment was only supposed to take me to Southern Uzbekistan, or more precisely, to the Surkhansk foothills of the Pamir and Altai mountains. There, a party of glaciologists from the Academy of Sciences was experimenting with a new method of melting glaciers by seeding them from the air with coal dust and soot. I spent part of the time climbing with the glaciologists, and the rest of it flying with the pilots of the Antonov agricultural planes used in the exercise.

Down beneath us was a green carpet of cotton plantations, criss-crossed with bright red patches of poppy fields. Early May is the time when poppies flower, and you could see streams of scarlet licking the mountains like flames, reaching to an altitude of two thousand meters, with only the snow of the eternal white peaks surveying their treasure. I don't know which brought the local farms greater profit— the giant cotton plantations in the valleys, or these mountainous fields of opium poppies, which are grown here for the pharmaceutical industry. Of course, I had heard a lot of fantastic stories about Afghan smugglers who were supposed to arrive here over secret mountain paths. If I hadn't had occasion myself to write a series of articles about our border police, and if I didn't know how jealously they guard every inch of our frontiers, then I might have been tempted to believe these wild stories myself. Anyway, once I had been drinking a while with Major Ryskulov, the head of the local border post, I asked him a point-blank question about these smugglers. He burst into laughter and said, "That's one of those tall tales, my friend! Not even a buzzard crosses the border around here without my permission!"

"And with your permission?"

"Somebody who crosses with my permission wouldn't be a smuggler," he said with a laugh and changed the subject.

The day before my visit was due to end, a few of the Charshanga helicopter pilots dropped me into the neutral zone between frontiers, a mountain valley filled with edelweiss. Of course, the duty officer at the local air-control tower asked us for the password and then began to swear at us for landing in the neutral zone without special permission, but I took the headset away from the pilot and began to serenade the anti-aircraft gunners with Vysotsky's song, *And in the neutral zone flowers of unusual beauty* . . . And Vysotsky is absolutely right. These edelweiss were as soft as a kitten's paw: I hadn't seen flowers as beautiful and downy as these during the whole ten days of my visit, and I'd been all over the Surkhansk mountains with the glaciologists.

So now I was carrying a whole pot of magnificent edelweiss back to Moscow—well, the pot was actually one of those black mess kits that scientists take into the field with them. All the members of the expedition had scratched their names on it, and the glaciologists had made it into a present for our newspaper museum. I didn't know which lucky lady I would present the flowers to in Moscow (I was out of love at the time), but knowing my amorous nature, I didn't think the edelweiss would stay in the smoke-blackened mess kit for long. Could I have imagined then that my next affair would have such fateful consequences for me? But I won't get ahead of myself. I'll merely say that I was returning with a whole bunch of edelweiss, a nose peeling from the sun, a black mess kit, and passes to enter the frontier zone and the tiny Charshanga agricultural airport, both signed by the Head of Anti-Aircraft Defenses, Central Asian Military District, General Fedoseyev. I also had a few notebooks filled with writing for a future article, and what was more, a healthy feeling of tiredness, caused by all that walking up and down mountains. Of course, I should have surrendered both special passes at the Chief Border Police Authority in Tashkent, but after the exhausting flight from Charshanga to Tashkent, via Samarkand, was it really worth traveling from the airport right into the center of town just to hand in a couple of documents at Anti-Aircraft Defense Headquarters, and then rush back to the airport to catch the flight to Moscow? Anyway, they could manage without those two passes, I decided, and you'd have to be a first class idiot not to keep such unusual souvenirs for yourself.

So I found myself sitting in the office of the director of Tashkent airport, who had summoned his chief ticket clerk to write a ticket to Moscow for me, and save me the bother of waiting in the monstrous line for the booking office. I was listening to a voice on Radio Moscow announcing, "The temperature in Moscow is plus four degrees, with low cloud and drizzle...", when I had a sudden idea. Why not visit my grandmother in Baku first, spend a few nights sleeping on her divan, do some fishing in the Caspian with my old friends, and start my article about the glaciologists? After all, it didn't make any difference whether I wrote it at the office in dark, damp Moscow, or at my grandmother's place in Baku!

"Excuse me," I said to the gray-haired ticket clerk, who was only too willing to ingratiate himself with a famous correspondent from the capital, "make out the ticket for Tashkent-Moscow via Baku, okay? I've just remembered that I've got some business to transact in Azerbaidzhan. When's the next flight to Baku?"

The ticket clerk looked inquiringly at his boss, but the latter couldn't have cared less where he sent the Moscow journalist off to. Just let him get out of the airport as quickly as possible so as not to notice the enormous crush for tickets in the departure hall and write a critical article about it in his newspaper.

"So you want to fly to Baku first?" said the airport director.

"That's right," I answered decisively.

And while the clerk was writing the ticket, I could almost feel the cool, green waves of the Caspian flowing into my soul, enveloping me in a weightless and translucent cocoon. It seemed more and more a good idea to go from wandering the sunbaked Uzbek mountains and dirty, soot-covered glaciers straight to my native Caspian where I would dive, swim and harpoon deep in those peaceful waters.

I could already taste the sea salt on my lips. I passed through the crowd waiting to get their tickets endorsed, handed my rucksack in at the check-in desk and went out towards the plane, carrying nothing but a small travel bag. The airliner was an old TU-104, standing close to the glass building of the air terminal, but passengers weren't allowed on yet, as the baggage was still being loaded. The latter consisted mainly of huge, unwieldy wooden boxes, which were technically forbidden to be transported by plane, and large, mock-leather suitcases, bound with string and peppered with little holes to prevent the fruit and vegetables inside them from perishing during the flight. After all these cumbersome objects, the baggage loaders handled my rucksack as if it were a beach ball. Then I watched them tense their muscles and lift an amazingly heavy, zinc coffin towards the plane.

Go on a journey with a corpse! Now I'm a modern, enlightened and educated man, but all the same: an omen is an omen, and I immediately remembered all the signs connected with a coffin. If a coffin is being carried towards you, that's a good omen, because it means that unpleasantness and misfortune are no longer lying in wait for you but have been removed from your path. But if a coffin accompanies you on your journey, that's a sure sign that fate is bound to play some dreadful trick on you.

Hell's bells! I thought indignantly. There was a rule against transporting dead bodies in passenger planes. They have to be taken in freight aircraft. I know the rules of Aeroflot. After all, I've been flying around the country for nine years without a break. Someone must have been bribed, without a doubt...

To distract myself from the sight of the coffin, I ran my eyes over the passengers who were assembling at the turnstile before walking out onto the airfield. There was a whole crowd of speculators with their great Caucasian peaked caps, their faces badly shaven, or not shaven at all, wearing dark, creased jackets, and taking green vegetables to the Baltic States. There was a round-faced major from the border police, looking as proud as a peacock, a couple of elderly women dressed in silken Uzbek dresses, and some fellow, dressed in mourning, wearing a small, black-framed photograph of his dead relative on his chest. But wait a minute! I looked more closely at the face of this man. Why, it was Ziyalov. Oleg Ziyalov, who had been in the same class as me at school in Baku! We were in high school together. We skipped classes to go to the movies together. I'd copy his homework for chemistry, and he'd do the same for me for literature.

"Oleg!" I said, as I stepped towards him.

It seemed to me that he froze for a split-second, without turning to face me (this is a natural reaction, after all, when somebody suddenly calls your name). Then I thought that he had to make a conscious effort to turn towards me. After all, he had just lost a relation, I thought, and it was obviously him transporting the coffin. In such a state of mind, it is difficult to switch to a different wavelength.

"Hello! It's me, Garin. Don't you recognize me?" I said, clearly seeing that he *had* recognized me. "Accept my condolences. Who is it you are burying?"

"My uncle," he replied very slowly, looking at me suspiciously at the same time, as if asking himself: does he *really* know me?

"Ziyalov! We were at school together! What are you looking at me like that for? It's me, Garin, you used to sit at a desk behind me at the back of the classroom. Remember?"

"Er, yes..." he said reluctantly, as if finding it difficult to remember. "That's right..."

His words didn't show any of the enthusiasm or the friendliness you'd expect on such occasions. I even regretted going up to him. After all, I hadn't changed so much over eleven or twelve years that he shouldn't be able to recognize me. In fact, he'd become fatter and somewhat flabbier than me. It wasn't that he'd aged, but, after all, there's no need to have folds of fat around your neck at twenty-seven. However, at this point they announced that passengers could board the plane, and started to let people through the turnstile towards it. I wandered off after Ziyalov, in the strange position of an old school friend who hadn't exactly been spurned, but who, nonetheless, had scarcely been acknowledged.

Well, I don't know, I thought. Perhaps this uncle of his was closer to him than a father, and that was possibly why he was in this trance-like state. I hadn't buried any of my close relatives yet, not my parents in the Ukraine, nor my grandmother in Baku, so I couldn't take offense.

"Oleg," I said, when the line had come to a halt in front of the steps up to the plane. "If you ever need my help in Baku or Moscow... Are you ever in Moscow?"

He gave me a long, hard look again, and took longer than he had to in remembering whether he ever visited Moscow or not.

"I was asking you whether you ever go to Moscow," I said again, trying to shake him out of this funereal trance. "I've got a job there with *Komsomolskaya Pravda,* so in case you ever need my help, write down my address. Or call me. The number of the editorial office is printed in every issue. You only need to mention my name..."

"Uh-huh," he said. "OK." And walked up the steps, showing the stewardess his ticket.

I was getting angry. Go to hell then, after all that, I thought. I was a well-known journalist, one of the best feature writers in the country, whose articles were translated by newspapers and magazines all over Europe, Africa and South America. Why, even Brezhnev himself had included me in his own personal press corps! Yet here was Ziyalov not wanting to exchange two words with me! I couldn't give a damn! He was burying his uncle: let him get buried himself! I couldn't care less! Only it was a pity he'd had to spoil my good mood. Just as I was beginning to look forward to scuba diving and shashlyks of gray mullet— grilled on a skewer kebab-style—by the seashore, this idiot Ziyalov had to come along with his coffin. Still, I'm exaggerating a little. One thing Ziyalov never was was an idiot. Chemistry, physics and geography were his really strong subjects, and the veranda at his house was always strewn with ancient tomes on palmistry and black magic. I remembered descending on his place once with some friends of ours from school and coming upon a strange scene. His ten-year-old sister, an incredibly skinny little creature with huge eyes and a black pigtail, was jumping rope, with a completely blank expression on her face. Her eyes were staring straight ahead, while she muttered automatically, "Five hundred and one, five hundred and two, five hundred and three..." Meanwhile Oleg, looking pale and tense, with dilated pupils and sweating intensely, was standing next to her, his eyes glued to hers, so that we couldn't figure out whether he was training her to be a gymnastics champion or whether he'd hypnotized her.

As I thought about this my feeling of indignation gradually faded, and I began to doze off in my seat.

And in all probability I wouldn't even have gone up to Oleg Ziyalov at Baku airport. I would have collected my rucksack at the baggage desk, taken a taxi and—farewell, former school buddy! I haven't seen you for twelve years, and I probably won't see you for another twenty, but still . . .

However, those of us in the third cabin were the last to leave the plane, and when I stepped down onto the hot and dusty Baku airfield, I realized that I wouldn't be able to avoid Ziyalov. There he was, waiting for the coffin at the baggage section, but he wasn't the one who caught my attention. Standing next to him were two other people, one of them a man of about fifty, featureless apart from having a mouthful of metal teeth, and on his right . . .

Forgive me, but the girl standing to his right deserves a fresh paragraph. I know that from the point of view of classical literature this may sound hackneyed, banal or even stupid, and . . . Call it what you like, if a person falls in love the first time he sees someone, it *is* hackneyed, banal and stupid, of course, but . . .

She was about twenty-two, with deep blue eyes and black hair tied up in a tight bun. She was wearing a blue-gray summer dress, and her whole figure exuded grace and harmony. That's it, my friends. I don't have anything to add, except to say that the vision of this figure outlined against a background of Ilyushin and Tupolev airliners, like some cheap Aeroflot advertising poster, was burned into my soul forever, despite all the fateful events which were to occur in the days to come.

Not all my faculties had deserted me, because I suddenly remembered from somewhere deep in my memory that skinny ten-year-old girl with the big, staring eyes who had been jumping with her rope and intoning, "Five hundred and two, five hundred and three . . ."

And then I went straight up to face those deadly blue eyes. I strode right across the pavement, despite the obvious displeasure of Oleg Ziyalov, who was standing next to me and eyeing me in an almost hostile manner. He could go to hell! I walked right up to her, to those eyes of hers. It was too late for her to turn away, as I looked into them and said to her, "I know you. You're Oleg's sister. Hello. My name's Andrey". And I offered her my hand.

She looked at her brother anxiously, but he said nothing, so she took my hand. "I'm Anya," she said.

Her grip was light and cool.

"Oleg and I were in the same class together at school," I said. "I saw you once at your house. You were playing jump-rope and saying, 'Five hundred and one, five hundred and two, five hundred and three.' Remember?"

She smiled and shrugged her shoulders. "I don't remember," she replied. "But if somebody was jumping rope, it must have been me."

Nodding in the direction of the plane, where I could see baggage handlers unloading the coffin from the hold, I offered her my condolences. Meanwhile I noticed that all three of them, including the older man, who was twisting a set of car keys around his fingers, had become very tense and had their eyes glued on the coffin. However, at a sign from Ziyalov, the man walked over to the baggage handlers. At that moment I noticed that Anya had come to the airport to meet her uncle's coffin in a light summer dress, not the dark clothes usually worn by somebody in mourning. This gave me the justification to open my bag, extract the pot of edelweiss and offer her the entire bunch of downy, beautiful flowers.

"Anya, these are from the Pamirs. I realize that this is neither the time nor place, but . . . I hope I'll see you again."

Then I turned towards Ziyalov. "May I call you some time?"

"Uh-huh," he muttered, none too certainly, and took his sister by the hand. Good grief! They were so different! He led her out of the baggage area, following in the footsteps of the porters, who were carrying the coffin towards the exit, assisted by the fifty-year-old man. The four of them were obviously finding the coffin a heavy burden. You might have thought that the Ziyalovs' uncle weighed two hundred pounds. I tapped Oleg's elbow. "Come on, let's give them a hand," I said. "Here, Anya, hold this," and I passed her my bag.

"Stop!" Ziyalov said rudely.

"What do you mean? Let's give them a hand."

He shook his head. "No, I'm not allowed to." And I suddenly remembered that he was right. According to custom, close relatives are not supposed to touch the deceased's coffin. But this didn't apply to me, so I thrust my travel bag into Anya's hands, caught up with the baggage handlers and put my shoulder to the heavy zinc coffin. Of course, this was not done so much to help the porters, as to busy myself in front of the woman with whom I had fallen in love and to whose house I might get invited, or at least to the funeral . . .

Whatever the reason, I put my shoulder to the coffin and we carried it through the turnstile, past the crowd of people waiting to meet the other passengers, and headed on outside, towards a car that was waiting on the station square. Suddenly, some six-year-old boy, with his arms spread out and making a humming noise like a plane, ran into one of the baggage handlers, the one on the left and in front.

It wasn't so much the boy's weight as his momentum that pushed the man from under the coffin, as if somebody had pulled away a support, and the heavy zinc box suddenly lurched forward. The other man in front, left on his own, let go of the coffin as he moved his shoulder to one side, and the enormous object hurtled to the ground in an almost upright position.

The crowd of passengers were suddenly hushed. "Good God!" someone said as the coffin hit the ground, fell forward once again and finally landed sideways on the asphalt, bursting a seam in the process. Nobody moved—not me, not the porters, not the crowd. Everybody expected the body of the dead man to suddenly fall out of the coffin. It appeared unavoidable, but it didn't happen. What did fall out were dozens of paper packages. Some of them had broken open with the impact, scattering tiny pieces of plastic, packed in bundles, all over the ground. Each piece was about the size of a postage stamp and stained with some brownish oily mark!

We were stupefied! One of the baggage handlers bent down cautiously, picked up a whole bundle and turned it

over in his hands. "What's this then, naphthalene?" he said
with a Caucasian accent.

I saw Ziyalov's male companion back away silently behind the crowd, his metallic teeth clenched tightly, his eyes
fixed firmly on the shattered coffin, which was still spewing
tiny pieces of plastic all over the roadway. Then one of the
passengers bent down, picked up a bundle, rubbed one of
the brownish grease marks with his finger, put it to his nose,
sniffed it, and suddenly said with a loud laugh, "Naphthalene,
my foot! It's opium!"—and, grabbing a whole armful of
the bundles, began to stuff his pockets with them.

You should have seen what happened next! The people
who had just been standing in muted sorrow before the coffin
now suddenly rushed for it, snatching up bundles of opium
as they did so. One of them forced the lid of the coffin up
a little further, grabbing more packets from inside it. It was
pandemonium! Those who had managed to fill their pockets
or clutch large piles to their chests weren't able to get back
through the hordes of people behind them. Taxi drivers,
flower sellers, speculators—all joined in, and everyone was
getting crushed. If it hadn't been for the sound of a police
whistle, I don't know whether I would have come out of it
alive. The militia didn't yet know what it was all about, of
course, but, figuring that somebody was getting murdered
at the epicenter of this swarming rabble, they rushed in
towards us, raining blows as they went and blowing their
whistles at the same time. It was this, rather than the fists,
which finally brought the crowd to its senses. People picked
up what opium they could and rushed off in all directions.
The baggage handlers ran off too, and I alone remained, at
the center of events, not yet understanding what had happened and still looking around for Ziyalov, his sister and
the fifty-year-old relative. But there was no sign of them
anywhere. I thought I could see a minibus disappearing at
the edge of the square, the same one that we'd been carrying
the coffin towards. But I was wrong. There was a different,
cloth-capped moustached Azerbaidzhani sitting at the wheel.
I looked around me in panic. Anya had been carrying my
bag containing all my notebooks, papers, passport . . . And
at that very moment a black-moustached Azerbaidzhani

militiaman put his hand on my shoulder and said, in a strong
accent, "You are under arrest."

*12:57 hours*

"One p.m., Moscow time!" came a voice from behind the
wall in Baklanov's office, reminding me that it was time to
go for lunch.

*"What* time is it?" I asked myself in panic, looking automatically at my watch. I'd become absorbed in all these
documents when I should have been getting an investigation
team together as quickly as possible.

"No. I'm not going to lunch, I'm sorry," I shouted to
Baklanov. Then I picked up the telephone. The people I
needed most urgently now were Investigator Pshenichny,
whom I didn't know, and that old bloodhound, Lieutenant-
Colonel Marat Svetlov. They already knew the details of
the case. I had to get them. There wouldn't be any problem
about Pshenichny, but as for Svetlov...

I dialed the number of the Moscow River Prosecutor's
Office and said, "This is the USSR Prosecutor's Office
speaking. Special Investigator Shamrayev here. I need to
talk to Investigator Pshenichny."

This was enough to make whoever was on the other end
of the line pause for a moment, and then say in an obliging
rush, "You want him to come to the phone?"

People always make fools of themselves when they're
talking to anybody of higher rank. I've caught myself doing
it. What else would I want him to do, if I was phoning him?
I didn't want to exchange witticisms with the Moscow River
Prosecutor, so I waited while the voice at the other end of
the phone bawled, "Quiet! Where's Pshenichny? Tell him
to get over here! There's a call for him! From the USSR
Prosecutor's Office!"

Half a minute went by, and just as I was beginning to
lose patience a voice said, "Hello. Investigator Pshenichny
here."

"Hello," I said. "My name's Shamrayev, Special Investigator at the Chief Public Prosecutor's Office. I need to see
you as soon as possible."

"About the Belkin case?"

"That's right. What time is best for you?"

"When do you want to see me?"

"When? To be honest, right away." I tried to make it sound less like an order from above as an ordinary request from a colleague. I don't know whether he detected this or not, but at least he didn't start making awkward objections. Instead, he replied quite simply, "I can be there in forty minutes. Where's your office?"

"Fourth floor, Room 418. Thanks. I'll be expecting you."

Well, Pshenichny certainly appeals to me so far! I happily dialed "02", the Moscow Militia number.

"Operator, get me CID Department 3, Head of Section 2."

"Svetlov? One minute, please."

A few seconds later I could hear a woman's voice saying, "Kulagin's Department. Secretary speaking."

"Get me Svetlov, please."

"And who is calling?"

"Tell him it's Shamrayev."

I didn't have long to wait. Svetlov lifted the receiver immediately. "Hello! What's going on with you?" he said in his cheerful familiar way.

"Hello, colonel," I replied, to show that I knew all about his recent promotion. "How are things? Are you buried in paperwork? Are you still alive?"

"Well . . . Do you want to go out and meet some women?"

Uh oh, I thought, down to basics right away, as usual.

"Well, we can go and meet some women, too . . ." I replied. I wasn't sure how to broach the subject so I thought I'd draw things out a little.

"But you don't need detectives to help you with women, do you?" he asked. "Don't forget that I'm not a detective anymore, but a bureaucrat, an office drudge," he went on lightly. Despite his promotion, he was still as trivial a conversationalist as ever.

"OK, drudge! But couldn't you abandon your papers for a couple of hours, get into your special colonel's police car, start your sirens, and tear over here to Pushkin Street?"

"With sirens, hmm? What's this—an order? A request? What's happened?"

"Nothing terrible. But I do need to see you."

"All right," he said in a businesslike way. "I'll be over right away."

People like Svetlov thrive on intrigue and excitement— even in their everyday lives. I was certain that he'd arrive within ten minutes.

Then Baklanov's inquisitive face appeared at the door.

"So what was that about serving people?"

"What?" I said, uncomprehendingly.

"I was asking you whether you felt fed up being everybody's servant."

He was quite right. I'd completely forgotten about our earlier conversation. That's what's known as getting into a case.

Baklanov continued. "Do you want to drink more beer in protest?"

"No," I replied, "I can't any longer. People will be here any minute."

"So you're doing it?"

"Yes."

"OK. In that case I'd better go and ask for some work to do, too. Here I am, back from vacation, and people seem to have forgotten I even exist."

BELKIN'S MANUSCRIPT
(continued)

## Chapter 2
## The Baku Drug Addicts

Sashka Shakh was keeping an eye open for the militia or vigilantes, while Sickly Simon was on the lookout for somebody, preferably a woman, wearing a gold watch or carrying a purse. If he found a likely victim, he'd give the signal to Rafik Gaikazyan, distracting the victim while Rafik grabbed the spoils.

This was ordinary "work" for them. It had a certain element of risk to it, to say the least, and they were all experts at their trade. But that day they were out of luck. What they'd taken that morning turned out not to be a gold watch but an ordinary gold-plated watch-case, and Tolik Khachmas, unfortunately, was no fool. They were long-standing customers of his, and Tolik wouldn't even give them enough hash for a single joint. Meanwhile, the morning rush hour had passed and by now, after 10 a.m., only housewives would be in the trams, traveling back from the market, their bags full of green vegetables, eggplants, chickens and radishes. And stealing a radish just isn't worth it!

Shakh could feel the first stiffening in his joints. It was tolerable at the moment, but in half an hour's time, unless he could get a fix, this aching feeling would begin to stab at him, bring unbearable pain to his eyes. He had to steal something as quickly as possible for a fix, one of those lifesaving, greasy brown drops of opium on a piece of plastic film.

At last! There was a No. 7 tram with a trailer turning out of Basin Street into Lenin Street, with Sickly Simon hanging off the platform of the first door in the trailer. Nobody has shut the door of a Baku tram for as long as anyone can remember—not only for ventilation but for the convenience of the passengers. Anybody can jump on or off a tram while it's in motion. This is the way it's done, and even elderly Azerbaidzhanis sometimes jump off as a tram slows down to turn a corner.

Sickly Simon was hanging off the platform of the trailer and nodded his head slightly in the direction of a man in glasses, who was hanging on beyond him. Shakh noticed the gesture and could see the Seiko watch the man was wearing, even though he was some distance away. He quickly moved forward, and in a series of long strides caught up with the tram. There was no way of undoing the watchstrap and letting the Seiko fall into his outstretched palm. It was one of those bracelet jobs, so getting hold of it wouldn't be easy. Grabbing the handrail, Shakh jumped onto the platform and shoved Simon forward, so that he pushed the man with the Seiko back towards Rafik, who was waiting for him inside.

"What are you shoving for?" Simon shouted, ready for a fight.

"Shut the fuck up," Shakh said, pushing him again.

"You son of a bitch!" Simon snapped, moving his hand threateningly towards him.

The man in glasses, of course, moved further inside the tram to get as far away as possible from these thugs, but Rafik pushed against him from behind, while Simon shouted from the platform, "Rafik, they're fucking with us!"

And now the two of them, Rafik—over the head of the man in glasses, who was getting in his way—and Simon, began to pound Shakh on the head and shoulders. Shakh, in the meantime, feigning rage, grabbed hold of Simon and began to push him off the moving tram.

"Let's get off and fight it out, you bastard!" Shakh shouted.

The main aim of the scuffle was to create a crush around the man in glasses, and when he tried to get away from the three brawlers, one of them would grab the arm with the watch for a moment and push it under his own arm. By the time the victim pushed himself away from the fight, the watch would no longer be around his wrist.

Everything went beautifully, without a hitch. The General hadn't spent a month training them for nothing. He was as good a professional as you could find in the best theatrical schools. He was the king of the Baku criminal fraternity. I don't mean that he was the leader of every single drifter, drunk, pickpocket and out-and-out thug who swarms over this enormous city with its million inhabitants. What I mean is the gang of professional, hash-smoking thieves that he created himself. As recently as three or four years ago, when Shakh was in high school, he was still filching Bulgarian cigarettes from his father, who, as a colonel in the border police, could get them at the officers' stores. He and his pals would go and smoke these cigarettes on a small hill behind the Sabunchinsky railroad station. They could play hookey there, and the bushes that concealed this hill from the rest of the world was an ideal place for them to hang out in and smoke. They could daydream, swear as much as they liked or read the dog-eared pages of books like *One Hundred and Forty Ways of Indian Lovemaking*. Beyond the fence, at the foot of the hill, was a humpyard with freight trains constantly coming and going. If you had nothing else to do, you could spend hours watching trucks loading and unloading, listen to the loaders exchanging foul language with the traffic controllers, or follow all the customers as they scurried around looking for their boxes and containers...

But one day the General turned up on the hill. Of course, nobody knew his nickname then. As far as Shakh and his friends knew, this was simply some old joker coming up to them to talk. (Anybody over forty was a "joker" to them.) Anyway, here he was, and he told them that he was an unarmed combat trainer looking for young men to join his class. He looked them all over, but didn't choose anybody in particular. Instead, he saw that somebody had a pack of cards and offered to teach them how to play the Russian gambling game called *sekka*. The boys had played cards for money before, just to amuse themselves, but the stakes had never been more than thirty or forty kopecks. But after the General's first appearance, things began to change. The stakes grew higher, and the boys took more and more risks. At first the General would always lose. He was easily and even happily parted from his money, and after playing for an hour he might leave the lads with eight or nine roubles. He would then leave, saying he had some business to attend to, and they would continue to play against each other, splitting the money which he had contributed to the game in the first place. The next day, the one who ended up winning would reappear, showing off a new pocket-knife or Cuban cigar which he had bought with the money. A couple of years later, when Sashka had become one of the General's close assistants and had been given his nickname, Shakh, or the Shah, he realized that the General's regular losses of eight or nine roubles a day were actually the opening moves in a carefully calculated psychological game. First of all, the General would begin by getting them used to handling money, and not only the lads who gathered together on this particular hill, but the members of twenty or thirty similar groups elsewhere in Baku. Adding them all together, he would probably lose 200 or 300 roubles a day, but this wouldn't last very long. Once he had them used to taking risks for higher stakes, he would gradually win his money back, and soon the whole macro-gang, consisting of boys in their last year or two of school all over Baku, was in debt to him. And somehow it would turn out that the boys in greatest debt were the strongest ones, the leaders of their group. Although the General didn't demand repayment in the beginning, the feeling that they were in debt nonetheless made them dependent on him, unable to break away. After that the General began introducing them to drugs, hashish for the most part.

At first they were afraid to inject themselves with morphine, and limited themselves to hash. But once they were used to the hash, and had no money to buy it with, the General would start to bring them pharmaceutically-produced morphine or drops of opium on strips of film. Gradually he got them accustomed to it. He also showed them how to use a hypodermic needle, and then they'd inject morphine and opium into their veins, getting high in the little public garden next to their hill.

And on it went. The General was in no hurry. He would observe and sometimes, for a joke, show the boys how to steal a watch off someone's wrist without their noticing, use a razor blade to cut away someone's back pocket with a wallet, and other tricks of the pickpocket's trade. He would always forbid them to try anything like this in real life. But there was no stopping the boys. They needed a lot of money now, not just to play cards or repay debts, to the General and to each other, but also to buy hash, opium and morphine. There's no stopping the hardened addict, especially if he's young and not yet out of his teens.

At length, as if yielding to their pressure, the General split them up into groups of three and began to teach them to become professional thieves. As a result of what he taught them and the money they owed him, they had become forever in his debt, literally—his permanent assistants, obliged to share their spoils with him on every occasion. The General spent a month training them—a whole course in the art and science of being a thief. It included both theory (thieves' law) and initiation ritual. Then the whole town, and especially its tram routes, was divided up strictly between the groups of three. According to Shakh's arithmetic, there were about thirty trios beholden to the General. His boys were at work along practically the whole tram network. And it was an exciting, vital life, meeting your friends at an agreed street corner in the early hours, checking out two or three trams in the morning rush hour, whipping a couple of watches and a wallet or two, and then heading straight to the Drama Theater in the middle of town. There, in his usual place, you'd find Tolik Khachmas, a hash and opium dealer.

The lads would never hoard very much of their loot. They didn't have the patience. They would just take as much as they needed for a couple of fixes or two or three joints. In the morning the hardened smoker doesn't think about a pack of cigarettes to last the whole day. His mind is fixed on a single cigarette, or even on one long puff. What happens later, when the high begins to pass, doesn't matter. It'll be lunchtime by then, the trams will already be filled with people during the midday rush hour, and there'll be pickings enough to get a new fix . . . And so it goes all day long.

Only once did they steal, not for money or drugs, but for the sheer hell of doing so. This was a real art-for-art's-sake occasion, when each of them exerted himself to the limit of his professional ability. It had happened the previous summer, during the Neftyannik–Ararat soccer game. This game was to be a historic battle between Azerbaidzhan and Armenia, with political, cultural and nationalist overtones. Indeed, it was one of the only legal expressions of the ancient tribal enmity between the Azerbaidzhanis and the Armenians. It couldn't be ruled out that, if Ararat won, the whole city of Baku would witness an Armenian massacre. That's obviously what the authorities thought too, because troops were pulled into town the day before the game, and there were reinforced military patrols, with six men apiece, openly walking the streets.

On the day of the game, it was obvious that the trams going to the stadium would be fantastically full, and it would have been a crime not to take advantage of such an opportunity. So the General organized a competition between all thirty groups to see who could steal the most watches that day. The lads took up the challenge with grit and determination, especially since the General had promised the victors a unique reward—a real Browning automatic.

They were due to count up who'd stolen what at 9 p.m. in the Malakansky Gardens in the center of town. Once all the groups had gathered together, each trio began to unload its takings on a park bench. One lot had filched eighteen pairs of watches, another twenty-three, and a third group twenty-seven. This was the work of Shakh's team, but even they were outclassed by Arif, nicknamed Mosol, whose trio had taken twenty-nine pairs. So the General presented the revolver to Mosol's group. It was a tiny, lady's version, without any bullets. "That doesn't matter," said Mosol. "It's a Browning, and that's the most important thing. We'll get some bullets!" Then the General, with a quiet chuckle, opened his briefcase and emptied his takings into the general pile. Without anybody's help he'd managed to take sixty-nine watches in one day. That's work for you!

But on the day I am describing, the routine on the tram went as smoothly as clockwork. In a short scuffle lasting only twenty or thirty seconds, Simon and Rafik managed to crowd in on the man in glasses so much that he pushed his way further and further into the tram out of fright. However, the wrist with the watch on it seemed to become accidentally stuck under Rafik's elbow, and as the man attempted to dislodge it, Shakh deftly undid the bracelet with a fingernail. Nothing else was necessary. As he moved his arm, the victim in glasses slipped his wrist out of the bracelet himself, and the watch fell, like a ripe fruit, into Shakh's waiting palm.

"Got it!" Shakh whispered to Simon, before shouting, "You son of a bitch!" at him and pulling him off the platform, as if dragging him away for a fight. Rafik jumped off after them, and in full sight of the passengers in the departing tram, they carried on the scuffle, with Rafik trying to keep them apart—but only for as long as it took the tram to disappear around the corner. Then Shakh took the watch out of his pocket and all three of them admired their prize— a real Japanese Seiko. If they were to line up at the State Commission store, they'd make a hundred roubles in half an hour. But they wouldn't bother, of course. They needed some opium and hash right away, and although Tolik Khachmas wouldn't give them more than fifty roubles for the watch, it wouldn't make any difference. *If* he was still in his usual spot and hadn't slipped away yet. It was already eleven o'clock, after all.

Without a word, all three of them set off by their usual route, across Station Square towards the Drama Theater in the center of town, when suddenly Shakh froze. The others stopped too.

There on the sidewalk in front of them, leaning against a street lamp and crying bitterly, just like Snow White in the fairy tale, was a seventeen-year-old girl, exceptionally pretty, with light-blue eyes and obviously not from Baku. A small suitcase stood by her feet, and she had an open travel bag in her hand. The Baku sun was beating down on her ash-blonde hair, its rays shimmering in a faint rainbow—an effect they had never seen before, as if each hair were able to refract the sun's light into wonderful colors. And, just like a child, she was trying to use her fist to wipe away tears she couldn't hold back.

"What's the matter?" Shakh asked as he walked towards her.

"N-n-nothing . . ." she said through her tears.

"What are you bawling for, then?"

She raised her blue eyes to look at him, and Shakh's heart skipped a beat.

"I've . . . I've . . . lost my money . . . and the . . . address . . ." she said.

"What address? How did you lose it? Where do you come from?"

"I've . . . I've . . . just got off the train . . . from Vilnius . . . I've come to visit my aunt . . . I just got off this minute . . . I had a purse . . ." and she showed him the bag which she was carrying. "My money was in it, and my passport, and my aunt's address . . ." And then she started wailing again.

"Wait a minute," said Shakh, taking her by the arm. "Did somebody approach you?"

"No," she said. "Although a boy did help me carry my things at the railroad station . . ."

"What did he look like?"

"Nothing much. He was tall with black hair . . . So what?"

"Was he wearing a peaked cap?"

"Yes, he was. So what?" she asked, looking at him again with those great blue eyes of hers.

The boys looked at each other. "It must have been Mosol," Rafik said confidently. The station was Arif Mosol's beat, and all three of them realized that it must have been his doing. Shakh looked down at the stolen Seiko. It was a quarter to twelve.

"What time did the train arrive?" he asked.

"At eleven o'clock. So what?"

"It doesn't matter. Let's go." And, taking her suitcase, he headed resolutely for the taxi stand.

"Where are we going?" she asked in amazement.

"Let's move!" he said to Rafik and Simon. "How much money was in the purse?" he asked her.

"Eighty roubles for the trip home," she replied. "But where are we going to?"

"Get in," he said, opening the door of an empty taxi. There was no time to lose. After filching the purse, Mosol would have immediately taken out the money and thrown away the purse and its contents, probably in a trash can, or perhaps in the street. But where? He looked around the square he was standing in, imagining what he would have done with the purse, to get rid of the evidence as quickly as possible. But how was he to know where and when Mosol had lifted the purse? He might have done it on the platform. No, there wasn't much that could be done. He'd have to find Mosol immediately, and with eighty roubles, there was only one place where Mosol could have gone, of course— to Tolik Khachmas.

"Drama Theater," he said to the driver, and practically pushed his surprised accomplices and the blue-eyed crybaby into the taxi. "What's your name?"

"Lina."

"And your last name?"

"Braknite."

"What?" he asked again.

"Braknite, Lina Braknite."

"I see. OK," he said, committing it to memory. "My name's Sasha, Sasha Romanov. Don't forget. And I'm your cousin."

"Cousin?" she repeated.

"Yes. We'll have to play it like that. If anybody asks, you're my cousin." Then he turned to Rafik and Simon. "Understood?"

"OK," they replied, already guessing what he was going to do. Then he added for their benefit, and in Azerbaidzhani, so that Lina wouldn't understand, "And if anybody gives me away, I'll . . . I'll . . ." But he couldn't bring himself to swear in her presence, even in Azerbaidzhani. His tongue simply wouldn't form the word. In any case, it didn't matter, as Rafik and Simon fully understood what he meant.

"So why didn't your aunt come to meet you at the station?"

"I don't know . . ."

"Can you remember her address?"

"No . . ."

"What about her name?"

"Sure, I know that. Her name is Nora Gustavovna Braknite," she said, looking at him with the trusting gaze of a child who has found the firm hand of an adult to hang on to.

And it was this expression, this trusting belief that he, Sashka Shakh, would help her in this strange and unknown city, which made him feel, perhaps for the first time, that a woman had faith in him as a man, as someone who would protect her. It filled him with such resolution that even were Mosol to meet him with a loaded gun, nothing would stop him.

The taxi came to the Drama Theater.

"Stay here," he said to Lina, and he almost ran down the narrow alleyway between the buildings, towards the half-hidden shady courtyard behind the theater, the place where Tolik Khachmas usually hung out. Thank God, he was still there. Sashka silently offered him the Seiko and saw Tolik's eyes gleam. "How much will you give?" he asked.

"Made in Odessa, I suppose?" said Tolik in a drawling voice, trying to lower the price.

"Khachmas, don't mess around. I'm in a hurry. It's not junk, you can see that for yourself. It's the real thing. Have you seen Mosol?"

"What if I have?" Tolik replied, examining the watch, and admiring it.

"I need to see him. Has he been here today? With cash?"

"Yes, he's been . . ."

"How long ago?"

"I'm not sure . . . Ten minutes ago . . . I'll give you forty roubles for it," he said, naming his price.

"Give it back," Shakh replied, making a grab for the watch.

"Not so fast. What's going on?"

"Nothing. I'm going to Mamed. I need money."

"Don't you want any hash or anything?"

"I need money, bread, dough, got it?" Sashka said angrily and impatiently.

"How much?"

"Fifty. And if you let me have it, I'll take enough for two joints from you, or even three." He was remembering about himself too. He had to get enough for Rafik and Simon; he had to get rid of them as quickly as possible, to stop them from saying anything in Lina's presence that she didn't need to hear. The third pellet he would hide somewhere for himself and smoke it when Lina wasn't around. After all, he couldn't smoke hash in front of her, but he couldn't *not* smoke it either. His bones and joints would start to ache terribly.

"I'll give you forty," Khachmas said.

"Oh, give me that, you fucker!" Sashka shouted, tearing the Seiko from Tolik's hand.

"Wait a minute! What the hell is going on with you anyhow?" asked Khachmas in amazement. He'd never seen Sashka so excited. "Here, take these," he said, producing three tiny pieces of hashish from his jacket lining, and handing over thirty-five roubles as well.

"Who gave you the money? Was it Mosol?" Sashka asked, pointing towards the rouble notes.

"What if it was?"

"Was it eighty roubles he gave you?"

"None of your business. Whatever he gave me, it's my money now," Tolik said, just in case. "You've got your reward. Now get lost!"

He was right. Nobody has the right to look in somebody's pocket, especially if there's stolen money in it! Sashka stuffed the notes into his own pocket, closed his fist over the pellets and went back to the car, gesturing to Simon and Rafik as he did so. They immediately scrambled out of the taxi, and Sashka deftly slipped the two portions of hash into Rafik's hand without being noticed. Then he said, "Go off somewhere, only don't go up the hill. You haven't seen me today at all, OK? OK!" And he dived into the car, saying to the driver as he did so, "Drive us to Armenikend, the Stalin Palace of Culture."

The palace was in the Armenian quarter of Baku, and although it had long ago been renamed after Yury Gagarin, nobody in the city called the palace by its new name. Behind it was another public garden with a hill—only this hill was the domain of Arif Mosol.

When the car started moving, Sashka took Lina by the hand and said, "Don't worry. It's going to be all right. Look, there's the Malakansky Gardens, and now we're coming into the center of town. Over there is the Nizami Museum..."

The taxi hurtled down the main streets, up towards the hilly area of old Baku. As they reached the top of steeply ascending Lenin Street, Lina looked around and gasped in awe. The enormous greenish-blue saucer of the Caspian lay beneath them, and around it the city dipped down to the water's edge in narrow terraces with green, flat roofs, dotted here and there with modern, whitewashed houses, public gardens and parks. The sails of boats from the Yacht Club gleamed white in the middle of the sea.

"It's beautiful!" Lina said. "And everybody told me that the sea was black, polluted with oil. Look—it's green!"

The car came to a halt outside the Stalin Palace of Culture. Sashka left Lina sitting in the taxi, crossed the street and entered the public garden. Mosol and his bunch were there, in their usual place. They were sitting back on a park bench, feeling fine after a fix of opium. When Sashka went up to them, Mosol opened one eye very slightly, and then, just as lazily, a second. They had never been enemies, but then they'd never been friends either. Each had his own area, and each observed the rules, never crossing onto the other's turf. Of course, there was scarcely any love lost between these lads from Armenikend and the boys from the center of town, but there was no open enmity between them either. There had never been an opportunity, I suppose.

This was the reason for Mosol's surprised and expectant expression.

"Hello," Sashka said, looking at all of them and feeling his knees go weak with envy. There they were, all of them high as kites, having smoked or injected their fill and now experiencing that indescribably airy, fluid feeling of euphoria and buoyancy, that unbelievable feeling of joy and well-being which no words could convey.

"Salaam," replied Mosol.

"I've got some business to discuss with you," said Shakh.

"OK," came the reply.

Sashka looked at the two boys sitting on either side of their chief. They had also opened their eyes suspiciously, and Sashka could see the torpid gaze of their drugged pupils. All right, there was no way out of it. He'd have to speak in their presence, too. After all, Mosol hadn't come to him. He'd visited them. In their garden.

"OK. An hour ago you took my cousin's identity papers from her at the station. Makhanya was supposed to meet her, but she couldn't because she's sick, and I was ten minutes late. There was some money in her purse, too, but the money's yours now, and I'm not asking for it back. But I do want the purse back, or for you to let me know where you chucked it."

Mosol stared at him for a long time and you could see that native wit of his stirring in the depths of his black, Armenian eyes. Sashka could read in them the way Mosol was willing himself out of his drug-induced state, freeing his brain from it and coming out with the only response which he could muster: "And what if she isn't your cousin? Then what?"

"I tell you, she is. She's sitting outside in a taxi. You can go and ask her, if you like."

"Huh. Why bring the girl into it?" Mosol laughed. "It's you I'm asking. If she's your cousin, that's one thing, but if she's not, that's another. Am I right?" he asked his two cronies, who burst into helpless fits of laughter.

Sashka stood there, waiting calmly. Of course, Mosol wouldn't do anything for anybody for nothing. At the very least he'd boast to people that Shakh had stood before him asking for a favor.

"OK, that's enough. Shut up, you guys!" Mosol yelled suddenly at his companions in Armenian. Then he addressed Sashka. "I threw away the papers and the purse, you know yourself..."

"Where?" Sashka asked impatiently.

"In the courtyard where they used to sell kebabs. You know where I mean?"

Shakh knew. Mosol meant the yard next to the station. Only which dumpster had he thrown them into? There were nine or ten there at least. It was a huge courtyard, and as many as a hundred families use those things for their garbage.

"I know the place," he replied. "Only which dumpster did you throw them in?"

Mosol laughed slyly and spread out his hands in a gesture of helplessness.

"I don't remember . . . you know, I *was* in a hurry. Maybe the third one, or the fourth . . . Huh?" he said, turning towards his companions.

Those clowns had started to laugh, like hyenas, at the thought of Sashka Shakh rummaging in dumpsters, looking for his little cousin's passport.

"OK, that's enough!" Sashka said. "Thanks, Mosol." He was about to go when Mosol stopped him.

"Wait a minute, Shakh." He thrust his hand into his pocket and pulled out some crumpled rouble notes. Then he did the same with the other pocket, slowly, as if to make a point and to show that he was producing all the money which he had on him. Spreading them out on the park bench, he smoothed out each note, counting aloud as he did so. "Twenty, twenty-one, twenty-two roubles—and forty kopecks. Here you are. Take it, Shakh."

This was what Sashka had feared, that Mosol would give him all the money left over from Lina's purse.

"No, didn't I say the money was yours? You didn't know she was my cousin," said Shakh, resisting the offer.

"When I didn't know, I took it. When I found out, I gave it all back. Can you all see?" he said to his companions.

They nodded. They could see that Mosol had dug deep into his pocket and given every last kopeck to Shakh, because Shakh had said that the money belonged to his cousin.

"Take it. If it's your cousin's money, that's enough for me. I believe you. Take it."

Sashka knew he had to take the money, and the moment he had it in his hand, Mosol said, softly but firmly, "You've accepted it. Everybody saw you. But if she turns out to not be your cousin, then I've got a claim on you. Right?"

"OK, Mosol," Sashka said as lightheartedly as he could. "OK. Goodbye."

And he went off towards the taxi. Those unlucky twenty roubles were burning a hole in his hand. Because of the money, Mosol now had a claim on him. In any place, at any time of day or night, in front of any person, Mosol could now do what he liked with him—beat him up, cut him with a razor blade, stab him, or even kill him, and according to the rules of the criminal fraternity, Sashka would have no right to offer resistance. He'd taken the money, he'd put his seal to the fact that Lina was his cousin, and if Mosol could prove this was baloney, then he would have a claim on Sashka.

Shakh went up to the car, saw Lina's anxious eyes—they were like snowdrops, or the eyes of a child's doll—and, suddenly aware of gentle emotion, overcame his depressing thoughts. She had faith in him and was anxious for him, so what did some jerk like Mosol matter? He could go to hell with all those "claims" of his!

Sashka sat in the taxi and said to the driver, "Take us to the station, the courtyard where they used to sell kebabs."

"Let me see the money first," came the sudden reply. "There's already twenty-five roubles on the clock. Are you going to be able to pay?"

"Don't worry, I'll pay. Here, take this," he said, emptying all the money he'd got from Mosol onto the front seat, along with the twenty roubles from the cash he'd received from

Tolik Khachmas. "Is that enough for you? Let's go!"

"Have you given him all your money?" said Lina, alarmed.

"What if I have?" asked Shakh.

"I want something to eat..."

Damn it! That soft Baltic accent of hers, those eyes, that hair, that trustfulness! God knows what was making his head spin, Lina or the fact that he'd not only not had a fix all day, but that he hadn't had a single hit of hash!

"But we've got to find your passport."

"Yes, I know..." She spoke so softly that he really did begin to think that she was related to him, a cousin or something.

The car came to a sudden halt by the yard next to the kebab house. Lina wanted to go with him, but he left her in the cab again. Having her rummage through garbage dumps with him was all he needed! He zipped in quickly, behind the gate, towards the yard and the dumpsters.

Dozens of bright blue and green flies were buzzing around the piles of old food and refuse. Nearly an hour and a half had passed since Mosol had tossed Lina's purse and passport into one of the dumpsters, along with her aunt's address. True, the latter wasn't very important. You could always find somebody's address from the local information office, but getting a new passport wasn't easy at all.

Sashka walked firmly up to the first dumpster, frightened away a cat that was sniffing around it, and overturned it with a single jerk. The refuse fell out, along with a second filthy cat that had been digging around in the middle. It ran off like a bat out of hell. Sashka overturned another dumpster, and a third. Then he turned to those on the other side of the entrance. He had to hurry. If he was seen by one of the people who lived in the block, there might be a real problem...

Thank God! There it was! He could see the red corner of a Komsomol membership card sticking out from under some pieces of bread. He bent down, raked through the trash and extracted the Komsomol card, a new passport and a piece of paper folded in four—her aunt's address. Written in large, almost childlike letters was *Aunt Nora, No. 6 Agayev Street, Buzovny, Baku.*

When he had read the address, Sashka held the piece of paper in his hands for a few moments, then crumpled it up and threw it back into the trash.

Armed with the passport and the Komsomol card, he walked out onto the street and watched Lina's eyes light up with gratitude.

"Here they are," he said, handing her the documents. Then he told the driver to take them to his own address— No. 8 Melnichnaya Street.

He didn't know what his mother would say, but there was no way out. As far as Mosol and the whole gang was concerned, she would have to live in his family for a few days as a cousin.

He could feel how long it was since he'd last had a joint— the day before! He desperately needed to smoke hash. He remembered that he had some in his pocket and he slapped his forehead mentally. What a dope he was! He could have had a hit behind the gateway, when he had been searching for her passport! But how could he do it now? Not with her around. She'd smell it.

His mother was at home, and she stared at Lina and her suitcase in amazement. But Sashka led her off to the kitchen, and they had a short business discussion. His mother had known for a long time what her son was getting up to, and it made her very sad. She would cry, beseeching Sasha to give up drugs, while doing her best to keep it secret from his father. The last twenty-four months had seen her age ten years, and she could only pray to God that Sasha wouldn't get arrested before he was called up for the army. She saw the army as the only thing that would save her son. Then suddenly this blue-eyed girl, this seaside doll, makes an appearance. You only had to look at Sasha to see that he was head over heels in love with her. And his mother saw that God had sent her this as an opportunity to save him. She scarcely inquired who or what she was. It was enough for Sasha to mention a few preliminary details, like the railroad station and her aunt's lost address, for his mother to say, "All right, she can live with us for a whole month if she likes, but on one condition, Sasha—that you don't leave her alone for a moment."

"But Mom, I've got things to do . . ."

"Do them with her, then," said his mother. "Go wherever you like, only take her with you. Show her the town, take her to the movies, the beach. But remember, a girl like that can't be left by herself in town for a moment. You know better than I do what could happen to her."

He did. Only Azerbaidzhani girls could walk the streets of Baku freely without encountering any problems. All the others knew that at every street corner, on every tram, in every store, somebody might lay hands on them, grab them by the breasts, pinch their bottom—even in broad daylight. And after dark it wasn't safe to enter the parks unless there were at least ten of you together. He could see how his mother was purposely capitalizing on this, but he accepted the conditions. What other choice did he have?

"Sasha, give me your word that you'll stop injecting yourself and smoking this garbage. If you can do that, it'll be all right. She can stay here with us. All right?"

"OK, Mom."

"No, not 'OK'. Give me your word, your simple word as a man."

Sashka could feel the aching in his joints. His whole body was beginning to suffer from withdrawal symptoms, and in his pocket he had his salvation—the pellet of hash. Looking his mother in the eye, he said, "All right, I give you my word."

An hour later he had locked himself in the bathroom and switched on the shower to make as much noise as he could. Trembling with impatience, he crumbled the tiny pellet of hashish in his hand, mixed it up with tobacco and stuffed it all into a Belomor cigarette. Then he stood by the open window and took several short puffs. The feeling of relief and relaxation spread through his muscles, and tears came to his eyes. If he could only give himself a shot right away. Maybe he should tell everyone to go to hell, go down the fire escape to the street, and run to the corner of Vurgun Prospect and Ketskhoveli Street, where Kerim would be hanging out. He would take the whole twenty roubles for a shot of opium, because it wasn't the local type. It was imported from Central Asia, or even Vietnam. But that

didn't matter. Sashka had the twenty roubles after all...
He could slip into a nearby gateway and inject himself with
Kerim's syringe—and everything would be all right. He'd
get high...

No! Stop! That was enough! Was he a man or a spineless
creep? He crushed the unfinished joint in his hand, threw
it in the toilet, and pulled the chain. Then he spent a long
time washing himself under the shower, and rinsing out his
mouth, to get rid of the hash smell.

An hour later, when he and Lina were entering the Nizami
cinema, the best in Baku, to see a new comedy film, Sashka
came face to face with the man in glasses, the owner of the
Seiko which he had stolen earlier that day. He turned out
to be the manager of the theater, and Sashka saw him go
into his office to call a militiaman or vigilante. Sashka had
a few seconds to make up his mind whether to run away or
not. But where could he run with Lina? And what expla-
nation could he give her? The internal phone had started to
ring. Out of the corner of his eye Sashka saw the ticket
collector answer it. He grinned. They were already blocking
the entrances, it was too late to run away. He looked Lina
in the eye and said, "Listen, I'm about to get arrested. Not
for anything serious, just for a fight I got involved in. Stay
at my place as long as you like, and tell Mom that I'm
keeping my word. They'll release me. And wait for me,
you hear?"

A militiaman on duty was already approaching them.
They moved into the auditorium, but the militiaman grabbed
him roughly by the elbow.

"Wait a minute! Stop! Come with me," he said in an
Azerbaidzhani accent.

"What's the matter?" Sashka asked, feigning surprise.

"Nothing. You'll find out."

Lina froze, wide-eyed with fright. Sashka said, as he
was led away, "Don't be afraid. Our address is No. 6 Melnichnaya Street. Go home."

An hour later Sashka Romanov, nicknamed Shakh, was
being held at Baku Police Headquarters in a preliminary
detention cell. Twelve people were sharing the cell with
him, all arrested that day for various reasons, or lack of

them, and one of them was me, Andrey Garin, special correspondent of *Komsomolskaya Pravda*.

*The same day, 13:15 hours*

That was it. Belkin's manuscript broke off at that point. I placed a sheet of paper on the desk in front of me and wrote the following: "1. A middle-aged man between fifty and fifty-five years old, with no distinguishing marks except a mouthful of metal teeth, was at Baku airport and at the Kursk railroad station in Moscow. 2. Did the drug-filled coffin exist? Check it out. 3. Summon Aina Silinya from Riga . . ." It was likely that Aina was Lina Braknite, Sashka Shakh's girlfriend. And Shakh himself was "Sultan". As Belkin had been "Garin" in his manuscript, this meant that all the names were fictitious. This wasn't the case for the factual details, however: I found these immediately convincing. Of course, one would have to be cautious and recheck each fact at least ten times. Writers aren't judicial investigators, after all. They are not obliged to make an exact record of reality. They can alter the facts, mix them up, and even invent them. But the pages which I had read contained so many authentic, or at least probable, details that to ignore them would be a sin. I was glad that Pshenichny had found these notebooks of Belkin's. The only problem was that he hadn't found more of them. I wrote on my sheet of paper, "Belkin's notebooks—*Komsomolskaya Pravda* offices." This wasn't a plan of investigation, or even the first outline of one, only a few notes to jog my memory.

Just then Svetlov appeared.

"May I?" he said before entering. He was dressed in his short-sleeved uniform, his new lieutenant-colonel's epaulets and a peaked cap. Although not tall, he was well built, a stocky bundle of energy with a cheerful expression and resolute, intelligent eyes. Taking off his cap, he rubbed the beads of sweat from his receding hairline and entered my office. "How are you, boss?" he asked.

"Still alive," I replied, shaking his hand and motioning him to sit down in the chair next to my desk. "Have a seat.

Do you recognize this?" I said, showing him the file of case No. SL–79–1542.

He opened the file and glanced at the first page. His face registered disappointment. "Um-hm. I sure do. The diamonds are still in my safe."

"Are they high quality?"

"They're incredible! I've never seen anything like them. Should I give them to you? I'd suggest you find out from jewelers who they used to belong to. I haven't done it yet, but if you're taking the case over..."

"Wait a minute," I said, interrupting him. "You know about the corpse and the jewels, but do you know the identity of the other man who was abducted?"

"Another speculator, I suppose," he replied with a shrug. "But it's none of my business. I've got enough going on. The Moscow River Militia are dealing with it now, I think. But how did you get involved?"

"Sit down and read this," I said, handing him the file. "Only read it carefully and all the way through, especially the manuscript..."

As I handed it over to him I noticed once again that the first page was typed carelessly with plenty of mistakes, while the remaining pages were flawless. It was as if they'd been taken out of a typing pool, although Pshenichny had written in his report that he had removed them from Belkin's apartment.

Svetlov began reading. After a few minutes he undid the top button of his shirt, loosened his tie, lit up a cigarette and asked, without interrupting his reading, "Listen, you wouldn't have any cold beer, would you?"

"No, we don't keep any here," I said, with a laugh. "But we can always go out when you're done. There's a bar next door."

I heard a knock at the door. I said, "Come in," and looked at my watch. It was 1:30 p.m., almost forty minutes since I'd spoken on the phone to Pshenichny. He entered and introduced himself. "Hello. I'm Pshenichny."

He turned out to be younger than I had expected, a tall, lean, thirty-two-year-old with fair hair. His features were sharp, like the poet Alexander Blok's, with serious, light-blue eyes. As he entered the office I noticed that he limped slightly on his left leg. I got up to shake his hand and said, "Igor Iosifovich Shamrayev. May I introduce Lieutenant-Colonel Svetlov..."

"Hello, we know each other," Svetlov said. Without interrupting his reading, he raised his hand. Pshenichny shook it and sat down on a spare chair. He'd examined my office the moment he walked in, noting everything about it: me, Svetlov and Belkin's file on the desk. This was just the kind of person I needed, and perhaps even better than I'd expected, since he was younger. Thirty is the best age for an investigator. He's already got experience, yet his enthusiasm for the job hasn't dried up. As strong as a horse—but as stubborn as a mule.

"OK! Got it!" Marat Svetlov said, slamming the last page of Belkin's manuscript down on the table. "You need to fly to Baku and start from there. The drug addicts are there, along with the General and Ziyalov. The names are all invented, of course, but there's enough to go on—who was in the same class as Belkin, who used to copy whose essays, and so on. Nothing difficult there. And it has to be done! They're already transporting these drugs by plane in coffins! Unbelievable!" Svetlov was so worked up that he'd risen and was pacing the length of the room. "But what do you need me for? That's what I don't understand."

"Well, you read it yourself in the file. Investigator Pshenichny thinks it's important to set up a special team to investigate this case. And I agree with him. That's why I've included him in the team, along with myself and you and your section."

"Me? You must be crazy! Shcholokov will never let you have me! You know how he gets on with your boss!"

"Even if I'm investigating this case on behalf of the Central Committee? I've got to find Belkin before the eleventh, in time for him to accompany Brezhnev to Vienna. And the law says that I can request any member of the CID to become part of my team."

"You just try! 'The law says' my foot!" he mimicked my words. "They'll palm some incompetent fool off on you, and you won't be pleased with the results."

"All right, we'll talk about it later," I replied. "But what I'm interested in first of all is whether or not you *want* to work with me on this. Just look: drugs, diamonds, a murder and the kidnapping of a special correspondent. There's a full house for you. Right up the alley of a sleuth like you, I think. And an extra promotion wouldn't be bad either, would it?"

"Okay, okay, you got me," said Svetlov with a laugh. "You know how to get someone hooked. There's only one thing missing."

"What?"

"There's no woman involved."

"What do you mean? There are two of them, at least! Anya Ziyalova, who Belkin fell in love with at the airport, and Lina, the girl Sashka Shakh fell for."

"I doubt it," said Svetlov, grinning. "This one falls in love, so does that one. It sounds too much like fiction to me. Now, a coffin full of drugs—that's something different ... No writer would think that up! Or the fact that he got arrested himself..."

"None of it happened," Pshenichny said softly.

We both turned around to look at him. He'd already taken his briefcase and was removing some kind of document from it.

"Here's the cable I received from Baku Militia Headquarters," he said, placing it before us. I picked it up and read it out loud.

"TELEGRAM

"To Investigator Pshenichny, Moscow Prosecutor's Office

"IN CONNECTION WITH YOUR REQUEST NO. 3341 DATED JUNE 1 1979, WE HAVE TO INFORM YOU THAT A PAINSTAKING CHECK OF FREIGHT TRANSPORTATION DOCUMENTS FOR BAKU AIRPORT HAS ESTABLISHED THAT THE LOAD TO WHICH YOU REFER (A ZINC COFFIN CARRIED ON FLIGHT NO. 315 TASHKENT/ BAKU ON MAY 12) NEVER REACHED BAKU STOP FURTHER EXAMINATION OF THE DOCUMENTATION INVOLVED HAS REVEALED THAT NO SUCH LOAD REACHED BAKU ON ANY FLIGHT DURING THE WHOLE OF MAY STOP

NOR DOES THE BAKU MILITIA HAVE ANY INFORMATION
ABOUT ANY ILLEGAL PARTY TRANSPORTING NARCOTIC
SUBSTANCES (OPIUM) FROM CITIES IN CENTRAL ASIA VIA
BAKU AIRPORT STOP AN EXAMINATION OF THE RECORD OF
PEOPLE DETAINED IN BAKU HAS REVEALED THAT THE
*KOMSOMOLSKAYA PRAVDA* CORRESPONDENT VADIM BELKIN
NAMED BY YOU WAS NOT ARRESTED IN THE CITY DURING
MAY AND WAS NOT PLACED IN THE PRELIMINARY DETEN-
TION CELL STOP THE SECOND PERSON MENTIONED CITIZEN
YURY RYBAKOV WAS DETAINED FROM MAY 12 TO 16 ON
SUSPICION OF BEING INVOLVED WITH OTHERS IN A CASE
OF THEFT BUT WAS RELEASED THROUGH LACK OF EVI-
DENCE STOP CONCERNING THE WHEREABOUTS IN BAKU OF
THE CRIMINALS NICKNAMED THE GENERAL AND MOSOL
WE HAVE TO ADVISE YOU THAT THE BAKU CID HAS NO
INFORMATION ABOUT INDIVIDUALS BEARING THOSE NAMES
STOP FURTHERMORE A CHECK OF THE RECORDS OF SCHOOL
NO. 171 FOR 1967/69 CARRIED OUT AT YOUR REQUEST HAS
REVEALED THAT NO PUPIL WITH THE NAME OF OLEG ZI-
YALOV WAS REGISTERED IN THE SCHOOL OVER THAT PE-
RIOD STOP HEAD OF THE BAKU CITY MILITIA STOP COLONEL
N. MAMEDOV
JUNE 4 1979"

"So there you are..." Svetlov said slowly, narrowing
his quick, intelligent eyes and lighting his pipe, something
which was completely out of keeping with his plump, round
face. The match burned his fingers. He shook his hand up
and down, but kept puffing on the pipe anyway and blew
a large cloud of smoke. "So there you are," he said again.
"I don't like it. The further you go into the forest, the
murkier it gets. One side is lying—either Belkin or the
Baku militia. Now, Belkin is a professional liar, like any
journalist, but the incident with the coffin did take place,
I'd lay money on it. And the fact that there's no mention
of the coffin in any of the airport records doesn't surprise
me. Belkin himself writes that coffins are not allowed to
be transported on passenger flights, so someone was probably bribed to register it as a container or suitcase. And
Colonel Mamedov is trying to pull the wool over our eyes,

of course. You can smell the drugs here half a mile off. And even if Belkin invented it all from start to finish, you can't get away from the fact that Rybakov *did* inject himself with drugs and that he *was* carrying a suitcase containing diamonds. You won't get jewels like those in exchange for a shot of opium, but for a whole coffin full of the stuff, now that's something different . . . OK!" he said, thumping the desk with the palm of his hand. "There's one way I can start getting involved in this case, but we'll have to get going immediately." He looked at his watch. "It's already 2. Since one o'clock my boss, CID Chief Minayev, and our new deputy minister, Churbanov, have been inspecting the work on getting the Moskva swimming pool ready for the Olympic Games. They do the same thing every day, it's become a ritual, because the baths have got a great sauna. Churbanov is Brezhnev's son-in-law. In the five years since he got married to Galina Brezhneva, he's moved from being a lousy adviser to the Central Committee of the Komsomol to being Deputy Minister of Internal Affairs. And that's why he'll do anything if Belkin is really needed by Brezhnev. So let's go to the sauna. The two of them should be nice and warm by now!"

Once he'd made up his mind, Svetlov moved into action, like a dog when it's unleashed. His idea about Churbanov was a pretty good one, though I was far from clear about how we should approach Brezhnev's son-in-law, or about how we could explain our sudden and unexpected visit to the sauna. But I was acquainted with Churbanov myself. He'd been an external student at the Moscow University Law Faculty about ten years before, and I'd been giving a series of seminars on the Soviet legal process there at the time. I began to get ready to go.

"What about me?" Pshenichny asked.

I moved my typewriter forward on the desk, slipped in a piece of official Prosecutor's Office notepaper, and typed out the following:

### TEMPORARY IDENTITY CERTIFICATE

This is to certify that Comrade Valentin Nikolayevich PSHENICHNY, Investigator for the Moscow River Dis-

trict Prosecutor's Office, has been seconded to the USSR
Public Prosecutor's Department as member of an investigation team, and that he is carrying out the functions
of Special Investigator.

USSR Chief Public Prosecutor
R. Rudenko

As I removed the paper from the typewriter, I said to
Pshenichny, "Go downstairs to Vera Petelina's office and
tell her that I'm asking for this to be signed as quickly as
possible, either by Rudenko himself or by one of his deputies. Then go to see Prazdnikov in the Supply Office and
tell him that we need a special car equipped with a radio-
telephone link for a week. After that, you can wait for us
here and write up your ideas for a plan of investigation.
When the identity certificate is ready, call your office to tell
them that Rudenko has seconded you for ten days. OK?"

*The same day, 14:30 hours*
The usual teenage chaos was going on at the Moskva swimming pool on Kropotkinskaya Street. A few dozen girls and
boys were playing ball, racing each other, picking each other
up and flirting generally. Young female swimmers from a
special sports school were being trained on the paths around
the edge of the pool. And, as usual, the place was surrounded by curious visitors from the provinces. The Moskva
swimming pool is one of the city's prime tourist sights.

But few people know that the real sight at this pool is
the marvelous sauna. Access to it is restricted to the party
and government élite. It has dry steam, Finnish equipment,
Czech beer, Volga crayfish, export vodka and Russian masseurs. Yury Churbanov was there, the husband of Galina
Brezhneva, stepfather to her married daughter and step-
uncle to her nephew. But he was young-looking for his forty-
two years, and didn't have the appearance of someone's
step-uncle. We found him relaxing in the dressing room
with the hefty masseur, Stasik, toning up the muscles of his
suntanned and slightly flabby body. Next to him, and receiving the same treatment, was the head of Moscow CID,

General Minayev. The two of them were looking out the window at the young swimmers from the sports school with obvious interest. The girls were fourteen or fifteen years old, a ripe age for admiration.

I had already explained my request to Churbanov and Minayev. Brezhnev's favorite journalist, Belkin, had to be found in the next four days, and this could only be done with the help of Svetlov—*if* the CID would be kind enough to help out their colleagues in the Public Prosecutor's Department. Minayev immediately saw what I was aiming at, furrowed his brow and said, "In that case, why don't you let us take over the whole case, if you can't manage by yourselves? You see, Yury, they keep their own investigation branch. The Public Prosecutor's Office has got more than 30,000 investigators scattered throughout the country, but as soon as something serious turns up, they're immediately asking the CID for help!"

But Churbanov already seemed to have a good grounding in the nature of Soviet power. I'm sure his father-in-law had told him of the principal strategy for maintaining the balance of power between the three main investigative organs (the KGB, the Interior Ministry or MVD, and the Prosecutor's Office) allowing none of them to acquire absolute authority. While Rudenko, Shcholokov and Andropov are competing, they are a danger to each other—but not to Brezhnev. But as soon as one of them gains the upper hand ... Churbanov was the agent of the Brezhnev family in the Interior Ministry, somebody whose appointment as deputy minister Shcholokov was forced to accept. And Churbanov showed a lively interest in the Belkin case.

"Yes, I know Vadim Belkin! Quite a guy! I got to know him in my days with the Komsomol Central Committee. Agh! That hurts, Stasik! Comrade Shamrayev, could you pass me some beer from over there? Have some yourself. It's German and tastes fantastic. I don't like Czech beer. It's too sweet, but German beer is just right. So what are these diamonds you've found, Marat?" he said, turning to Svetlov.

Although I think I'd be right in saying that this was the first time Churbanov had met Svetlov, he was already calling him by his Christian name. I could see how it jarred Svetlov, and a tiny shadow of anger passed over his face. But this disappeared immediately and he said, "They're fantastic diamonds, very rare ones. Pendants and earrings mainly, and obviously very old. I think that if we were to show them to experienced jewelers, we'd be able to locate their former owners and through them find out..."

"And where are these jewels now?" Churbanov said, interrupting him.

"In a safe at my office on the Petrovka," Svetlov replied. "They're evidence in the case."

"Well, why didn't you bring them along with you to show us?" asked Churbanov. "You're an odd fellow! I know! Let's go into the steam room again, then we'll go and look at these jewels and make up our minds."

### 15:25 hours

The legendary Moscow CID can be found in the left-hand wing of the also legendary building at No. 38 Petrovka Street. The ground floor houses the canteen and an enormous hall with panelling down an entire wall, commemorating in gold letters the names of CID men who died in the war and in operations to neutralize the enemies of Soviet power. The first and second floors contain the CID itself, with all its departments and sections. The people that work there are simple, noisy folk, not like the types you'll find at our Prosecutor's Office or at the KGB. At these they all give themselves intellectual airs and are very formal in the way they address each other, always talking in quiet, measured tones. It's the opposite in the CID, where everybody uses bad language all the time, whether they are interrogating suspects or talking to each other. They're not bothered about literary style in the slightest, and informality is the style. That's why Svetlov always talks about his section as the "boys."

We were sitting in Svetlov's office on the second floor, Minayev, Churbanov, Svetlov and me, as well as Pshenichny, who had been summoned from the Prosecutor's Department. Svetlov removed a black document-case from the safe and emptied the diamond and gold jewelry onto his desk. All those pieces, of the most delicate craftsmanship, really *were* something to see. I'd worked on several jewel cases in the past, but it had been a long time since I'd seen such exquisite pale green chrysolite or such delicate gold settings for the diamonds, fashioned like a bunch of grapes or a sprig of roses. The only place I'd seen anything like them was in the Diamond Museum. There could be no doubt that the value put on this jewelry in the official report, one hundred thousand roubles, was a gross underestimate. This was not an unusual precaution on the part of the CID valuers, though, since it meant there would be less of a problem about responsibility in any aftermath.

Churbanov looked at Svetlov. "Are you sure that these haven't been stolen from a museum?"

"Yes," Svetlov replied. "We've checked. Nothing like this is missing from any museum. But, as you can see, it's not a complete collection. There are no rings or necklaces."

Churbanov was turning the most luxurious item around in his hands—a gilded brooch in the form of a rose, decorated with chrysolite and diamonds.

"My wife, Galina Brezhneva, likes these a lot," he said. "I'll hang on to this one until tomorrow to show her."

Then he turned to Minayev. "You can pick it up from me tomorrow. All in all, I think we ought to give them the chance to find Belkin and the rest of the collection. Leonid Ilyich really does read some of Belkin's articles sometimes and after Vienna he intends to write another book, so he'll need people to help him with it. And if these baubles turn out to be part of a complete collection," he continued, nodding in the direction of Svetlov's desk, "then they'd make a suitable gift for the CID to give Galina Leonidovna on her birthday."

"And when is that?" asked Minayev, very interested.

Until now Major-General Pavel Sergeyevich Minayev, a tall man of fifty with fair hair and delicate, nervous features, had been listening rather sullenly to my explanations about the Belkin case. He would occasionally scowl at Svetlov, obviously preparing to yell at him for bringing Churbanov into it. But when Churbanov himself mentioned that the CID might be able to make a personal gift to Galina Brezhneva, Minayev's attitude changed. You don't need much intelligence to realize that the father would be at the daughter's birthday celebrations too, and if Minayev were able to attend, bearing such a gift...

"In October," Churbanov replied, "so there's still plenty of time..."

He stood up and slipped the gold brooch into the inside pocket of his new general's uniform.

Minayev turned towards me and said, "Svetlov and his whole section are at your disposal. But have it put in writing, and get Rudenko to sign it." Then he turned to Svetlov and added, "Come directly to me for whatever you need, understand?"

"Understood, Comrade General."

*15:35 hours*

The three of us, Svetlov, Pshenichny and myself, were now alone. At last we could get down to brass tacks. There was a great deal of painstaking work ahead of us, and one of the seven days we had at our disposal had already flown by. I'd done nothing to advance the investigation, except to set up this team with Pshenichny, Svetlov and his section. Still, that wasn't terribly bad going.

"Igor Iosifovich," Pshenichny announced, "car, registration number MK 46–12, is down below and equipped with a radio telephone, as you requested. I've drawn up a plan of investigation," he added, placing a standard-issue exercise book on the desk in front of him. "May I read it out?"

"Wait a minute," Svetlov said. "There are a few things which have to be done first." He shouted to his secretary through the half-open door. "Zoya! Tell Ozherelyev to come and see me!"

"Here I am," said the imposing, dandyish figure of Major Ozherelyev.

"Now listen," Svetlov said imperiously. "Check the CID and MVD card indexes. We need a man who answers the following description: aged between fifty and fifty-five, with no distinguishing features apart from a mouthful of metal teeth. Unfortunately, we've got nothing else to go on."

"But Marat Alekseyevich..." the major said beseechingly. "Half the Soviet Union has metal teeth. My own father has metal teeth."

"That's the first thing," Svetlov went on, not listening. "The second thing is this. Look in our card index to see whether we've got anything on a *Komsomolskaya Pravda* correspondent, Vadim Belkin."

I looked at Svetlov in astonishment.

"It's just a precaution," he explained. "We ought to check up with the KGB, too, but I don't want to be in their debt. They've probably got something on him, since he works for a newspaper, but it would probably be something political rather than criminal. And the third thing is this," he said, addressing Ozherelyev again. "Choose somebody to go down to Baku for two or three days. In fact, send a couple of men, to be on the safe side. What they have to do is simple: get Aeroflot to supply lists of the passengers on flights between Tashkent and Baku on May 12 of this year and check on them against the list of pupils at Baku School No. 171 for the years 1967 to 1969. If even a single name corresponds on both lists," he explained to Pshenichny and myself, "then that's our man. That's it. Report back in twenty minutes," he said to Ozherelyev.

Then he turned to the two of us again. "Good. Now we can continue our conversation. I hope I haven't taken anything from your plan, Valentin."

I realized that although Svetlov was putting on something of an act to show off his quickness and efficiency, he'd done everything correctly. Or so far at any rate. His idea of checking with Aeroflot was a good one, although not foolproof. There were thousands of people sharing the same surname in Baku and Tashkent. There were any number of Gasanovs, Mamedevs, Bagirovs and so on—as many as there were Ivanovs and Petrovs in Moscow. Not one but a dozen names on the lists might match up. Even so, it was an approach that deserved to be followed up.

Pshenichny smiled at Svetlov, his left hand poised above his plan of investigation on the desk. "I asked Aeroflot for details of the passengers between Tashkent and Baku on June 1, as soon as I'd finished reading Belkin's manuscript. But I haven't received a reply yet."

"There will be one now," Svetlov replied. "If someone from the CID gets on to them, they'll move pretty quickly."

I could see that Svetlov wasn't perturbed in the least by the fact that Pshenichny had had exactly the same idea. As a person who had ideas all the time, he didn't begrudge them in others or guard them jealously for himself.

"All right, Valentin, let's have it," I said. "We're listening."

Pshenichny arranged his notes more conveniently and began. "From the very beginning we need to establish why Belkin was abducted, or at last sketch in possible reasons. I think that either he knew something about the drug smuggling and diamonds, or that he was on the point of finding something out about it. And you can't rule out the possibility that they were kidnapped by a rival gang. After all, the people who abducted Rybakov and Belkin almost certainly murdered Rybakov . . ."

"That hasn't been proven," Svetlov interjected. Until now he had been listening to Pshenichny, silently but impatiently, since he was a person who preferred action to discussion. Pshenichny, on the other hand, was the complete opposite—he was a pedant with a penchant for meticulousness and logic. Fate couldn't have presented me with a better combination of talents.

"It hasn't been proven," Svetlov repeated. "There's no guarantee that Rybakov was murdered. He lost the document case, jumped out of the train after it, and hit his head against a stone—and it could all have happened under the influence of drugs."

"I've had a talk with the forensic experts," Pshenichny said. "They think that somebody hit the kid over the head with something and smashed his temple. But he fell out of the train onto his chest. Whatever happened, we have to find Belkin and Rybakov's kidnapper. And what clues are there so far? An ambulance—without a registration number, unfortunately. And a few medical orderlies, possibly in disguise or possibly the real thing. One of them had metallic teeth and was obviously not an ambulance man, if you assume that he was the same person who met the coffin at Baku airport."

"And what about this Aina Silinya from Riga?" asked Svetlov, obviously following his own line of thought. "Are she and the Lina Braknite mentioned in Belkin's manuscript one and the same person?"

"Unfortunately, Aina Silinya left Moscow on May 30, immediately after identifying the corpse, and I didn't find Belkin's manuscript until the thirty-first. So I wasn't able to ask her any questions connected with it. Besides, after identifying the corpse she was in a state . . . But Rybakov's parents, who arrived by plane to claim their son's body, confirmed that a girl by the name of Aina did live with them from May 12 to 18."

"I see," Svetlov said. "Then we need to bring Silinya to Moscow again, that's one thing. And make urgent inquiries at the Kursk railroad station, that's another. The place is always full of riff-raff—thieves, alcoholics, pie-sellers. I'll lay odds that we can come up with somebody who witnessed the kidnapping, and not just one person either."

"All right, I'll make a note of it," I replied. "Summon Aina Silinya back from Riga. And—find people who witnessed the abduction at Kursk station. We'll decide who does what in a minute. What else?"

"Third point," Pshenichny continued in an even voice, thereby implying that the first two mentioned by Svetlov had already figured in his own plan. "Apart from the main terminus itself, we need to go down the line 100 or 150 miles in each direction from Moscow River station questioning all the railroad employees who were at work on the night Rybakov was murdered. Perhaps somebody saw him with some other people. At the same time, we ought to check what trains traveled through Moscow River station that night . . ."

"You realize what you want us to do?" Svetlov interrupted. "Question all the guards? It'll take a year. What we need is to think of some lightning strikes in all directions. Note this," he said to me. "Get some jewelry experts to examine the valuables. I'll see to that myself."

"Is that it, Valentin?" I asked.

"No. We need to question the journalists at *Komsomolskaya Pravda*. Knowing that I'd seized some manuscripts and books at the apartment, including Solzhenitsyn's *Gulag Archipelago*, one of Belkin's friends at work removed all his papers from the office, I think. And a continuation of Belkin's notebook may have been among them. It's no coincidence that the one we have is marked No. 1. This means that there may be a notebook No. 2."

"OK," I said. "We'll stop exchanging opinions now, and divide the work—in a comradely fashion. We've got as much time at our disposal as we would have in a lightning chess match, so let's deal with the most important parts first. One or two of your boys, Marat, can take care of Aeroflot by flying to Baku and also checking out School No. 171. You can put them in the picture and give them Belkin's manuscript to read. That's the first thing. I'll look after *Komsomolskaya Pravda* and the whereabouts of the remaining notebooks. Svetlov can get the jewelry and diamonds identified. And Valentin can deal with the Kursk railroad station. That should give us enough to do today and tomorrow morning. Unless there's an emergency, we'll meet again tomorrow afternoon here in my office. Any questions?"

"Come in, Ozherelyev," Svetlov said in the direction of my half-open door. Obviously, from his vantage point, he'd been able to see the figure of the major through the crack in the door.

Osherelyev opened the door with his back and came in carrying an enormous pile of CID files in his arms. He banged them down heavily on the sofa and shook the dust off his uniform.

"Phew!" he said. "There are no less than seventy-two known criminals aged fifty and with metal teeth. Lieutenants Rogozin and Shmuglov are going to make the trip to Baku. And here's what information we've got on Vadim Borisovich Belkin, *Komsomolskaya Pravda* correspondent, born 1952."

"Where does the information come from?" Svetlov asked. "Us or the MVD?"

"The MVD, First Special Section," Ozherelyev replied, holding a typewritten sheet in his hand.

"Read us what it says," Svetlov ordered.

"It's a report by the Interior Minister of the Yakutian Autonomous Republic, Lieutenant-Colonel Khalzanov.

\* \* \*

"To the Head of the USSR MVD First Special Section, Major-General Yegorov. I have to inform you that on January 16 1979, while he was on an official visit to the town of Mirny in the Yakutian ASSR, *Komsomolskaya Pravda* correspondent Citizen Vadim Borisovich Belkin, while under the influence of alcohol, took part in a brawl between workers of diamond factory No. 7 and the kitchen and waiting staff at a restaurant. When apprehended, he used vulgar and abusive language. Further investigation was halted at the request of the editorial staff of *Komsomolskaya Pravda* in view of the inexpediency of bringing Citizen Belkin to trial. I am appending standard form No. 1 concerning crimes committed, for registration in the Central Card Index. Lieutenant-Colonel Khalzanov, Interior Minister, Yakutian ASSR."

Svetlov and I exchanged glances. First drugs, then diamonds, and now this—fun and games in Yakutia. Never a dull moment where Belkin was concerned! But what made him visit such places?

*16:20 hours*
"It is twelve days since your colleague, Vadim Belkin, was kidnapped. Either he has already been murdered, or he is in the hands of the criminals..."

I was seated in the office of the chief editor of *Komsomolskaya Pravda,* Lev Aleksandrovich Korneshov. The chief administrator, Stanislav Granov, was there, too. Korneshov's vast writing desk was strewn with piles of manuscripts, galley proofs, and the pages, I realized, of tomorrow's edition. Similar printed pages were pinned to the wall. Korneshov was a small man with auburn hair and gentle, brown eyes. He was about forty or even a little less, while Stanislav Granov was no more than thirty at most.

"On instructions from the Central Committee," I continued, "the USSR Public Prosecutor's Office has set up a special investigation team to discover the whereabouts of Belkin as quickly as possible. One of our best detectives, CID Section Head Lieutenant-Colonel Svetlov, is a member of the team, along with several experienced investigators and CID operatives. I am in command of the team. We know that as a result of his particular employment, Belkin had access to such things as drugs and Yakutian diamonds as well as border crossing-points. I want you to understand me clearly. The interests of the state compel us to consider every possible version of events. Could Belkin, of his own free will or otherwise, have been involved with dealings involving drugs, cut and uncut diamonds, or whatever? The youth kidnapped at the same time as Belkin and murdered two days later was a member of the underworld. He was a drug addict, and next to his body we found a document case containing jewelry of extreme rarity and value. We might be able to find the solution from the notebooks which Belkin kept during his assignments around the country. Here is the first of them, which we removed from his apartment. Look at it. 'If I don't put down an account of all the terrible things that have happened, I'll have to go and drown myself in the Caspian.' It is possible that he has described everything that happened to him. But the second notebook, which could be a continuation of this one, has disappeared. And we believe that it went astray here, in your editorial offices . . .''

Korneshov picked up Belkin's notebook and began to read it with the speed of a professional, whose eyes rapidly peeled the words from the page. He passed the sheets over to Granov, one by one.

Meanwhile he said to me, "Continue, please. I'm listening."

"We must find the remaining notebooks," I said.

"Do you share the opinion of the investigator who carried out the search of Belkin's home, which is that one of our employees removed these documents?" he asked, not looking up from Belkin's notebook.

"I didn't put it like that. But work it out for yourself. On May 31 Investigator Pshenichny found a copy of Solzhenitsyn's *Gulag Archipelago* at Belkin's home, as well as manuscripts written by Belkin himself, the tone and content of which was occasionally far removed from what you find in the newspapers. His neighbors, who were called upon to act as witnesses at the search, were also employees of your newspaper—that is to say, friends of Belkin. There is no doubt that at least half the staff of *Komsomolskaya Pravda* could have known about it within the hour, including one or more colleagues of his who may have decided to remove Belkin's other notebooks from the investigator's attentions, just in case. You never know what might have been written in them, after all. What if they contained something anti-Soviet? You can follow their line of reasoning. But although the motive may have been friendship towards Belkin, the actual result has been to hinder our search for him."

At this point the two of them finished leafing through Belkin's manuscripts and then exchanged a short glance. Granov said, "I'll be back in a second," and went out of the room.

"Do you want to question Loktyova and Zharov?" Korneshov asked. "They were the witnesses."

"No, that wouldn't lead anywhere. Let's assume that they told four friends of theirs, who then told four others, and so on. You'd have a geometrical progression, and before you knew where you were, my whole team wouldn't be enough to question all those who know. No, there's no point in following up that line of thought. The notebooks could either have been taken by friends of his, or . . . did he have friends in the office?"

"Half the editorial staff, if not more."

"Or else taken by enemies, so as to cast suspicion on him. We can't rule out the possibility that somebody doesn't like the investigative organizations and wants to throw a wrench in the works. It sometimes happens. But we are carrying out the instructions of the Central Committee, and I'm relying on your assistance."

"In a nutshell, what you're saying is that you need to cross-examine the whole staff. All right. Why don't you start with me?" he suggested mildly, but with a hint of challenge in his voice.

"OK," I said with a smile, realizing full well, of course, that he had been expecting a different response, something on the lines of "What on earth do you mean? You're above suspicion!" and so forth. "Belkin hadn't been in the office for a whole week, and yet nobody noticed his absence.

Why? Doesn't he have to come to work every day?"

"Technically, yes, of course. But you know, with journalists like Belkin . . . He'd only just returned from an assignment and was supposed to be writing it up . . . And it's not easy to do that at the office. So . . . you understand, we turn a blind eye."

"Lev Aleksandrovich, if it weren't for these lapses in discipline, if somebody had noticed that Belkin was missing on the day he was kidnapped, or at least the day after, we shouldn't be in such a hurry now. Meanwhile, Brezhnev is going to Vienna on the fifteenth, and it was only on the fourth that we started to look for this member of his press corps. In my opinion it would be in both our interests not to waste any more on inter-departmental sniping, but to co-operate with each other. I don't need to cross-examine the whole staff, as you put it, but simply to have a chat with them. Talk to them all at the same time—and as quickly as possible."

He waited a moment before replying, as if weighing all the pros and cons.

"All right. I see what you're driving at." Then he bent down and pressed a button on his intercom. "Zhenya, I want an emergency meeting of all the staff in the Blue Room in ten minutes. And I mean *all* the staff, without exception."

He looked up at me. "What else?"

"Belkin's personal file," I replied.

"Zhenya, get Belkin's personal file from First Section," he said into the intercom. "What else?" he said again to me.

"That's all for the time being," I replied. I had what I was after. The editor understood that, whether we found Belkin or not, whether the latter turned out to be a victim or an accomplice in the crime, it was better for him, Korneshov, to co-operate with my team now, and not defend the honor of his profession. At that moment Granov, the chief administrator, came back into the room. He was carrying some long, narrow sheets filled with fresh newspaper print.

Korneshov looked at Granov in amazement. Granov, meanwhile, began to explain.

"I had to go to the printing department to get a copy made. There's no copy of the article anywhere in the editorial office. They're all with the censor." And he set the galley proof before me. "This is Belkin's last article, dictated over the phone from Baku. It reproduces word for word what he wrote in the second chapter of the manuscript, except that it lacks the final paragraph. That's why we didn't know that Vadim had been arrested and was being held in a preliminary detention cell."

"The Baku Militia have informed us that they never arrested Belkin," I said. "But tell me, did he usually make things up in his articles?"

Korneshov replied. "Well," he said, "it's difficult to say. Probably not. It's a moot point. A journalist's choice of actual detail is a subjective affair. This article probably errs on the side of generalization, maybe even exaggeration. Did you talk to him about it?" he asked Granov.

"Yes. He said that it was all true, apart from the names of the people involved. He also reckoned that he'd most likely be bringing Shakh to the office in a few days' time. And that was all. The next day he disappeared."

"Shakh was the fellow who was kidnapped at the same time as Belkin and found dead two days later," I said. "But I'll explain all this in more detail at the emergency meeting."

I looked at my watch. Ten more minutes had passed. A secretary with pink varnished nails, about forty but trying to look younger, appeared at the door of Korneshov's office. She had Belkin's personal file in her hands.

"In about a minute everybody will be assembled, Lev Aleksandrovich," she said softly, placing Belkin's file in front of me.

Without opening it, I said, "Tell me, what happened to him at Mirny, in Yakutia? Something to do with a fight in a restaurant, wasn't it?"

"Yes, I know," Korneshov replied. "But Belkin's no drunk, that's for sure. Sooner or later every journalist comes back from an assignment with a charge like this hanging over him. It happens to investigators too, you know. The correspondent catches somebody fooling around with the books or stealing merchandise, and before you know where you are, before he even has time to return from his trip, there's an anonymous or collective letter on your desk denouncing him. And do you know the funny thing? None of these letters ever comes from an individual. People usually tell the truth when they write in their own name. But this doesn't happen. People always write collective letters in these instances. They always get together, so as to make it more credible."

"But a fight did take place in this case. It's registered in MVD files," I said.

"Of course it did. A few diamond workers gave some cook a going over because he'd served them with rotten venison. In my opinion, they were right to do so—though that's between ourselves, of course. And Belkin was present when it took place. He even wrote an article entitled *A Brawl*—that was to be the headline. And it wasn't too bad. A shame the censorship wouldn't pass it. So, you see, Mirny's got its own mafia, too, and they cooked up the whole story, as far as it concerned Belkin. That's *our* opinion, anyway. If we acted otherwise, nobody would be able to work in our profession anymore. And until you prove that Belkin was really mixed up in some criminal dealings there . . . We're willing to help you, but as for getting Belkin accused of something—I'm sorry, you'll have to go elsewhere."

I didn't know whether he was saying all this exclusively for my benefit, or whether he was relying on Granov telling the whole staff about how the editor-in-chief defended his employees and so on. All the same, I felt some sympathy for him.

"Let's go," he said, getting up from his chair. "They'll all be in the Blue conference hall by now. Please remember that we've interrupted production of the newspaper, and that even the typesetters have been dragged away from the printing room . . ."

"I understand," I said.

In the Blue conference hall, the famous room where *Komsomolskaya Pravda* arranges meetings with distinguished cosmonauts, composers, performers and travelers, I found myself confronting about fifty people, the entire staff of the newspaper at work that day, including typists, stenographers and messengers. Men and women, teenaged girls and boys, many of them tanned young journalists who had traveled thousands of miles in the course of their work—and all of them looking at me with the mixture of irony and interest typical of old hands who have seen everything in their time.

I explained to them as quickly as I could what I knew of the affair. I didn't mention being a "special investigator" or try to portray myself as a Sherlock Holmes, but simply explained, in as few words as possible, the facts about the kidnapping of Belkin and Rybakov, the latter's death, the reasons for the search of Belkin's apartment and what it had revealed—his manuscript describing the Baku drug addicts and the disappearance of the remaining notebooks. I said that I wasn't interested in who had taken the notebooks or for what reasons. It was simply that they were absolutely essential to the investigation, if we were going to find Belkin's kidnappers and Belkin himself while there was still some hope of finding him alive.

"If the person who removed these notebooks doesn't want to declare himself or herself," I continued, "then I suggest the following solution. I see that there is a telephone in front of me. I shall sit by it for half an hour. During that time the person who took the notebooks can call me anonymously and tell me when and where I can find them. I give you my word, as a party member, that I will not carry out any investigation into who it was who removed the notebooks. If only because there is no reason for me to do so," I said with a smile. "I have been instructed to find Belkin, and I don't want to waste time on extraneous matters."

Nobody uttered a word. One was smoking, another was looking absent-mindedly out of the window, and another had already risen and was impatiently asking the chief editor, "Is that all? Can we go?"

"One more thing," I said. "If anybody can add to my knowledge about Belkin, about his enemies—if he had any—his links with any suspicious individuals, or simply about what he was doing the day before he disappeared or anything like that, then even the most insignificant detail could be of great assistance to the investigation. For this reason, I ask anybody who knows anything at all to approach me during the next half-hour or call me in my office at the Public Prosecutor's Department."

They all began to move their chairs and crowd towards the exit with obvious relief, laughing skeptically and talking among themselves as they did so. It seemed they were all preparing to leave the hall, every last person. But a lanky girl, who couldn't have been older than seventeen, wasn't able to resist asking the following question. "Look," she said with a blush, "everybody knows that you found a copy of *Gulag Archipelago* at Vadim Belkin's apartment. And everybody knows that for keeping *samizdat* publications, books by Solzhenitsyn, Avtorkhanov and all the others you get a sentence of at least three years. Right? So if you do find Belkin, you'll send him to jail, right?"

It was a question I had been expecting. I had been *hoping* that somebody would ask it, and now someone had, thank God! Everybody stopped in the doorway, waiting for the answer. This was obviously the main obstacle to their helping me.

"No," I said. "You're wrong. I base my argument on the fact that you, as workers on the ideological front, need to know the weapons of your opponents, that is, the methods of Western propaganda. This is why I can see nothing criminal in the fact that Belkin had a copy of Solzhenitsyn's work at his apartment. Those whose job it is to know these things are allowed to do so. I doubt that he's read Solzhenitsyn aloud in the Moscow metro." This caused a few people to smile. "In any case, we're not talking about abstract points of law at the moment. What's at stake is the life or death of one of your colleagues. Even if his manuscripts do contain something ideologically unsound or unprintable, I promise you, indeed give you my word, that this will not affect his future."

"If he has one," the young woman noted.

"Yes, that's right," I replied. "Provided we take urgent steps to ensure that he has one."

It looked as if I had lost. I could see the skeptical smiles again. Everyone's eyes looked distrustfully at me. With no other questions, the staff went out of the conference hall, leaving the chief editor, the administrator and myself standing alone. I could read an unspoken question in Korneshov's eyes: "Well, what next? What else can I do for you?"

"Do you need us now?" the administrator asked.

"No. Thank you very much. I'll sit here by the phone, as I said."

"We'll go back to our offices then," said Korneshov. "If you need anything..."

"Yes, of course. Thank you," I replied.

And they left, closing the door behind them. I lifted the receiver to make sure the phone was working, then replaced it and began to wait. I didn't feel like reading Belkin's file. The meticulous Pshenichny had read it before me, and if there was anything in it, he would have extracted it.

Time passed. There was no sound, either of a phone ringing or of a door being opened. There were three minutes left to go before the half-hour was up, then two, then one. I decided to stay on for another five minutes, but it was obvious my experiment had failed. People's aversion to the organs of justice, ingrained during the long years of Stalin's rule, went deep, and there was no way investigators could dissipate or overcome their distrust of the militia and the Public Prosecutor's Department by simple heart-to-heart talks or by offering their word of honor, as I had done. These newspaper workers were afraid of compromising their friend and of becoming undercover agents and informers themselves. They were afraid that their own homes might be visited the next day, their apartments searched and their manuscripts taken away. And we could do it, too. What's the point of denying it? You can twist the law any way you like, after all, and you can always find a reason for entering anybody's home. Not that you really need one! My God! Find me something that isn't rotten in *this* state of Denmark! Still, what is to be done? Throw in the towel?

As I followed this bitter train of thought I watched the orange-yellow sun slip silently behind the rooftops, still waiting for a miracle to happen, for the sound of footsteps outside and for someone to knock at the door. But the

miracle didn't occur. I could hear telephones ringing somewhere in the distance, and the sound of people tapping away
at typewriters in the typing pool. I started to gather my
papers together, including Belkin's manuscript with its slop-
pily printed first page and its immaculately typed continuation, when I suddenly had a vague idea.

I got up, leafed through Belkin's notebook, tore out the
dirtiest and least decipherable page from somewhere in the
middle and walked out to the typing pool, past rooms marked
*News Department* and *Students' Office,* past journalists who
eyed me with cold curiosity.

The door to the typing pool opened easily, at the touch
of a hand. The room was bathed in light from the setting
sun as well as by fluorescent lighting from above. In it were
eight typists, all tapping away at their electric typewriters
as if they were machine-guns. As I entered, the noise stopped,
and everybody looked at me questioningly. The women were
of different ages, but all took pains with their make-up.
There they were, sitting at their humming machines, like
so many tailor's dummies, their hands poised over the key-
boards.

Raising the sheet of paper which I had torn from Belkin's
notebook into the air, I addressed them in the lively, almost
familiar tone of voice that I use with the typists back at the
Public Prosecutor's Office. "Girls! Who knows Belkin's
handwriting? I'd like to get half a page typed out..."

Nobody said anything, but somebody automatically looked
in the direction of a well-proportioned, dark-haired woman
dressed in a green summer dress, who was sitting over by
the window. That was enough for me. As I walked towards
her, I could see she was already beginning to blush.

"Be so good as to type out this page for me. What's your
name?"

"Inna," she said softly, suddenly turning pale as she did
so.

I pretended not to have noticed anything and laid the
sheet of paper on the desk in front of her. "Here. You won't
find it difficult."

Without a word she removed what she had been typing,
inserted a new sheet and moved Belkin's page a bit closer.

The room filled again with the sound of the secretaries typing away diligently—possibly *too* diligently. A moment later Inna's typewriter joined in. Without looking at the keys, Inna's eyes were focused solely on the flow of Belkin's script, while her fingers flew over the keyboard without hesitation. It was the place where Belkin describes how he fell in love with Anya Ziyalova the first time he met her at Baku airport. Looking at Inna out of the side of my eye, I could see her face darken and her teeth clench as she typed out the text. When she had finished, she tore the sheet from the typewriter and handed it back to me.

"Thank you very much," I said, in as off-hand a way as I could manage. "I was worried. I couldn't decipher all of it. Thank you once again."

And with that I left.

Of course, I could have cross-examined Inna on the spot. But I didn't want to hurry, and I especially didn't want to question her at the office. It was six o'clock, and the two hours remaining until the end of the working day were hardly crucial. A quick look at the list of internal telephones revealed that there was only one Inna among the typists—Inna Vitalyevna Kulagina—but that was all I needed. Outside the building my black Volga was waiting for me.

In it, reading *Anna Karenina,* was Seryozha, my driver. I'd known him for some time, as he'd been employed by the Prosecutor's Office for almost three years. I picked up the radio telephone, dialed CID Headquarters on the Petrovka, and through them got through to the Moscow Address Office. "Kulagina, Inna Vitalyevna, aged twenty-five or twenty-six, an employee of *Komsomolskaya Pravda,*" I said to the voice at the other end of the line, and a moment later was told her address: "12 Parkovaya Street, House 17, Apartment 73."

"Listen," I said to Seryozha, "I don't need you until eight o'clock. Go and get something to eat, or do what you like. I'll take a walk around here, as I need to be here at eight anyway."

"Do you mind if I earn some money?" Seryozha asked.

"That's your business," I replied. What Moscow driver doesn't earn some money on the side by giving lifts to passengers in his spare time? And what department doesn't turn a blind eye to it?

"Get in touch with me by radio through CID Headquarters if you need me," he said, switching on the engine. Now that he had some time to earn some money on his own behalf, he didn't have a moment to lose.

I had walked as far as the newsstand at the corner, wondering where to head next, and whether or not to have a shashlyk at the kiosk on Leningrad Prospect, when someone suddenly spoke behind me.

"Excuse me. May I talk to you for a minute?"

I looked around at the sound of this quiet, female voice. There, in her green summer dress and with her black hair cut short over her dark eyes, was Inna Kulagina. And I had been planning to phone her in a hour to arrange a meeting after eight!

"I need to tell you something. I have those notebooks."

"I know you do, Inna. But where do you have them? At the office?"

"No, at my apartment. Only . . ." she mumbled, suddenly stopping short.

"Only what?"

"I don't know . . . There are some phrases in them, you see . . . I'm afraid that . . ."

"Inna, let's go around the corner. Your office windows are above us right here, and maybe you don't want anybody to see you."

"It doesn't matter now," she said, almost in despair. "The other women in the typing office have guessed everything by now."

"There's nothing to fear," I said, taking her by the arm and moving her around the corner in the direction of the Circus Training School. A group of cheerful young circus performers were heading towards us. They were talking and laughing excitedly as one of them gave an imitation of somebody. "And they nearly failed him for doing it," we heard him say as we walked past them. I suddenly thought how it was June and the final examinations would be taking place in the Training School right about now. Somewhere in there was a former "client" of mine, Vasily Kozhdayev, once known as the Gypsy, the Professor, Blackie and the King of the Bird Market, and now head of the illusionist and trick department of the Circus School.

"Listen to me, Inna. Is there anything anti-Soviet in Belkin's papers?"

"I'm not sure..." she replied helplessly.

"OK. I promise you that anything not relating to this case won't appear in the account of the investigation. When can I get these notebooks?"

"Perhaps I could bring them to you tomorrow?" She seemed to regret talking to me already.

"No. 1 need them today. Do you want us to find him?" I asked her point-blank. "I mean—find him alive, if he is alive?"

"Yes, of course!" she replied softly. "He's always getting into trouble like this... I used to tell him..." Her voice already sounded tearful, and it would have been awkward if she had burst into tears on the spot, in front of all the passers-by. I quickly altered my tone of voice.

"Now, now. Everything will be all right. OK, we'll meet here on this corner at eight o'clock, and then we'll go to your apartment to pick up the notebooks. OK?"

"It would be better to meet near the metro station," she said. "Everybody from the office will be around at eight o'clock. Let's say we'll meet outside the Belorusskaya metro at 8:15, by the entrance to the Circle Line. All right?"

"Suits me," I replied. "I live near the Izmailovsky Park, not too far from you."

"You do? And how did you find out that it was me...?"

"Because he typed out the first page of his notebook himself. It was done hurriedly and with lots of mistakes. But as for the rest... Somebody was at his apartment and typed the rest out for him—somebody who knew his hand-writing very well and was a good typist into the bargain. Did you type it while he was there? Did he tell you anything about Shakh?"

"No," she said, shaking her head. "I didn't see Vadim at all this time around. He flew in from Baku and didn't even look in at the typing pool. He never even phoned me. And after that he wasn't around at all—not for one day, then for two, then three. I couldn't wait any longer, so I went over to his apartment. I've got the key . . . I've had it since . . . well, you know . . . I arrived there quite late and stayed up all night to finish typing what he had begun . . ."

I pictured this young woman sitting up all night in Belkin's bachelor pad, waiting for the person she loved to return from somebody else's apartment or wherever she thought he was, and instead of jealousy, hysterical scenes, throwing furniture and crockery around the place and all that other nonsense that you see in the movies, there she was, quietly and submissively typing away at his diary, at his description of how he'd been away on an assignment and had fallen in love one more time with a local beauty, following her around all over the place. The loyalty of Russian women!

"Then his apartment was searched," she continued, "and the book by Solzhenitsyn was confiscated. When I was told, I was so afraid . . ."

"That the next day you removed all the notebooks from his office?"

"No, on the same day. I worked until eight o'clock after all, and the search took place at six or seven. Half an hour later the whole office knew about it. I stayed in after everybody else and . . . listen, he won't get into trouble for having a copy of Solzhenitsyn at his place, will he?" she asked, almost beseechingly.

"I promise you! I said I give you my word!" I said, beginning to lose my patience.

"All right," she said. "I'll see you later."

And she went back into the newspaper building. I imagined how she would feel during the next two hours. Wondering how to kill the time, I wandered along to the Circus Training School. Something was egging me on (curiosity and the lack of anything else to do, most likely) and so I went into the building. The trained eye of the janitor immediately picked me out of the stream of young people wandering in and out of the school.

"Where are *you* going?"

I had to produce my red Public Prosecutor's Office identity card.

"I want to see Vasily Nikolayevich Kozhdayev."

The brick-red features of this obvious boozer immediately changed. "Go on in, please. He's in the arena, supervising the exam. Go down this staircase." And then he started obsequiously showing me the way.

"Did you work in the circus once yourself?" I asked, as we went.

"Who? Me? Once I did . . . I used to fight in the ring with Korolyov, when I was young. I used to win medals. And after that I started throwing weights around—empty ones, of course . . ."

"Did you begin to hit the bottle?" I asked, unintentionally holding on to him as we descended a dark spiral staircase leading to a passageway under the training arena, specially constructed for trick performances.

"Well," the janitor explained, "you know how it starts. First you have a small one to get a little loose, then you take another, then another . . . There weren't any of these drugs around in those days. There's Vasily Nikolayevich . . ." And he raised his hand to tug at the pants leg of somebody sitting directly above us. I lifted my head a little and could see that this trap door was immediately below the desk where the examination panel was sitting. And there, swaying on a rope over the arena, high above their heads, was a boy, playing the violin with his feet and juggling firebrands of some sort in his hands.

"Vasily Nikolayevich!" the janitor shouted, pulling again at the leg of a light-colored and well-ironed pair of slacks. Kozhdayev's familiar gypsy features looked down from above, and he saw who I was.

"What brings you here, old friend?" he said, raising his black eyebrows in amazement.

A moment later I was sitting at the desk with the rest of the panel, made up of famous stars of yesteryear who had now become teachers at the Circus School. It was funny to hear these former clowns, riders and jugglers, whose names were familiar to me from the circus posters of my youth, now addressed as "professor." It was particularly funny in the case of Kozhdayev. He'd reacquired the title which he used to carry in the Bird Market, I thought, as he gave me a humorous, sideways glance with those fiery black eyes of his.

After the young juggler-violinist Shimansky, it was up

to the teenaged twins, Nadya and Olya Tsuryupa, to perform, and after them the young clown Ivan Urema. After
him came Boris Nezhdanny, a conjuror equipped with playing cards and tennis balls. The names of Urema and Tsuryupa sounded vaguely familiar, and I looked at Professor
Kozhdayev in puzzlement. He literally started laughing in
my face.

"Don't you remember?" he said, slapping me on the
back.

And then I did remember. Fifteen years ago the names
of Urema and Tsuryupa had been on the tongues of the
entire Moscow CID. Urema had been a talented trainer of
bears, as well as being an expert safe-breaker, while Tsuryupa was a handsome gigolo, able to pick up, soft-talk and
seduce even the most upright lady in less than two minutes.
The next morning the victim would phone the militia and
explain in horror that all her jewelry, money, household
silver and gold had disappeared. Yet no one would ever
testify that she herself had brought a strange man to her
apartment the previous night.

"You've got it!" Kozhdayev said with a laugh, when we
were talking in his office later. "It's the same Tsuryupa and
Urema, except that it's their children, of course. I transferred
them from their world to this. I write to all my talented
friends, former friends, that is, and ask them to let me have
their children. And often they don't know where their children are, so I have to search for them myself. Take a look
over here . . ."

He opened a safe and pulled out a long, narrow drawer.

"This is my card index," he said proudly. "Just like at
the CID, filed according to names and nicknames."

"You wouldn't have a general in there, I suppose?"

"A general? I know one person nicknamed the General,
only he died six years ago in the mines of Temir-Tau and
didn't have any children. Kravtsov was his surname. I only
file the names of people with children."

"No," I said, "this is somebody else. Here, look at this."

I placed the first two chapters of Belkin's manuscript on
his desk. While he was reading them I flicked through his
card index with interest. Some of the Christian names, sur-

names, and nicknames I knew or half-knew. The others were completely unfamiliar to me. But each card was complete with names, addresses and ages of the children, along with details of their talents and the dates when letters to them were sent and answers received. I looked at the former Gypsy and King of the Bird Market with respect. This was a valuable task which he was performing secretly and without any seeming desire for gain or glory. Some Belkin or other should write a big article about it in *Komsomolskaya Pravda* or *Yunost*.

Kozhdayev read the last page of Belkin's manuscript and looked at me.

"Is there any more?"

"No, but there will be."

"You know that all the names in it are invented? I've never been to Baku myself, so it's beyond me. It seems to contain a lot of nonsense, like a movie. But the part about competing to see who could steal the most watches, that rings true ... I think that could be Salo, otherwise known as the Chief. Nobody could filch watches like him, and nobody could be as mean, either. Getting these kids in a jam, so that they had to start working for him, sounds like his style. I wouldn't be surprised if he turns out to be the one who is behind the drug-peddling there, so as to get rich two ways using the same gang."

"What does he look like?"

"Difficult to say, really. Nothing out of the ordinary, just like the guy described in this story. On the other hand, he's got metal teeth, and I don't remember Salo having any. Still, maybe he has some now. I haven't seen him for twelve years. The bastard! Here I am battling over every kid, and there he is, ruining them by the dozen!"

"So you think that the General and this guy with the metal teeth are one and the same person?"

"Sure they are!"

Twenty minutes later I was in Svetlov's office at No. 38 Petrovka. Captain Laskin and I were going through the pile of CID files that Ozherelyev had thrown on the sofa. By the time we'd waded through twenty of them we finally came across the following entry under the column headed

*Names Used when Committing Crimes*. There it was: *The Chief, Salo, The Godfather, Kurevo*. Then we looked at the record card which was pinned to the file:

> Gridasov, Semyon Yakovlevich, born 1926, sentenced four times for robbery and theft under Articles 144 and 155 of the RSFSR Criminal Code. Height 5'8". Light-blue eyes, whitish hair, medium build. Distinguishing marks—metal crowned front teeth. May 17, 1973, escaped from Strict Regime Colony No. 402–77, Irkutsk Region. Present whereabouts—unknown.

*The same day, Monday, July 4 (after 21:00 hours)*
BELKIN'S MANUSCRIPT
(continued)

Chapter 3
The Preliminary Detention Cell
So I was arrested at Baku airport because of that crazy coffin filled with opium.

What does a person feel the first moment he's under arrest? The first thing you want to do is to twist your shoulder free from the militiaman's grip and shout, "Are you nuts? Do you know who I am?" At the same time, you want to thrust your hand into your pocket and get your red *Komsomolskaya Pravda* identity card, with the initials of the All-Union Leninist Komsomol Central Committee embossed in gold letters upon it. Any policeman would change his expression and would give you a salute the moment he saw it. A powerful weapon! It opens the door to exclusive restaurants and warehouses and even—women's hearts! Armed with such a document, you can do anything. Invite a beautiful woman to see a closed performance of a foreign film at the House of Journalists or at the House of the Cinema, arrange a holiday at a hotel reserved for the élite, get meat at Yeliseyev's, buy imported clothes at a special department in GUM, order a table at any restaurant, smoke Marlboro cigarettes and drink Scotch whisky bought at the editorial canteen, break the driving regulations and even tell the traffic cop where to go! You can do whatever you like under the protection of the good old red card! But just as the Baku militiaman was taking me by the arm and saying, "You are under arrest," I suddenly remembered in horror that this particular magic wand of mine, which I had used to get out of trouble many times, was currently with Anya Ziyalova and her brother. So were the rest of my papers, the notebooks which I had kept during my trip to the Pamirs, my electric razor and a few other items. And the Ziyalovs' trail was cold. There I was, dressed in an old, threadbare cowboy shirt, unwashed jeans and dirty sneakers—one of your ordinary plebs, a nobody.

I looked over towards the baggage section.

"Hey, my rucksack is over there with the luggage..." I said to the militiaman, trying to make him see reason.

"Who cares? Get going!" he shouted, pushing me roughly into the Black Maria. It was one of those special vans they move suspects and prisoners around in, with all the windows curtained off.

"Now wait just a minute!" I said in a rush. "I'm a journalist from Moscow! I work for *Komsomolskaya Pravda!*"

"Have you got any papers to prove it?"

"They were in my travel bag, and that's disappeared. But maybe they've been dropped somewhere..."

"Disappeared!" he said, mimicking my accent. "You just watch it! Correspondent, my ass! You're a speculator! And you were carrying opium! Maybe even a smuggler! Come on, come on, get into the van! And shut up while you're at it."

Deprived of my red card, and my passport, I suddenly felt naked and weaponless. I'd become an ordinary person, just like that: a cipher, a nobody. And when he simply heaved me into the van like an animal, I had a sudden, sharp awareness of how terrifying, how dangerous it can be to be just an ordinary person...

But a few minutes later, when the bus was on its way and I could see out through the bars of the tiny rear window, I grew a little calmer and even began to take stock of my position with a certain interested detachment. I was being taken from the airport into town. Everything would work out in the end, and meanwhile I was caught up in an unusual adventure. It would make a marvelous newspaper article. I immediately thought of a number of possible titles. *Coffin without a Corpse, The Flying Drug Peddlers, Report from a Prison Cell* . . . The office would throb with excitement, and *Izvestiya* and *Literaturnaya Gazeta* would be green with envy!

Still, these militiamen were idiots all the same, I realized. Instead of setting up roadblocks and apprehending Ziyalov and his beautiful sister—God! Could she really be mixed up in this drug-running too?—instead of blocking off all the rail and sea links, questioning the baggage handlers, impounding the documentation relating to the coffin and so on, instead of taking urgent measures like these, which even I, a forensic ignoramus, could see were essential in such circumstances, they'd arrested the first person they'd seen. And now they were wasting more time by taking him off somewhere. Although my rucksack was lost, the police would probably seize it eventually, and the baggage office was hardly likely to give it to anybody else in the meantime. On the other hand, my travel bag with all my papers was gone . . .

I'd never entered Baku under arrest before. We were already passing through Chorny Gorod, a suburb of the city filled with low-roofed houses and rows of oleanders lining the streets. Soon we'd pass the Sabunchinsky railroad station near my grandmother's house. It was good that I hadn't sent her a telegram about my arrival, or else she would have been in a state of total panic by now. We turned to the right, so that meant they were taking me to Militia Headquarters, opposite my old school on Ketskhoveli Street. Amazing! Here I was, former top student, pride of the school, now working in Moscow for *Komsomolskaya Pravda,* arriving at the school gates in a Black Maria and being escorted into Militia Headquarters to be interrogated by a half-literate, Azerbaidzhani police captain.

"Name?" he asked, poised to fill in the preliminary report.

"Andrey Garin."

"Where do you live?"

"Moscow," I said, making a slight attempt at imitating his accent.

"So you live in Moscow, but you spend your time smuggling drugs between Tashkent and Baku? Don't you think we've got enough drugs here already?"

Not bad! He's got a sense of humor!

"So there's a lot of drugs in Baku?" I asked.

He looked at me, pretended not to have heard the question, and went on, in a lazy drawl. "Let me see your papers."

"They were in my travel bag, which was lost at the airport. I asked the militiamen to search for them, but . . ."

I hadn't yet figured out what to do. Should I give away the Ziyalovs, or not? He was an old school-friend of mine, after all, and I'd fallen in love with his sister. On the other hand, how would I get myself out of this mess over the coffin if I didn't tell him that it was the property of my friend and why I'd offered to carry it?

But while I was wondering whether to ask to see the officer in charge and prove that I was the person I said I was, or whether to play along with them for the time being so as to get better material for my article, the decision was taken out of my hands.

"Where do you work?" the captain asked.

*"Komsomolskaya Pravda."*

"What's that? A co-operative association?" he asked uncomprehendingly.

"It's a newspaper!" I said indignantly. "You *can* read newspapers, I suppose?"

The captain got up slowly, in an almost idle way, came up to me and suddenly, without hesitation, smashed me so hard on the ear that I fell on the filthy office floor, which was covered with cigarette ends. What had he done? And why? What right did he have? . . . Stunned, and grasping my head, I managed to get to my feet again. He returned to his seat.

"If you talk to me like that again," he said, "I'll tear your head off. Understand? Go and sell your drugs in Moscow, not around here!"

I stared at him silently, trying to remember every detail about him—that arrogant face of his with its protruding, Caucasian eyes and his receding line of black hair. You'll grovel at my feet, you bastard!

"Now then," he said, "where do you really work?"

It was time to end this charade.

"I want to talk with the Chief of Militia," I said as calmly as I could.

"In a minute," he said with a laugh. "As a matter of fact he's waiting for you! So, you don't work anywhere, you're just a speculator. Which address are you registered at?"

"I will give further information only in the presence of the Chief of Militia. Or the Public Prosecutor."

He looked me in the eye, waited a moment, then pressed some button or other on his desk. I could hear a buzzer outside, and immediately a duty sergeant appeared at the door. The captain nodded in my direction. "Take him to the Preliminary Detention Cell! You stupid Moscow prick!" he shouted at me with contempt. *"Gyotveran!"*

Ever since I was a child I have known that the Azerbaidzhanis hate the Russians even more than they hate the Jews and the Armenians, regarding them as the agents of an occupying power. But for somebody in a government institution, and the militia at that, to call someone by the Azerbaidzhani obscenity for "homosexual", and to display anti-Russian prejudice so plainly and openly, well . . . I'd never encountered that before. On the other hand, he had no reason to watch what he said. Who was I, after all? A drug trafficker! As he told me himself, they had enough drug peddlers of their own. I am certain that if he had arrested some Azerbaidzhani trafficker, it would have been a different story. At least he wouldn't have hit his fellow countryman as he hit me, that's for sure. He had a Muscovite in his clutches . . . So even if I really was a journalist, why not beat me to a pulp anyway? If I'd had my *Komsomolka* identity card with me, it would have been another matter. But without it I could be killed, and nobody would be called to account.

I was led down a brown-painted corridor, lined with barred basement windows so that all you could see were the feet of passers-by. In the distance I could hear the shouts of boys playing soccer in the yard of my former school. The duty sergeant led me up to a door, pushed me through it, and waited outside it.

I was already expected. The usual rough hands rummaged in the pockets of my jeans, and only after that was over did a burly Russian sergeant-major order me to take off my shoes and jeans and untie my belt and shoelaces.

I did as I was told, and waited. Painstakingly and calmly, almost phlegmatically, the sergeant felt the elastic of my underwear and then emptied the contents of my pockets all over the table. There was a half-empty pack of cigarettes, a handkerchief, and eight roubles (the rest of the money from the Pamir assignment was in Anya Ziyalova's hands, along with all my papers). Then, just as carefully, he felt the seams of my jeans. After that he gave me back my clothing, apart from my belt and shoelaces. He counted up the number of cigarettes in the pack—there were six left— thought for a moment, and then said, "OK, you can hang on to these. You'll want to smoke!"

I got dressed and took the cigarettes.

"Let's go," he said.

The corridor seemed to continue endlessly, but now the office doors were replaced by metal ones with spy-holes and bolts. I counted six of them. The sergeant-major tiptoed up to the fourth door, looked through the spy-hole, and uttered some silent obscenity. Then he shot the bolt with one sudden movement and opened the door.

"Fulevy!" the sergeant shouted into the cell. "Give me those cards at once!"

"What cards?" came the reply from the cell.

"Go on in," the sergeant said, nodding towards the cell, and I went in. It was covered with dust, with rows of double bunks along the walls and a dirty, barred window high up on one side. In one corner, not far from the window, was a latrine, and in the other a small cistern filled with water, with a mug attached to it by a chain. This was the sum total of the "furniture" in the cell. Somebody was asleep on one of the upper bunks, while the other occupants, eleven in all, were lying or sitting on the lower beds. One of them, a skinny fellow, aged about forty with Tartar eyes and wearing a sweater of some kind, tried to argue with the sergeant.

"What cards, sergeant? What are you talking about?"

"Stop playing around with me," the sergeant-major said

quietly. "Let me have the cards or I'll call Bagirov."

I realized that Bagirov was the captain who had just belted me on the ear. I could already feel the bruise above my temple.

"I'll call Bagirov, I'll call Bagirov," the Tartar said mockingly, passing a pile of tiny pieces of paper, about the size of a matchbox, to the man sitting next to him. These were the "cards," nothing but pieces of paper torn from a notebook. "Shakh, you give them to him. He can go to hell!"

Shakh took the cards and went up to the door, eyeing me for a second as he did so.

"You might give me a book to read or something..." he said to the sergeant.

"Let me have them, Sashka, come on," came the reply. "So you're a reader, eh?"

He took the cards and asked, "Are they all here?"

"They are, apart from the Queen of Diamonds."

"Where's that?" asked the sergeant.

"I screwed her," said Fulevy from the other end of the cell. "And now she's sucking off the cripple." He started laughing at his own joke. Then the whole cell joined in, apart from the cripple in question on the top bunk. The lower part of his leg had once been severed and sewn back on.

Sashka Shakh smiled too.

The sergeant smiled good-naturedly, looking first at Fulevy, who was laughing away, then at the others, and finally at Sashka. He was not allowed to enter the cell except in the company of at least one other guard. Sashka was still standing by the doorway smiling. Suddenly the sergeant kneed him in the groin so hard that he bent double and immediately caught a premeditated blow to the chin from the same knee. This second blow was not a hard one, but it was enough to lay Sashka out flat on his back. At the same time the sergeant slammed the door shut, bolted it noisily and walked away, without even peering through the spy-hole. We could hear his unhurried footsteps recede down the corridor.

In this way, he had his revenge on Fulevy by hitting Sashka. What a bastard!

I looked at the prisoners. None of them, not even Fulevy,

got up to help their seventeen-year-old fellow inmate. He was writhing around on the floor, pressing both hands to his groin and gasping for breath. His bloody mouth was twisted in a noiseless scream. The others simply stared at him, as if they were watching a circus act. Amid the tedium of prison life this was choice entertainment!

I pulled the end of my shirt out of my jeans, tore a piece off, went up to the cistern and tried to moisten it. But the cistern turned out to be empty. I went up to Sashka and started to wipe the blood off his face with the dry piece of shirt.

"Get away, you son of a bitch!" Fulevy snarled suddenly.

I hadn't expected this, and turned towards him in surprise.

"Get away from him! Take your hands away, you stool-pigeon!"

"Are you crazy or something?" I asked.

Fulevy raised himself from the bunk and walked up to me. I could see that he was chewing on something in his mouth, but I couldn't understand why he was moving his cheek muscles so vigorously. By the time I realized that he was simply gathering saliva, it was already too late—he suddenly spat a loud and juicy gob right into my face.

I'd never had that happen to me before! Forgetting that I was a famous journalist, I lost all self-control. Using the same trick as the sergeant, I kneed him in the groin, and then, when he was staggering from the blow, hammered both fists into his neck. As he fell, the bastard caught me by the legs, and we rolled around on the floor of the cell, covered in spit as it was. He tried to bite me, but I managed to twist his arm and wipe my face on his sweater. I don't know how it would have ended if, at that moment, the door hadn't opened. Two new militiamen rushed into the cell, grabbed the pair of us, and dragged us past the smirking sergeant-major, along the corridor into the interrogation room—a different room this time. There were no windows in this one. And beneath those thick, concrete walls decorated with portraits of Dzerzhinsky and Kalinin, these two policemen began, methodically and professionally, to beat us up.

I immediately received three shattering blows—to the

jaw, the liver and, again, to the ear, and I fell senseless to
the floor. Fulevy lasted a little longer, I think, though I'm
not sure. The only thing I know is that they doused us with
water and then forced us to get to our feet and "make up".
We stood across from each other, still swaying, while the
militiamen, who were having a great time, said, "Tell him.
I won't hit you anymore, I swear!"

I said nothing, not because I didn't want to, but simply
because my jaw was hurting so much that I couldn't say
anything. I received another blow to the ear for my pains
and fell onto the cement floor again. They doused my face
with water and lifted me up. Through my clouded brain I
could hear Fulevy's voice whisper. "I w-w-won't h-hit y-
you any m-more . . ." His voice sounded very distant, as if
under water.

"Swear on your mother's grave!" they ordered him.

"I swear . . ."

"Now you!" they said, poking me in the ribs.

I mumbled something through my swollen lips, but they
still weren't satisfied and forced me to say it more clearly.
Then they hauled us back to the cell, and shoved us, not
even onto the bunks, but simply on the floor.

We lay there next to each other. Now it was Sashka
Shakh's turn to wash the blood from our faces with that
torn-off piece of shirt. But I was lost to the world and I had
only the vaguest notion of what was going on. It was probably two or three hours before I regained consciousness
completely. A light was on, fixed behind the bars of the
window just below the ceiling. I was lying on one of the
bunks, though I didn't know who had put me there. Sashka
Shakh was sitting above me and arguing loudly with Fulevy.
Through the drowsiness and aching that I could feel throughout my body, I could hear the murmur of their voices.

"Look, if he was an informer, they wouldn't have beaten
him up like that . . ." Sashka was saying.

"They beat up their own stoolies, too, so that us prisoners
will believe them more easily," Fulevy replied.

"Sometimes, but not as much as that! What are you
talking about, Fulevy? Just look what they've done to him."

"Well, how the fuck should I know?" came the reply.

"Only why did he rush to wipe the blood off you? He even tore up his own shirt. What a performance! So I decided that he was a stool-pigeon. What did they arrest him for?"

"But you didn't even ask him . . ."

"Yeah, then this fucking mess happened. You got a cig?"

"Let's smoke his—there's one left."

I realized that they'd taken the cigarettes out of my pack. I desperately needed a smoke, so I managed to croak in a hoarse whisper, "Cigarette . . ."

Sashka put it in between my lips, and I took a long, greedy drag on it. And it was as if some great weight bearing down on my shoulders was suddenly gone. I opened my eyes.

"Who are you?" Sashka asked. "What were you picked up for?"

I said nothing, but kept smoking.

"Can you hear me?" asked Sashka, but I took no notice.

"Listen, pal," Fulevy said, touching my shoulder. "I thought you were a plant. But they gave you a worse going-over than me. So I owe you one, OK? What did they take you in for? There are one or two in here for fifteen days, petty stuff, you know. One of them could take a letter out with him. Any good to you?"

"Uh–huh," I mumbled.

"Hey, you! Bookkeeper!" he shouted, giving the guy asleep in the next bunk a poke in the ribs. He looked like a typical middle-aged alcoholic. He woke up with fear in his eyes, ready to do whatever he was asked.

"Write this down," Fulevy ordered. "Now tell him what you want to say," he said to me. "He's got a brain. He *is* a bookkeeper, after all, and he'll remember it now, and then tomorrow, when he's at work, he'll write it down and send it wherever you like. They take him to work right from here. You dictate what you want him to write, and he'll remember."

I realized that Fulevy wanted to test me again, but I couldn't give a damn any longer. It was time for me to be getting out of here. Idiot! I'd had enough of being immersed in real life!

Now which paper would publish an account of everything

that had happened to me? I looked at the bookkeeper, who was wide-eyed with fear. I expect I looked the same myself.

"Get hold of a telephone directory. Look up two numbers. The first is that of *Komsomolskaya Pravda*'s journalist department, where you'll find Izya Kotovsky. The second is the Azerbaidzhani Central Committee's Propaganda Department, where you'll contact Kerim Rasulov. Tell them that I'm here. My surname is Garin."

"So who *are* you?" asked Fulevy, dumbfounded.

Instead of replying, I said to the bookkeeper, "Have you understood?"

"Repeat it all!" Fulevy said, kicking his leg.

"Get hold of a telephone directory," said the bookkeeper, "and look up two numbers, the *Komsomolskaya Pravda* journalist department, where I'll find Izya Kotovsky, and the Azerbaidzhani Central Committee's Propaganda Department, where I'll contact Kerim Rasulov. Tell them both that you're here and that your name is Garin."

"Well, is it right?" Fulevy asked, not without a hint of pride. "So who are you then?"

"I work for *Komsomolskaya Pravda*," I said.

"Are you a writer?" asked Fulevy, interested.

My swollen lips started to grin, but I immediately groaned with pain.

"Well, I'll be damned!" he said. "Give them a description of our life here. You could write a whole novel about what I've been through. Will you do it? I'm begging you—please write about it. Look at this!" He opened his mouth and pressed down his lips to reveal a mouthful of metal teeth. "See these? I had all my teeth knocked out when I was being transported, before I was even fifteen. And what for? For nothing! Look here!" He showed me his arm. It was covered with needle marks. "See that? I've been on drugs for fifteen years. Yes, I could tell you my life story, and you could write a novel about it as good as anything by Tolstoy. And what have they nabbed you for?"

I told them—about the drug-filled coffin and about Ziyalov. The only thing I left out was his sister. I didn't want to get her mixed up in it.

"A whole coffin filled with opium! Not bad!" said Fulevy,

who was completely amazed. "You see how they use us, Shakh? Why, it'll have been worth a million roubles at least! Christ knows, maybe even two million! That's the kind of money they earn, those people! Listen, writer, are you going to tell them all about it? Are you going to write about the going-over they gave you? Huh? Christ, they've bitten off more than they can chew with you, the shits! As for you, bookkeeper, if you don't make the phone calls he's told you to, then don't come back here, OK? And if you snitch, I'll get you, even if I have to do it from Kolyma, understand? I'll cut your throat, get me?"

"I get you . . ." the bookkeeper said, moving fearfully a little further away from us.

The whole night, while the other inmates were snoring away, Fulevy and Shakh told me their stories. As well as being a drug addict, Fulevy was a housebreaker who moved around from city to city. The morning before he'd been caught red-handed robbing the apartment of the chief engineer of the local tube-rolling factory. He already knew that they'd pin ten years on him under Article 144, Section 3. The other thing that was in doubt was whether he'd be sent to the Baikal-Amur Railway Colony, Vorkuta or the Naryn Hydro-Electric Power Station.

Then we discussed Sashka's story. According to Fulevy, his case presented no problem at all. In fact, his only crime was that he'd jumped onto the platform of a moving tram. After that two guys, whom he didn't know, started to push and kick him off the platform. He'd tried to defend himself and pulled them off the platform too. There *was* a man with glasses nearby but as for a watch . . . What watch? Where did it come from? *I* was supposed to have taken your watch? What are you talking about? In any case, Citizen Investigator, how could I have taken his watch, if he says himself that he saw me being attacked by the other two? I'm supposed to have done it while I was being beaten up, is that right?

Fulevy gave such an accurate, lifelike and detailed description of how Sashka should defend himself during the investigation that, looking ahead, I could see that all Sashka would have to do at the cross-examination would be to repeat the answers his cellmate had prepared for him.

The next morning, after the three fifteen-day merchants had been taken off to work (including the bookkeeper), Sashka was summoned for cross-examination. When he came back he had a huge package in his hands, containing a round Caucasian loaf, some grapes and a short note saying, "We'll be waiting for you. Mom and Lina."

But we'd hardly started in on the parcel when I was called for questioning myself. The very fact that the guard was now taking me straight to the first floor seemed to signal a change in my situation. The corridor was no longer painted that dull brown color (I realized now why brown paint had been used on the floor below—so as to make the blood less obvious, if any of it splashed on the walls). No, the corridor on the first floor was painted light green and there was a carpet running along it. It was obvious that they wouldn't beat anyone up here, if only to prevent the carpet getting stained with blood.

The furniture in the investigator's room was far better than the standard office issue. There was a good desk, bentwood chairs and even a refrigerator in the corner. Sitting at the desk was a youngish-looking man with light-blue eyes and dressed in an ordinary suit. He was writing something.

"Take a seat," he said, motioning me towards a chair. I did as I was asked. Without raising his head, he continued to write for another four or five minutes. Then he placed his signature at the bottom of it, raised his eyes and sat back in his chair.

"Hm . . . yes, so you're Garin? From *Komsomolskaya Pravda?* And how can you prove it?"

I decided to say nothing, pure and simple. To make my point.

"Well, why won't you say something?"

The fact that I had been brought to a normal office, where somebody was addressing me fairly politely, spoke for itself. The bookkeeper must already have phoned Izya Kotovsky or Rasulov at the Central Committee, or perhaps he'd phoned the two of them.

"Well, why won't you answer?" he persisted.

Without looking at him, and fixing my eyes on the wall,

I said, "I don't know who it is I'm talking to."

"Ah..." He sat back in his chair and said in an offhand way, "And why should you? Let's assume that I'm the investigator. It doesn't matter very much for the moment. We'll just have a little chat, not for the report. Now look. Somebody helps the baggage handlers unload a coffin from a plane and carries it to the airport exit. Right? On the way the coffin accidentally falls and splits open. It turns out that it contains drugs. That person is naturally arrested and taken off to Militia Headquarters. But while being placed in a cell pending further investigation of the case, he insults a militia officer and threatens to have everybody locked in jail. He says that he's a journalist working for *Komsomolskaya Pravda*, although he has no papers with him to prove it. You see, everything has been entered in the report." He pointed to it. "After that, the said person has scarcely entered the Preliminary Detention Cell when he picks a fight with some of the other criminals and attacks the prisoner nick-named Fulevy. You see, Comrade Garin, ours is a democratic country, and you don't have the right to insult the militia and beat up prisoners, even if you really are a newspaper correspondent..."

I said nothing. If they had the testimony of my fellow inmates, it must mean that the fifteen-day merchants had given me away, or maybe the bookkeeper had, the son of a bitch. He hadn't phoned anybody, but had simply reported our conversations the previous night to the militia. He would undoubtedly receive a reward for his information. They wouldn't send him back to the same cell again, that went without saying.

"Well, I'm waiting," my investigator said.

"I will talk only to the Chief of Militia," I replied.

"Only the Chief, hm?" he said, smirking. "What's your patronymic?"

"You know it already, I think."

He grinned. "Quite right, we do. Andrey Borisovich. More than that, I've read some of your articles—about the Arctic zone. Siberian workers and geologists, and the like. And I must tell you that I'm a great admirer of your work. You write very well. But... nobody has the right to attack a member of the militia. You attacked a captain, no less. Here's his report. What shall we do?"

"Let the courts decide," I said, looking him in the eye.

"Let them decide what, exactly?"

"My case," I replied. "Let's have it tried in open court, and then we'll see who laid hands on whom. Let's invite *Komsomolskaya Pravda* and the Central Committee Propaganda Department to send along some observers..."

He said nothing for a few moments, but simply stared at me. Perhaps he was revising his opinion of me, or weighing what to do next.

"Hm... Yes... You're a strange man, Andrey Borisovich. Don't you know that the militia are never brought to court in our country? Although, of course, we do make mistakes, too. We're only human, after all, aren't we? The only people not to make mistakes are those who never do anything. Even the newspapers make mistakes. You and I know, don't we? They might write about somebody one day, saying that he's a first-class worker, a hero of labor, and then he turns out to be a petty thief the next. He's been fixing the books, or something like that. The Anti-Fraud Squad has a whole file on him. But the newspaper doesn't get taken to court, eh? You see, Andrey Borisovich, you and I know what we are about. Yet here you are, going on about court, open sessions, the Central Committee Propaganda Department! Besides, you have yet to prove that you and Ziyalov weren't in cahoots with each other. Why did you arrive in Baku with him? What is he to you?"

"I was at school with him," I replied. "That's all."

"Well, that remains to be proved."

He got up and began to walk around the room, lighting a pipe as he did so. I couldn't help smiling. He reminded me of Stalin. His features were very different, of course, but as far as his movements and manner of speaking were concerned, he was the image of the Great Leader.

"OK. This is how it looks to us. Two former schoolmates are transporting a consignment of drugs from Tashkent to Baku. One of them is an employee of a national newspaper who happens to get caught. The other one manages to escape, present whereabouts unknown. But only for the time being. We'll find him, of course. What are you smiling at?"

"Nothing," I replied. All the same, it was amusing. He sounded like Stalin, too!

"You're wrong to smile. Drugs offenses are very serious. According to the Decree of April 25 1974 entitled *Intensifying the Struggle against Drug Addiction,* drug trafficking is now considered an especially grave offense. We could keep you under arrest for up to nine months while the investigation is proceeding. And bear in mind that no editor would be able to help you then. You see, you'd have to spend nine months in cells similar to the one you've just been in—with criminals, murderers and homosexuals for company. At night they could do anything they liked to you. Eventually, of course, it might turn out that you were innocent after all, but meanwhile . . . Take Fulevy, for instance. Did he bother you last night? He's a queer, after all, and if you won't do the kind of things he tells you to, he'll strangle you. And if he doesn't, somebody else will. I can't give you a cell to yourself, even if you are a journalist. But . . ." and at this he turned his smiling eyes towards me, "It's your choice, in fact. We could let you go after all . . . eh? How about leaving here on the spot, going home, taking a shower, catching up on some sleep, lying on a beach for a few days—and then flying back to Moscow? How about it?"

The bastard! He knew just the approach to take with me! I could see the gentle green waves of the Caspian in my mind. After spending such a terrible night on a prison bunk, I could imagine myself immersing my tortured body in the healing, salty waters of the warm sea, and then lounging on the sandy beach, roasting in the sun and drinking cold beer . . .

As if reading my thoughts, my questioner opened his refrigerator, which contained a few bottles of Czech beer. Can you imagine? I was dumbfounded at the coincidence. Meanwhile, he gave me a smile and took out a couple of bottles. I could see tiny droplets of icy water glistening on them. He placed them on the desk, and then opened them up by pressing their metal caps underneath the lid of the desk. He poured some out into two glasses.

"Here you are. It's Czech beer, just like you'd get at Sokolniki Park in Moscow."

I admired his flawless psychological approach. I took the glass, emptied it in one gulp, and said, "Who are you? This isn't your office, is it?"

"What gives you that idea?"

"You wouldn't have opened the bottle like that if the desk belonged to you."

He smiled.

"Andrey, let's call each other by our Christian names. We're the same age, and we both work in the same system, although in different sectors. Look, we made a mistake in your case. Our boys were too hasty. And they'll apologize to you. I'll call them in presently. The captain and his two sergeants will crawl on their knees in front of you, if you like. Should I call them?"

I said nothing and he pressed a button underneath his desk. The duty officer immediately appeared at the door.

"Send for Captain Bagirov—right away," he ordered.

The guard disappeared, and my "investigator" continued to look at me silently. Then he said, "Finish your beer, or else it'll get warm . . ." He opened another bottle and poured some into my glass.

I am not sure, but according to the laws of literary narrative, if this story were being written by Victor Hugo or even the detective story writer Yulian Semyonov, the hero— that is to say, me—would hurl the glass away, or at least spit the beer out into the face of the "investigator". He would then be led away to the cells, to get beaten up once more, either by the militiamen or criminals. But I am not Victor Hugo, or Yulian Semyonov, or Shtirlits, the famous detective, for that matter. Also, it was by no means clear what I would be kept in for. So I wouldn't betray Ziyalov? But they already knew his surname, it appeared. To write an article about prison life, then? But the paper would hardly be likely to print it. Anyway, there I was, sitting in the room with the "investigator" and waiting for Captain Bagirov to arrive. I hadn't said either "yes" or "no" yet. In fact, I didn't know what he wanted from me, or why he had become suddenly so polite . . .

The door opened and Captain Bagirov entered the room. I recognized the same slightly protruding, arrogant Azerbaidzhani eyes, the beads of sweat on his receding hairline, and the black moustache.

"Allow me, comrade..."

"As you were, captain!" the "investigator" barked suddenly, obviously unwilling to have his name or rank revealed. "Shut the door." When Bagirov had done as he was told, the "investigator" went up to him and said softly, "You swine, you're a disgrace to your uniform! Why the fuck do you think you're paid your salary? Why do you have those stars on your epaulets? I could tear them off you this minute! You should be able to tell the difference between shit and a prominent worker, that's what you're paid for, you understand me?"

"I understand you, comrade..." Bagirov said quickly.

"And leave out the 'comrade' bit. Do you know who you raised your hand against yesterday?"

"I have no idea..." Bagirov said in a thick sweat.

"You apologize now. Go on! Ask his forgiveness. And if he tells you to get on your knees, you'll do it, understand? Otherwise I'll have you drummed out of the force on the spot! You have any children?"

"Yes, two, comrade..."

"Shut your mouth! Either your children will go starving because you've been cashiered, or you beg Comrade Garin to forgive you. OK?"

It was a hideous scene. Without asking why, or even thinking, this bull of a captain suddenly fell to his knees and crawled over to me, grasping his Adam's apple. "I beg you, Comrade Garin! Forgive me. I promise I won't do it again! I swear by my mother's grave!"

I could see the "investigator" looking at me out of the side of his eye, waiting for my reaction. Meanwhile, kneeling in front of me was the supposedly repentant hypocrite of a captain. The whole scene was so repulsive that I turned to the "investigator" and said with a feeling of disgust, "OK, that's enough! Stop it!"

"Do you forgive him?"

"Yes."

"Thank you, comrade," Bagirov started mumbling to the "investigator". "Thank you . . ."

"That's enough!" said his superior, apparently repelled by the spectacle himself. "Leave us alone now!"

When the door had closed behind him, the "investigator" said, "Should we summon the two sergeants now?"

"There's no need," I said. "What do you want me to do?"

He offered me a Marlboro. "Have a cigarette. What do I want? I want you to forget about the whole business. Nobody beat you up, and in fact you haven't even been to Militia Headquarters. We'll find Ziyalov. He's a crook — but the whole case has nothing to do with you. So why should you get mixed up in it? You'd be dragged along to the investigation, you'd have to give evidence in court, and so on. Do you really want that? Look, I'll tear up all the reports of your cross-examination, as well as the testimony of your cellmates. You haven't been here at all, OK? Otherwise it'll drag on and on. How you got arrested, where you were taken, how and why you were released, and so on. I'll tear it up, OK?"

"Wait a minute," I replied. "Ziyalov has the bag containing all my papers. How can I get out of here if I don't have any documents? I need to get my passport back, as well as my *Komsomolka* identity card. I'd better put in an official request, or else he'll get picked up carrying my passport . . ."

"Quite correct! But how do you think I found out that you really are the journalist Andrey Garin?"

"From the bookkeeper," I replied.

"Well, from him, too," he grinned. "You're absolutely right. But before that happened, a woman phoned last night and said that items belonging to a correspondent of *Komsomolskaya Pravda* were to be found at baggage locker No. 23 in the marine station."

He opened one of the drawers of his desk, took out my travel bag and passport, and pushed them across the table at me. "What do you think? Who is this woman?"

I looked at him in silence.

"I don't know either," he said. "Some anonymous person. The duty officer who spoke to her just had time to make a note of the number of the locker, when she hung up. But she did say one other thing—that you weren't mixed up in anything. But that doesn't matter now . . ."

Of course, I knew who it was that had phoned—Anya Ziyalova. But why tell *him* that? Apart from loathing and the desire to get away as quickly as possible, I felt completely empty. I checked the documents in my travel bag. They were all there—passport, newspaper card, driver's license, my Union of Journalists membership pass, and even my money! I got up from my chair.

"I can go now?"

"If we've reached an agreement, then of course you can! Now, you'll agree to let me tear this up?"

He was still holding the transcripts of my cross-examination and the reports of my cellmates. I was convinced that they were only copies, but I didn't care.

"Yes, go ahead," I replied.

He tore them up, first into four, then into eight, and made a big display of throwing the pieces into the wastebasket.

"Excellent. So you haven't been to Baku Militia Headquarters at all, about anything? Correct? You've forgotten all about the incident with the coffin and about Ziyalov, too. Right?"

"Yes," I said, forcing myself to agree.

"Thank you very much!" he replied, offering me his hand. But suddenly he appeared to remember something. He opened the drawer of his desk and got out a file bearing the inscription, *GARIN, A.B. Agent's Dossier*. He opened the faded gray file and extracted a yellow sheet of paper from it. He passed it over to me. Looking at it, my heart fell into my stomach. It was a parody of a famous poem by Lermontov, in my handwriting and composed more than ten years ago, in reaction to the events in Czechoslovakia in 1968:

And you, with flames and shrapnel, you common
    Kremlin rabble,
Remembered for our fathers' agony and death,
Have crushed the heart of freedom

That was in Bohemia's cities, beating still.
You gannets, greedy crowd, that cluster round the throne,
Butchers of liberty, art and choice,
Have forced your laws with tanks and fire,
Stifling any voice of peace and human right.
Now you, you base manipulators, listen to another law,
The people's law that waits and speaks from history,
Not to be corrupted by jingling sounds of gold.
It has in mind *your* future mind, of action or intent.
So resort to scorn or slander it in vain,
No second chance.
Nor ever will your own black blood be payment
Fit to drown the blood of freedom drained from Prague.

Thank God the poem was unsigned.

He grinned as he took the piece of paper from me.

"I'm sure this isn't your poem. In your youthful enthusiasm you simply copied it down from someone else. Those were passionate, heady times, I remember. So let it stay in our files. We haven't even passed it on to the KGB. But if you don't keep to your agreement . . . Remember, this little piece of paper could ruin your whole career. No Lermontov will be able to help you. Do we see eye to eye?"

A moment later I walked out of Baku Militia Headquarters onto the street outside. The bright noon sun blinded my eyes. I stopped and listened. I could hear the hum of traffic in the streets. I could hear teenagers kicking a soccer ball around in the yard of my old school, swearing away in Azerbaidzhani, Russian and Armenian. An old man selling ice cream was dragging his stand along the street, castors squeaking as he did so.

"Ice cream for sale!" he was shouting. Meanwhile, outside Militia Headquarters, some valiant Azerbaidzhani militiamen were dozing away, ready to drive off in their Volgas at a moment's notice. As I wandered along Red Army Street, down towards the Esplanade and the sea, I felt violated and useless, like a woman who has just been raped. Not even when that bastard Bagirov struck me in the ear, or when Fulevy spat in my face, did I feel as sick and as used as I did at the moment I was released into the sun.

Oleg Ziyalov was the one who must have given them that poem ten years ago. That was why they were shielding him today, I thought. Oleg Ziyalov was probably one of their agents...

*The same evening, 22:30 hours*

No, there was certainly never a dull moment where Belkin was concerned!

I was at 12 Parkovaya Street, on the twelfth floor of a whitish tower-block, sitting in the one-room apartment of *Komsomolka* typist Inna Kulagina. It had a tiny entrance hall, a minute kitchen and balcony, and one room measuring seven and a half square yards. I had an identical place myself in an identical white tower-block just by the Izmailovsky Park metro station. If it weren't for the signs of a woman's hand—the lace curtains in front of the open windows, the comfortable sofa with Inna curled drowsily up on it, waiting for me to finish reading Belkin's manuscript— if it weren't for all these admittedly significant details, I could easily have imagined that I was at home, sitting at my own desk and thinking about some utterly routine matter. The table lamp highlighted the pages of Belkin's neatly typed manuscript, a glass of strong, lukewarm tea and a small glass bowl containing my favorite cookies. This was all I had agreed to have when we arrived at Inna's apartment.

But I didn't eat any of the cookies, because I didn't want to wake Inna up with my crunching. Above the sofa was a photograph of a laughing, eight-year-old girl, Inna's daughter by an unsuccessful or "difficult" marriage, as she put it. At the moment her daughter was at a summer camp, organized by *Komsomolskaya Pravda,* at Bolshevo, near Moscow. There was a photo above the desk at my apartment too—it was of my twelve-year-old son, Anton... Still, we mustn't get distracted. Let's examine the "pickings from the goose", as my Jewish grandmother used to say—that is, what was left from the third chapter of Belkin's manuscript. I had a few thoughts about what I had read so far. In the first place, he had definitely been arrested and held in a preliminary detention cell—despite what we had been told by the Chief of the Baku City Militia. Only somebody who has actually been in one could have described the cell and its inmates in such detail. I'm no literary critic, of course, but even an investigator like me could tell that in the first chapters Belkin was still attempting to maintain the journalistic tone, probably thinking that he would write a story which could get past the censorship. He exaggerated some things, but others he kept quiet about or played down, all with this in mind. However, when he started to describe the way he had been beaten up in the detention cell, there was no stopping him. He described everything in the order it must have occurred, with a mixture of bitterness and hate. That was why the third chapter contained many more exact details and was much truer to life. But who was this so-called investigator? Someone the same age as Belkin, with light-blue eyes, who had the power to strip a militia captain of his rank. No, it wasn't just the Chief of Militia, it was somebody higher up. He smokes a pipe like Stalin and has the same intonation—so that means he can't be Russian. Stalin had a Caucasian intonation. Of course, he really shot Belkin down with that Lermontov parody. It's true: nothing is ever forgotten in our "state of Denmark". A poem written years ago by a thoughtless boy lies in the archive of the Azerbaidzhani Interior Ministry, until its hour finally arrives. A brawl which took place at some restaurant in Yakutia is the subject of a secret report placed in a CID Special Department archive. I couldn't help wondering what they had on me, and where. The USSR Prosecutor's Department is charged with keeping an eye on the work of every organ of state, including the MVD and the KGB, but once a year the latter gets to work on us, too. For a week or more they tap the people we know, our friends, and the nature and content of all the conversations we hold. And all this information, along with reports provided by various special agents, are placed in my file at the KGB Fourth Special Department. Nobody knows precisely when he or she is going to be worked on, not even the Chief Prosecutor himself, but we all know that it happens, at the very minimum once a year...

I bent down cautiously, and took the bottle of *Chornye*

*Glaza* wine, which Baklanov had brought back with him from his vacation, out of my briefcase. Of course, when you've had thoughts such as I was having you really need to drink something a little stronger, but this would do for now. I was glad I'd carried it around with me in my case all day. I had a penknife-and-corkscrew with me, too! So it was easy enough to open the bottle without making any noise. And it wasn't difficult to get a glass from the sideboard . . .

BELKIN'S MANUSCRIPT
(continued)

Chapter 4
The Sea-nymph

A quiet little island in the green Caspian Sea, forty feet long and two hundred feet wide. Or, if you don't like that, then imagine whatever you like. The island is forty minutes by car from Baku, if you follow the road to Bilgya. Just before you reach the village of Rybachy you turn right, drive down an old dirt track for about a mile, and there you are! By the sea, on an empty, sun-drenched beach. Before you is a chain of tiny islets, just rock and sand, and totally deserted. There's nothing for miles around, apart from a few fishing boats and the tiny village of Rybachy—a cluster of simple wooden houses. If you look beyond them you see the sloping shore of the Caspian disappearing in the heat haze, with Bilgya and its complement of beaches, summer houses and sanatoria hidden somewhere beyond.

But in this spot there is nobody, only the sun, the sand and the sea. When I dive in, equipped with my harpoon, the water is cool and gentle. Oh, if I could only live forever in this submarine world, with its emerald light, its coral, its yellow flowers and silver fish! Forget about newspapers, salaries and trips to Vienna! Just imagine disappearing under the water and returning to the life we came from, a world without governments, militia, moral codes for builders of Communism and lines for smoked sausage! The land beneath the waves has gardens and a sun of its own, and life there is completely natural . . .

This was the fourth morning that our special correspondent, Izya Kotovsky, had driven me here in his Zhiguli. He then went on with his business and left me in the same place until evening. He would ask no questions. He didn't try delving into my soul, but simply returned every evening, and I fed him shashlyks of freshly caught gray mullet. We'd sit there quietly eating and discussing trivia like tomorrow's weather or the soccer game between Spartak and Dynamo. Izya was great. He looked after me, as a doctor would a patient. He'd bring me on trips to the sea, as if he were one of my parents, and then would take me back to his bachelor apartment on the Esplanade, and we'd spend the evening drinking liquor, or sitting in the little shashlyk house in the Baku fortress.

Of course, some of life's usual conversations, smells and noises succeeded in getting past this protective shield, but I didn't want anything to do with any of it. There I was, one of the best journalists in the country, the representative of one of the Soviet Union's greatest national dailies, and some lousy prick of a militia captain had managed to hit me in the face, and some idiot policeman had kicked me in the heart and liver. Then the next day they'd sealed my tongue with their hypocritical apologies and a childish poem à la Lermontov. What use is your freedom if you have to keep your mouth shut like that? Is that freedom? Go to hell, all of you, with your articles, typewriters, editorial phone calls, telexes, prizes awarded by the Union of Journalists, and all that shit!

My God, why didn't I enter the Geography Faculty, like half of my class at school, and eighty percent of our Geographical Society at the Pioneers' Palace? I could have found employment as a geologist or glaciologist, in the mountains, in the swampy forest lands, in the tundra, or wherever you like. What the hell use was it being a talented journalist if you had to be as silent as a fish? You'd be better off becoming a *real* fish, like this gray mullet here, or maybe a dolphin.

The green waves of the Caspian rocked and comforted me. My fits of anger and impotent rage lessened as the sea lulled and gradually healed me. Then, on the fifth day, She appeared. From the depths of the sea, from the silvery bubbles and the froth of the waves, I suddenly saw a tall, suntanned body moving, hair spread out in the water. I was dumbfounded and almost let the snorkel slip out of my mouth. She was virtually a mystical apparition, this sunbronzed nymph armed with a small harpoon who dived to reach reefs and weeds where I would never have dared to follow, even for the tastiest-looking mullet. The quiet ripples from her flippers and the tell-tale silvery bubbles of air were all that I could see of her. So I swam around the surface, waiting for her to reappear.

And she did reappear, but not where I was expecting her. She surfaced much further away, almost by my island. I saw her emerge on the shore, take off her flippers and sit down at the bonfire which I had made. I swam to the shore myself. By the time I caught up with her, she was already roasting lumps of fresh mullet over the fire, and there were another three large fish lying next to her harpoon. She was sixteen. I can see her now, with her lithe, ripe figure, grown used to the sea, and her firm breasts and thighs beneath her narrow, tight bikini. I can see her damp, sun-bleached hair, and her round face with its snub nose and brown eyes, following me closely, as I reached the beach, took off my flippers and diving mask and wandered exhaustedly towards the fire. My skin had begun to peel from sunburn, and I felt awkward. I quickly donned my shirt, so that my pampered, city-dweller's body wouldn't get completely scorched by the hot noon sun. But she didn't say a word. She just looked.

After I had put on my shirt and shorts, I lay down by the fire and recovered my customary, slightly ironic journalist's aplomb.

"Where are you from?" I asked.

"Over there," she said, nodding towards the tiny village. "Here. Take this." And she offered me a piece of grilled mullet on a skewer.

What more can I tell you? The two of us were alone on the island, and within an hour our bodies had entwined on the sand, our mouths joined in long, deep kisses. She gripped me with her strong, firm thighs, the brown of her eyes melting behind closed eyelids and her half-open lips breath-

ing in short, loud gasps. Then, when we tired of making
love, we lay naked in the water, lazily moving our flippers,
touching each other with the tips of our fingers. We were
like two fish, two dolphins, two sea creatures who had met
in the water and surrendered to each other, silently and
according to nature's law. That's all. And once we'd rested,
we tackled the grilled fish, tomatoes and black bread which
Izya Kotovsky had left me that morning. And we embraced
again.

An hour before Izya arrived, she swam off to her village.
She appeared again the next day, and this went on for four
or five days. I think I am right in saying that, in all that
time, we didn't spend more than twenty minutes talking to
one another. The rest of the time was spent with the sea,
the sand, the hot stones beneath our backs, sex—and then
once again the sea, that warm, green font of ours!

But, by the fifth day, I began to get tired of it all.

Nature is somehow generous with women. A single
woman can go without men for years on end, seemingly
keeping her temper, composure and even her cheerfulness.
But it's not like that with men. Only a woman can cleanse
the dross from our minds and dissipate our feelings of tiredness, irritation and anger. And so it was that this mistress
of mine succeeded in purging my body and spirit. She re-
stored me to life by dissolving all the bitterness I felt at
being humiliated by the Baku Militia. Everything else, my
sober realization of how powerless I was when confronted
by the system, and my feelings of aversion both for myself
and my profession—all this disappeared. By the third day
of our love, I was back to being the witty, ironic, metro-
politan super-journalist, and by the fifth I was like an impatient racehorse, champing at the bit. Neither the sea, nor
underwater harpooning, nor my sixteen-year-old mistress
were able to satisfy this new urge of mine—the need to
act, to drive or fly somewhere, to write something and get
it published. In short, to make my mark on the world. Lying
next to her or diving into the cold, dark depths beneath the
rocks, I was no longer thinking about her or about the next
shoal of silvery mullet, moving here and there in the distance. Instead, I was thinking of the one form of vengeance

open to me, if I were to get my back at the Baku Militia. I would go among the Baku drug addicts myself, using all my journalistic experience, and I'd get at the drug traffickers through them. Then I'd write a detective novel about it, in which everything would be fact apart from the actual names used and a few odd details. And the first chapter of it would be my article for *Komsomolskaya Pravda* about the everyday life of addicts in Baku. I'd give a detailed description of their lives, twenty-four hours a day, and it would cover Sashka Shakh and Co., Mosol, Fulevy and others like them. I could already see the article in my mind's eye, as a blood-hound can scent its quarry. All I needed was to see with my own eyes what Sashka Shakh and Fulevy had described to me that night in prison. I needed to see and describe the way these fifteen-year-olds started their "work" every morning, on the trams, at the railroad stations, and in the markets; stealing purses, filching watches and cutting holes in bags; and in the evenings how they mugged lone pedestrians in darkened streets—all with one purpose in mind: to get drugs in exchange for the money they steal. I had to describe how they get high by smoking hash or shooting opium.

Nobody in the whole history of Soviet journalism has ever described such a thing! I'd be the first, and I'd do it! It would suit our newspaper right down to the ground. It was aimed at Soviet youth, after all, and this article about fifteen-year-old drug addicts would cause a sensation, an explosion among all the newspapers.

On the sixth day I simply failed to turn up at the island. I felt young, self-confident and obstinate again, as I went back to "normal" life. And this time I plumbed the depths in another sense, for it was an easy matter to discover Sasha Romanov's address and telephone number from the Central Inquiry Office. I phoned his mother, kicking myself for not doing so earlier. I didn't know where he was, whether he was still in prison or at large.

Sasha came to the phone himself. His case had gone just as Fulevy had said it would. He'd been freed because of "lack of evidence". After a couple of minutes we agreed to meet at the main entrance to the Esplanade.

And then Sasha asked, "Perhaps I can come with Lina?"

I hadn't reckoned on including a girl in my journalistic plans, but I was interested in seeing the person who had succeeded in curing Sashka of his drug addiction in sixty seconds flat. In any case, she could figure in my story in her own right.

They appeared on the Esplanade, holding each other's hand, like children, or rather, like two creatures who had discovered a whole new world in each other. There was Sashka Shakh, strong, suntanned and dressed in a sports shirt and a pair of Odessa jeans. And there was Lina, a skinny girl with deep-blue eyes, legs like skittles and wild, blonde hair falling down to her shoulders. Whether they were walking down the Esplanade with me, surrounded by people and baby carriages, or sitting squashed together under a canvas awning at an ice cream parlor, they were always together and only together, as if their love cut them off from the rest of the world.

When they were in such a state, what was there for us to talk about? Sashka could neither hear nor understand anything. In fact, he was scarcely capable of it. I kept trying to engineer situations that would allow me to spend a minute or two with him by himself. I talked Lina into riding a children's merry-go-round, and while she was spinning with the five-year-olds, explained my idea to Sashka as quickly as possible—how I wanted to be introduced to the addicts, spend a few days with them, smoke, play cards and even take part in a robbery so as to write an article about it all in *Komsomolskaya Pravda* later. But this made no impression on him at all. He seemed to be in another dimension. He'd said farewell to the underground world and had entered another, and all I could get out of him was a promise to help me with my plan, but only after Lina had gone away.

"When will that be?"

"In three days."

"Where is she living? Is she still at your place?"

"No, at her aunt's."

"So you're not spending all your time with her? When she's at her aunt's, you could help me."

"No, I'm sorry. I go to see her first thing in the morning . . ."

Throughout this whole conversation, he'd done nothing but follow her with his eyes, as she'd been spinning on the merry-go-round, and wave to her every time she came by. I realized there was nothing more I could do. It was useless talking to the love-stricken Shakh. Love *can* make people pretty stupid!

"OK," I said, changing the subject. "Where's Fulevy now?"

"He was due to be transported somewhere in Siberia a couple of days ago. They've raised his old case again."

"Where?"

"I don't know."

"Sasha," I said, "what do you mean? You were in the same cell as he was, you used to share cigarettes—and now you say you don't know where he is. Maybe he's still there, and I could get something through to him..."

"And what about you?" Sashka said, suddenly turning towards me and forgetting about Lina for a moment. "Didn't you share a cell with him, too?" he asked point-blank. "Didn't you get beaten up with him? And where did you disappear to, when they let you go? You might at least have smuggled him in a pack of cigarettes. But now...you need me in order to write your article, so you've remembered him too!"

He was right.

I looked him in the eye. How could I explain to him? Even if I were to recount every detail of my conversation with the "investigator" on the first floor of Militia Headquarters, it still wouldn't justify my behavior. And why had I forgotten about my fellow prisoners as soon as I was released? Why didn't I arrange for something like fruit, cigarettes or books to be sent to them, maybe through Izya Kotovsky? I looked at Sashka and said, "You're absolutely right!"

"That's it, you see. It's the same thing..." And he grabbed Lina's hand as she ran up to him. "See you later."

"Goodbye!" Lina said, eyes sparkling. With that, holding each other's hand, they walked away down the tree-lined Esplanade, without looking back. They had forgotten about me the moment they said goodbye.

* * *

Chapter 5
Shots at Sandy Beach

What can stop a journalist—I mean, forgive me if this
sounds unexpected, a professional—once he has sunk his
teeth into an assignment? I borrowed some old jeans, a faded
T-shirt and some sneakers from Izya and changed into them.
Dressed in these ordinary clothes, I took the tram for Armenikend and the Gagarin Palace of Culture. Once off the
tram I easily found the overgrown, shady gardens where
Sashka Shakh visited Mosol on the day Lina arrived in Baku.

The gardens were empty aside from a handful of five-
year-old Russian urchins who were playing with a couple
of slightly older kids. But I wasn't discouraged. I looked
around. On the other side of the gardens I could see some
so-called "Khrushchev slums"—four-floor apartment buildings with balconies that had at one time been different colors,
but which were now all reduced to the same unidentifiable
hue. The clothes I was wearing meant that I could pass
myself off as one of the locals, so I went up to one of the
older kids and said, "What's your name? Seryozha?"

"No, I'm Alik," he said in surprise.

"What's your family name?"

"Krasavin."

"Which block do you live in?"

"That one there," he said, pointing towards one of the
buildings.

"Do you get teenagers fooling around here too?"

"You mean the ones who smoke hash?" one of the other
youngsters said in a businesslike voice.

"Yes."

"They come here later, after lunch."

"And where do they live? In these buildings, too?"

"No, they don't come from our buildings," Alik Krasavin
said.

That was enough. I didn't think that Mosol and Co. could
live in these buildings, so close to the place where they
smoked hash and shot opium. Otherwise, any one of them
could have been seen by his parents. Sashka Shakh lived
on Melnichnaya Street, and it wasn't by accident that he'd

chosen a spot near the Sabunchinsky railroad station for his hideout, five tram stops away from home. So that meant that they were hardly likely to know all those who lived around here.

I sat down on a bench in the shade and began to wait. I can't say that I found it tiring. It was a beautiful summer day, a little on the hot side, but there in the shade of the trees and the luxuriant oleander bushes, some of them more than six feet high, it wasn't hot at all. It was actually re-assuring and peaceful. I think that I had even started dozing when I heard voices in the bushes behind me.

"Let me have that needle. Give it to me!"

"Wait a minute, there's some asshole sitting over there."

"Fuck him! Stop farting around. Give me a light!"

I didn't move, but kept sitting as if I was asleep.

I heard a match strike behind me, and then, after a short pause, the sound of voices again.

"For Christ's sake, what are you doing? I'll do it myself . . . Give me the joint!"

The heady, heavy, honey-like smell of hashish wafted over from the bushes, and without any warning, even to myself, I suddenly sneezed extremely loudly.

I could hear people laughing behind the bushes. I turned around. The thick oleanders hid from my sight whoever was laughing, but it was certainly my gigantic sneeze that they were laughing about. I figured that this was the time to see them, so I strode through the bushes. In a tiny clearing three yards square, completely surrounded by shrubbery, five boys, aged between thirteen and sixteen, were sitting together in a circle. They were Azerbaidzhani, Armenian and Russian. One very skinny boy of about fourteen had rolled up his sleeve. He was holding his thin arm out in front of him with fist clenched and veins bulging, while the other hand was clutching a syringe filled with a cloudy-white solution. He was trying to inject the large needle into his vein just below the elbow. But the vein had become hardened and glassy through overuse. He kept trying, but he couldn't inject the needle into his body, and it kept slipping off. As a result a stream of blood was slowly trickling down his arm and dripped past his elbow onto the ground. Neither the boy nor any of his companions paid any attention to it. They hardly even noticed me. Only one of them got up as I approached, while the others kept their eyes fixed on their comrade's efforts to inject himself, and took greedy puffs at the joint of hash that they had between them.

"Let me have a hit!" the lad with the syringe shouted, pursing his lips. They gave it to him, and he inhaled deeply. This seemed to calm him down, as he suddenly managed to penetrate the vein. He drew some of his own blood up into the syringe, threw his head back, closed his eyes and then started slowly to squeeze the mixture of blood and opium into his vein. I could see that he wasn't the only one to experience a feeling of relief. The others did too. The feeling was almost palpable. It was as if they were also feeling the drug.

"What do you want?" asked the youth who had got up when I appeared. He was a strong-looking Azerbaidzhani lad of sixteen, with a shock of wiry hair.

"Can I have a hit?" I asked.

"Where you from?"

"From Moscow, give or take a mile or two. I'm here on vacation at my cousin's, Krasavin. You know him? He lives in that block over there. Does anybody need any jeans, American ones?"

"Are you a speculator or what?"

"Well . . ." I said evasively.

Meanwhile the syringe had been passed to one of the others, and he pulled a "shot" from his pocket—a piece of film with a greasy spot of opium on it. He removed the opium with the blade of his knife, stuck it on the end of a matchstick, scraped it into the mouth of the syringe and dissolved it with ordinary water from a mug. Then he violently clenched his left fist a few times, forced blood into the vein, and raised the needle above his forearm, just below the elbow. I could see that his skin was covered with red injection marks, just as Fulevy's had been.

"So, what about the jeans?" I asked the boys. But jeans were the furthest thing from their minds at that moment.

"You'll have to ask Mosol," one of them said lazily.

Then they lost interest in me, and Ramiz, the one I had

been talking to, took the syringe and prepared to inject himself. I sat down on a rock next to them. I probably looked a little tense, as one of them said to me, "What's wrong? Haven't you ever seen it before?"

"Don't people shoot opium in Moscow?" asked another.

"Are you kidding?" somebody answered on my behalf. Then he said to me, "Do you want to have a game of *sekka?* You got any money?"

I had only played the game once in my life, on the Yamal peninsula in the tiny Nenets fishing village of Novy Port, about 125 miles from Dikson Island. I had to spend six days with airmen in the tundra, waiting for a blizzard to end so we could fly on. We cooked some fish soup out of white salmon and sturgeon caught in the Ob, we drank booze and played all the card games any of us knew. Now this knowledge came in handy. I had eight roubles on me, so I sat down to play with the ones who weren't on opium, but were only smoking hash. I decided that my article about drug addiction in Baku would begin like this: "To the Chief Accountant of *Komsomolskaya Pravda.* I request payment for the following expenses incurred in connection with my recent assignment: (a) 8 roubles 40 kopecks—lost at cards; (b) 6 roubles 12 kopecks—spent on drink; (c) 23 roubles—spent on drugs; (d) 16 roubles—cost of a pair of pants torn as I was trying to get away from a police inspector." I would follow this with a detailed, almost hour-by-hour account of how I spent my time. I was with these boys for almost ten days, playing *sekka,* smoking hash, hanging around the streets, running away from the militia, forcing money out of automatic lemonade dispensers, selling my jeans to somebody for 30 roubles . . . I saw them inject themselves, steal watches on crowded trams and cut away the back pockets of shoppers lining up for butter and buckwheat. Hanging around with these boys, I soon got a picture of their everyday lives and habits. Since they needed to save their money for drugs, most of them would go without eating almost anything for days on end, relieving their pangs of hunger by chewing a cheap piece of halva, or maybe sherbet. But it wasn't only their everyday life which interested me. I wanted to discover who was behind the pushers, how all these Tolik

Khachmases, Arif Zelyonys, Magomed Gogols, who sold hashish and opium almost openly all over Baku, were supplied. But, however strange it may seem, none of the addicts themselves ever asked themselves exactly how the sale of the drugs was organized. Obviously there was a professional supply network behind it, but the boys were so conditioned and stupefied by the actual drugs that they never looked further ahead than the next pellet of hash or shot of opium.

I consoled myself with the thought that I would be able to contact Ziyalov through these drug peddlers (I had been informed by the Baku Address Office that Oleg and Anya Ziyalov had officially left Baku six years earlier and that their present whereabouts were unknown). But none of my attempts to get in with Tolik Khachmas, Magomed Gogol or any of the other pushers had any success. They would coldly and sharply interrupt everything I asked, and any attempt I made to get into conversation with them, or even to stand near them for more than a few moments, ended the same way: You've got your shot or joint—now get lost! They would even start moving their feet impatiently, as if they hadn't been able to go to the toilet for an hour and a half or more, so anxious were they to get rid of this unwelcome customer as quickly as possible . . .

I still had hopes of meeting Mosol, though—and, of course, the General, who hadn't been mentioned by the boys at all. When I succeeded in moving conversation in this direction, it turned out that they hadn't seen him recently at all. There was even a rumor going around that he'd been thrown in jail. But Mosol had told them that that was nonsense, and that the General simply had other business on his hands. Mosol himself was also busy, they told me. He'd fallen for some girl and had been following her all over the place. He hadn't been seen at his usual place for the last week or so.

Mosol finally put in an appearance on the third day, towards evening. He was no older than seventeen, a thin fellow, but strong and wiry with sharp, intelligent eyes. Despite the hot weather, he was dressed in Soviet-made jacket, jeans and sneakers. He stepped through the bushes, where we were playing *sekka*, and looked us over. Suddenly he pointed to me and said, "Who's this?"

"One of us," Ramiz replied, shuffling the cards. "He's a speculator from Moscow. He's been hanging around with us for the last few days."

"OK. Give me a joint and finish the game," he said to Ramiz authoritatively. "I need you. You too, Sikun."

Ramiz and Sikun were probably the strongest members of the gang. Mosol took several hits off the joint, threw himself down on the grass, and said in a dreamy, boastful voice, "I've had enough! Today we're really going to get Shakh!"

I was listening intently, but gave no outward sign of it, merely continuing to play that stupid game. Mosol finished the joint, and then looked at his watch. Ramiz and Sikun stared at him in silence, waiting for his orders.

"It's early yet," Mosol said to them, obviously displeased. "At seven we'll take the tram to Sandy Beach. That's where they hang out, I've learned. They're going away tomorrow. Fuck 'em!" he said, making an obscene gesture. "Cousin, my asshole! I'll give him a *real* cousin!"

He was lying on the ground, eyes narrowed and lips pressed tightly together. Suddenly he jumped up and gave the order.

"Let's go!" he said. "And let's get some wine! It'll make his girl go with more of a bang!"

And he went off with Ramiz and Sikun.

A few minutes later I yawned, pushed away the cards with a bored expression, and said, "OK, that's enough. I'm fed up with playing . . . I'm going home to sleep . . ."

Out on the street I shouted to the first driver who came along. It was a private Moskvich. It was the same here as in Moscow. Any driver was willing to drive you around for money.

"Take me to the Esplanade!"

"You got any cash?" asked the driver.

"Yes. I've got some. Come on. We've got to move!"

"There a fire somewhere, or what?"

"Almost."

Five minutes later we were outside Izya Kotovsky's apartment block.

I could see that his blue Zhiguli was parked outside, so I ran up to the third floor. Izya wasn't at home, but there, under the mat as always, was the key to the apartment. I rushed into the living room and ran to the telephone. It was already a quarter to seven, by my watch. Sashka wasn't at home, of course! The phone just kept ringing.

I went over to Izya's desk and rummaged through the drawer. Car drivers usually have a second set of keys and keep them in a "secret" place. Izya's desk was the repository for everything he owned, from medicines to screwdrivers and pliers. Emptying the entire contents of the drawer on the floor, I managed to find the keys. I changed quickly into an ordinary shirt and slacks, grabbed some money and my identity papers and tore out of the apartment. It was ten to seven.

A moment later, without a driving license or anything, I was rushing down the Esplanade towards Sandy Beach. I remembered that Mosol had won a Browning automatic in the General's competition, so that meant I had to get to Sashka before he did. Under the front seat, beneath my feet, was a car repair kit, the only weapon that Izya, ever cautious, carried with him.

Now that I had my *Komsomolka* identity card with me again I felt at ease, even driving somebody else's car. I'd show these cloth-capped Azerbaidzhani roadhogs some Moscow driving! I approached every set of traffic lights just as it was turning green, so that I was able to accelerate away in second gear towards the next set of lights without stopping. I went down April 26 Street, past the Nizami cinema and the familiar offices of the *Bakinsky Rabochy* newspaper, where I had worked for three years before joining the *Komsomolka*. If they only knew—Artur Gurevich, Alyoshka Kapabyan, Nina Krylova and all the rest in the office—if they only knew who was zooming past outside! It was quite possible that Izya Kotovsky was there at that moment, hanging around idly in the photo lab . . .

April 26 Street led me into Chorny Gorod. I knew the route well, as it led towards the airport. About three miles before Bilgya I had to turn right, towards the sea. I was doing seventy-five miles an hour, easily overtaking cars and

Aeroflot buses, with the electric railroad embankment running along beside me. I could already see that I was ahead of Mosol's seven o'clock train, and I slowed down a little, when suddenly . . .

The engine died. The car kept moving down the highway, losing speed as it did so. I looked at the instrument panel. Hell! Out of gas! The hand on the gauge was pointing towards zero and the red warning light was flashing. What an idiot I was not to have looked and filled up in town!

Cursing my stupidity, I drove over to the shoulder, got out and rushed to the gas tank. I unscrewed the lid and looked inside—there might have been some left, by some miracle, after all. No! It was empty. In desperation I started to wave down passing motorists—you never know, one of them might have been able to give me some gas by siphoning it out of his own tank. But now, of course, I was being passed by the same drivers whom I had just overtaken so insolently. They sped by, wearing smiles of sweet revenge. One of them stuck out his tongue at me, another gave me the finger.

At that moment the electric train flew by too. And Mosol was in it, I had no doubt, accompanied by Ramiz and Sikun. Rattling over the joins in the rails, the carriages zoomed along the embankment and disappeared into the distance.

I sat back helplessly in the driver's seat. Then I tried hailing a car again—but it was no good. The main road to the airport is a government highway, and vehicles are not allowed to stop on it. So even if somebody could have given me some gas, he wouldn't have done anyway. Why risk losing your license? I sat in the car dumbly. Should I run to Sandy Beach? Don't be stupid! It would take you half an hour to get there. There were oil rigs stuck along the road and everywhere else, as far as the eye could see. With their great cross-bars pecking away monotonously at the bore-holes, they seemed to be echoing my own thoughts: "I-di-ot! I-di-ot!"

I'm not sure, but around twenty minutes had passed when a police car screeched to a halt. It carried the marking of the State Automobile Inspection. A young Azerbaidzhani police lieutenant got slowly out. He was already smiling

broadly at the thought of the large fine he would extract
from me for halting on a government highway.

"What's wrong?" he drawled as he came up to me. "Show
me your papers."

I looked at him, realizing that only he could save me
now. But I had to choose the right tone of voice when dealing
with him. Without saying a word, I got the red *Komsomolka*
pass out of my pocket, with the magic words *Central Committee of the All-Union Leninist Komsomol* branded in gold
on the front. I showed it to him, and he immediately changed
his tone.

"Are you waiting for someone?"

"Look, lieutenant, this is what happened," I replied. "A
really stupid thing. I'm out of gas. Siphon me a couple of
gallons, will you?" I continued, nodding towards his police
Volga. "I'll pay you for it."

The lieutenant shook his head sorrowfully.

"Don't insult me. *Komsomolskaya Pravda* can have a
couple of gallons from the militia without paying! Do you
have a siphon?"

How did I know whether Izya carried a siphon with him
or not? I opened the trunk. It turned out that he didn't even
have a spare tire, let alone a siphon. The lieutenant looked
at me reproachfully.

"OK," he said, and using his police baton, waved down
a passing car. A few moments later our cars were positioned
back to back, with his gas tank next to mine, and a siphon,
borrowed from the third car, connecting the two. We were
blocking traffic, of course, but it didn't matter. I must have
received half a tank's worth out of the police Volga.

Despite what he'd said, I was about to reach into my
pocket to pay him, but he stopped me with a look of dis-
approval. I realized that he would take offense if I offered
him money again. I shook his hand, jumped into the car,
and roared off down the highway. Now that I had the bless-
ing of the militia, I could jam my foot on the accelerator
as hard as I liked. The speedometer lurched to the right:
75, 80, 85 m.p.h. . . . The car was light, without any drag
even in the trunk, and I thought its wheels might suddenly
leave the asphalt and fly into the air. Yet at the factory

testing track the makers had told me that a Zhiguli would hug the ground even at very high speeds, unfortunately.

It was getting dark very quickly, so I switched on my headlights and swung smoothly across to the old dirt road which disappeared in the direction of Sandy Beach. The rail line ran alongside, and in the distance I could see the dotted lights of the train standing at the terminus. Without thinking twice about Izya's car, I pressed my foot down hard on the accelerator again. I had to keep both hands on the steering wheel and keep my back firmly pressed against the seat so I wouldn't hit my head against the roof of the car, with all the jolting going on.

I was sure that I knew the place where Sashka and Lina would be. Sandy Beach was a spit of land leading into the sea, and it ended in two cliffs called the Stone Saddle. Beyond them was the tiny Lovers' Bay. Hidden from the gaze of others, generations of sweethearts had gone there to kiss and make love. I had kissed my first girlfriend there, as a matter of fact...

The train moved out of the station and headed towards me. That was it! Would I be too late?

Seconds later I was driving up to the empty station, which had just said farewell to its last day-trippers. It was deserted, station as well as beach. The dirt road came to an end there too, and from here on, as far as the Stone Saddle, there were only dunes and wet sand. I turned left towards the water's edge and, raising fountains of water with my wheels, headed for Lovers' Bay. When I emerged by the Stone Saddle, I saw what I had feared: there, on the deserted beach, Ramiz and Sikun had Sashka Shakh pinned to the ground. He'd already been beaten up and Ramiz was holding a knife to his neck, to stop him interfering, while down by the water, Mosol was trying to rape Lina. She was biting him and twisting and turning like a snake, with her knees tucked tightly to her chest. But Mosol was forcing her arms open and striking her with his fist, which was clutching the revolver.

"I'll kill you!" he was shouting. "You're mine! I've won you! I'll kill you!"

With his free hand he kept trying to pull his pants down.

I switched on my headlights again, sounded the horn, and drove the car straight towards this pair of bodies, struggling together on the wet sand. In the gloom they couldn't tell who was at the wheel. Was it the police, a private motorist, vigilantes? Out of the corner of my eye, I could see Ramiz and Sikun abandon Sashka and run out past the Stone Saddle. But as for Mosol . . .

He wasn't one to lose his head at crucial moments. Blinded by the headlights coming at him, he jumped up, pressed Lina to his body, and put the Browning against her head, slowly and clearly, so that whoever was in the car could see what he was doing.

I slammed on the brakes. The car swerved to a halt in the sand two yards from where Mosol and Lina were standing. The blinding light of the headlamps still prevented him from seeing who was in the car. From the driver's seat I could see the two of them very clearly. There was Lina, bruised and almost naked, dressed in a torn swimsuit. I could make out her childish breasts, her shapely legs and her blonde curls. And there was Mosol, badly bitten, with his pants hanging down, gripping Lina tightly with one hand and pressing the revolver against her face with the other. Seeing that the car had stopped and that the meaning of his gesture was understood by whoever was inside, Mosol paused, then began moving slowly to one side, out of the headlights, dragging Lina behind him. I sat motionless in the car, my face pressed forward as hard as possible against the windshield. If only he would run off and leave her alive! Just as Mosol moved out of the light, a body rushed towards him in the darkness and knocked both Mosol and Lina to the ground. At the same moment I heard a shot, and suddenly the windshield shattered into a thousand fragments, all over my face, my shirt, my pants. Sashka Shakh had attacked him, and as he fell, Mosol had pulled the trigger. The bullet had hit the windshield and smashed it. I don't know what reflex mechanism was at work, but I just managed to shut my eyes before the slivers of glass shot into my face. I'd probably blinked out of fear when I heard the gun, and it probably saved my sight.

I could hear a fierce fight going on outside on the sand,

but couldn't open my eyes due to the splinters of glass. I managed to open the door and feel my way out of the car. When I got to Sashka, Mosol was already zig-zagging away over the sand dunes and Sashka was firing at him with the Browning automatic. "Don't Sasha! Don't!" Lina shouted. But he pushed her away with his free hand and took aim again. In the heat of the moment I seemed to hit him harder than I had intended, as he groaned and dropped the revolver. He immediately picked it up again with his other hand, however, and started shooting into the darkness at random, in the general direction which Mosol had taken. Lina and I hung on to him, preventing him from running after Mosol. He kept trying to break free from us, crying out hysterically, "Let me go! I'll kill him! Let me go!"

I had him in a full nelson, while Lina was kissing him tearfully and trying to calm him down.

"Sasha, it's all over. No more, no more..."

Almost naked, her face wet with tears, she clung to him, inadvertently pressing into my arms, which were locked around Sashka's neck. I could feel her breast, stomach and shoulders against my elbows.


Chapter 6
A Dangerous Decision
That night Izya Kotovsky's apartment virtually became a field hospital. I used iodine, witchhazel and sticking plaster to ease and cover the cuts, bruises, scratches and other injuries that Sashka and Lina had acquired, then saw to my own wounds, which fortunately were light. Meanwhile Izya, overwhelmed by the loss of his Zhiguli windshield, was wandering up and down the room with a cold compress on his head, wailing like a Jew at a funeral. "Where on earth will I get another windshield like that?" he said. Then he clicked his tongue and started all over again. "Where, where, where will I get another windshield? There aren't any for a Zhiguli *anywhere*! It would have been better if you'd burst all the tires! Or wrecked the bumper! Actually, on second thought, you can't replace bumpers either! Oh, I don't know ... It would have been better if you'd smashed the head-

lights! Where, oh where will I get another windshield?"

"Izya, it wasn't me who broke it! We were fired at! Somebody was taking a pot-shot at me! One or two inches to the right and I would have been killed. Look at these marks on my face. Nice, huh? And all you can think about is your windshield! I'll buy you a new one, for Christ's sake!"

So I swore not to leave Baku until I had replaced his windshield. We'd visit the garage manager the next day. If we had no luck there, then we'd go to the Ministry of Transport, and then to the Propaganda Department of the Azerbaidzhani Party Central Committee if we had to. But whatever happened, we'd get that windshield! By hook or by crook!

"I don't know," Izya said, shaking his head sadly. "I don't know at all. What I do know is that tomorrow I'm supposed to drive around the area taking photographs of leading cotton-growers, and that I have nothing to drive! In any case, there haven't been any windshields like those in Azerbaidzhan for the last eight months! Gurevich, director of the Azerbaidzhani Telegraph Agency, totalled his Zhiguli, and what happened? His car has been sitting in the garage for six months! Or look at Orudzhev, the Rector of the University. He was in a crash. They took him to the hospital. By the time his fractured leg was healed, his car had been repaired and given a new coat of paint—but guess what? He couldn't drive it, because they didn't have any windshields! What am I going to do? What the hell am I going to do?"

Sashka Shakh couldn't stand it any longer. He disappeared into the kitchen and came back with one of those rubber things—I don't know what they're called—one of those big rubber suckers with a wooden handle that you use for clearing blocked sinks.

"Izya," Sashka said, "go and ask your neighbors to lend you another one of these for a few minutes."

"What for?" asked Izya, startled.

"Do as I say. I only want it for five minutes, but I need it badly."

Izya shrugged and went next door. A few moments later

he reappeared with another rubber sucker. Sashka took both of them and went outside.

"Where are you going?" I asked in surprise.

"I won't be long. Look after Lina."

Lina had a blanket over her and was asleep in Izya's bedroom, curled up on his bed. To calm her nerves and make her go to sleep, we had persuaded her to drink a double brandy. Now she was stirring in her sleep and mumbling something through her swollen lips. She was sweating and her hair was stuck to her forehead.

Sashka returned after five minutes, carrying a Zhiguli windshield, held between the two rubber suckers.

"What's that?" Izya asked in disbelief.

"It's a windshield for your car," Sashka said, placing it on the floor and carefully pulling off one of the suckers with the edge of his knife. After that, the whole sucker came away in his hand easily, and he passed it over to Izya. "You can give it back to your neighbors."

Izya was looking at me, then at Sashka, with horror in his eyes.

"You mean you've removed this windshield from another car?!"

"Not from one of those on your street, so don't worry. I got it around the corner," Sashka said. "What's the big deal? Nobody saw me. And the car wasn't from Baku, it was from Kyurdamir. They're speculators, and they won't even try to get a new windshield. They'll buy themselves a new car."

"For Christ's sake!" Izya said, beginning to pace the floor again. "If I get arrested tomorrow . . ."

"For what?" Sashka Shakh asked.

"For stealing this!"

"But were you the one who stole it?" Sashka asked deliberately.

"Unbelievable!" Izya said. "Absolutely unbelievable . . . !"

"Listen, Izya. A windshield like this costs 200 roubles on the black market. I've never stolen one before because that's the monopoly of the boys in Chorny Gorod. So if anybody at the garage asks you where you got it, say that you bought it in Chorny Gorod. That's all—and stop getting worked up. You'd be better off giving me a reward! Now take that sucker back to your neighbors!"

When Izya had gone out, Sashka said, "I need to talk to you, but not when he's around. Can we go for a walk?"

"All right. But why don't you call your mother first, so she doesn't worry about you not coming home."

"She'll survive," Sashka said, brushing my suggestion aside with total lack of sympathy.

Ten minutes later, as we were walking along the sea front, I began to understand the reason for the cruel tone that had been in his voice. The water in the fountains along the Esplanade, turned down at night, could still be heard bubbling away. On the other side of the granite embankment lay the silent Caspian, divided into two by the reflection of the moonlight. In the Esplanade gardens the oleander bushes were giving off a heady scent, while the paths were strewn with ripe berries from the black and green mulberry bushes. Here and there in the darkness beneath decapitated street lights you could just about make out the brownish outlines of lovestruck couples, sitting motionless on park benches. Sashka and I wandered from path to path as he told me his story.

"I've decided to leave Baku. Forever. I love Lina, and she loves me. We want to live together—always. I told my mother that I wanted to move to Vilnius with Lina. I can't stay here. If I do, I'll start to shoot opium again tomorrow and steal things on the trams. I know everybody here, and everybody knows me. There's no getting away from it. Either I nail Mosol, or he nails me. I told my mother this yesterday morning. That I had to go away with Lina— forever. I want to rent a room or an apartment in Vilnius. Then we can marry, and I'll get some work and finish at night school. Whether I then go to college or join the army, I'll decide later. To cut a long story short, I asked my mother to give me some money, or at least lend me a couple of thousand roubles. So I could get to Vilnius, find an apartment, and start a new life there. You should have been there for what happened next. She called her all the names in the book! 'Baltic bitch', 'sleazy whore' and anything else you can think of! She hadn't fed and clothed me for seventeen years, she said, just to give me over to a whore! It would have been better if I'd stayed in prison! She reckoned she'd denounce me to the militia herself and get them to lock me up again before she'd surrender me to that 'dirty bitch'. And what was the reason for all this? Two fucking thousand roubles!"

"Wait a minute!" I said. "I don't think it was because of the money. It's that you're only seventeen, and that's pretty young to get married."

"That's our business," said Sashka harshly. "Understand? We're not children. We're both seventeen, and already living with each other as husband and wife. But why should we have to do it in secret, hiding away in other people's apartments, or on the beach? We want to live like normal people, we've got nothing to hide. Are we supposed to have stolen something? I love her, and she loves me. That's all. I asked my mother to lend me two thousand. I know how much she and Dad have stashed away in the bank. What will *they* do with all that money? Who are they saving it up for?"

He stopped talking. We were walking past the Yacht Club. The pointed masts of the yachts were outlined against the black and yellow patchwork of the moonlit sea, looking like the fins of some gigantic prehistoric fish. Our footsteps were swallowed by the quiet warmth of the southern night. Sashka said nothing for a long time, and I didn't hurry him. I realized that he hadn't dragged me out for this long walk just to complain about his mother. At last he started talking again, only this time in a different, much calmer voice.

"So, in a nutshell, she didn't give me the money. Not even enough to buy me a ticket to Moscow. But I got the money from someone else. The General. Of course, he doesn't give money away for nothing, but this will be the last thing I do for him. I know that I shouldn't be telling you this, that you're a newspaper guy and all that. But you did save my life, and Lina's, and I've got no one else to ask. If something should happen to me, if I should get caught and locked in prison, please help Lina wait for me. Will you do it? Will you help her?"

"What kind of job is it you have to do, Sasha?"

"I can't tell you."

"OK. But you're being stupid. You're willing to trust me with looking after the person that means more to you than anything else, the girl you love, and yet you won't trust me with knowing about some deal between you and the General. It's your funeral."

"OK. I'll tell you. Although . . . although I shouldn't, but still . . . There you are! Only you have to give me your word that you won't tell anybody else. Otherwise they'll get both of us. Give me your word!"

"OK. I give you my word."

"The General says to me, 'Here's a thousand roubles in advance, and you'll get ten thousand more when you've done what I ask.' And this is what it's all about. He wants me to take a case full of money to Moscow. When I get there, I've got to exchange it for a rucksack of drugs at a prearranged place. So I take the money to Moscow and get a rucksack of drugs in return. With a rucksack I'll look like a student. I then bring it back to Baku on the train, hand it over to the General, and fly back to Lina in Moscow. I'll only have to fix her up with a room in a hotel and think of an excuse for disappearing for three or four days. Can you help me?"

What a fine mess! A *Komsomolka* correspondent helping drug dealers! Still, wasn't that the reason I'd decided to explore this side of life in the first place? But how could I be sure things weren't closing in on Sashka Shakh? Taking part in this operation was enticing, of course. I'd be able to describe it in my second article for the paper. But Sashka Shakh could get eight years for sure. Hold on, Garin! You've already been in a detention cell . . . You'd better stop now, and stop Sashka . . .

"Sasha," I said, after a short pause. "Let's start from the beginning with the reason for all this. You need money to start a new life in Vilnius, right?"

"But I'm not going to borrow any from you!" he said immediately.

"And I'm not offering you any. I don't have that kind of money. Though if I did, why shouldn't you borrow it? But that's not the point. I've got another suggestion. Let me get you a ticket to Moscow. The newspaper will pay. You can then give me an interview at the *Komsomolka* office—you can tell me everything that you told me that night in detention. If you like, we can change your name. In the interview you can tell me that you're renouncing your past and starting life all over."

"No. I'm not going to squeal on anybody!"

"Wait a minute," I said, annoyed. "Nobody's asking you to..."

"But if I'm supposed to name the guys I used to go around with, do drugs with..."

"You can change their names, too. It makes no difference to the reader whether Ashot was involved with you, or Rasim. It's the story that matters. After the interview the *Komsomolka* will be responsible for you *and* Lina. The Komsomol Central Committee in Lithuania will be able to get you an apartment and a job. We'll even arrange your wedding for you. We'll make you a hero, and for the first few months we should be able to help you out with money too—I mean, the newspaper and the Komsomol. I'll take responsibility for it. I can see the headlines now: former drug addict falls in love with Vilnius girl and begins a new, honest, normal life. Another coup for Andrey Garin! Of course, it won't be as sensational as it would have been if I'd written an article about secret drug-running, but all the same, it won't be bad. The Central Committee's Propaganda Department on Staraya Square prefers positive material like that in any case. It wasn't a fluke that my last three articles earned me the personal thanks of Zamyatin, the head of the Central Committee's Ideological Section. And now that the battle against teenage crime and drug addiction has become almost a national problem, it's time for the newspapers to start talking about it. And something positive like the article I've been outlining might be just the thing to break the censorship taboo on the subject."

But I'd let my imagination run ahead of me to no purpose.

"It's already too late," Sashka said. "He's already given me the money."

"You can always give it back."

"No, it's not a question of taking it or giving it back. I

already know the background to the whole thing. I worked for the General for two years, but I didn't know that he got us all addicted to drugs so he could sell more drugs to us. And it turns out that Tolik Khachmas, Magomed Gogol and all the other dealers get all their stuff from him, the General. I didn't know about this before, but I do now. Even if I were to give him all the money back right now, it wouldn't make any difference. In fact, it would make it even worse, because I wouldn't be really involved in it, but I know all about it. They'd kill me if I tried to get out now. So I'm already mixed up in it, thanks to my mother," he said with a sarcastic grin. "Andrey, I trust you. If you can help me, I'll let you. If not, I haven't told you anything at all, OK? Otherwise they'll get both of us, me and you. We're not talking about Mosol with an old Browning, but about the real thing. Don't forget that!"

## Chapter 7
### (Untitled, unfinished)

The next day I flew to Moscow. On the General's orders Sasha and Lina took the train to avoid the baggage search which takes place at every airport these days.

The General accompanied Sasha and Lina to the station to hand over the case containing the money. He bought them two sleeper tickets on train No. 5 from Baku to Moscow and ordered them to place the case with the money inside the larger suitcase containing Sasha's belongings. He was to stow this beneath the lower bunk and not leave it for the entire journey. On arriving in Moscow, they were to go straight from the station to the Hotel Tourist, just beyond the Exhibition of Economic Achievements in the north of the city. They were to head for Block 5, place twenty-five roubles in each passport and be given two single rooms in exchange. After that they were to sit in one of the rooms and wait for a phone call. In an emergency, if there were no rooms in the hotel or something like that, they were to take a taxi at 6 p.m. and travel to the Circus box office, next to the Central Market for Collective Farm Produce.

I didn't like the sound of it and was getting fed up with the whole deal. First, the Pamir mountains with coal dust and glaciers, glaciologists, poppies and edelweiss. Then the descent from those ethereal heights into the Baku detention cell and getting beaten up by the police. Then a spell of harpoon hunting, the brief encounter with the sixteen-year-old nymph, four days of uninterrupted sex. Then drug addicts again, stealing on the trams, the fight at Sandy Beach, the bullet that missed my temple by half an inch. Wasn't this a little too much for a three-week newspaper assignment? Not to mention the effort of writing two articles over the same period and keeping a fictionalized diary!

Still, never mind! I've been digressing. The day after the fight and my nocturnal conversation with Sashka Shakh, I took the plane to Moscow. I hadn't even visited my grandmother on Bondarnaya Street, even though that was the reason why I had flown from Tashkent to Baku in the first place, to have a few days' relaxation at her apartment. Some relaxation!

In Moscow I went from the airport straight to the offices of *Komsomolskaya Pravda*. The chief editor's secretary, Zhenechka, was sitting at her desk in the room next to Korncshov's. She was over forty but like all secretaries liked to be paid compliments and given presents, however small. I got a ballpoint pen out of my pocket and gave it to her. It was one of those with a top filled with some kind of pinkish-colored transparent liquid and a swan swimming in the middle of it. Made in Baku, it was the last word in artistic taste.

"Zhenechka, that'll go with your mother-of-pearl fingernails," I said. "You can only get them in Baku."

"Thanks very much," she replied, taking my hand and motioning me to come closer.

I went to the other side of the desk and stood over her. From above her, through the modest cut of her regulation gray dress, I could make out "two hills with a hollow between them," as I had heard in a French film somewhere. Say what you like, but Zhenechka had a beautiful bust! She read my thoughts and said in a reproachful voice, "Andrey!"

"Amazing!" I replied impudently. "A bust like yours, and you're still allowed to walk around in public! Unbelievable!"

"This trip of yours has driven you crazy or something! But listen—and keep it to yourself. I read your article about the addicts yesterday. Is it really true? It sounds terrible!"

Ah! So that meant the editor-in-chief already had the article.

"And did you really smoke hash with them? Tell me about it!" she went on, pestering me. "Is it nice? Did you bring any back with you for us to try?"

"Zhenya!" Now the reproachful tone was on my side. "What is this need for sensual gratification? Ask the foreign correspondents—they'll send you some LSD from New York!"

"OK," she said, with a wave of the hand. "Are you going to write any more?"

Well, if the chief editor's secretary was asking me about a continuation, then I could sleep easily. I nodded towards the boss's leather-clad door. "Is he in?"

"No. He's gone to the Central Committee with your article. Only I haven't told you anything about it."

"The Central Committee? Which one? On Khmelnitsky Street or Staraya Square?" I asked, meaning had he gone to the Komsomol Central Committee first, or straight to his patrons, Zamyatin and Suslov, in the Party Central Committee, who are in overall charge of ideology?

"To Khmelnitsky Street," she replied. "Did you know that you have finally been confirmed as a member of Brezhnev's press corps? There are three from *Pravda,* and two of ours, you and Agaryshev from the Foreign Section. You're to receive instructions from Zamyatin and Suslov on the twelfth. Then there'll be lunch with Brezhnev on the fourteenth. Then you fly the next day."

Suddenly the telephone rang and she lifted the receiver. "Chief editor's office."

I smacked her a kiss somewhere near the ear and went off to my office, waving a copy of my article. It was all turning out very well. The piece about the glaciologists, 370 lines, was appearing in tomorrow's edition. What I'd written about the drug addicts was already being given an airing in the Komsomol Central Committee, and on June 15 I was due to fly to Vienna to cover the Brezhnev—

Carter talks. I'd show those Baku militiamen where to go!
Tomorrow I still had to go to the station, meet Sashka Shakh
and persuade him to give an interview to the newspaper.
After that I could fly to Vienna ...

*The same evening, 23:50 hours*

That was the point where Belkin's manuscript broke off. I
laid the final page to one side and began to think. Certain
things had become more clear, but others were as confused
as ever. Gridasov, alias the General in Belkin's version but
the Chief in real life, had given Sashka Shakh (or rather,
Yury Rybakov) a case full of money, which he was to
exchange in Moscow for a rucksack filled with opium or
some other drug. But why had Gridasov turned up in Moscow before Shakh and Lina and been waiting for them at
the Kursk railroad station at the moment they arrived? It
couldn't be ruled out that the exchange was to take place
right there at the station, of course, instead of at the Hotel
Tourist or at the Circus on Tsvetnoy Avenue. But what
Gridasov hadn't envisaged was *Belkin's* arrival at the station. He'd already seen him at Baku airport, so he knew
who he was and what he did. Belkin was getting in their
way. He was messing up their arrangements and was becoming dangerous. So they kidnapped the two of them. OK.
Let's say that I've more or less reconstructed a logical version of events, but where does that get me? How are we
going to find Belkin? And who are the other three who took
part in the kidnapping? This Chief or General has already
been on the run for six years. He could do the same for
another six, but how would we find him? We have to get
the other three kidnappers too, and how do we do *that?*
How do we recognize them? We have to interview Aina
Silinya, damn it! In all the confusion, I'd forgotten to send
a telegram to the militia in Riga, asking them to send her
to Moscow as soon as they could find her.

   Forgetting that I wasn't at home, I took out a cigarette
and lit a match. Then I suddenly remembered and started
to curse myself. It was too late. Inna had woken up and
jumped nimbly off the sofa.

"What time is it?"

"About midnight. Inna, what's the name of your Baku correspondent?"

"Rady Sverdlov. Or Rady Aukhman, but Sverdlov was his mother's name. Vadim calls him Kotovsky in his story."

"Inna, may I phone from here?"

"Of course."

I got through to the inter-city exchange, gave the password for the Prosecutor's Office, and asked them to connect me with the *Komsomolskaya Pravda* correspondent in Baku immediately.

"Inna," I said, "sit down and have a second glass of wine. It's a very good one. A friend of mine brought it back from his vacation today. I've been dragging it around with me and now it's going to come in handy."

"Hello," I said into the receiver. "Comrade Sverdlov? This is Investigator Shamrayev speaking, from the USSR Public Prosecutor's Office. I'm sorry to be calling so late. I understand Vadim Belkin was living at your apartment from May 12 to 23, and I'd like to know . . ."

"At my apartment?" said the voice in bewilderment. "Belkin at my place? What are you talking about? I haven't seen him for a year or so. Last summer it was . . ."

"What do you mean?" I was dumbfounded. "He was in Baku from the twelfth."

"Yes, I heard what you said. He was just passing through. But he didn't get in touch with me. It may be that he tried to phone me, but I was traveling around the region at the time. Now that it's summer there's a lot of work . . ." His voice sounded apologetic but firm.

Well, how do you like that?

"All right, I'm sorry I bothered you." I hung up. I looked at Inna.

She hadn't touched her wine. She was standing there in the middle of the room, her figure lit up only by the lamp on the desk. In the semi-darkness I could see those deep, black eyes of hers, full of anxiety for Belkin. He had abandoned her, and she obviously felt hurt by it, but she continued to love him all the same.

"What did he say?"

"He said he hadn't seen Belkin since last summer. Inna, did Belkin like to make things up? Sit down and try some of the wine. OK. Did he . . . ?"

"It tastes nice," she said, sipping it. "Did he make things up? I don't know. When he used to tell me stories about his assignments, it always sounded very smooth and slick, like in a book. And even if it wasn't true, you wanted it to be. But what do you think? Is he still alive?"

She asked the question quickly, point-blank. What could I say to her?

"I'll be honest with you, Inna. I'd like to know that myself." I could see her eyes lose their sparkle, so I added quickly, "Inna, I've only been working on the case for one day. Since early this morning. And we already know that the General is really Semyon Gridasov, otherwise known as the Chief, aged fifty-three, height five feet eight inches, with pale-blue eyes, and so on. The CID are looking for him all over the country, and between you and me, from tomorrow every prisoner in every prison in the Soviet Union will be asked whether they know anything about Gridasov. That's what we call investigating a case."

Hope reappeared in her eyes, and so did her respect for me as a person. I didn't tell her, of course, that the CID had been looking for Gridasov for six years nationwide without any success. But I must confess that I didn't want to make a positive impression on her, as a detective who knew what he was doing, the kind she might see in a TV series. I'd like to know what those "experts" would say if it suddenly happened that a manuscript describing a whole series of major crimes turned out to be nothing but lies. If Belkin hadn't been living at Sverdlov-Kotovsky's apartment, then there hadn't been any sixteen-year-old nymph at Rybachy Island. There hadn't been any masquerade with Belkin changing into a T-shirt and a pair of old jeans, or visiting the drug addicts on that "hill" of theirs. He hadn't chased after Mosol in a Zhiguli and there had been no shoot-out at Sandy Beach. He hadn't had that nocturnal chat with Sashka Shakh, so he couldn't have known that Rybakov and Aina Silinya were traveling to Moscow. The Baku Militia deny the story about the coffin or that Belkin was ever arrested, while Rady Sverdlov is supposed to have never seen Belkin in Baku at all. So was Belkin there, or not? If it weren't for Rybakov's corpse, if it weren't for the General—Gridasov—abducting Belkin at the station, if it weren't for the fact that Belkin dictated his two articles over the phone to the *Komsomolka* office, and if it weren't for Inna's anxious black eyes, here in front of me, then you could wonder whether Belkin existed *at all* . . .

Inna and I had another glass of wine. We agreed that I would keep her informed of what was happening, and that she would call me if she discovered anything new. Picking up Belkin's manuscript, I left for home. The unfinished bottle of *Chornye glaza* was standing on the table, and Inna insisted I take it with me. But I refused.

"We'll finish the bottle when it's all over, and we've found Belkin," I said. "We're neighbors after all. I live next to the Izmailovsky Park."

Then I walked from 12 Parkovaya Street to Izmailovsky, thinking more about Inna than about Belkin.

# Part 2

*Tuesday, June 5 1979, 12:15 hours*
During the first half of the day nothing much happened. I sent the Riga Militia an urgent telegram, requesting them to send Aina Silinya to Moscow as soon as possible. Then I gave detailed instructions to Svetlov's two "boys" who were flying to Baku: first, they were to check the passenger list for the Aeroflot flight from Tashkent to Baku against the records of School No. 171, where Belkin had been a pupil; second, they were to carry out low-key unofficial inquiries among the baggage handlers at Baku airport to see whether this business with the coffin actually had taken place; third, they were to make contact with the Baku underworld and find out what they could about Gridasov, alias the Chief. This was more than enough work for two men, especially if you took into account the fact that they would be operating in a foreign city and unable to call on the aid of the local police. The moment the door closed behind them, I started in on all the boring paperwork which no investigation, however important, can do without.

Baklanov tried to drag me off to a bar again. He obviously wanted to talk about his new case over a brew, but I had no time. There was enough for me to do, setting up my own investigation.

Baklanov went off by himself, somewhat offended, and I started tapping away at my typewriter again. Suddenly the door opened with a bang, and Marat Svetlov came boisterously in.

"Damn, damn and damn again!" he shouted, as he stomped into the room. He looked sweaty and dishevelled, and his shirt was unbuttoned. "What the hell did we take on this work for? I finally get to visit the old woman and she's dead as a goddam doornail! It's fucking amazing!"

I didn't understand a word he was saying, so I stared at him, waiting for him to cool down. A minute or two later he'd calmed down, and I got to hear his "amazing" story.

After sending his two subordinates to Baku that morning, Marat Svetlov had assembled his remaining staff at ten o'clock sharp, to give them instructions for the day. His section was basically concerned with unraveling particularly difficult murder cases and other dangerous crimes, so he didn't touch those men who were following up important, fresh leads in other cases. This left him with five detectives at his disposal, and he gave each of them a pile of photographs. They were like shots from a museum collection. A photographer from the CID Technical Department had taken photos of the brooches, pendants and earrings found in Sashka Shakh/Rybakov's document case. Svetlov ordered his men to pay a visit to every store in Moscow that buys and sells gold and diamonds, and also to question any black-market dealers, fences or other riff-raff they knew, in case somebody could identify the owner of the valuables. Each of them was assigned five or six stores in the outskirts, while Svetlov himself went downtown.

When he reached the Sretenka, Svetlov parked his car outside the Sports Bookstore. With a small case in his hand, he walked over to the doors of a gold and diamond merchant on the same street. He called the manager from behind the counter and went with him into a back room. This was the first place Svetlov visited, so he asked the manager to give his opinion on the merchandise before him. Seeing all those filigree brooches and pendants decorated with chrysolite, mother-of-pearl, garnet and diamonds, Giltburg clapped his hands in appreciation. "Marat Alekseyevich, where did you get these from? They must come from a museum . . . No, I have never touched or even seen anything like it. We came across this kind of thing during the war, confiscated abroad, but even so—nothing of this caliber . . ."

Svetlov was no further along after this visit than he had been before. But he didn't give up. He went to one of Moscow's oldest jewel stores on the Stary Arbat, then he visited places in the Krasnaya Presnya district and in Stoleshnikov Lane, and even looked in on the specialists at the

State Diamond Museum. But aside from being told that the jewelry was the work of a single hand and probably no later than the nineteenth century, he didn't uncover a thing. Not even Moscow's oldest and most experienced jewelers had ever seen these particular brooches and pendants before.

Svetlov interrupted his travels at noon, to have lunch in the restaurant of the Union of Artists building. When he had finished and was walking out to Gogol Avenue, Svetlov suddenly clapped his hand to his balding head. "Christ! How could I have forgotten?!" He was standing near the famous Kropotkin bread store. The same building was also where Emmanuel Isaakovich Sinaisky, one of Moscow's most experienced jewelers, had lived since the Revolution.

Svetlov ran up the stairs to the first floor. The blackened copper nameplate was still there: *E.I. Sinaisky, Jeweler*. He rang the bell impatiently.

"Marat Alekseyevich, old friend. What a pleasant surprise!"

Svetlov was melodramatically embraced and ushered into the apartment by an elderly man, smartly dressed, the image of the famous singer Alexander Vertinsky. A young woman in the apartment was quickly motioned to serve them snacks. These were washed down with brandy, vodka and kirsch.

"She's my niece from Vladikavkaz, Marat Alekseyevich," Sinaisky whispered confidentially. "You mustn't get the wrong idea." (He had a slight stammer and pronounced his r's in the French manner.)

He then went on to examine the jewelry with a magnifying glass, while entertaining Svetlov at the same time with stories drawn from his seemingly inexhaustible store of anecdotes.

"Now, where did you get these treasures from? Tell an old man."

"You're asking me?" Svetlov said in the same casual tone. "Why do you think I've come to see you?"

"No, seriously. You must have caught a pretty big fish?"

"We don't bother with small ones, Emmanuel Isaakovich."

"Yes, I can imagine! So what do you want from me?"

"Have you ever seen these pieces before?"

"Well, that's a pretty specific question, I must say! Listen, Marat Alekseyevich, I've retired from business now. I live a quiet life on my pension and the few shekels I managed to put together while I was at work. Of course, some people will tell you that Sinaisky is a crook, that he's rolling in money and has seen to it that his children are well provided for too, *and* his grandchildren and great-grandchildren. You'll always find there's someone around ready to tell tales about you. And then they'll start to harass an old man. But can I rely on you to protect me from such slander on this occasion, Marat Alekseyevich?"

"Of course," said Svetlov, smiling. He was prepared to make a trade. If the old man was making a few conditions, it meant he knew something.

"Well, let's drink to it then, old friend." He beckoned to the woman. "Be an angel, er . . . niece, and fill up our glasses, will you . . . ?"

They drank a toast to "friendship and mutual understanding." Then Sinaisky began. "Since you've already arrested the last person to own this jewelry, I see no harm in filling you in on its past history. The woman is honest in any case, and there can't be any charges to bring against her. She's been living on her family's jewels, which had been hidden for years. She leads a modest, quiet life. One of these things gives her enough to survive on for a whole year."

"Who are you talking about?"

"My very oldest customer, Olga Petrovna Dolgo-Saburova. She's over ninety-two years old and very lively. Longevity runs in the family. She comes from aristocratic stock. Her younger sisters got away from Petrograd in a naval cruiser in 1917 and are still alive and kicking somewhere in Rome. They run a guest house there. She didn't go with them, but had the family valuables stashed away somewhere. These are some of them that you've brought along today. None of them are in museums. Do you know who made them? The master jeweler Aleksey Trofimov, a serf of theirs. And she's been living on the proceeds from them through all these years of proletarian rule. There was one break, of course—from '37 to '56. She was supported by the state then, so to speak. But after they let her out, she'd invite me to her room on Meshchanskaya Street about once a year. And I used to value the jewels for her. It might have even been a bit more often to begin with. After she was let out of the camps, she became very fond of men, you see, but that all came to an end—ten years ago or more. Not completely, I admit, but after all, being ninety-two years old is no joke! Pour us out another brandy, will you angel?"

"So who used to sell these jewels for her, then? You?"

"Not me, no, certainly not! She used to sell them herself. All I would do was name her a price and take my commission—three percent, as according to the law. The thing was that my valuation was reliable. The buyer would often rely on my judgment himself, or so she told me many times."

"So who was the buyer? Do you know him?"

"Marat Alekseyevich! We seem to have misunderstood each other. I thought that you'd arrested him, and might even have been intending to show him to me. For years I've been wanting to meet the person who accepted my valuation for all these things without a quibble. The countess always kept his identity a secret for me, you see. And now it turns out that you're looking for him yourselves."

"We are," Svetlov admitted. "Where does she live, Dolgo-Saburova, I mean?"

"I can't get out of that one. Apart from the time she was in prison, the Countess Olga Petrovna Dolgo-Saburova has spent the last ninety years in her own former residence on First Meshchanskaya Street. These days it's called No. 17 Peace Prospect. Out of the whole three-story house they left her one single apartment, if you can call it that—one room only, on the top floor. Would you like some more brandy?"

"Please don't be offended, Emmanuel Isaakovich, but it's time for me to be going."

"Are you going to call on the countess? I dare not delay you in that case. Angel, pour Marat Alekseyevich one for the road."

Twenty minutes later Svetlov was at the street in question, and ten minutes after that he discovered that the occupant of apartment No. 47, Olga Petrovna Dolgo-Saburova, had died the week before and that the apartment was now occupied by a man named Rakov, a plumber/locksmith who worked for the Housing Department.

Svetlov rushed off to the Housing Department and burst into the director's office.

"Where are the belongings of old Dolgo-Saburova?" he asked. "Who arranged her funeral? And where is the locksmith who moved into her room?"

"We buried the old woman ourselves, at the Housing Department's expense," replied the plump woman director. "She has a nephew, somewhere or other. He works on the railroad as a sleeping-car superintendent, I think. We did try to phone him, but he was away on duty. We had to transport her body to the Vostryakovskoye Cemetery at our own expense."

"Where are her belongings? How can I get into the room? Where is your locksmith?"

"What belongings are you talking about? All she had was a filthy mattress and a bunch of old clothes. I'm not sure, but Rakov has probably thrown everything out already. I barely managed to persuade him to take the room, and temporarily at that. They won't sign on with you for anything less than a two-room apartment these days. He moved in yesterday."

After finding the locksmith, Svetlov and the director managed to enter Dolgo-Saburova's former room. It was empty, aside from a half dozen bottles of vodka, ready for a housewarming party.

"Where's her furniture? Where are all her belongings?"

"Furniture?" said the locksmith. "It was a pile of old lumber, not furniture! I took it all down to the garbage dump this morning—photograph albums, a Bible, and a mattress, stinking of urine. I cleared everything out and opened the windows, to get rid of the stench. The dump is over there. Come on, I'll show you."

When Svetlov, the locksmith and the director arrived at the Housing Department garbage dump, they could see the flames of the bonfire that was already consuming old Dolgo-Saburova's photograph albums, Bible, bed linen, clothing and mattress. The latter was a dirty gray, and the men standing around the fire poked it to make it burn a little quicker. Then something strange happened. The mattress cover broke open and out burst brooches, pendants and earrings, adorned with rubies, diamonds and chrysolites. There weren't very many of them—maybe seven pieces in all—but what they lacked in quantity they made up for in quality! They should have been in a museum!

"Here they are!" Svetlov said, pouring them out on my desk. "You see what an unlucky bastard I am! The old countess could have lived another week, damn her! Then we would have known who she was selling these trinkets to!"

I looked at him silently, and then asked, "When did the countess die?"

"On the twenty-eighth. So what?"

"Don't you find that a little strange? It seems an odd coincidence! The old woman sells the jewelry to someone. On the twenty-sixth Sashka Shakh dies in possession of the same jewelry. Then, two days later, the old woman herself dies all of a sudden, with the rest of the jewels still in her mattress."

"Well, she had to die sometime, I guess," Svetlov said, though he could already see the direction my thoughts were taking.

"Of course," I replied. "But why should it have happened right after the death of the person who had part of her collection? And what kind of guy is the railroad employee nephew of hers, who didn't even attend the funeral? Have you found out?"

"Yes. His name is Herman Veniaminovich Dolgo-Saburov. He's a sleeping-car superintendent with the Kursk line. I don't know anything else about him."

"Well, that's something."

Just then the telephone rang. It was Pshenichny.

"Igor Iosifovich, you couldn't drop in at the Kursk station, could you? I've found somebody who witnessed Belkin's abduction."

I looked at Svetlov for a second.

"Yes, we'll be over immediately," I replied. "And can you do something else for me, Valentin? Make a note of the following: Dolgo-Saburov, Herman Veniaminovich, a sleeping-car superintendent on the Kursk line. Find out anything you can about him—what trains he works on, his duty roster for this month . . . whatever you can."

* * *

*15:00 hours*

The Kursk station is not only the most modern in Moscow, it vies with the main station in Bucharest for the title of largest rail terminus in Europe. Silent escalators, flashing signs, endless rows of baggage lockers and the longest ticket lines in the world! During the summer months the place looks more like an army camp on the move. Thousands of people are running through the halls and up and down the escalators. Everywhere you look, people are sitting or lying on seats and benches, on the floors and in the underground walkways, and the lines outside the women's rooms stretch a hundred yards or more.

Svetlov and I forced our way past all the suitcases, bags, pails, baskets, children, old men and other passengers aged somewhere in between, until we reached a door bearing the legend, *Railroad Militia*. The Kursk branch of this organization looked as beaten up as its sister offices at the Kazan, Pavelets and every other Moscow terminus. Still, turning even the most modern office into a pigsty seems to be an unavoidable feature of militia work.

The duty office was filled with the customary oak benches, occupied by the usual number of tramps, pickpockets, drunks, prostitutes and speculators, as well as howling children and passengers who had gotten lost or who had had their belongings stolen. Some had been detained by the militia, others had come by themselves, or brought somebody along with them. And all these passengers were either shouting, cursing or demanding something, or else trying to justify themselves to the duty officer, a red-cheeked captain with a triple chin.

"Comrade Captain, it's three days since I lost track of my wife in this chaos. We were standing in different lines and lost sight of each other. She's been robbed, or worse, I know it . . . Help me find her, I beg you . . ."

"Listen, sir. I was carrying three sacks of dried apricots, mine, you understand, to sell at the market. I went up to this pretty, fair-haired girl, you see, and said, 'Look after this for me, will you, my dear, I need to go to the toilet.' And what do you think happened? When I came back ten minutes later—no girl, no sacks of apricots, no suitcase. How such a girl could have even lifted three heavy bags, I don't know..."

"So I said to them, 'Look, I'm carrying Polish cosmetics to Odessa for my friends.' I didn't want to, of course, but they kept on asking. 'Our train is going any minute,' they said. 'You can always buy more. You can get whatever you like in Odessa, but there's nothing up in Norilsk, where we live...' Well, I felt sorry for them... And then the sergeant comes along and says, 'Selling goods on the black market, my friend?'"

Amid such confusion, with suitcases, children, fiancées, husbands and wives disappearing or getting lost all the time, I could imagine how Aina Silinya's story about the kidnapping of her fiancé and a newspaper correspondent had been received: "Never mind, it's no big deal. Your fiancé will turn up. He's probably gone off to down some vodka somewhere..."

Svetlov and I had just introduced ourselves to the duty captain when Pshenichny suddenly appeared out of nowhere. He looked exhausted. His cheeks were sunken and his eyes were red from lack of sleep. But from the way he behaved, moved and answered questions, you could tell he was in his element.

"Have you been here long?" I asked.

"Almost twenty-four hours, since last night," he replied. "Let's go."

Dragging his left leg slightly, Pshenichny led us into a corner office. We each lit a cigarette, and he started to tell us what he had succeeded in discovering in the last twenty hours or so.

To find witnesses to the attack on Belkin and Yury Rybakov, he had had to question the people who hang out in the station square all the time. Porters, taxi drivers, militiamen, stall-holders, petty speculators, and so on: these were the people Pshenichny had talked to during the past twenty hours. He'd gone over every inch of the square as methodically as if he was ironing a shirt. He'd talked to literally dozens of people—from traffic controllers to ice cream merchants and flower sellers. Pshenichny had gone from person to person as if he were following the links in a chain certain that someone, somewhere in this square, had witnessed what no one else seemed to have any inkling of. After meeting lots of people who said, "I don't know", "I don't remember", "I didn't see", "I didn't hear", he finally encountered an old porter who said that, although he hadn't been on the square himself at the time it happened, he had nevertheless heard the fortune teller, Zemfira, threaten her demanding children with the words, "If you keep on asking for things, I'll hand you over to the ambulance men, and they'll take you away, just like they did to those loonies."

Pshenichny arrived at the militia office just as citizeness Zemfira Sokolova was being transferred to the preliminary detention cell after a two-hour interrogation. This turned out to be more difficult than one might have imagined, however. As the duty officer's assistant was trying to shove the gypsy woman into the cell, he was suddenly surrounded by all eight of her children, who started pulling him in all directions, rummaging through his pockets and grabbing his shoulders. They pretended to cry and then started biting him.

Pshenichny took her into a room containing a picture of Lenin, and began to question her himself. Zemfira remembered the incident, and confirmed that there had been four ambulance men and that the car they had been dragged into had been an ambulance. But she couldn't remember what the ambulance men looked like, however hard she tried. On the other hand, she did say the following:

"When the ambulance drove off, a drunk came up and said, 'They're picking people up off the streets, just as they did in '37!'"

"Who was this drunk?"

"I don't know his name, but I see him every day. He visits Lidka's to get beer."

Lidka, the woman who ran the beer stall by the suburban ticket office, immediately recognized the drinker in question, from Pshenichny's description that he had gotten from the fortune-teller.

"Lev Pavlovich is the one you're after, for sure. He comes every day at three, regular as clockwork. Hang around, and you'll see him!" Pshenichny spent the next hour sitting near the beer stall and waiting for a tall, elderly, fair-haired man to turn up, carrying his own metal tankard for beer. Lev Pavlovich Sinitsyn finally arrived. He was a teacher from the Surikov Art Institute and one of Lidka's regular customers.

When she'd filled his container and he'd ordered another mug of beer to boot, Sinitsyn, with great dignity, went off with Pshenichny to talk.

"How can I help you?" he asked.

Pshenichny explained what he wanted. Rubbing the palm of his hand up and down the side of his glass, Lev Pavlovich began to tell his tale in a thoughtful, unhurried way. Yes, he could remember that morning very well. His annual vacation had just begun, and he'd come for his beer at an unusual hour. He'd just finished lining up for some anchovies at the fish store. He was walking past the taxi stand on his way to the beer stall, carrying his fish and his empty tankard, when he suddenly saw something strange. An ambulance drove up to the end of the taxi stand and stopped. Then four men got out, two of them medical orderlies dressed in white coats, and another two in ordinary clothes. They grabbed two young men and a girl who were waiting in the line for a cab. The girl either managed to get away from them, or they let her go themselves—Sinitsyn didn't remember. He didn't recall the number of the car. On the other hand, he remembered very well what struck him most about the whole incident. It wasn't the fact that people were being seized in broad daylight, and that this reminded him of 1937. "What's so surprising about that?" he asked with a sad smile. "History's a tragedy when it first happens, but a farce when it repeats itself." No, what struck him was the fact that one of the ambulance men was the former European middleweight boxing champion, Viktor Akeyev. On the other hand, as he later thought, why shouldn't a former boxer get work as an orderly in a mental asylum if he wanted to?

Pshenichny kept Sinitsyn at the police station, and then phoned me. Now this same tall, fair-haired individual was seated in front of Svetlov and myself at the station.

"Are you certain that the man you saw really was Viktor

Akeyev? How did you recognize him?" I asked, after Sinitsyn had repeated his story to us.

"Well, my dear fellow, I *am* an artist after all!" he replied. "Four years ago, before he won the championship, Akeyev spent a whole semester posing for my students. I've sketched his face, his every muscle, at least a hundred times. Still . . ." He sounded a little uncertain. "I *was* sure at the time. Even though he was wearing dark glasses and a cap, I *thought* that it was him. Still . . . How shall I put it?"

"Wait a minute, Lev Pavlovich!" Pshenichny said with a start. Until then he'd been proud of his discovery. "There wasn't any doubt in your mind at the time that it was Akeyev, was there?"

"No, and there isn't any now, but . . ."

"But what?"

"Well, I don't know. There's something strange about it—a boxing champion turning into a medical orderly . . ."

We let Sinitsyn go home, and Pshenichny gave me the information about sleeping-car superintendent Dolgo-Saburov, which he'd gathered from the Railroad Personnel Department. Then I sent my persevering assistant home too, so that he could get some sleep. The last twenty hours had knocked him out, although he wouldn't admit it and begged me to give him something else to do. I ordered him to go home. He lived in Mytishchi, a suburb of Moscow, and planned to get there by train. I could just imagine what it would be like for him to go home in a crowded compartment, so I ordered my driver Seryozha to take him home in the car.

Meanwhile, Svetlov was already on the phone to the Central Address Office to find out where Akeyev lived. A moment later his face changed. "What do you mean, he's in detention?"

When he had a further reply, he put the receiver down and said, "Akeyev left Moscow a year ago after being convicted and sent to a prison camp."

So much for our artist! It looked as if the results of Pshenichny's twenty-hour stint had just gone up in smoke. It was just as well that he'd gone home to bed. But I didn't want to believe that this was true, so I phoned the CID First

Special Department and received the following information: "Akeyev, Viktor Mikhailovich, born 1942, last worked as a boxing instructor at a children's special sporting school in the Lenin district of Moscow. Former address: 70 Lenin Prospect, Block 11, Apartment 156. On January 24, 1978, convicted by the Lenin District People's Court under Article 191/1, Part 2, and Article 206, Part 2, of the RSFSR Criminal Code, and sentenced to three years' imprisonment. Serving his sentence at strict regime penal colony No. UU–121 at Kotlas, Archangel region."

The old artist had been wrong. Akeyev couldn't have been locked up at the strict regime prison camp in Kotlas *and* simultaneously wander around Moscow dressed as a medical orderly. And if he'd escaped from the camp, there would certainly have been a note about it in the information I had from the CID Special Department.

All the same, if you looked at what we'd gained rather than what we'd lost, we at least knew now that one of the "orderlies" resembled former boxing champion Akeyev, and that, of course, would help us put together an identikit picture of him. Svetlov looked at me rather dourly when I suggested that we check out all the ambulance depots in Moscow to see if anybody recognized the picture. It wasn't much to go on—some kind of ambulance, and a person resembling the boxer Akeyev—but what else could we do? We had nothing else to go on.

Without any enthusiasm, and more downcast than hopeful, we started to examine the information received from the Railroad Personnel Department on Citizen Dolgo-Saburov, superintendent of sleeping-car team No. 56, operating between Moscow and Central Asia. Reading his duty roster, we came upon the following curious detail: May 26, Train No. 37, Moscow–Tashkent, manned by team No. 56, departed on its regular trip from Moscow at 5:05 a.m." We exchanged glances and then got a copy of the railroad timetable from the officer in charge at the militia station. It certainly looked significant. Train No. 37 had passed through Moscow River station at 5:30 that morning. And at 6:15 the linesman had found the body of Rybakov near the platform!

Svetlov gave a long whistle. What were we to make of this? Furthermore, the same duty roster revealed that on May 24, the day Belkin and Rybakov were attacked at the Kursk station, superintendent Dolgo-Saburov wasn't on his usual route. Instead, he was resting in Moscow between trips. This made Svetlov exchange a further glance with me. We hardly spoke. True, according to the same information, on the day of his aunt's death, the nephew was already a long way from Moscow, approaching Aktyubinsk, and that held us up a bit.

"Well . . ." said Svetlov, rolling his eyes. We were already in the Personnel Department, leafing through Dolgo-Saburov's personal file. "It's like this . . . He's a bachelor, living by himself, and he doesn't arrive from Tashkent until the day after tomorrow. I think we should search his apartment."

We both understood that there were no legal grounds for conducting a search. The only things that Dolgo-Saburov was guilty of so far were that he was the old countess's nephew and that his train passed through Moscow River station on the night of May 26. "So what?" would be the response of the Public Prosecutor; he'd simply put the search warrant to one side without signing it.

On the other hand, what has legality got to do with it if a special investigator and a CID section head want to take a look in somebody's apartment? You can twist the law any way you like, after all . . .

*17:30 hours and subsequently*

At 5:30 in the afternoon, Svetlov and I were at Smolenskaya-Sennaya Square, in the building which houses the Arrow cinema. Seven stories up is the two-room apartment Herman Dolgo-Saburov inherited from his parents when they died. We took the cinema manager and the ticket collector as witnesses (they didn't have anything to do while the show was running, after all), and then we forced open the door to Dolgo-Saburov's apartment. A quick glance was enough to tell you that this sleeping-car superintendent was living well beyond his means. The place had a Western radio, a color television and an expensive bedroom suite. There was the usual mess that you find in any bachelor apartment. A handful of Western magazines lying on the sofa with pictures of naked girls, as well as the overall feel of the place, indicated that Dolgo-Saburov didn't waste his time between trips. A cupboard in the bathroom contained packets of Indian and German contraceptives (with "ticklers" and without), and there was somebody's bra there, too. There were more porno magazines in the kitchen, as well as packs of erotic playing cards. The cocktail cabinet and the refrigerator contained Armenian cognac, Scotch whisky, Rigan balsam and export vodka—in other words, something for everyone. The refrigerator contained fish, an open pot of caviar and an impressive birchwood bucket filled with a honeycomb weighing at least seven pounds. This fellow lived a pretty good life, to put it mildly, and was obviously spending a lot more than the 160 roubles a month he received as his salary. Still, what rail attendant ever lives on his official earnings? Even a child knows they're all involved in black market dealings of some kind or other. At a time when there is a scarcity of so much, in a country as massive as the Soviet Union, rail attendants aren't unlike general suppliers to the rest of the population, and we could see from the example of Dolgo-Saburov, they didn't do too badly as a result.

But even the most careful search of the apartment failed to reveal what we were after. There were no diamonds stashed anywhere, no hard currency, nothing out of the ordinary at all, in fact, unless you counted the porno magazines and *samizdat* copies of *Moscow–Petushki* and *Sex in a Hundred Easy Lessons*.

An hour later our search of Dolgo-Saburov's apartment was coming to an end, which was just as well, as our reluctant witnesses were becoming impatient. We drew up a report of the search according to the rules, got the witnesses to sign it and came out on the street empty-handed.

We felt tired. A whole day's work had been wasted. We were less the brilliant detectives than we were simple idiots. We were like blind kittens, wandering around near a saucer of milk with no way of finding it.

"He's got some pretty decent cognac up there!" Svetlov

said hoarsely, putting his hand in his pocket to dig out some money. "I have fourteen roubles. How about you?"

"Ten," I replied, not bothering to check. I always know exactly how much money I have on me.

It's difficult to believe that a special investigator and a CID section head would only have twenty-four roubles between them. It seems ridiculous, especially these days, when there's bribery staring you in the face wherever you look, but . . . what can I say? It is growing less common all the time, but you still *can* come across honest people, though you feel a little embarrassed to talk about it, as if you were poverty-stricken or uneducated or something. It's as if you had something to apologize for.

In any event, we felt we had to wash away the failures of the day with something stronger. After all, why should those dim-witted rail attendants spend their time stuffing themselves with caviar and having a good time with girls (the porno magazines and the woman's bra in the bathroom weren't there by accident!), while two normal, virile forty-year-olds like us should live like monks? Like hell we would!

Egging each other on, we drove off in Svetlov's CID Volga and soon pulled up outside the Prague Restaurant on Arbatskaya Square. As always, there was an enormous line outside the front door with a sign saying *No seats available* behind the glass door. A doorman, dressed in braid, was standing behind it, like a statue. So we pushed open the door as if we owned the place, calmed down the doorman by showing him our identity papers, and were led upstairs, like a couple of foreigners, by the obliging head waiter. We could have a separate room, sit down next to the band, or even have a table at the very top, in the so-called "winter garden" with its fountains. Such honored guests as ourselves could sit wherever we liked.

But we didn't need too much. We took a quiet table in the winter garden and, aware of our limited resources, gave our order to the waiter.

"A bottle of vodka, roast beef and salad. Can we keep it down to twenty-four roubles?"

"Absolutely, Comrade Colonel," the waiter replied with a smile. Svetlov looked at him in surprise, but the waiter had already disappeared.

We looked around us. There was soft music coming from the main restaurant below. A group of students, all young women, was sitting three tables away. A little further away, at tables set along the wall, was a larger group, all men, dressed in sober business suits. Either they were celebrating the passing of somebody's dissertation, or they were making a presentation.

The atmosphere of a restaurant always raises your spirits, especially the thought of having something to drink, and, in this case, getting to know the students who were sitting nearby. Svetlov and I both straightened our backs and looked like eagles. That miserable twenty-four roubles of ours wouldn't allow us to have a really good time and treat the girls, but all the same, we could ask them to dance, and we'd see how things turned out.

Suddenly—I don't remember what Svetlov and I were talking about, probably his men in Baku, and how if they didn't put their finger on anything, we might as well give up—suddenly I noticed something unexpected and stopped speaking. The waiter was placing a three-tiered dish of *hors d'oeuvre* on our table, like at a banquet when you simply help yourself. There were ripe Bulgarian tomatoes and Nezhin cucumbers, pickles and olives, pressed and unpressed caviar, fillet of sturgeon—more than I can describe. Then a bottle of vodka appeared in a silver ice bucket, some three-star Armenian cognac and some Gurdzhuani wine.

"Wait a minute!" Svetlov said to the waiter. "What are you doing? We only ordered vodka, salad and roast beef. This isn't our order."

"Don't worry, Comrade Colonel," the waiter replied, smiling as always. "It's just that we want to give you a little treat."

"Wait. I told you that we've only got twenty-four roubles."

"Now, Comrade Colonel . . ." the waiter replied in a reproachful voice. "What are you talking about? We know each other, after all. Relax. In about twenty minutes I'll be serving you sweetbreads, mushrooms and shashlyks of fresh mutton *à la* Kara. It's all being cooked by our chef Stukozin just for the two of you, Comrade Investigator. Do you remember him?"

"Stukozin?" I repeated, trying hard to remember. I seemed to recall that he'd been mixed up in a case involving floating restaurants sailing up and down the Volga. Yes, that's right. Stukozin and a few other cooks had been quietly fixing the books, without ever really overstepping the mark. At least they hadn't served people rotten meat, so I'd taken pity on them. They'd been treated separately from the rest of the group involved, who were dyed-in-the-wool criminals, and "transferred to a workers' collective for re-education". Well, what do you know! I had no objection to eating his mushrooms! Stukozin was in my debt, after all. If it had gone differently, he would have been completely finished. I could easily have gotten him five years in the place where ex-boxer Akeyev was serving his stretch even now.

"Of course! I remember Stukozin!" I replied, brightening. "Say hello to him for me!"

Now I was on equal terms with Svetlov. We'd both done each other a favor—he through his reputation as a CID officer, I through my prestige as a special investigator. In any case, it cheers you up when people recognize you in restaurants and pay back old debts, especially when they do it with such style . . . I'll have to visit the kitchen afterwards, I thought, and exchange a few nice words with the cook. Meanwhile, Svetlov and I dug in on the feast. Half an hour later, after we'd made short work of the *hors d'oeuvre* with the aid of a bottle of vodka, Svetlov and I were in top form, talking with the girls at the neighboring table, dancing with them, and then persuading them to join us. They were very willing to get to know us, too. They were all external students at the Co-operative Institute, and they'd come to Moscow from Donetsk and Voronezh with the express purpose of not wasting any time while they were here. I found myself with a plump, dyed blonde, aged twenty-three, while Svetlov went for a sultry but dizzy brown-haired woman. He was soon calling her his "little babe." Every now and then she would pass her tiny pink tongue over her delicious, full lips, and I could see Svetlov's eyes glaze over dreamily.

Everything was going as it should—the dancing, the girls, the grilled mushrooms "*à la* Public Prosecutor", as Svetlov dubbed them, the piping-hot sweetbreads, the Caucasian shashlyks, all downed to the accompaniment of Armenian cognac and Georgian wine. The only sour note was the succession of official toasts coming from the party across the way. "To the health of our deputy minister!" "To the achievements of our directorate!" was all we could hear coming from that direction.

Svetlov couldn't stand it anymore, so he said to the waiter with some annoyance, "Just who *are* those individuals over there?"

"They're from the Health Ministry, Comrade Colonel," the waiter replied in almost military fashion. "The one on the left is Petrovsky's deputy—Edward Sarkisovich Balayan. He used to work in the KGB before he went to Health. He knows a thing or two. They're celebrating receiving some official prize for making a new drug to be used by the cosmonauts."

"OK," Svetlov said with a magnanimous wave of his hand. "Let them keep celebrating, then. Only I wish that Balayan wouldn't keep ogling our girls."

It was true. Balayan was about forty-five with a broad, gray streak running through his thick black hair. His dark-brown, velvety eyes came to rest too often on our table, examining us calmly, closely and at considerable length. I didn't like this at all. To get my back on him, in front of everyone, I grabbed my blonde around the waist with one hand, and placed my other in comradely fashion on the shoulders of Svetlov's "little babe."

"Isn't it about time we went back to my bachelor pad, colonel?" I said in a lusty, suggestive voice. "We can dance there, and listen to some music. The night is young."

Whatever we said, the girls couldn't believe that Svetlov was a militia colonel and that I was a special investigator. But we didn't press the point. Instead, we both made an "honest confession"—that we were stomatologists from a local clinic, and I even promised to fix one of the "little babe's" teeth when I got home.

All in all, it was the kind of conversation that you usually have in restaurants. At one point my blonde from Voronezh said it would have been better if we had been sportsmen. She "adored" sportsmen and her fiancé was the third best boxer in Voronezh. He was a boxing instructor at a special children's sports school.

"Just like Akeyev," I couldn't help saying. They didn't know who he was, so Svetlov explained.

"Viktor Akeyev is a good friend of ours. He was the former middleweight boxing champion of Europe. He's been touring abroad now for more than a year, and Igor misses him terribly," he said, nodding towards me with a broad grin.

"I think you may be able to see him," the waiter said suddenly, as he was serving us with ice cream and iced coffee.

Svetlov and I looked at him sharply.

"He's back from abroad," the waiter continued. "He had lunch here on Thursday."

"Who did?" I said, leaning forward as far towards the waiter as I could.

"Viktor Akeyev, of course, the former boxing champion," he replied.

"Are you sure?"

"Comrade Investigator, I do believe that you're insulting me!" he said. He was smiling, but his eyes had narrowed, and he looked offended. "He had lunch here—at the table over there. His hair was closely cropped. He was dressed in a new gray Hungarian suit and a light blue shirt without a tie. What else? He had two women with him. One was about twenty-three years old with dyed brown hair. She was about five and a half feet tall and had a northern accent. The other was about twenty-two or twenty-three, too, with dark blue eyes, sort of like Natasha Rostova in Tolstoy's novel."

Our "girls" shut up immediately. They became very serious, looking first at Svetlov and me, then at the waiter. But it didn't take the two of us very long to recover our composure.

"Where's the telephone?" I asked. He showed me directly into the head waiter's office. I quickly phoned the duty officer at the Main Directorate of Corrective Labor Institutions and gave him some instructions. He was to contact the local office in Archangel by VHF radio and check whether

Akeyev was still at the camp or on the run. Three minutes later I received the following reply: "Viktor Akeyev, prisoner No. 1533, at corrective labor institution No. UU–121 at Kotlas, was released for good behavior and first-class work and transferred to a government building site in the same city until the end of his sentence. He is to be found there at the present time."

"Thank you," I replied—and immediately called Aeroflot. "When is the next flight to Kotlas?"

"At 10:40 in the morning."

"Isn't there one before that?"

"It left an hour ago."

I returned to the dining room, fully convinced that our "girls" would have already left in fright. But to my surprise, I found them both drawn very close to Marat, their eyes full of enthusiasm and interest. After all, it's not every day you get to meet a real colonel from the CID!

"And we thought you were pulling our legs," said my blonde. "We thought that you were a couple of store managers or speculators, and we wanted to lead you on. But now..."

She looked at me enthusiastically and seemed much more respectful than before.

"You're flying to Kotlas tomorrow," I said to Svetlov briefly in response to his questioning look. "We can do the rest of it later. Well, what now? Time to go home, ladies. Where are you staying? We can drop you off..."

"What do you mean?" my blonde said indignantly. "Who was it that said, 'We can dance and listen to music. The night is young'?"

Meanwhile, the "little babe" licked her lips and, looking Svetlov straight in the eye, "This won't do, Comrade Colonel!" she said. "It's leading girls on, only to disappoint them. You picked us up, bought us drinks, danced with us—then what? You're supposed to be a member of the Moscow CID. If you're not careful, I'll go off with Balayan!"

So we had to answer for our Don Juan act. Svetlov's CID Volga was parked outside my place at Izmailovsky Park all night. In the morning, Svetlov, looking the worse for wear, phoned his wife, told her some story about urgent business and zipped off to Petrovka headquarters to arrange his official trip to Kotlas.

"We haven't managed to catch any criminals yet," he said, as he was leaving, "but what about gonorrhea . . . !"

*Wednesday, June 6, noon*

REPORT OF THE EXHUMATION AND AUTOPSY CARRIED OUT ON THE BODY OF CITIZENESS O.P. DOLGO-SABUROVA On June 6, 1979, at the request of Comrade I.I. Shamrayev, chief investigator at the USSR Public Prosecutor's Office, I, A. B. Kogan, forensic expert at Mortuary No. 3, Moscow City Health Department, Forensic Section, carried out an exhumation and autopsy on the body of Citizeness O.P. Dolgo-Saburova at the Vostryakovskoye Cemetery, in the presence of Comrade Shamrayev and witnesses.

The results of the autopsy are as follows:

The presence of vomit in the respiratory tract, of colorless abrasions around the mouth, and of small scratches and contusions around the nostrils, show that death occurred as the result of asphyxiation caused by the blocking of the mouth and nose.

The victim may have been smothered through having an object like a pillow pressed tightly over her face.

The conclusion of the autopsy is that the death of Citizeness O.P. Dolgo-Saburova was caused by violent means and was *not* the result of natural processes, as indicated in the medical report and death certificate issued by the Dzerzhinsky Register Office in Moscow.

Forensic expert A. Kogan
Signatures of the other persons
present . . .

I sat staring at the report, thinking of all the effort I had gone to in order to get it. But what the hell use was it to me, now that I had it? Getting the body exhumed and forcing a forensic expert to carry out an autopsy usually takes a week, at least. The experts all turn out to be busy a week in advance, you can't get hold of any gravediggers at the cemetery, and so forth. But today I had managed to get it all done in three hours, at considerable cost to my nerves and my pocket (you had to give the gravediggers enough money for a bottle of vodka, after all). But the main thing was that it had deprived me of a whole morning. And for what? Certainly, my suspicion had proved correct. The old woman had been suffocated to death two days after the murder of Shakh/Rybakov. But who killed her? And what did it have to do with Belkin?

I couldn't make heads or tails out of it, no matter how hard I tried. I could clearly see that, apart from giving me extra work—here was one more crime to be solved—the investigation hadn't progressed at all. What else did we need to do to discover this journalist, damn him! This was the third day we'd been looking for him. In terms of the amount of time available to us, today and tomorrow should see the end of our preparatory work. We would then be in a position to use all our information to begin getting firm, qualitative results, but...

I needed to see Aina Silinya badly! I could then show her pictures of Akeyev, Gridasov and even the nephew Dolgo-Saburov, and if she recognized even one of them as a kidnapper, I'd be able to pull all the threads together. But if she didn't, and none of the three turned out to have been at the Kursk station that day, then that would mean that all of our work over the last seventy-two hours had been a waste of time and we'd have to start from scratch.

I lifted the receiver and ordered an urgent call to the Militia Chief in Riga. The password used by the USSR Prosecutor's Office never fails with the operator. Twenty seconds later I could hear the soft voices of the Riga operators, and then the sing-song, Baltic accent of Lieutenant-Colonel Robert Baron's secretary. I don't understand a word of Latvian, but I could guess what was being said. The operator was explaining to the secretary that there was an urgent call from the Public Prosecutor's Office in Moscow.

At last, the lieutenant-colonel lifted the receiver, and I said to him without waiting for his hello, "Listen, colonel. What is it you want? Do you want Churbanov or Shcholokov to get in touch with you personally?"

"What's the problem?" he asked.

"Yesterday morning I sent you an urgent telegram, and sent another by phone last night. I need to question the witness Aina Silinya. I asked you to ensure her appearance in Moscow this morning. But it's already twelve-twenty and I haven't heard a thing from you."

"Unfortunately, Comrade Investigator, the person whom you wish to question is not in Riga at the moment."

"Where is she?"

"Her neighbors reported to the local divisional inspector that she had gone away on a trip with her parents to the coast."

"Where to exactly?"

"They didn't say, Comrade Investigator . . ." Baron spoke Russian with an accent, but there was a certain mocking tone in his voice, as if to say: All right, we carry out your requests, of course, and we do what we are told, but on the other hand . . . Don't order us around, we've got our own republic, after all.

I had no time to play at being polite with him. "Listen to me, colonel," I said. "The job I'm doing is connected with Comrade Brezhnev's imminent meeting with Carter in Vienna. You and I have a very limited amount of time at our disposal. Aina Silinya must be here in Moscow today, even if you have to check the whole coastline near Riga to find her. Do you understand?"

He said nothing. He needed time to think things through again. Would he really have to check the whole coastline, or was there a chance that he might get out of it?

"Does Comrade Shcholokov really know all about this case?" he said cautiously.

"Not only Shcholokov," I replied, "but Rudenko, Suslov and Andropov too. Which one of them would you need to get a telegram from, if you're going to find the girl?"

"Well, that's not necessary . . . I don't know . . ." the colonel murmured indecisively, realizing that it was better not to force me to go to Shcholokov or Suslov in order to get a telegram. If every militia chief were to ask a minister to confirm the authority of his special assistants, it would lead to an explosion of anger by the authorities. Especially if I were to carry out a task on the direct instructions of the Central Committee . . .

"And please don't forget, colonel," I said, "I am acting on the direct instructions of the Central Committee, and every hour could be crucial. Those who help to bring this case to a successful conclusion won't be forgotten, either. Do you get my drift? I need her today. I'm not kidding!"

First show the big stick, then offer the carrot—it never fails.

"All right," said the colonel, changing his tone. "I'll see to it today, personally. Where can I call you?"

Of course, once it was a question of early promotion to the rank of full colonel, Baron would see to the matter personally, that very day. I gave him the number of my own office and apartment, as well as that of Rudenko's secretary and CID Third Section, where one of Svetlov's men was always on duty.

"Can I take her into custody, if she refuses to come along of her own free will?" Baron asked.

"Of course. I'll prepare the necessary warrant. Formal niceties have to take second place in this investigation."

From that moment Lieutenant-Colonel Baron and the Riga Militia would start scouring the whole surrounding coastline. I imagined that half an hour later the resort of Yurmala would be swarming with agents and informers of all descriptions, all of them employees of the Latvian MVD.

I hung up. Now it was a question of waiting—of waiting for Baron to find Aina Silinya, for Svetlov in Kotlas to find something out about the boxer Akeyev, for the CID men in Baku to come up with something too, for train No. 37 from Tashkent to arrive in Moscow tomorrow with Herman Dolgo-Saburov on board, and finally for Pshenichny's team at the Kursk station to come up with somebody who witnessed the murder of Yury Rybakov that night (or could it have been an accident?).

I was feeling sleepy—I started absent-mindedly rolling up some papers that were lying on my desk. After a night on the floor, you feel more like sleep than work. Of course, a call from Baku, Kotlas, or at least from the Kursk station would have got me going. For some reason, I didn't believe that they would pin down Ziyalov simply by comparing the lists of Belkin's former classmates with the list of passengers on the flight from Tashkent. Probably because it would have been too simple, and I've never been given anything *just like that* in the whole of my life. There was another reason, too. I didn't believe what Belkin said anymore, or what he wrote in his manuscript. If he had lied about Sverdlov, then why shouldn't he also have lied about Ziyalov being in his class at school . . . ?

I don't know whether I was still awake or nodding off as I thought about all this, but some instinct suddenly made me lift my head and look towards the door. There, standing in the doorway, I saw Roman Andreyevich Rudenko, Chief Public Prosecutor of the USSR. Dressed in a marshal's uniform and with his hair smoothed down, there he was, staring at me silently with those flat blue eyes of his, as if he were listening to my thoughts or reading them from a distance. When he saw me look up, he started to smile.

"I don't detect much spirit," he said.

About once a month, as part of the new trend towards greater democracy, the Chief Public Prosecutor would walk through the offices himself, talking about this and that with his employees, showing interest in their personal lives and working conditions. But this obviously wasn't the only reason for his visit today.

"Hello, Roman Andreyevich," I said, getting up from my chair.

"Hello," he replied, walking up to my desk and staring at me closely. "Why are you looking so under the weather today? There are bags under your eyes. It's the life bachelors lead, I suppose. Been having a wild time?"

I tried not to breathe near him, so that he wouldn't catch a whiff of brandy and vodka.

"Now, what time would I have for wild living, Roman Andreyevich? That's quite a case you've dropped on my head."

"And how's it going? What can I tell the Central Committee? Will we get Belkin back, or not?"

"Well, we're still looking for him. We've found somebody who witnessed the kidnapping, and we think we know the identity of one of the kidnappers."

"'We're still looking for him', 'We think we know'!" he said, mimicking my voice. "I don't detect any enthusiasm in your voice, Igor Iosifovich, or any resolve. It's not good enough. And don't forget that you've only got four days left. Perhaps you need some more assistance? Where are the rest of your team—Svetlov and that . . . what's his name?"

"Pshenichny," I prompted. "Svetlov is in Kotlas at the moment, looking for a convict. And Pshenichny is combing the Kursk rail line. He's looking for anybody who might have witnessed the murder of Belkin's friend from Baku."

"I don't know, I don't know . . ." he said, tapping his fingers on the desk. "You're running the case, so you've got a better idea of what's going on, but . . . here you are with one of your teammates off in Kotlas, and the other one is looking for witnesses to a murder. Look, the murder's not going to run away, you know. But Belkin we need *now,* and preferably alive. Otherwise, what am I going to tell the Central Committee? That we can't find a person in our own country?"

I said nothing. All I could do in my position was keep silent and wait. And even if he were to give me more assistants, what would I do with them?

He lifted the receiver and began to dial. Then, as though his thoughts were elsewhere, he rather abstractedly stuck his pencil into one of the holes and stopped the dial halfway around.

"How did you get hold of Svetlov?" he asked suddenly, staring me right in the eye. "Did Shcholokov say you could have him?"

So *that* was why he had come! And that was why he'd turned the dial on the phone and had stuck his pencil in it. How funny! The Chief Prosecutor of the USSR is afraid that the KGB might be bugging the phones at his office, so he decides to disconnect one of them for a few seconds, just to be on the safe side! And at the same time, we both had to pretend that I hadn't understood or even noticed what he was doing.

I told him as quickly as I could what had happened with Brezhnev's son-in-law, Churbanov, and about the diamond brooch which he had taken away with him to show Galina Brezhneva. The Chief Prosecutor listened with obvious satisfaction. In the end, he even deemed me worthy of praise.

"That's wonderful!" he said. "Shcholokov won't go against Churbanov, of course, so they won't take Svetlov away from you now. But bear it in mind that both Shcholokov and Andropov will be very pleased if we *don't* find Belkin. So one of them may try to slow you down. Be really careful, and don't make any mistakes!"

He let the dial on the phone return to its usual position, and then came out with a peremptory remark, addressed to me, but obviously said for the benefit of anybody else who might have been listening in.

"There's no point in you wearing out the seat of your pants by sitting around in your office all day. You've got to get on with investigating the case at hand. Good luck." With that he left.

I lifted the receiver again and listened. There was the usual dial tone, nothing special. That didn't prove anything, though. You can't tell whether a phone is being tapped or not just like that, of course. OK, that was enough sitting around for one day. It was time for action. The Chief Prosecutor had given me a warning, and that was the most he could do. Svetlov was a long ways off in Kotlas, but I did need to help Pshenichny out. I dialed the number of the head of Militia at the Kursk railroad station. I got his number direct by looking it up in the MVD internal telephone directory. Somebody answered immediately.

"Colonel Maryamov speaking."

"Good afternoon, colonel. This is Shamrayev from the Chief Prosecutor's Office. You don't happen to know where my assistant, Investigator Pshenichny, is at the moment?"

"He's in Podolsk, Comrade Shamrayev. Your team has set up a temporary headquarters there. We've had all our people working on it since early this morning, down the line as far as Serpukhov. Everybody has been pressed into action, Comrade Shamrayev!"

"Good, colonel. You couldn't come over here, could you?"

"I'm ready to come if you need me. I'm at your disposal."

"I'll pick you up in ten minutes."

*At the same time, in Kotlas*
"It's prostitution, Comrade Colonel! No doubt about it! Look

at these girls. I know they look like angels. What would you say they were? Students and members of Komsomol? No way! They're nothing but whores, who do it for three roubles."

Lieutenant-Colonel Svetlov had driven from Kotlas airport to camp No. UU-121, where he arrived right in the middle of an argument in the office of the camp commander, Major Smagin. Five pretty teenage girls, aged between fifteen and eighteen, and all with enticing lips, were huddled together on the major's sofa, listening to him heap abuse on them, but not afraid of him in the least. They weren't prisoners, but students at the Kotlas Technical School, who were free to come and go as they pleased.

"What am I going to do with them, colonel?" Smagin sighed. "Can you imagine what they've been doing? We don't leave any guards on duty in the wood-felling area at night—all the prisoners are inside the camp. So these young ladies sashay along and hide in all kinds of places. And they wait. Later on, at six in the morning, the area is cordoned off by soldiers, and an hour after that the prisoners are brought in to chop down the trees. As soon as they see their chance, these fucking cunts make their move. Goddammit! They can suck a guy off the French way, and they go through a hundred prisoners a day, hitting them for three roubles a shot. Komsomol members, I'll be damned! It probably takes a prisoner a whole month to save up the money, kopeck by kopeck, and they suck it out of him in two minutes . . . Well, what do you want me to do with them, Comrade Colonel?"

Svetlov, exhausted by his own adventures the previous night, had barely managed to grab a couple of hours' sleep on the plane. He looked away and shrugged his shoulders impatiently. He had no time to worry about these students. All three of them—Major Smagin, Lieutenant-Colonel Svetlov, and the deputy camp commander, Captain Zharikov, an irritable-looking man with nicotine-stained buck teeth—all three knew perfectly well that there was nothing anybody could do about these girls. Since the Article about prostitution had been removed from the constitution in 1936 (there was no such thing as whoring in the USSR!), the worst thing that could happen to the girls was a fifteen-rouble fine for "violation of public order". Of course the girls knew this. That was why they were listening so calmly to the major's ranting. They weren't afraid of threats. Finally, Major Smagin sent them out of the office. When he found out about the purpose of Svetlov's journey, his face changed.

"Akeyev? He's been released from direct custody and is working on a building site. They're building a big chemical plant. He's been assigned to the site manager there, and doing work as a welder. What about him?"

"Are you certain that he's in Kotlas? Where's the site manager's office?"

"I'll get a car and drive you there myself."

Svetlov declined the major's offer to accompany him. He took the car and drove across Kotlas in the direction of the building site. When he arrived, he avoided talking to the manager's secretary, a big-bosomed woman not yet twenty, who was dressed in a miniskirt. She was an ex-prisoner, released on parole too. He walked right past her and went straight into Captain Chabanov's office. A few minutes later it emerged that, although Akeyev was registered at the site as a welder, his real job was to act as a "fixer" or "go-getter", someone who could get hold of spare parts for machinery and other things that were in short supply at the building site. It was in connection with this that he was sometimes sent on official business to Archangel, Kirov, and even Moscow. Who could be better at hustling than a famous sportsman, a former European boxing champion?! The chief engineer at the plant had just sent Akeyev to Moscow to negotiate purchases at the Ministry of Industrial Construction with the site manager's knowledge.

It took Svetlov another hour to get the salary office at the plant to make copies of all Viktor Akeyev's travel documents, so Svetlov could establish when and where he had been away on business. It turned out that he spent more time in Moscow than in Kotlas, and that his trips were often extended by the Ministry itself while he was in the capital. He'd gone off on his last trip as long ago as the beginning of May. However, the chief engineer at the plant, Kogan, was very satisfied with what Akeyev had achieved.

"I don't know about him being a boxer or a welder, but what I do know is that if I had five or six fixers as good as Akeyev, I'd get this chemical plant built in a third of the time. He even managed to get Gosplan to waive the quotas on ferro-concrete reinforcements. Imagine!"

When he had the documentation he needed, Svetlov, hoping he'd be in time to catch the last flight to Moscow, rushed back to the airport.

Captain Zharikov was waiting for him. Svetlov looked at him in surprise.

"May I have a few words with you, colonel?" Zharikov said in a gloomy voice.

"Of course."

"It's about Viktor Akeyev. I couldn't talk at the camp office, you see. The walls have ears. It concerns Major Smagin, the camp commander..."

"Hold on a moment. I've got to get my ticket checked."

The Pechora-Kotlas-Moscow flight was late as usual, so there was time to talk.

"Smagin wants his daughter to marry Akeyev," said the captain. "She's head over heels in love with him, and can twist her father around her little finger. That's why Akeyev has been released on parole and transferred to the chemical plant. At the moment they're both in Moscow, at the Hotel Peking."

"How do you know?" asked Svetlov, surprised.

"As soon as you left the camp, Major Smagin tried three times to book a call to the hotel, to talk to his daughter. I think he wants to warn them about your visit. Only he couldn't get any reply from her hotel room."

"Thank you," Svetlov said. "Come with me." And the two of them hurried towards the airport post office. There was an inter-city telephone booth there, and Svetlov immediately dialed No. 38 Petrovka, dictating the following message to his deputy, Major Ozherelyev: "Place a tap on the phone of Yelena Vasilyevna Smagina at the Hotel Peking. Don't connect any inter-city calls. Have Smagina put under immediate observation, as she may be in touch with Akeyev."

Akeyev wasn't entitled to stay at a hotel, as he didn't have a passport. But a big enough bribe would enable him to spend any number of nights with his mistress, even at the Peking.

"Thank you very much, captain," Svetlov said. "The country will not forget you. I'll inform the Main Directorate of Corrective Labor Institutions of your scrupulous devotion to duty."

"But I haven't told you everything," Zharikov replied, as melodramatically as ever. "Our camp is supposed to be a model of its kind and is always having official visits. Everywhere you go there are placards saying 'Honest labor is the way to freedom' and 'Support the moral code of builders of communism' and so on. But it's a fraud! Smagin is always being too easy on the prisoners. He's even set up an orchestra, and the result is . . . Look!" And he opened his fist to show what he had been clutching throughout the whole conversation: two ampoules of morphine.

"I seized them from the prisoners during our last search," he said. "And this is what they came in. I found it in the trash."

Zharikov produced part of a small cardboard box from his pocket. It had a factory label bearing the words *Chief Pharmaceutical Authority, Moscow.*

"As you can see, they came from Moscow. And I have no doubt that they were brought here by Major Smagin's future son-in-law, Viktor Akeyev."

*Yes,* Svetlov thought, *Captain Zharikov wants to become a camp commander very badly. He'll soon take care of things!*

He thanked the captain again, said that he'd inform the prison authority of his good work without fail, took the ampoules and the label, and departed for Moscow.

*At the same time, in Moscow*
*Secret*

To Special Investigator
USSR Prosecutor's Office
Comrade I. I. Shamrayev

REPORT

Today, June 6 1979, I, V. Pshenichny, acting Special Investigator at the USSR Public Prosecutor's Office, along with a group of police operatives from the Railroad Militia, questioned all those rail employees who were at work on the night of May 26 1979, when Citizen Yu. Rybakov was killed.

Thirty-two militia agents took part in the operation, and a total of 214 people were questioned, at stations and halts on the Kursk railroad between Serpukhov and Moscow. Each person questioned was shown a photograph of the deceased, Yu. Rybakov, and identical pictures of the persons presumed to have kidnapped Rybakov and Belkin—Citizens S. Gridasov, V. Akeyev and H. Dolgo-Saburov.

The results of the operation were negative. None of those questioned was able to provide any additional information about the death of Yu. Rybakov...

A tank or a tractor would have been envious of the energy Pshenichny had. Sitting in the headquarters of the Railroad Militia at Podolsk, he was about to finish writing this report when he heard the voices of some railroad personnel walking by outside his window.

"But why haven't they questioned the cleaners? They work nights, too, after all..."

"That's all we need!" another voice said.

By this time Pshenichny had already risen from his chair and jumped over to the window.

"Hey! Wait a minute! What cleaners?"

Fortunately, all the cleaners at Podolsk lived in railroad wagons, on sidings not far from the station. It was late in the evening and the rest of us, including Colonel Maryamov, Pshenichny's assistants and myself, had long since gone home. But Pshenichny was a man of conscience, and he went off to question all the cleaners. When he was near the end of his last interrogation, chance intervened in the form of a night-watchman named Sytin, the common-law husband of the cleaner that Pshenichny was questioning. As he was listening to Pshenichny's insistent voice asking, "Do you remember whether you were on duty on the night of May 26?", Sytin, an unprepossessing dwarf of a man, suddenly said,

"Listen, chum, stop bothering her and listen to me. I remember that night very well. It's my name-day. You can check it in my passport. Pelageya was ill in bed that night, women's trouble, you know. So I did her shift in Tsaritsyno instead, except that I wasn't at the station. I was walking along the tracks, talking to the engineers of a freight train that had stopped at the points. It was carrying new Zhiguli cars straight from Tolyatti. I remember it well. That's why I was talking with them. The signals changed to green, just as a clock was striking midnight or one o'clock somewhere. As the signal changed, this guy jumps onto the track carrying a briefcase or something in his hand. He was breathing hard, like he was running away from someone, and his shirt was sticking out of his pants. 'How can I get to Moscow?' he asks. And how *would* you get there when the last train for the night had already left? 'Climb up onto the freight train,' I says. 'It'll be leaving any minute, and you can arrive there with the cars.' And that's what he does. The train had just started to move when a car drives up and two men jump out. 'Have you seen a guy with a case?' they ask. 'What do you want to know for?' I say. 'He's escaped from the hospital. He's soft in the head.' Well, the fellow hadn't looked well, to be sure. Then they say to each other, 'He must be on the train, there's nowhere else for him to go.' And they jumped on too, as the train was beginning to pull away really fast..."

### INVESTIGATOR PSHENICHNY'S REPORT
#### (continued)

... Additional questioning of the cleaners at the Podolsk rail complex has revealed that on the night of May 25–6 the cleaner Pelageya Sinyukhina was away sick, and her co-habitee, the night-watchman Nikolay Nikolayevich Sytin, was deputizing for her at Tsaritsyno railroad station. The latter testified that between midnight and one o'clock on May 26 he saw a young man, carrying a document case, climb onto a passing freight train, followed by two men in pursuit who also jumped up on this same train. From the photographs which he was shown, N. Sytin recognizes the young man as Yury Rybakov and his pursuers as Semyon Gridasov and Viktor Akeyev. Their identification was categorical. Records of the cross-examination and the identification procedure are appended.

> Acting Special Investigator
> V. Pshenichny

June 6 1979

*The same day, 21:45 hours*

URGENT TELEGRAM

Moscow, USSR Public Prosecutor's Office
Investigator Shamrayev
(copy to Lieutenant-Colonel Svetlov, CID)
AFTER CHECKING LISTS OF PUPILS ATTENDING BAKU SCHOOL NO. 171 BETWEEN 1967-9 WE HAVE NOT DISCOVERED ANY SURNAMES CORRESPONDING TO THOSE OF PASSENGERS ON TASHKENT FLIGHT STOP TOMORROW WE WILL SEARCH FOR AND QUESTION BELKIN'S FELLOW PUPILS TO ASCERTAIN WHO HIS FRIENDS WERE STOP ACCORDING TO HIS GRANDMOTHER, S. M. BELKINA, AND HER NEIGHBORS, VADIM BELKIN WAS NOT AT THEIR APARTMENT BLOCK DURING MAY STOP YOURS, ROGOZIN, SHMUGLOV

*Thursday, June 7 1979, 03:45 hours*
As the poet said, "This day witnessed what a hundred more will not."

During the night I was awakened by the phone. It was Svetlov at the Peking.

"The girl has come back drunk and has gone to bed."

"Which girl, where?" I asked, still half-asleep.

"Well, she isn't back in your place, don't worry! Lena Smagina I mean, Akeyev's mistress. She arrived back at the Hotel Peking so drunk that she couldn't get the key in the door. Then she went to bed. Before this, according to Central Telegraph, her dad tried to call her twice from Kotlas. But I've blocked all inter-city calls to her room so they won't connect her to Kotlas. As you're in charge of the investigation team, I want to know whether to arrest her now and interrogate her, or to lead her on and observe her."

"What do you think you should do?"

"Well, in my opinion, we can always arrest her any time. But if she really is in love with Akeyev, she may not confess and betray him. So I would prefer trying another line. I'll put Ozherelyev on to her, as soon as she wakes up. If you have no objection, that is. He can tell her something he shouldn't, and we'll wait to see the reaction. OK?"

I know that this is a favorite trick of Svetlov's. Sometimes he calls it "forcing the issue", sometimes "casting bait". In fact, it's the purest form of provocation: you incite the criminal to commit a series of actions in which he incriminates himself. So what? Let him try. Our moral code (if you can call it that) allows us to adopt these tactics in the struggle against crime.

"All right," I said. "Only don't overplay your hand or let it drag on too long. We need Akeyev urgently."

"And what shall we do about Dolgo-Saburov, the old woman's nephew? Are you going to follow up on that angle?"

"Of course I am! I told you that somebody smothered the old woman to death. When the Tashkent train arrives at 5:50, Pshenichny and I will search Dolgo-Saburov's wagon."

"Well, you'd better get up then. It's already 3:45."

*The same day, a few minutes after 07:00 hours*
The search of wagon No. 5 on Moscow–Tashkent train No. 37 had already lasted more than an hour—with no tangible results. The passengers had gone home long ago, and the train itself had left the Kursk station and was now standing in the Kalanchevskaya hump-yard. The attendants had taken the sheets off to the laundry, while Pshenichny and myself, accompanied by three inspectors from the Railroad Militia, were busy with the sleeping car and Dolgo-Saburov. The inspectors were doing the search of the actual wagon, since there is no way one investigator could do that by himself. You have to know the detailed layout of the

carriage and possible hiding places. Meanwhile, Pshenichny and I were questioning Herman. Did he know that his aunt had the family jewels in her possession? What were his relations with her? When did he find out about her death? Herman Dolgo-Saburov was a lean thirty-year-old, with brown hair, sharp features and a prominent chin. He was irritated and angry, but he gave precise answers to all our questions and didn't appear to be concealing anything. Yes, he had known that his aunt possessed some old family jewels. He'd also known that she sold the occasional brooch and lived on the proceeds. Well, what would you expect an old woman to live on? No, he'd never laid any claim to these valuables. Why would he have done so? He had enough to live on anyway. He knew nothing about her death, and he was hearing about it from us for the first time. Who did he suspect of the murder? He shrugged his shoulders. Nobody, he thought, though heaven knows. The old woman had had admirers up to the age of seventy, if not later. She liked to amuse herself with men, so maybe one of her former lovers had . . . But in any case, it wasn't him. He couldn't identify the jewelry from photographs, because he'd never seen it. His aunt had never shown him.

The inspectors removed various items of food from the refrigerator and from a hatch in the floor. These included two boxes of fruit and grapes, a side of mutton and a wooden bucket filled with an amber-yellow honeycomb.

"What are you carrying the fruit for?" I asked.

"What do you mean? To eat it, what else? Can you get grapes like that in Moscow?"

"And the mutton?"

"To make shashlyks, what else?"

"And the honey?"

"It's from the Altai. It's the best cure for any cold. Besides, honey helps my liver. I've got an inflamed gallbladder."

I finished the cross-examination. What more could you get out of him? Empty-handed, Pshenichny and I went off to the nearby Hotel Leningrad to have some breakfast. Seryozha, my driver, was still reading *Anna Karenina* and asked me another question.

"Igor Iosifovich, where in Moscow was a hotel or res-

taurant called the England? Oblonsky had lunch there. I
know all the inns in Moscow, I think, but the England . . ."

I didn't know where it was, either. It was the Peking
which interested me at that moment, not the England. I
contacted Svetlov over the radio phone and discovered that
Lena Smagina was still asleep, but that Major Ozherelyev
had already moved into the room next door.

*The same day, 09:30 hours*
"Mercenary jack-asses—that's who's looking after our interests in the Central Committee! A bunch of incompetent
womanizers! I'll be goddamned if Shevtsov, Titov, Pavlov
and the rest will ever tell the Politburo how things really
are. For eight years I've been asking them to give us emergency powers to deal with drug trafficking. So what happens? Not a fucking thing! The country is being torn apart
by drug addiction, prostitution and VD, but everybody acts
as if the place is like a fucking convent! Of course, under
Stalin and Khrushchev the place *was* clean, but now it
seems, wherever you look, there's nothing but fucking im-
morality, alcoholism and drugs . . ."

I had never heard anybody in a government office make
such frank observations, and certainly not from the lips of
an attractive young woman, spiced with such vulgar language. But this was Nadezhda Malenina, a thirty-three-year-
old former gymnastics champion with fair hair and a well-
preserved figure. She now held the rank of major in the
militia and was the head of the recently formed narcotics
section of the Anti-Fraud Squad. She was married to a
professor at the General Staff Military Academy, who was
particularly close to Marshal Ustinov, the Defense Minister,
so she could say publicly what we usually only utter in the
privacy of our own homes, amid a tiny circle of friends—
and even then only after we're on our third or fourth bottle
of vodka . . .

"The country is being plundered from top to bottom,
young people have no beliefs or principles, teenagers are
shooting dope into themselves, and all the newspapers do
is blather on about universal happiness and how everything
is flourishing. Strong government, that's what we need! In

Central Asia, the Caucasus, the Crimea—whole fields are used to cultivate hemp and opium, and there are millions of organized criminals out there selling the shit. In Simferopol there's an opium poppy by every telegraph pole. People grow them for profit. Come here and have a look at this!"

She had an easy, familiar way of talking to me, as if she'd known me for a hundred years, although I'd heard of her existence only an hour ago, when I had decided to bring the Anti-Fraud Squad in on the investigation. After all, Svetlov had brought two ampoules of morphine back with him from the camp at Kotlas, and they had a definite place of origin: Chief Pharmaceutical Authority, Moscow. It turned out that because of the ominous growth of drug addiction in the country, a special narcotics investigation section had been set up as part of the Anti-Fraud Squad.

Malenina turned to the wall and pointed to a map of the USSR. It had a large number of tiny flags pinned to it, all in the south of the country. "Look! These flags indicate the whereabouts of opium poppy fields in Turkmenistan, Uzbekistan, the Caucasus, the Crimea and the Amur basin. They're all on collective farms, of course, run by the state for the pharmaceutical industry. But do you think I got this information through official channels? Like hell I did! Both the Ministry of Health and the Ministry of Agriculture were as shifty as Jews at a marketplace. You know the reason? Because they've all been bribed. If there are poppy fields belonging to collective farms, that must mean there are private holdings in the same place, with the produce sold on the black market. There's stealing everywhere! Nobody works anywhere these days unless they can swindle the state out of something! I know what I'm talking about, too . . . !"

I smiled inwardly. I don't know about anywhere else, but the Anti-Fraud Squad really should know what's going on. They even take precautions against bribery in their own offices. Their investigators don't have individual rooms to work in. They have to sit two or three to an office to prevent each other from taking unofficial payments. As if there weren't other places where you could pocket a hefty bribe from some big noise in the underworld! If that weren't the case, then where did these Anti-Fraud Squad investigators get their imported suits from, their Italian shoes, their Bulgarian sheepskin coats and the various culinary delicacies that you can't get anywhere else? As they investigated all aspects of economic consumption in the country, the employees of the Anti-Fraud Squad had become one more élite caste of well-heeled, elegantly dressed government inspectors, with the manner and appearance of respectable and prestigious guardians of the law. This made Nadezhda Malenina stand out all the more, of course, with her vulgar language and her links with the military group around Ustinov. It also meant that she was able to rise above bribery and corruption herself, thanks to the superior rations that her general husband had access to.

"I guess I got carried away. What you're interested in is what I can actually do for you in a concrete way. Two things, I think—and not so much for you as for myself. I've been sniffing around this Pharmaceutical Authority myself. In the State Arbitration Department I found a lot of complaints from the Defense Ministry's Medical Directorate, alleging that military hospitals were receiving consignments of drugs containing large shortfalls in the number of ampoules. Four or five of them were broken in each box. The thing to do is to go and check whether the damage occurred while the drugs were being transported, or whether the broken ampoules were substituted during the packaging. That's what I did. I planted some of my people at the factories, who reported that it was physically impossible for the women who did the packaging to substitute broken containers—they do everything in full view of everybody else. It turns out that what's needed is a full inspection of the main warehouses where the drugs are stored, but I don't have permission to organize one. It's out of the question, they say. You can't interrupt the supply of medicines to the hospitals. But I've got them where I want them, now that you've given me these ampoules. I'll get the warehouses shut down for inspection. As for the coffin you mentioned, you'll know soon whether it was filled with narcotics or not. And if it was, I'll be able to turn all Central Asia upside down to find who did it!"

"Two CID men have been in Baku since yesterday, but they're not investigating the business with the coffin at the moment. They'll look into it in a day or two."

"And I should think so, too! What next, the scum! Soldering drugs in a zinc coffin! What the hell won't they think of next?" Malenina said, not without a hint of admiration. "By the way, I did get one thing done. Every large airport is now equipped with dogs who are trained to sniff out drugs. Until now they used to carry hashish and opium quite openly, stuffing it in their suitcases. Even now they're finding ways around it, though—by sealing the hash in wax, or stuffing opium into honeycombs! Holy Ch-rist! There isn't a dog alive that can sniff that out."

I suddenly turned pale. Only two hours before, in Dolgo-Saburov's coach at the Kursk station, I had seen a wooden bucket containing Altai mountain honey, and the day before yesterday I'd seen a similar birchwood bucket filled with the same stuff in the refrigerator at Dolgo-Saburov's apartment. And I—idiot that I was—had taken Dolgo-Saburov and his complaints about his bad liver at face value!

The color had obviously drained from my cheeks as Malenina suddenly asked, "What's wrong?"

"Nothing," I replied hoarsely. "I'm all right. Only I've just remembered that there's something very urgent which I have to do."

*10:20 hours*

I rushed out of the building and ran across the sidewalk to where my Volga was parked. I pulled open the door and plumped down into the front seat, right next to the driver.

"Smolenskaya-Sennaya Square, as fast as you can! The Arrow cinema!"

To coin a phrase, I'd fallen for it hook, line and sinker. Fancy holding buckets full of opium and honey in your hands on two separate occasions and not even probing the honeycombs with a fork or something! And now all I could say was, "Let's move, Seryozha! Step on it!" But what was the point? The old countess's nephew would no doubt be expecting me!...

All the same, I opened my briefcase and pulled out a

pile of forms. There was one for practically every contingency—arrest warrants, search warrants, you name it! I hurriedly filled in one of the latter for Dolgo-Saburov's place. Then I needed some witnesses, though this search, like the one before it, was far from being legal, since we had no charges to bring against Dolgo-Saburov—yet. I couldn't break the law at every step. I had to observe due process in some ways, at least.

"Stop over by the Military Registration Office," I said to Seryozha, nodding towards a brick building on the corner not far from the Arrow cinema. A group of close-cropped new recruits stood milling around outside the main entrance. I rushed past them, went up to the duty officer, stuck my Prosecutor's Office identity card in front of him and said, "Quick, I need two witnesses urgently! Anybody will do!"

Whether it was my tone of voice that impressed him, or the identity card, I don't know, but he made no complaint. Instead, he suddenly shouted, "Zakharyev and Kupala, come here immediately!"

Two young sergeants placed themselves at my disposal and got into the Volga.

"Let's go," I said to Seryozha, and we sped off immediately.

The soldiers, who were obviously fresh from a sergeant's training course, looked around curiously and said, "Where are we going? Is it far?"

We'd hardly gone one hundred yards before the car came to a halt.

"Follow me!" I said. "As fast as you can!"

The elevator *would* have to be in use, of course. Some delivery men were bringing a new set of furniture for one of the tenants.

Swearing under my breath, I started to run upstairs towards the seventh floor. By the time we reached the landing on the sixth, my heart felt like it would burst, and I had to pause for breath while the two sergeants stared at me expectantly. Finally, we reached the door of Dolgo-Saburov's apartment on the seventh floor. I rang the bell, while the two sergeants, true to all rules of police behavior, stood by the wall on either side of the door. There was no reply, of course. I rang again and again, but it was a waste of time. I saw a light appear behind a peephole in the door of the next apartment, but it only lasted a moment and then went off. I rummaged around in my briefcase and got out a penknife. I wasn't going to fool around now, so I shoved the knife into the lock as firmly as I could. Finally the lock gave. But one look at the apartment was enough to prove that Dolgo-Saburov had gotten wind of things the last time I'd appeared. The hi-fi equipment and color television were gone. There were no Western porno magazines and not even the *samizdat* copy of *Moscow–Petushki*.

I headed straight for the kitchen and opened the refrigerator. There was no honeycomb, of course. To the bewilderment of the sergeants, I irritably kicked the box of Uzbek grapes—they were the same ones we'd found in the train that morning—sat down at the table and started to drum my fingers. I needed to regain my composure. What the hell did it all mean? Dolgo-Saburov was involved in illegal drug trafficking. That still needed to be proved, but let's assume for the moment that it was true and that he really was carrying opium from Central Asia to Moscow. What did that have to do with Belkin? Or Akeyev? Or the General? Or the murder of the countess? If he could prove that he was away from Moscow and on duty at the time of her death, and if we'd missed the chance to catch him redhanded with the opium, then we had nothing on him. Still, he really had skipped fast. He'd removed all his most valuable possessions, as if he were about to be arrested or flee the country. It stood to reason that the first thing he would do would be get rid of the narcotics. Even as I had urged Seryozha to drive faster along the Garden Ring Road, I'd had no doubt about that. Still, I had at least hoped to find him home and put him in the detention cell for a few days, just to be on the safe side. But now, as I looked around this half-empty apartment and saw Dolgo-Saburov's belongings thrown all over the place, I realized that his haste could mean only one thing: that the countess's nephew had really taken me for a ride—and disappeared himself!

I rose from the chair and walked into the bedroom to make a phone call. Just as I was reaching for the receiver, the phone began to ring. I froze. Should I answer the call or not? Could it be Dolgo-Saburov himself at the other end of the line, calling to see whether we'd appeared to carry out a second search? Or maybe it was somebody phoning Dolgo-Saburov? What should I do? Curiosity finally got the better of me and I lifted the receiver after the fourth ring.

"Yeah?" I mumbled, as if still half-asleep.

"Hello, Herman." It was a young woman speaking.

"What?" I asked slowly.

"What's the matter, darling? Are you still asleep?"

"Uh-huh," I muttered.

"Well, wake up and listen carefully to what I've got to say. Are you awake?"

There was a box of matches next to the phone. I got one out and ignited it right next to the receiver, so that the person at the other end would hear the sound. Then I started to cough, as if I'd just had a hit of a cigarette.

The ruse seemed to work; the woman gave a sarcastic laugh.

"Stop coughing into the phone, you bum," she said. "Now, listen to me. Katyukha says that the CID has circulated photos of the boxer and the old man all over Moscow. Police at all the railroad stations and exit roads have been alerted. Can you hear me?"

"Uh-huh."

"What do you mean, 'Uh-huh'? What are you mumbling for?"

I could hear caution creep into her voice. I realized that I'd have to say something properly.

I gave another cough. "My throat hurts. Well?"

There was a suspicious silence at the other end of the line. I had nothing to lose. So as not to prolong the silence, I said, "Well? What's happening with the journalist?"

The dial tone was the only answer I got. I carefully put the receiver on the table next to the phone.

"Don't replace the receiver," I said to the two sergeants who had been watching me. Then I rushed out onto the landing and rang the bell to the apartment next door. I held the button down until somebody came.

A light appeared at the peephole again. "Public Prosecutor's Department!" I shouted. "Open the door! I need to use your phone! Quickly, it's an emergency!"

I could hear the sound of locks being opened, and an old crone opened the door slightly. I pushed forward and literally tore into the room.

"Sorry, ma'am, but where's the phone?"

Then I saw it myself, before she had a chance to reply. I dialed the number of the secret Central Telephone Surveillance Department at Zubovskaya Street. "Hello—is that the duty officer? Password—'defense'. Shamrayev speaking. Find out immediately which phone 244–12–90 is connected to. And for Christ's sake, move it!"

Until you replace the receiver you are still connected to the phone where the call originated. That's how the Moscow telephone system works. This meant that I might be able to trace the phone that had just been used to contact Dolgo-Saburov. It was a pity that I'd frightened her off, of course. If only I could have prolonged the conversation a little, I might have been able to find out more and, at the very least, discovered whether Belkin was still alive or not. It was also a pity that the nephew had disappeared. But at least one thing had been proved: he was mixed up in this whole mess. Dolgo-Saburov, the boxer and the "old man", whoever he might be: they all had something to do with it, and each of them must have known where Belkin was being held.

The Moscow Militia had three photos to work on: those of Belkin, Gridasov and Akeyev. The boxer was obviously Akeyev, so that meant that the "old man" must be Gridasov. Still another nickname! I tried to imagine who it might have been that was phoning now. "Katyukha says that the CID has circulated photos of the boxer and the old man all over Moscow." That meant that the criminals had somebody called Katya working for them in the CID. Great! You couldn't move without them knowing about it! But in which department could this "mole" of theirs be working . . . ?

What are these telephone engineers doing, giving birth, or what?

As if replying to my thoughts, I suddenly heard a voice say, "Are you listening? Number 244–12–90 is connected to a telephone booth at the Universitetskaya metro station. Shall we disconnect it?"

A telephone booth! Of course, the woman knew what

she was doing! She wouldn't slip up by using a private number!

"OK, disconnect it," I replied, "but have number 244 – 12 – 90 tapped."

This meant that all calls to Dolgo-Saburov's place would be recorded and their origin traced.

"Do you have a warrant?" the duty officer at Surveillance asked.

"As far as you're concerned, yes," I replied. "I have full authority from the Chief Prosecutor. I'm acting on instructions from the Central Committee."

I slammed down the receiver, without waiting to hear the reply. There was no point in wasting time with those idiots! I trudged back into Dolgo-Saburov's apartment. The sergeants were still standing by the telephone, staring at it hard, as if it might explode at any moment. I sat down next to it and phoned Svetlov's section at the Petrovka.

"Duty officer Lieutenant Krasnovsky speaking."

"This is Shamrayev. Where is Svetlov?"

"Colonel Svetlov is in the Incident Room talking to the Hotel Peking, Comrade Shamrayev. Is it urgent?"

"What's going on at the Peking, then?"

"The suspect appears to be waking up."

"I see. And where's Pshenichny?"

"He's here with me questioning people who resemble the suspects."

Poor old Pshenichny! He always gets the hackwork — and he's really had a lot of it from me on this job! Thousands of copies of photographs had been distributed to the Moscow Militia, the State Automobile Inspection and MVD secret agents — informers and stool pigeons of all descriptions, bartenders in such doubtful places as the beer-bars at Sokolniki Park or on the corner of Pushkinskaya Street and Stoleshnikov Lane. All of them were now on the lookout for Belkin, Akeyev and Gridasov. I could just imagine how many so-called "lookalikes" were being stopped now at every railroad station and traffic inspection post — or simply on the street or in restaurants. And they were all being taken in to the Petrovka, where Pshenichny would be examining them and their identity papers. With any luck he was being assisted by Aina Silinya, the artist Sinitsyn, and the night-watchman Sytin.

"Any news from Baron in Riga?" I asked.

"We got a phone call to tell us that Baron had gone to Yurmala on the coast. They'd found the witness there, but she was unwilling to go to Moscow."

"I see. Take a note of this. All police stations in Moscow are to be circulated with photographs of Herman Dolgo-Saburov. I'm speaking from his home now. Have some men sent over right away to relieve me, as I want to lay a trap for him. Get Minayev to issue instructions to have this phone tapped—number 244–12–90. Get a second squad ready at his aunt's apartment, as he may turn up there. The address is: 17 Peace Prospect, Apartment 47."

"We don't have enough men right now, Comrade Shamrayev," the lieutenant said beseechingly.

"Tell Minayev. He'll provide them. Tell him that it was me who asked. But you have to send at least a couple of men here right away!"

"All right. Will that be all?"

"Yes."

I hung up and said to the two sergeants, "Look, boys, I know that you're here as witnesses and that I don't have the right to use you in an operation, but there's no choice. If anybody should turn up before the militia do, we'll all help grab him. OK?"

*10:47 hours*

Lena Smagina had just woken up. She was lying luxuriously on one of the Hotel Peking's big double beds and smoking a Winston cigarette. The bright June sun was penetrating the closed venetian blinds, and the noise of traffic from the Garden Ring Road came from below. A cigarette first thing in the morning often does more to revive you than a cold shower, especially after spending a night as she just had. Lena thought it was a shame that Viktor wasn't allowed to stay in the hotel with her yet. Instead of that, he had to spend his time hanging around somebody else's apartment, keeping an eye on the expensive Finnish furniture and other crap that belonged to his boss. They were real bastards in the Central Committee and the Council of Ministers! What harm would it do to release Viktor once and for all, give him a passport and the right to live in Moscow? Still, one of these days it would happen, and not very long from now—just as soon as Viktor's boss returned from his trip abroad. Then they'd be able to lead a normal life together—vacations by the sea, visits to the theater and the best restaurants, a new car...

She looked at her Japanese watch and gave a start—the hotel buffet would be closing in ten minutes. It was time for her to get up. Lena forced herself to get out of bed, gave her face a quick cold water rinse and slipped on an American dress which she had bought in the Beriozka store for special foreign-currency certificates (she got those on the black market, of course). She ran a comb through her hair and then rushed to the buffet. Fortunately, it was on the fifth floor, the same as her hotel room. As she was going along the corridor, she was almost knocked over by a tall, good-looking officer, a major in the MVD. He'd come out of the room next door so fast that he'd simply bumped into her.

"What are you getting under my feet for?" she said in a rather insolent tone. The fact that he was an MVD officer didn't surprise her. This wing of the hotel belonged to the Interior Ministry, and you were always coming across MVD personnel and their families from all over the country.

"I'm so sorry," he said. "I was told the buffet was open until eleven. Is that right?"

"Yes, that's right. Come with me. I'm going there too," she said, immediately adopting the patronizing tone that she used when talking to officers in Kotlas. Aside from that, she'd been there many times before, and he was obviously a newcomer.

"I haven't seen you here before," she said. "There was a woman inspector from Krasnoyarsk living in your room."

"I'm from Odessa. Major Smorodinsky. Eduard is my first name, Eddie to you. What's yours?"

"Lena."

"Glad to meet you, Lenochka. Hey, we know each other now!"

"Is this a great event in your life?"

"Who knows?" he said with a smile. "The ways of the Lord . . ."

He may be good-looking, thought Lena to herself, but he's soft—not like my Viktor.

They reached the buffet. Lena ordered an aristocratic breakfast—caviar with French toast, Turkish coffee and an almond pastry. You could tell immediately that the major was from the provinces, though. He ordered all kinds of pap—vinaigrette salad, four sausages, *kefir,* a mashed potato and lemon tea.

Lena and the gallant major sat down at the same table. With both cheeks stuffed full of food, he began to tell her all about himself, just like Khlestakov in Gogol's *Government Inspector.* His stories all added up to the same thing: that there was nobody in the whole MVD more intelligent, courageous and resourceful than Major Smorodinsky. First he gave her a graphic account of how he managed to penetrate a group of speculators who were smuggling all kinds of foreign goods into the country by sea: sheepskin jackets, jeans, French perfume, you name it! Then he explained how he had risked his life uncovering an illegal wool factory. Then he told her something else that sounded more like a scene from a detective movie than anything else. He'd arrived at the Militia Academy yesterday to take the summer exams as an external student, and everybody had been given photographs of three men. Two of them were of extremely dangerous criminals being sought by the police all over Moscow. The other was of a well-known journalist, very admired by Brezhnev. He was supposed to accompany Brezhnev on his trip to Vienna in a few days, when suddenly—it's amazing what happens!—some men had abducted him in the middle of Moscow in broad daylight, and nobody knew where they had taken him. So now Major Smorodinsky had the chance to do a favor for Brezhnev by finding his favorite journalist. The day before, the Rector of the Academy, General Krylov, had gathered all the students together and told them that all examinations were postponed for a few days, so that they could join the Moscow Militia in hunting down the kidnappers and finding the journalist. The person who tracked him down would be sure of earning the personal thanks of the Central Committee and an early promotion. The major was convinced that it would be him.

"How will you go about finding them, that's what I'm curious to know," said Lena, wondering how to get rid of this tiresome fellow.

"Easy. Look at these." He got the three photographs out of his pocket and put them on the table in front of Lena. Staring up at her from one of them were the features of her own beloved Viktor, younger than he was now, and dressed in a track suit.

"A nice-looking fellow, isn't he?" Major Smorodinsky said, interpreting her obvious interest in the photograph. "That's the former boxing champion Akeyev. Together with this other one, an escaped criminal called Gridasov, they kidnapped the journalist and some youth who they then proceeded to murder outside Moscow..."

Lena was no longer capable of coherent thought. In fact, she could hardly even focus on what was in front of her. She felt a lump in her throat. All the time Smorodinsky was talking, she felt colder and colder. Her Viktor was being hunted by the entire Moscow Militia! That was why he was spending his time sitting in there and didn't want to go out on the street any more than he had to!

She managed to recover her composure for a moment, just as the talkative major happened to mention that, if the kidnappers were to hand over the journalist now, so that he could accompany Brezhnev to Vienna, they'd have half of their sentence commuted. But since they didn't know this, the major had the chance of earning himself another promotion. He'd been seconded direct to the CID. He'd soon teach them a thing or two...

Smorodinsky would have gone on and on like this if Lena hadn't interrupted him to say that she had some important business to attend to.

"What sort of business can *you* possibly have to attend to, Lenochka?" the major replied. "I know. You've got to buy some clothes at the GUM Department Store! You think I don't know how pretty girls spend their time?" After that he talked Lena into meeting him at seven o'clock that evening for dinner at the hotel restaurant.

"OK, I'll come," said Lena, saying anything, if it meant that she could get away from Smorodinsky. She had no intention of keeping her promise, of course.

When she finally said goodbye to the major, she ran back to her own room. What should she do now? She had to tell Viktor right away! She had to save him! She grabbed the telephone and dialed the first three figures of his number—242. But then she remembered: Viktor didn't answer telephone calls. The apartment block was inhabited by high government officials, and probably all their phones were bugged. So his "boss" had forbidden him to use it. Her phone was probably being tapped too, she thought. After all, this was an MVD hotel. In fact, perhaps she was already being followed and that fool major had told her the story and shown her the photographs on purpose. She suddenly went cold. No, it couldn't be. Take your time, don't panic. After all, she was the one who'd started up the conversation in the corridor. And you could tell he was just a provincial bumpkin from all that garbage he ate in the buffet. All the same . . .

Lena cautiously went to the window and looked outside. Everything seemed quiet on the Ring Road below. There was nobody standing on the street looking up at her window. She went back and peeped outside the door of her room. She saw only the chambermaid, Mariya Ivanovna, vacuuming the corridor. Everything seemed normal. Lena breathed a sigh of relief. She had to get to Viktor and tell him everything that had happened. But she'd have to be careful and check that she wasn't followed. She *was* the daughter of a prison camp commander, after all . . . It wasn't so easy to put one over on her. She knew all about the militia's little tricks . . .

*Secret*
CID Third Department
To Head of Second Section
Lieutenant-Colonel M. A. Svetlov

REPORT

On your instructions, I, Major V. S. Ozherelyev, and a group of men under my command have been observing the movements of Citizeness E. V. Smagina, resident at the Hotel Peking, room number 626. I myself occupied the adjacent room, number 627, and pretended to be one Major Smorodinsky on study leave from Odessa, here to take examinations at the Militia Academy. I made the suspect's acquaintance as she was about to have breakfast in the hotel buffet. There I appeared to show her by chance the photographs of Belkin, Gridasov and Akeyev. The first two were not recognized by the suspect, but when she saw the picture of Akeyev she displayed great emotional duress. During the rest of the conversation I attempted to provoke her into getting in touch with Akeyev. I also suggested to her that those conducting the investigation would react favorably to Belkin's voluntary return.

Immediately after the end of the conversation, Smagina returned to her room, where she attempted to contact somebody by telephone. However, she abandoned the attempt after dialing the first three digits—242. At 11:30 a.m. the suspect left the hotel and headed down Gorky Street in the direction of the Central Telegraph building.

*11:45 hours*

I was sitting in Dolgo-Saburov's apartment waiting for the CID men to arrive. I had nothing else to do, so I began to leaf through a photograph album. Svetlov and I had noticed it during our first search, but hadn't taken much interest in it then. It consisted mostly of photos of girls in swimsuits and various shots taken at work: of the sleeping-car attendants from Moscow–Tashkent train No. 37, together with the restaurant-car staff from the same train. They were photographed in front of the wagons with Herman Dolgo-Saburov himself in the foreground embracing the chief steward from the dining car. Inserted at the back of the album was a black envelope containing a handful of color photographs, all of a striking, brown-haired girl on the Black Sea coast. One was of her standing in front of some palm trees, another showed her in a group of smiling vacationers, sunbathing. In another she was licking an Eskimo ice cream, and in the last one she was cutting Dolgo-Saburov's hair on the beach. He was sitting in a chair, and her hands were poised above his head holding a pair of scissors and a comb. On the back was the following: "To Herman, I hope you won't forget! Zoya the Enchantress, Sochi, Hotel Zhemchuzhina, May 1979."

Well, that was something to go on, in any event! Now where the hell were those CID men? Every second was valuable, and I was hanging around like a dog on a leash.

I left the two sergeants by themselves in the apartment. They knew what they were doing, and I'd given them permission to eat as many of Dolgo-Saburov's Uzbek grapes as they wanted. Meanwhile, I walked next door to talk to the old woman again. I showed her the photos of the girl.

"Excuse me, ma'am, do you know this girl?"

"I don't know anyone," she said, pursing her lips and looking blank. You could understand her, I suppose. Why should she get involved with the police, and then have her neighbor take it out on her? She could have told me a lot about Dolgo-Saburov's comings and goings, of course. After all, it was no accident that a light appeared at her peephole every time there was the slightest sound out on the landing. Still, as far as I could see, she only *observed* what was going on. She probably wouldn't have known any names.

I picked up her phone and dialed Colonel Maryamov of the Railroad Militia.

"Colonel! This is Shamrayev speaking."

"What can I do for you, Comrade Investigator?" Maryamov said in an obsequious voice.

"In May of this year Dolgo-Saburov was in the Caucasus, in Sochi. What I want to know is whether he was on leave, or not. Did he go by train on a free travel warrant, or did he fly?"

Once a year all employees of Soviet railroads are allowed to travel with their families to any point in the USSR free of charge. Most railmen use this for their vacation, of course, and this was what I wanted to find out as far as Dolgo-Saburov was concerned.

"If you stay by the phone, I can let you have that information in a minute or two. I just need time to call the Finance Office."

"All right, colonel, I'll wait."

It took less than a minute.

"Can you hear me, Comrade Investigator? According to the file, sleeping-car superintendent Herman Dolgo-Saburov was away on leave from April 29 to May 6. Free travel warrants for Sochi and back were issued in his name and that of his wife, Zoya Kirilenko."

"His wife? But he's a bachelor!" I exclaimed.

"There's something about that in Dolgo-Saburov's application: 'Since I am intending to marry Citizeness Zoya Kirilenko in the near future, I request that she should be regarded as a member of my family for the purposes of issuing the warrants.'"

"So who is Zoya Kirilenko? Do you have any information?"

"Certainly. Her passport number is series XXIII—LS645217, and her home address is 27 Dybenko Street, Apartment 8. She works as a men's hairdresser at the Enchantress beauty salon on the Novy Arbat."

"Colonel, the Motherland won't forget you!" I said jubilantly. "Hang on, I'll get back to you." I pressed for the dial tone and immediately contacted Directory Inquiries.

"Operator, can you give me the number of the Enchantress beauty salon on the Novy Arbat?"

"241–28–82," she said, rattling off the number.

Then I phoned the salon. It was busy, of course, but I kept calling again and again. Meanwhile, with the other ear, I listened for any noise on the landing outside, in case the "nephew" should appear. At length I got a reply.

"Enchantress beauty salon."

"May I speak to Zoya Kirilenko, please?"

"She's not here at the moment. She's at a customer's. She'll be back after four o'clock."

"What do you mean: she's at a customer's? I thought she worked at a hairdresser's."

"I mean that she's working at a client's home. This isn't a hairdresser's, don't forget, but a beauty salon. Who is calling?"

"The Kursk Railroad Finance Office. In May she traveled to Sochi with an employee of ours, Herman Dolgo-Saburov. Do you know him? I need to ask them something in connection with the travel warrants they were given."

"Do you have the auditors in, or something?" the voice at the other end of the phone asked abruptly.

"What if we have?" I replied, adopting the same tone.

"Call after four anyway. They'll both be here then."

"What do you mean, both?"

"Zoya and Herman, of course. He came back from work today and called earlier to find out when she'd be around."

"Thanks very much, doll," I said. "You're worth your weight in gold!"

I was exultant. I looked at my watch. There was a long time to go until four o'clock, but I still had an enormous number of things to do. A minute earlier I'd been planning to arrest the fellow, if he came back home, but now my plans had changed. It was essential to remove all traces of the search in case he looked in at his apartment before four o'clock.

I rushed back next door. My two sergeants had already consumed a fair amount of the grapes, but there was still half a box left, thank God! I then performed a simple operation. I placed a pile of old newspapers at the bottom of the box, covered them up with the remainder of the grapes and—*voilà!* The box was full again. I didn't think Dolgo-Saburov would be worried about the grapes, but it was essential that nothing appear to have been tampered with, at least at first glance. The soldiers looked at me in astonishment, but I had no time to explain the reasons why I was doing this, especially as the CID men would appear at any moment to relieve me.

"Comrade Shamrayev, CID squad, three men at your disposal. I'm the senior officer—Lieutenant Kozlov."

"Lieutenant, I asked Krasnovsky to get a tap placed on this phone immediately."

"It's all been done, Comrade Shamrayev."

"Good. This is what I want you to do. I want one of you to stay in the neighbor's place next door. If Dolgo-Saburov shows up, make sure that the neighbor doesn't get in contact with him. If he calls, there's nobody at home. Got it?"

"Yes, Comrade Investigator."

"And I want the other two to keep a secret watch on the building from outside. I don't want him arrested, just followed. OK?"

"Yes, Comrade Shamrayev."

"That's all. Let's leave now."

I looked around one last time. Everything seemed to be in the right place, and even if we had moved one or two things, was he likely to notice? After all, he'd left the place in a mess himself. I removed the photographs of Zoya the Enchantress from the album, along with a couple of others depicting the rest of his workmates, and walked out of the apartment.

The CID men disappeared. One of them was at the wheel of an unmarked Volga, parked next to the entrance in the middle of a group of cars. I lost sight of the other detective completely. I said goodbye to the sergeants ("Thanks a lot! See you. Don't forget: you haven't been here, OK?") and walked quickly over to my own car.

"Seryozha, take me to the Kursk Station Militia Office, pronto!"

Before starting this game with the "nephew", I still had to run through various possibilities in my mind. If we were to arrest him now, what did we have on him that would make him confess? The drug-trafficking charge wasn't proven, and we hadn't managed to establish that he had anything to do with the murder of his aunt. The connection with Akeyev and Gridasov had emerged only twenty minutes earlier during a telephone call—and telephone calls effectively vanish into thin air: they are not admissible as evidence in a court of law. No, we'd have to crack Dolgo-Saburov by different means, using Svetlov's methods.

I lifted the receiver of the radio telephone and asked the Petrovka switchboard to put me through to Colonel Maryamov.

"Comrade Colonel, this is Shamrayev again. You've got some compromising material on the chief steward of Moscow–Tashkent train No. 37, I hope. Some black market dealings he's been involved in, or cheating some passengers?..."

"You'd better believe it! Was there ever a dining-car attendant who didn't serve less food than he should, or something along those lines? We've got files on all the chief stewards . . . On train No. 37 the restaurant car is run by someone called Irakly Golub. We've got all kinds of things on him. Black market dealings in caviar, smoked sausage, butter. Overcharging, sub-standard meat, serving booze after hours. There's enough there to put him away for five years. He's ready . . ."

"Wait a minute! I don't want him sent to jail. He can provide us with some very useful information," I said, smiling to myself. "Stay where you are, and I'll come and get you."

Everything was going smoothly. I lay back in the seat and switched on the car radio. It was time to listen to some everyday goings-on of the Moscow Militia. The loudspeaker immediately began to splutter a stream of police conversations.

"Central, Central! No. 8 here. At the northern exit to GUM there's a fight over women's boots!"

"Ostankino, Ostankino! A drunken driver in a dark, cherry-colored Volga has knocked over a pedestrian outside the Botanical Gardens. Registration not known. Car now moving towards the Altuferskoye Highway!"

"Central! Central! This is patrolman No. 108. I have detained a person at the Riga railroad station who looks suspiciously like the wanted prisoner Gridasov. He is carrying papers in the name of Heracles Isaakovich Shneyerson. What do you want me to do with him?"

"Hello, 108, take him over to Investigator Pshenichny at 38 Petrovka, Operations Room 10. Understood? Over and out."

I grinned. Who'd believe a suspect could have a name like that? It was like something out of a comic opera. But who knows?

"Central! State Automobile Inspection post on the Mozhaisk Highway. I have detained the owner of a Zhiguli named Yakov Alekseyevich Gridasov, aged thirty-four. He doesn't fit the description of the prisoner wanted by CID, but the surname is the same. Awaiting your instructions."

"Central! A drunk named Viktor Mikhailovich Akeyev, born 1916, has been detained at the Pavelets rail terminus and brought to detox station No. 31 . . ."

Moscow's multi-million population is hard at work. Or, if not, part of it is walking down the streets, traveling by metro, bus or trolley, sunbathing on the beaches by the river or lining up for ladies' boots or the first fresh tomatoes of the season. Meanwhile, at every rail and metro station and in every park, hundreds of informers, visible and invisible, secret agents, traffic police, and ordinary militiamen, are staring intently at every passer-by, comparing their features with those of the photographs hidden in their pockets. And this is only the tip of the iceberg. Inquiries are being made about which the general public knows absolutely nothing. Early this morning the governors of every prison in Moscow and the surrounding district instructed their stool pigeons and informers to turn conversations in the cells around to the subject of Viktor Akeyev and Semyon Gridasov—in case one of the prisoners had seen them, or knew where they lived and the people they associated with. On top of this, hundreds, if not thousands, of public-order vigilantes were being given photographs and information about the wanted men at police stations and assembly points all over the capital.

This is one of the Soviet government's great strengths. Whenever it wants, it can issue a single order which will activate—without delay—a huge army of informers, vigilantes, MVD agents, militiamen, the KGB and finally, in emergency situations, the regular army. Furthermore, it can isolate any city or even autonomous republic from the outside world in a matter of minutes, so that not even a bird can fly across the cordon without being noticed.

Today Svetlov and I had activated only the first layer of this system in the search for Akeyev and Gridasov, but even so, Moscow resembled a gigantic filter through which tens of thousands of people were passing.

Suddenly I heard an announcement over the air: "Attention all militia units and automobile inspection stations! Be on the lookout for the following person throughout Moscow and the Moscow region: name—Herman Veniaminovich

Dolgo-Saburov, occupation—railroad sleeping-car attendant, year of birth—1945. Photographs of the wanted man will be distributed later today. Physical description is as follows: height—five foot six..."

I grabbed the radio telephone.

"Central! Get me the Incident Room, Lieutenant-Colonel Svetlov! It's urgent!"

The reply came almost immediately. "Svetlov here."

"Marat, this is Shamrayev. Get it broadcast over the central network that Dolgo-Saburov isn't to be taken! If he is found, he is to be left alone and secretly followed!"

"Why? It's only an hour since you asked us to put out a general alert for him!"

"Listen to me! At four o'clock he's going to appear at the Enchantress beauty salon on the Novy Arbat to meet a hairdresser named Zoya Kirilenko. He's almost bound to turn up, unless he gets scared. So will you have a tap put on the hair salon's phone? At four o'clock I'm going to try out one of *your* favorite tricks."

"Ah, so you're taking a leaf out of my book!"

"That's right. And how are you getting on with the Smagina woman?"

"It almost worked first time. She rushed back to her hotel room and started to phone somebody. But she only dialed the first three figures—242—and then hung up. Anyway, 242 is in the Lenin district of the city, so I've put the whole local CID network there on the alert. Now she's heading towards downtown, either because she thinks she's being followed, or simply out of fear. And she hasn't made any more phone calls. But she's heading in the direction of the Lenin district. Give it another hour, and I hope everything will have calmed down and it'll be all right. We'll get Akeyev today, I promise you."

"All right, but don't count your chickens..."

"Hang on, I've got Riga on the phone. It's Colonel Baron. Shall I pass him over to you?"

"OK, but don't hang up."

After a few words from the operator, I could hear the soft Baltic accent of Lieutenant-Colonel Baron.

"Comrade Shamrayev? Hello. I'm speaking from Riga

airport. I've got Aina Silinya and her parents with me. On no account did they want her to travel to Moscow, so I've had to use coercion. They're going to fly with me now as long as you give your legal sanction."

"I do. What time will you be arriving?"

"At 2:15 p.m. Moscow time. We'll be coming into Vnukovo airport."

"Good. I'll have you met."

"Thank you very much. See you shortly."

I waited until he had hung up, and then I said to Svetlov, "Did you hear that?"

"Yes, I'll get one of the CID boys to meet them at Vnukovo. In fact, I'll do it now. Turning out to be a busy day, huh?"


*12:30 hours*

Lena Smagina was walking towards the Central Telegraph Office. At twelve-thirty she was supposed to meet Leva Novikov there. Novikov was a masseur working for the Spartak soccer team and a drug dealer into the bargain. Lena had been wandering around the center of Moscow for the last hour, waiting to hand over the packet of morphine which Viktor Akeyev had given her the day before. It was burning a hole in her pocket—or rather, in the bag which she had taken with her. As she was afraid of being followed, she couldn't get rid of it by simply throwing it away in a trash can. Of course, she should have flushed it down the toilet in her hotel bedroom, but she hadn't thought about the packet until her hand touched it, fumbling around in her bag for cigarettes as she was leaving the hotel. So, for the last hour, Lena had been trying to decide whether or not she was being followed. She was behaving like a character in a detective novel, suddenly turning back as she was crossing a street, wandering in and out of stores, taking the odd ride on a trolley and getting off when she felt like it, or simply sitting in Pushkin Square and watching the people around her.

She hadn't detected anybody following her, and she breathed a sigh of relief, deciding to ask Novikov for his advice on what to do next. Maybe he would go to Viktor instead of her, and tell him of the danger? At twelve-thirty she ran up the steps of the Central Telegraph building on Gorky Street and turned left into the section dealing with inter-city calls. She was supposed to meet Novikov next to booth No. 3—and there he was, alert and insolent, like most masseurs. But as soon as he saw Lena coming, Novikov began to move towards the exit. As he walked past her, he muttered to her without looking, "Look sharp! There's somebody following you!" Lena didn't stop, but kept walking up to the counter. Beginning to feel faint, she asked the girl whether she could get through to Kotlas. "You can dial direct from booth No. 16," came the reply. But Lena didn't bother to phone. What could she say to her father now? Almost on the point of passing out, she went out to the street.

What could she do? Feeling that she was about to start screaming, Lena went into a public restroom. It was the one in Arts Theater Street, and there was the usual petty black-marketing going on with women selling foreign cosmetics and contraceptive pills. Lena calmed down a little. The women were standing there offering eye pencils and various other items such as Polish and French make-up for sale, and nobody was arresting them. That at least meant that there were no militia around, and those who were following her had obviously stayed outside. She stood in line for the cubicles. Standing behind her, and breathing heavily, was a fat, asthmatic woman carrying a couple of string bags, both filled with frozen chickens and salami. She'd obviously lined up for three hours or so to get them at the Yeliseyev store on Gorky Street. Then a prostitute came in. Without looking at anybody, she went up to one of the black marketeers and said in a loud voice, without a trace of embarrassment, "Quick! You got any French ticklers? I have a customer waiting for me."

Lena went into the cubicle, sat down on the seat and burst into tears. Everything was going on as usual around her. People were buying and selling things on the black market, lining up for chickens and salami, window-shopping, or making phone calls home and abroad—and only she was out in the cold! She was being followed and might be arrested at any moment. And why? All because of a little bit of morphine and the 350 roubles she was supposed to get for it. What should she do? What? She undid the morphine. Inside were two smaller packets containing a hundred ampoules each. The simplest thing would be to flush them all away, but would these glass containers actually get flushed away? She tore open the cardboard packaging with her teeth and emptied the entire contents into the trash can next to the toilet. (It wasn't too pleasant, rummaging through a lot of used sanitary towels and toilet paper, but Lena wanted to make sure the ampoules dropped right down to the bottom of the can.) She tore the cardboard packets into tiny shreds and threw them into the can itself. By this time people were beginning to hammer impatiently on her door. "I'm coming out now," Lena said, pulling the chain. Outside she scrubbed her hands clean, dabbed at her tear-stained face, applied some eye-shadow, adjusted her hair and walked stoically up the stairs to face, as she thought, her imminent arrest. Let them arrest her now, she mused. They could all go to hell! She had no drugs on her now, and who could prove that the ampoules lying in the trash can had been left there by her, and not by someone ahead of her or behind her in the line?

She walked out onto the street and looked around. Where were they? They could arrest her now, if they liked.


*Secret*
To CID Third Department
Head of Second Section
Lieutenant-Colonel M. A. Svetlov

### REPORT
(continued)

Changing direction more than once, the suspect spent the next hour visiting the Central Telegraph building, where she inquired about making a phone call to Kotlas, and then the women's public restroom on Arts Theater Street. One member of the surveillance team, Militia Lieutenant M. Gorelkina, pretended to be a prostitute and entered the cubicle next to that occupied by the suspect. There she saw Smagina destroy two packets of morphine by emptying the ampoules into a trash can next to the toilet. When she left the restroom, the suspect walked apparently aimlessly down Gorky Street, crossed the Manezh and Red Square, and was unexpectedly lost by Lieutenant V. Sveshnikova somewhere in the GUM Department Store. In order to rediscover Smagina's whereabouts, members of my team stood in wait at all the exits from the store, but failed to find her...

### 12:52 hours

The chief steward, Irakly Kasyanovich Golub, didn't open his door for seventeen minutes. When Colonel Maryamov rang the bell at Apartment No. 64, 25 Mariya Ulyanova Street, in the Cheryomushki district of Moscow, there was no reply at all. It really did seem as if Irakly Golub had crashed out after his long trip from Central Asia. But we kept on ringing, forever, it seemed, and eventually he did wake up. He spent the next ten minutes pretending that he couldn't quite bring himself around. He seemed to spend an inordinately long time looking for the key, his dressing gown, his slippers and so on. We could hear him moving around on the other side of the door and found it easy to imagine what was going on. Having seen the Chief of the Railroad Militia, Maryamov himself, through the spy-hole in his door, the chief steward was scared out of his wits and didn't know what to do—whether to hide the valuables, set fire to the money or throw the jars of black caviar down the garbage chute. I figure he managed to do it all, considering the time he took to open the door! In any case, when we finally entered the apartment, there was a strong smell of burning even though all the windows were wide open.

"It's not polite to keep visitors waiting outside the door for so long," said Maryamov. "This is my friend, Special Investigator Igor Iosifovich Shamrayev. And ask us into the living room, for Christ's sake! What are you keeping us out in the hall for?"

"Of course. I'm sorry. Come on in."

Apart from his Georgian Christian name and patronymic, Golub also had a marked Caucasian accent. According to his file, which had been lent to us by the Anti-Fraud Squad's railroad section, Golub had been his mother's maiden name. She was a Ukrainian. His father was a Georgian, however, who had died on the White Russian front in 1944. So Irakly Golub had been a love-child practically conceived in battle. It seems strange, but despite this, he was a terrible coward. We didn't even have to show him all the incriminating evidence which the Anti-Fraud Squad had on him, or open the secret agent's report on his particular restaurant car. All Maryamov had to say was this:

"Listen, Irakly, this is what's going on. We've known for years about all the things you've been getting up to— speculating in smoked sausage, black caviar, butter, buckwheat, foreign cigarettes, *et cetera*. You take items that are in short supply from Moscow to Central Asia and bring back fruit and vegetables and so on. Do you want to look at your file? Or should we get to the heart of the matter right away, like old friends?"

Golub had probably decided that we were after a bribe, so he unbuttoned his shirt and asked, in a hoarse voice, "How much do you want?"

"What do you mean, 'How much'?" Maryamov asked uncomprehendingly.

I couldn't resist making a funny remark. "How much we can *give* you, or how much we can take from you?"

"*Take* from me," Golub said. You could tell just by looking at him that he was trying to figure out how much it would take to buy us off. He obviously couldn't make up his mind, either.

"Listen, Irakly," I said, "we're not going to *take* anything, but the court could certainly *give* you from eight to fifteen years under Section 3 of Article 92. The actual choice of camp would be the decision of the Corrective Labor Directorate, of course, but as you've spent all your time working in the south of the country, we would advise our colleagues on Bolshaya Bronnaya Street to send you north— to Potma, Magadan, Norilsk or somewhere like that..."

I was overdoing it a little, of course. I was carried away by my own eloquence. But on the other hand, Maryamov and I had reckoned that Golub would take some breaking. Instead of this, he immediately said, "I understand perfectly!

What do you want from me?"

"Something very simple. You've got a friend by the name of Herman Dolgo-Saburov. Later today we want you to pretend to meet him by chance on the street or at the Enchantress hair salon. One of our men will be with you. We want the two of you to invite Dolgo-Saburov to have a meal in a restaurant somewhere. That's all. All you have to do is talk him into going to a restaurant with you. Nothing else."

"Are you going to poison him?" Golub asked, showing a certain professional interest in the affair. I am certain that if I had said, "Yes, he's getting poisoned," Golub wouldn't have refused to sprinkle the poison into some Kiev cutlets himself, so long as he could avoid going to prison.

Ten minutes later, after shaving and putting on a light summer suit, Irakly Golub was sitting in my car, while I called Svetlov on the radio telephone.

"I'm bringing the bait now. What's happening with the girl?"

"At last!" Svetlov replied. "I've got some important news for you. The railroad police have tracked the nephew down at the Kalanchevskaya hump-yards. He's there now—on track 34 where there's a group of old, condemned wagons. It looks as if he's got a secret compartment or store in one of them. I don't know what. He's busy dragging out some boxes and stowing them in his Zhiguli sedan."

"What boxes?"

"I don't know. You can't get too close. There are railroad employees wandering around all the time. It *is* a hump-yard, you know. But I'll think of something!"

"As long as they don't let him know anything, OK?" I said. "And what's happening with the Smagina girl?"

"My boys lost sight of her in GUM. But I ordered the manager to put some foreign goods for women on sale, and to make an announcement about it over the relay. You should have seen what happened next! They started selling French underwear and eye-shadow. There are 600 women lined up already! And Lena's number 403. Good for her! She looked like a sleepwalker, but she's in line all the same!"

"You won't lose her again, will you?"

"You must be kidding! I've got four people shadowing her. If they lose her now, I'll kill them! Come on over, and we can decide what to do next—whether to let her buy the French panties or not."

"OK. I'm on my way."

Of course, I was very tempted to stop outside GUM *en route* to the Petrovka just to have a look at Lena Smagina myself, but there was no time. Instead we headed for the Incident Room at CID headquarters. Svetlov was waiting for us there.

*13:40 hours*
The Operations Section of the Moscow CID is in a three-story building to the rear of the famous No. 38 Petrovka. Few people know that this building, the wing of an old former private house, hidden away on Sredne-Karetny Lane, is now the operational headquarters of the whole Moscow Militia.

On the first floor there are recreation rooms for the investigators, dog handlers and other personnel who are on duty, sometimes for days on end. While waiting to be called out on a case, the officers can take a nap or play a game of chess or cards. Not that there is much time for relaxation. Something happens somewhere in Moscow every minute of the day—somebody will be stabbing his wife, robbing a savings bank or falling under a car. The loudspeaker down on the ground floor is never silent for long. No sooner has the message gone out, "Duty Investigator to the car pound!" than a veritable posse of new police Volgas or imported Mercedes, armed with the latest detection equipment, will be zooming through Moscow to the scene of any incident, headlights full on and sirens blaring...

But the main office of the Operations Section—its "brain"—is the Incident Room on the second floor. Here you can find the duty officers for the City Militia and the CID, along with their deputies and the officers in charge of various operational units. A huge, illuminated map of Moscow is mounted over an entire wall. There are smaller maps of the individual districts at a series of electronic consoles, as well as numerous pieces of communications equipment—

telephones, televisions and radios. Every piece of urgent information about the life of the city is channeled through this room. Here the various investigators and other experts are summoned and dispatched to the scenes of incidents and crimes all over the capital. Here covert surveillance teams are assembled and sent wherever they are needed. The officers put in charge of these aspects of militia and CID work are usually experienced detectives themselves, and their deputies—people of the rank and caliber of Marat Svetlov. You could have said that the work of the whole Operations Section required a lot of creativity if it hadn't been for the idiot in charge of the set-up, Colonel Shubeiko, a complete moron and superannuated party hack, a former political instructor in the army . . .

As our car turned into Sredne-Karetny Lane, the sergeant of the guard obligingly opened the metal gates, and we moved into the courtyard. The usual collection of drivers, dog handlers and other jokers sat on a bench outside the smoking room spending their twenty-four-hour shifts babbling about all the unbelievable rapes and *crimes passionels* which they had had to deal with. They were talking about the usual things now. As we walked by them on our way into the building, I could hear one of them saying, "First they raped her, then they shoved an empty champagne bottle up her . . . !"

As I headed towards the staircase, I came across a person whose face seemed amazingly familiar. I tried very hard to remember where I had seen him before, and suddenly it came to me. It was Belkin! The Belkin we were looking for! Yet this individual acted as if nothing were going on at all: he was simply heading for the exit. I was about to turn around and grab him when a door next to me opened and a voice said sarcastically, "Calm down, Comrade Shamrayev! That's not Belkin. He looks like him, but all the same he isn't him!"

I turned around and saw Pshenichny smiling at me. "That's the third time he's been brought in today. I had to give him a certificate saying he's *not* Belkin. Don't look at me like that! It really isn't Belkin! I've seen eleven Gridasovs and six Akeyevs so far today. I've just had a phone call saying that they're going to bring in three more of them. It's simpler with Akeyev, it's true. I've got Sinitsyn with me—you remember, the artist who witnessed the kidnapping at the Kursk station. He's the best Akeyev expert I have! Pity he doesn't remember what the other accomplices looked like . . ."

I stared at Pshenichny. Over the course of the last four days an extraordinary change had come over him. From a tired, overwrought district investigator, weighed down by the enormous number of routine cases assigned to him, he had turned into a calm, reliable colleague, self-assured and fully aware of his value to the investigation. His light blue eyes were attentive, but lacked the self-destructive expression you see in so many Russian eyes. You could see an immaculate white collar sticking out of his well-worn jacket. Everything about him seemed clean and meticulous. Working for the Chief Prosecutor's Office was obviously a major event in his life. I wondered if he had a wife and children. We'd been working together continuously for four days, but we hadn't even had time for a beer together. There was something wrong with that. It wasn't the Russian way of doing things.

I looked at my watch. "In about twenty minutes' time, Valya, Aina Silinya will be here. Show her photographs of all the principals—Akeyev, Gridasov, and Dolgo-Saburov. We're going to get two of them now. If she can identify them, then the case is ours—knock on wood! You have other photos for her to look at, right?"

"Igor Iosifovich!" he said reproachfully, and I realized that my question had been superfluous, even tactless. The law requires that, for identification purposes, you show a witness not just a single photograph, but a number of them simultaneously, and never less than three, so you don't influence the witness's reaction. Otherwise, the identification would be inadmissible as evidence in a court of law, and this sometimes happens with inexperienced investigators. But Pshenichny was obviously no novice.

"All right, Valentin. Here's the chief steward from train No. 37. Let him sit here with you. He's not allowed up to the second floor. What room is Svetlov in?"

"Incident Room, Igor Iosifovich . . ."

I left Irakly Golub in Pshenichny's hands and accompanied Maryamov up to the next floor. There was a lot of activity there today. There seemed to be several covert surveillance teams at work besides our own. The first eight rooms looked more like dressing rooms in a theater. One group was dressed up as senior air force officers, another as a band of bearded geologists from somewhere in the north, another as naval officers, and so on. To my amazement, I suddenly heard the familiar voice of my friend Baklanov coming from one of the neighboring rooms. "Unbelievable! Airmen, geologists, sailors—and all dressed in the same policemen's boots! That's a conspiracy for you!"

I looked past the door. Baklanov saw the look of astonishment on my face.

"Greetings!" he said. "I'm trying to nail a bunch of card sharks. They've been cheating our valiant officers when they return from service abroad, you see. They choose their victims the moment they leave the station at Brest and pick them clean between there and Moscow. But don't worry! We've got some well-heeled clients lined up for them! How are things with you?"

"I'll be in the Incident Room. Stop by."

As I entered I noticed the lively, restless figure of Marat Svetlov standing by an illuminated map of the center of Moscow. I could hear voices of both surveillance teams coming across the air simultaneously.

"Comrade Colonel! The suspect is still standing in the line. But the manager of GUM says that he only has enough French bras to last another five minutes!"

"Attention, colonel! The suspect Dolgo-Saburov has left his car at the corner of Lermontov Square and the humpyards. He's run into a telephone booth."

Svetlov immediately turned to one of his assistants. "What's the number of the phone booth on the corner of Lermontov Square and Kalanchevskaya Street?"

A series of diagrams appeared on one of the small screens, and we could see an electronic map of the intersection in question. The map showed you the entrance to every building clearly, as well as the name of every store and the telephone booth on the corner, with its phone number:

754–214. The assistant immediately called the Central
Telephone Surveillance Department at Zubovskaya Street,
ordering them to have a tap placed on phone number
754–214, and to have all conversations from it recorded.

A moment later we could hear Dolgo-Saburov's excited
voice. "Hello, Tolik? This is Herman. Need any stuff today?"

"What's today—Friday?" said the second voice.

"No, Thursday. But I'm tied up tomorrow. How much
can you take?"

"Uh-h-h, maybe 200 grams . . . Out of cash today . . . If
it was tomorrow . . ."

"How much do you have? Remember—I'm selling at a
reduced price today . . ."

"Two roubles, three at most . . ."

In Moscow business slang, that meant two or three thousand roubles. Meanwhile, Telephone Surveillance was able
to inform Svetlov's assistant on another line that the "subscriber" was phoning the Zhiguli beer-bar on the Novy Arbat.

In the meantime, Dolgo-Saburov had dialed another number, and we could hear his impatient voice again. "Robert,
this is Herman."

"How are you doing? Has something happened?"

"No. What makes you think that?"

"Well, today isn't Friday."

"I know. That's why I'm calling. I'm coming by now
with the goods. Will you be in?"

"And where would I get to? Come on over, that's all
right. As a matter of fact, I've just run out . . ."

Suddenly we could hear the dial tone and the voice of
the telephone engineer announcing, "The subscriber was
calling the Rioni shashlyk house on the Stary Arbat."

Then we heard the covert surveillance group over the air
again. "Colonel, he's going through his pockets. His money
has obviously run out, and he doesn't have anything to dial
with. Should we let him have a couple of kopecks?"

"Very funny," Svetlov said imperiously. "Just keep
watching him."

"When should we arrest him? At the beer-bar, with the
goods?"

"You won't be arresting him at all. Shamrayev has brought the bait. Who is going to go along?"

"It should be Ozherelyev, colonel. He's the best. Oh— the suspect is back in his car and is driving towards the Arbat."

"Ozherelyev has already set one suspect up today, and that's enough," said Svetlov. "I don't like him playing the same part twice in one day. After all, he's not Sophia Loren."

"Well, then you can do it yourself, colonel."

"OK, I'll think about it. Hello, GUM, can you hear me?"

"Yes, Comrade Colonel."

"Stop the sale of underwear now. Only don't let the suspect out of your sight, or I'll have you all put back on point-duty, understand me?"

Then Svetlov turned to me and filled me in on what had been happening.

"It's like this. The nephew kept drugs in a secret hiding place at the Kalanchevskaya hump-yards. It was very convenient—in one of those old wagons without wheels. You know, the ones that stand directly on the ground. There, in the middle of a pile of old clothes and lumber, he had boxes filled with packs of morphine ampoules. Why he decided to get rid of the stuff today I don't know. Perhaps those apartment searches tipped him off. Anyway, he loaded all this stuff into his car and drove off to the pharmaceutical warehouse on Lermontov Square. He was almost arrested by the Anti-Fraud Squad when he arrived, but I managed to warn them just in time. Malenina is inspecting the whole building, and the warehouse is completely closed. The Anti-Fraud Squad boys are swarming all over the place. I got one of our girls to dress up as a cleaner, and she managed to tip him off at the office by the entrance-gate. Now he's running around Moscow trying to unload his goods. By the way, the car he's in is registered in his aunt's name. He's got an official certificate to drive it, though. We got the automobile inspection to check his papers, after stopping him for passing on the right. Of course, what we really need now is a movie camera to photograph all his contacts, but where do we get one? There's only one camera for the whole CID, and Baklanov has grabbed it."

"Comrade Colonel!" said a voice over the radio. "The

suspect has just left GUM and is standing in line for a taxi."

"Is it a long line?"

"She's ninth."

"All right. Let her stand there for a couple of minutes, then get Fedotov to drive up. Is he available?"

"Of course, colonel. He's been on the job since this morning."

"Excellent. Put Fedotov in direct contact with me."

Tension began to mount in the room as one of the decisive points of the operation approached. That old CID hand, Tikhon Yegorovich Fedotov, was about to drive up to the taxi stand outside GUM. In the twelve years I've known him, and over the thirty years that he's been working for the Moscow CID, he has never failed. There's something about that enormous moustache of his, his corpulent, good-natured appearance, his simple, peasant face, that always has a calming effect on even the most suspicious criminal. They might suspect anybody and everybody, but somehow it never occurs to them that this cheerful old man is a police agent. When they get into his taxi, they immediately relax, and even if they had intended to cover their tracks and change taxis three times before going to the right address, they lower their guard in Fedotov's car and tell him to drive to their real destination right away. His taxi contained a hidden radio transmitter, so that all conversations could immediately be monitored by the covert surveillance team and at the console in the Operations Section. After a few seconds we could hear Fedotov's good-natured, northern accent coming over the loudspeaker.

"Central, this is Fedotov. I'm approaching the suspect now."

Then his tone of voice changed completely. "Wait a minute, comrades! Don't get into the car yet, please. Where are you going?"

"To Medvedkovo," said a man's voice.

"No. I can't take you there, sorry. It's my lunch break. And where are you going, honey?"

"Biryulovo."

"I can't go there, either."

By this time, Fedotov had obviously driven up to the

"suspect", Lena Smagina, and he threw her the bait. "Lenin District, South-West metro station, Lenin Hills, Cheryomushki ... any good to you?"

"I want the Frunze Embankment," a young woman's voice said.

"He's got her!" Svetlov couldn't help saying. "That's great, Fedotov!"

They couldn't hear our remarks in the taxi, of course, but we could overhear everything that Fedotov was saying to Smagina and the other people in the line.

"But comrade, can't you see? I've got somebody in the taxi already," Fedotov was saying to another potential passenger. "But I want to go to Cheryomushki, too," she was saying.

"Did you hear that?" Fedotov said. "She wants to go to Cheryomushki too! I don't know. Some people! Here I am, trying to get home for my beetroot soup, which will be getting cold on the table, and all they can do is push their way into the car! Now where is it on the Frunze Embankment that you want, honey?"

"No. 48, one of the red buildings," Lena Smagina replied. "Do you know them?"

"Of course! I *have* been driving a taxi for twenty-five years, you know. It's all high government officials that live there, retired ministers and so on. I remember taking Bulganin there once. He's getting on now. I wonder if he's still alive? Did you ever meet him?"

This was the way Fedotov worked. He'd start chatting innocently enough, but then he'd gradually wheedle out whether the passenger knew the people who lived in the building, or whether he or she was going there for the first time. Meanwhile, the conversation would distract the passenger from noticing how slowly they were driving along. Fedotov needed to let the surveillance group get ahead of him, after all, so that they could place observers outside the building.

"No, I've never met Bulganin," she replied.

"I bet he's dead by now," Fedotov said. "Maybe not, though. They would have given him an obituary in *Pravda*, wouldn't they? He used to be our prime minister, after all.

I always read the obituaries..."

"Could we go a little faster?" Lena asked.

"What for? We can if you like, only the traffic police don't like it very much. What do people say? More haste, less speed...?"

At that moment we heard a message from the second surveillance group following Dolgo-Saburov.

"Colonel, the suspect has parked his car outside the Zhiguli beer-bar. He's placed the box containing the morphine in a bag and gone in the bar. He's talking to the manager now. What are we to do?"

"How many are in the group?" Svetlov asked.

"There are eighteen of us."

"The 'nephew' is going to deliver to all his regular customers. You're not going to arrest anybody until I give the word. Just observe what's going on, and who he talks to, OK?"

"When are you going to have lunch with him, Comrade Colonel?"

"Not for another hour or hour and a half at least," Svetlov said, irritably. "We've got Akeyev going, for now."

"But colonel! What if the nephew wants to eat a little earlier? Let's say he goes into a restaurant before you arrive—what do I do?"

"I don't know. You'll think of something, that's what you're paid for. You could let the air out of his tires, or something... Anyway, make up your mind, it doesn't bother me. That's it. No time to talk. See you later."

Pshenichny entered the room and came over to me. "Igor Iosifovich, Aina Silinya has arrived from Riga with her parents and Lieutenant-Colonel Baron."

However much I wanted to stay in the Incident Room, I had no choice. I had to go downstairs and talk to the new arrivals. Lieutenant-Colonel Baron turned to me as I came down to meet him. He gave a few words of reassurance to Aina Silinya's parents, and then rushed off "to visit some friends". That's why he'd insisted on accompanying the Silinya family to Moscow, I expect. I arranged for a car to take the parents off to the Hotel Minsk. Aina stayed with me. She was a quiet, somewhat impassive girl with thin legs and big, greenish-blue eyes. It seems to me that eyes like that, which are fatally attractive for so many men, usually conceal a totally vacuous personality, although poetic, enthusiastic types like Belkin or Yury Rybakov are inclined to attribute all kinds of fantastic qualities to them.

Once we'd seen off Aina's parents and Lieutenant-Colonel Baron, Pshenichny and I took Aina into a smaller room, which had been placed at our disposal for the day, and showed her a series of photographs to see if she would recognize Akeyev, Dolgo-Saburov and Gridasov among these. She recognized Akeyev immediately and without any hesitation—"categorically", as we say. But she wasn't very certain about Gridasov and Dolgo-Saburov.

All the same, the fact that she had positively identified one of them meant that all the frenetic running around that Svetlov and I had been doing for days had been to some avail. We were about to pick up Belkin's trail, and were already hard on the heels of his kidnappers.

I turned to Aina Silinya and asked, "Did you see the *Komsomolka* correspondent Rady Sverdlov while you were in Baku?"

"Yes," she replied. "He lives on the Esplanade. We spent one night at his place, just before we left for Moscow. So what?"

"Valentin," I said. "Please make sure that that detail is entered in the report."

Then I went upstairs to rejoin Svetlov. Things were moving at breakneck speed. We should have called in the cinema people from Mosfilm!

*14:50 hours*

Lena Smagina was traveling to Vitya's. She was tired. It was stupid to spend the whole day dragging herself around Moscow, seeing everyone as a plainclothes detective or secret agent. She still hadn't been arrested, after all. She started weeping again in the GUM ladies' room, but then she went to a café on the first floor and had a cup of coffee and a sandwich. After that she spent two hours in line for some French underwear and felt more at ease. That idiot masseur must have been lying when he said she was being

followed. If they had really been hoping that she would
lead them to Viktor, then they would have stopped the
people lining up for underwear ages ago. What good would
it have done the militia to wait while she bought herself
some French panties? Lena considered herself an expert at
recognizing detectives. She had studied the line very carefully, and she hadn't been able to discover a single person
who resembled the types she knew from the camp at Kotlas.
In any case, if she had been followed, it was probably either
by some guy who wanted to get her in the sack, or by an
idiot like that major from Odessa, somebody she'd given
the slip to back in GUM or even earlier. Anyway, Lena
walked out of GUM towards the taxi and got into the first
cab that came along. She was hoping to stop at the Cheryomushki market and buy Viktor some grapes (he'd asked
her to bring some when she made her next visit in two
days), but when a taxi turned up that was actually heading
towards the Frunze Embankment, she gave up the market.
It wasn't worth it. Now was hardly the time to go buying
grapes! Once in the car she began to relax immediately. She
even began to doze off...

*Secret*
To CID Third Department
Head of Second Section
Lieutenant-Colonel M. A. Svetlov

### REPORT
(continued)

... After overtaking the taxi driven by Captain Fedotov,
our three special cars arrived at the address given by
Smagina: No. 48, Frunzenskaya Embankment. The
building had four entrances on the ground floor, so each
one was hurriedly covered by members of the surveillance team. When the suspect arrived, she paid Captain
Fedotov, giving him a ten rouble note and telling him to
keep the change. She then headed towards entrance No.
2, where she encountered Major Kuzmichova, who was
dressed as an old-age pensioner pretending to take her
Tibetan terrier, "Harry Truman", for a walk. The two of
them entered the elevator together, and Major Kuzmi-

chova was able to see Smagina get out at the sixth floor and ring the bell of No. 22. Nobody came to the door for nine minutes. Only when she began to disturb the neighbors by hammering on the door with her fists and shouting, "Vitya, open up, it's me," did the door open and a man's hand drag her inside.

Meanwhile, as soon as it became known which apartment Smagina was heading for, Lieutenant I. Z. Grinshtein from the Telephone Surveillance Department managed to lower an EPU-5 electronic microphone down to the window of the place, with the aid of the janitor who had been summoned for that purpose. From 15:07 hours onwards our group was able to overhear and record all sounds and conversations coming from the apartment, as well as feed them over the radio to the CID Incident Room. The relevant tape recordings are appended to this report.

*Tape recording*

MAN'S VOICE: Are you out of your mind, you fool?! Who told you to come outside the prearranged times?

WOMAN'S VOICE: But Vitya, listen! Is anybody here?

MAN'S VOICE: Of course not, idiot! You want to look around and check? You've raised the roof with your idiotic, jealous ranting! Did anybody see you in the hall?

WOMAN'S VOICE: Vitya, wait a minute! I haven't come because I'm jealous! The whole Moscow CID is looking for you!

MAN'S VOICE: So what? That means that somebody at the camp in Kotlas has squealed and told them I've extended my visit illegally. So what? What the hell point is there in you causing so much goddam panic?

WOMAN'S VOICE: Listen, Vitya, you've got it all wrong . . . !

At this point I returned to the Incident Room, where Major Ozherelyev's surveillance group was transmitting the monitored conversation. Until quite recently, two or three years ago, the CID, and the militia as a whole, hadn't possessed such technology. It had been the strictly secret preserve of the KGB. But now that we were on the eve of the Moscow Olympic Games, the KGB had purchased the latest American and Japanese listening equipment, and their old machines, which wouldn't work at distances greater than half a mile, had been passed on to the MVD. But thank the Lord for small mercies! Now, with the aid of a Soviet-made EPU-5 listening device, we were able to hear a conversation of crucial importance to the investigation.

WOMAN'S VOICE: You're wrong! They're looking for a journalist, who you're supposed to have kidnapped. And they say that you've murdered some teenage kid! Vitya! Is it true?

MAN'S VOICE: Shut your mouth, you fool! I haven't killed anybody! Who are "they", anyway? Who have you been talking to?

WOMAN'S VOICE: At the hotel this morning a major in the Odessa police tried to pick me up. He's a student at the Militia Academy. They were all given three photographs—yours, one of this journalist, and one of somebody else, who I think I remember seeing you with once. Vitya! Why are you mixed up in this business? Why!?

MAN'S VOICE: Wait a minute! Stop screaming! What else did he say?

WOMAN'S VOICE: I can't remember. I saw your photograph and I nearly went out of my mind!

MAN'S VOICE: Well, try to remember! What else did he say?

I bent towards Svetlov and asked, "Whose apartment is it?"

"We've already found that out," he replied. "It belongs to a Viktor Vladimirovich Sysoyev, head of the Chief Pharmaceutical Authority. He's in Geneva at the moment, at the head of a medical delegation attending an international symposium. His family is on vacation in the south, at Pitsunda."

Meanwhile, we could hear a woman sobbing violently

over the radio. "But Vitya, what's going to happen now? What's going to happen now!"

"Nothing. Everything is going to go on just as usual," said Akeyev, sounding angry but very self-assured. "In the first place, I haven't killed anybody! And in the second place, the boss will be home in a week's time and he'll get me out of all this shit. I'm not working on my own, after all . . ."

"Vitya, why don't we go back nice and quietly to Kotlas, *now!* You can finish your time in Daddy's camp, and nobody will know you've been to Moscow. How about it? Let's go?"

"Come on, come on!" Svetlov said impatiently. "Just leave that apartment . . ."

But Vitya Akeyev was not that stupid.

"How could you be such a fool?" he said to Lena. "If they're searching for me all over Moscow, it means that they'll be looking for me at the camp tomorrow. In any case, I can't leave here at all at the moment. What are you talking about? Are you sure you weren't followed? What's that car outside?"

"It was there when I arrived. Vitya, don't be afraid. My Dad was in the KGB. In any case, I wandered all over Moscow, checking to see if I was being followed. I was so frightened at first that I emptied all the morphine in a women's room, two whole boxes of it, one hundred in each. Because I thought I could see people following me everywhere. Then I calmed down, while I was in line for French underwear in GUM. Can you believe they ran out when I was only twenty places away in the line?"

"So how did you get here? By metro?"

"No, taxi. But don't worry. It was some senile old man who drove me here. I chose him carefully . . . !"

Everybody in the room suddenly collapsed with laughter. Despite his age, Captain Fedotov was a great one with women, and to hear him being called a "senile old man" meant that Lena Smagina had acquired a sworn enemy for life in the Moscow CID. As for Fedotov, he wouldn't shake off that description for a long time!

Meanwhile, the conversation in Sysoyev's place continued.

"Vitya, why did you kidnap the journalist?"

"That's enough, it's got nothing to do with you. It's just that the idiot poked his nose around once too often and persuaded that kid to squeal on us."

"And did you kill *him*, too?"

"Idiot! I've already told you: I haven't killed anyone. And stop whining, or I'll throw you out of the fucking apartment! Let's have a drink, that'll be better! What do you want? Brandy, vodka? I asked you to buy me some grapes."

"I know, Vitya. Only I was in such a state I couldn't be bothered with grapes. Do you want me to take a taxi to the market and get you some now?"

"No, we'll sweat it out here until the boss arrives... What do you want to drink?"

Then we could hear Major Ozherelyev's voice over the air. "We've missed our chance, colonel. She hasn't managed to get him out yet..."

"I know. I'm not deaf," Svetlov said rudely. "OK, let them have a drink and talk some more. Then we'll see..."

"You're so fucking dumb," Akeyev replied. "Here you are. Drink some brandy. There's nothing to be afraid of. What do you think I'm sitting here for? Guarding his wardrobe, or something? Listen! Out there in the kitchen, behind the slop-pail, is a safe full of diamonds, worth three million roubles at least! As soon as the boss gets back, we'll be able to buy our way out of anything. Half the ministers are his friends, and the other half are mixed up in this with him. Do you understand the country you're living in? All you have to do is support the people in power, and you're as safe as houses. Nothing can get at you after that, not the Anti-Fraud Squad, not anything..."

"Vitya, kiss me..."

"OK. Come here..."

Now all we could hear was the sound of passionate kisses, the squeaking of springs in the sofa, and breathing which got faster and faster. The CID men started to grin. Everybody looked at Svetlov and me. Then we heard Major Ozherelyev's voice, scarcely able to contain his amusement. "This is where the porn show starts, colonel. What are your instructions?"

"Shut your mouth and wait!" snapped Svetlov.

"Yes, colonel," said the major in an offended tone.

Meanwhile things were beginning to get juicy on the Frunze Embankment.

"Take my clothes off," the woman's voice whispered. "That's it . . . Take your time . . . Don't do it all at once. I want to be kissed . . . Don't move, don't move! God! How I love him! Look at him! Christ . . ."

"No, I'm sorry, but I can't work in these conditions!" said a middle-aged technician, Captain Shaginskaya, blushing deeply. As the rest of the officers shouted derisively, she left the room.

"Ozherelyev," said Svetlov hoarsely. "Take the strike group up to the sixth floor, and don't forget that Akeyev was a European boxing champion and may be armed. Open the doors very quietly, and only when they finish, at my signal."

"So they'll be finishing at your signal, huh?" Ozherelyev asked knowingly.

"You son of a bitch! I'll teach you to be funny with me! Just wait!" Svetlov said good-naturedly. "Now move."

"Yes, sir. Only can we listen a little longer? It *is* interesting, after all . . ."

Not that Lena Smagina had been quiet all this time. As is well known, women can be divided into several categories—those who say nothing, those who babble away and those who moan and cry out. Lena Smagina turned out to be one of the babblers.

"Take my breasts! My breasts. Please!" she whispered, breathing hard. "No, that hurts, Vitya. Let me go on top. Let me go on top! No, I'll do it myself . . . Oh! Ooh! That's marvelous! Oh, *God!* How wonderful . . . !"

The shadowing of this particular suspect had turned into a full-scale porno show, no doubt about it! The word soon passed around and people were shortly flooding into the Incident Room from all over the place. There were duty officers from along the corridor, engineers from the Technical Department on the third floor, officers from the recreation rooms on the first floor, and a whole horde of investigators and inspectors from the CID and the Anti-Fraud Squad, as well as dog handlers, criminologists, forensic experts and chauffeurs—they were all there! The whole Operations Department was listening in on the case!

"Do it again, Vitya, again! Oh, that's wonderful, wonderful. Oh!... Do it again...!"

"How long *can* they keep it up for?" asked Captain Pavlychko, one of the duty officers, indignantly. Then he looked at his watch. "He *has* been screwing her for twenty-three minutes, after all!"

"The other way around, you mean," somebody said. "She's been screwing him!"

He was right. Lena seemed to be insatiable.

"Do it again, Vitya, do it again! Don't stop! Only... do it slowly. That's right. That's right, darling... oh, I'm dying! Oh, *God!* Go deeper, deeper... Again... Here, let me turn around. Let me turn around... Oh, what are you doing? Oh, oh! What are you *doing?*" She said the same thing, louder and louder, quicker and quicker. "Oh, oh... I'm going to die... Oh... oh... oh..."

"What's going on here?" said an imperious voice. Everybody looked towards the door in surprise. There was a bewildered Colonel Shubeiko, the officer in charge of the whole Operations Department. All those not involved in our particular case rushed past him out of the room, leaving the rest of us and the pig-eyed Colonel Shubeiko to listen to Lena Smagina.

"Oh! What are you doing? I'm going to die!..."

"Is he strangling her, or what?" the colonel asked at last.

Neither Svetlov or I could resist it any longer. We burst out laughing and tried to turn it into a cough.

"Comrade Colonel," Ozherelyev said suddenly over the radio. "The strike group with Sergeant Afanasyev is in position. What are your instructions?"

"He's fucking her, colonel, if you'll forgive the expression," Svetlov said.

"Well, stop it at once!" Shubeiko ordered.

"I'm sorry, colonel, but you mustn't interfere with our work," replied Svetlov. "Ozherelyev, can you hear me?"

"Yes, Marat Alekseyevich. Only how long is this going to go on? We'll all have to drink a bottle of milk to restore our health!"

"OK. That's it. Who's going to open the door?"

"Technician Suzdaltsev."

"Good. Prepare yourselves."

To judge from what we could hear over the radio, it seemed as if events in apartment No. 22 were about to reach their natural conclusion.

"Now, Ozherelyev, go! Open the door! Only I want him alive! I'm on my way!"

Svetlov got his assistant to take his place at the console, and motioned Vanya Korovin, formerly a bear hunter and now a lieutenant in the Technical Department, to follow. The three of us rushed downstairs to the waiting CID Mercedes. We'd hardly had time to slam the doors behind us when the driver switched on the siren and we screeched out into Sredne-Karetny lane. The sound of our siren made the city traffic hug the side of the road in an effort to get out of the way, and we hurtled down the Garden Ring Road towards the Frunze Embankment.

*Secret*

To CID Third Department
Head of Second Section
Lieutenant-Colonel M. A. Svetlov

### REPORT
#### (concluded)

... Acting on your instructions received by radio, technician Suzdaltsev managed to pick the lock of apartment No. 22 without making any noise, and the strike group consisting of six men under my direct command entered the apartment silently. From the bedroom we continued to hear noises emanating from V. Akeyev and E. Smagina. When these stopped, we heard the sound of a match being struck and a man's voice asking Smagina whether she wanted to smoke. She refused, saying that she needed to go to the bathroom. We allowed her to enter the bathroom without hindrance and then rushed into the bedroom where we arrested Citizen Akeyev after a short struggle. We managed to place handcuffs on him. He had no chance to use the revolver that was concealed under the mattress. At the same time we apprehended E. Smagina in the bathroom. Akeyev hurled abuse at her, accusing her of "tipping us off." When she recognized me as the "major from Odessa", Smagina realized that our acquaintance earlier in the day at the Hotel Peking had been a set-up, and she fainted.

Special Investigator I. I. Shamrayev arrived on the scene, and on his instructions the two prisoners were dressed in their clothes. Lieutenant I. Korovin and Suzdaltsev then examined a cupboard in the kitchen. In it, behind a slop-pail, they discovered a well-concealed imported safe of new construction.

The prisoner V. Akeyev informed us that the combination to the safe was known only to the owner of the apartment, Citizen Sysoyev, who was on official business abroad at that moment. According to the two technical experts, it was impossible to arrive at the correct combination any other way, so Special Investigator Shamrayev gave instructions that it should be opened by using an oxyacetylene torch. However, the safe turned out to be empty. A painstaking search of the apartment revealed no other secret hiding place, nor were any valuables, foreign currency, narcotics or any other similar items discovered on the premises.

> Deputy Head of Second Section
> CID Third Department
> Major V. Ozherelyev

June 7 1979

The person most shaken by the sight of the empty safe was Akeyev himself. Neither his arrest, nor his having been "betrayed" by his girlfriend ("that fucking bitch", he called her), nor his own blunders ("I had a feeling that was a police car outside!")—none of these things had as devastating an effect on him as when police technician Vanya Korovin burned through the safe to reveal it as being absolutely empty.

Sitting in the kitchen, already dressed and handcuffed, Akeyev stared vacantly at the empty safe. Then he said, as if he couldn't believe his own eyes, "But the diamonds *were* there! I saw them myself!"

"When?" Svetlov asked.

Akeyev looked at me, then at Svetlov, Ozherelyev and the CID men crowding around in the kitchen. His brain was working feverishly, I could see that. He screwed up his eyes and clenched his handcuffed fists together, like the boxer he was.

"OK," he said. "Which one of you is the investigator? I want to make a statement to protect the security of the Soviet Union!"

He'd probably seen a similar scene in a movie or on television. When I said, "I'm an investigator from the Chief Public Prosecutor's Office," he coughed into his fist and said with a great show of bombastic emotion: "Today, June 7, I, Viktor Akeyev, prisoner and former European boxing champion, wish to make the following statement in the interests of the country's security! I freely admit that over the last two years I have been involved with criminals. I would also like to inform you that the Head of the Chief Pharmaceutical Authority, Viktor Sysoyev, away at the moment in the West on official business, has taken diamonds with him worth three million roubles or more, diamonds that belong to us!"

"Who is this 'us'?" I asked.

"The Soviet State," replied Akeyev solemnly.

"What do you mean? That you were guarding state property here?" I asked.

"He's a real bastard!" Akeyev exclaimed, forgetting his role as the savior of state property for a moment. "He got me to guard valuables that belonged to the whole gang, but what was I really looking after? An empty hole in the wall! Meanwhile, he goes abroad with the whole kit and kaboodle, damn him! Anyway, I'm making a statement, Comrade Investigator! You should call the KGB right now and get them to arrest him in Geneva. And you can take my statement as proof of guilt."

"But perhaps there never were any diamonds," Svetlov said.

"Oh, yes there were, Comrade Colonel. I saw them myself. Before he went abroad, I saw him put the box in the safe, with my own eyes. The box contained diamonds and hard currency. And we'd brought it over from the dacha.

The next morning he left for the West."

"Well, perhaps he hid them somewhere else?"

"Where? And leave me guarding an empty box? No, he took them away with him, Comrade Colonel. And they didn't belong only to him. They belonged to all of us, and I was supposed to be guarding them on everybody's behalf. Meanwhile he's having a whale of a time in the West, living on the proceeds, I tell you!"

"OK," Svetlov said. "We'll deal with the diamonds later. You tell me a few more things now that you've gotten started. Where's Belkin? Is he alive?"

"Belkin?" Akeyev asked.

"The journalist, the one you forced into an ambulance at the Kursk station, along with Sultan from Baku."

"Oh, *him!*" Akeyev said, shrugging his shoulders. "He was still alive when we were at the dacha. I don't know what happened to him after that."

"Which dacha?"

"The one that belongs to the boss, Sysoyev, in Tsaritsyno."

"What's the address?"

"Gagarin Lane, No. 72. Only you won't find him there now. After Sultan escaped, they took the journalist away."

"Where did they take him? And who did the taking?"

"Christ, I don't know, Comrade Colonel."

Svetlov turned suddenly to Ozherelyev and said, "Take a note of the address. Gagarin Lane, No. 72. Take some men and search the place right away!"

Then he turned back to Akeyev. "Are there any secret hiding places at the dacha?"

"There's one. In the garage, beneath the sink. Only you'll find that empty now. We brought everything here, I tell you."

Now that Akeyev had started to confess, he became very helpful and obliging, as often happens with criminals.

"Where could they have taken Belkin, and who took him?" Svetlov asked persistently. "And don't forget that Belkin is more important to us than the diamonds. If you help us find him, we'll reduce your sentence by half, I guarantee!"

"But I wasn't one of those in charge, Comrade Colonel! They didn't report everything they did to me. When this boy Sultan from Baku got away from the dacha, and the Old Man did him in on the railroad, our boss told us to clear out the dacha right away. I came here, but God knows what they did with the journalist. Probably the doctor took him away. He had been carrying out experiments on him, after all."

"Which doctor? What experiments?"

"You know, the doctor who started the whole damn thing. Him and the Old Man. The big bosses didn't know this, but the two of them were dealing in a little opium on the side. They were taking a coffin full of the stuff from Mara to Baku, via Tashkent, when a really stupid thing happened—the coffin fell open at the airport. It cost them two hundred thousand roubles to get the Baku Militia to hush the whole thing up. And everything would have been all right, if only this journalist hadn't gotten mixed up in it! Stupid bastard! He tried to get Sultan to spill the beans on everyone in *Komsomolskaya Pravda*. We arrived at the station with the goods to meet him, and there he is with a suitcase full of money. But guess who's waiting for him on the platform? The journalist again! So we had to push both of them into the ambulance, or else they would have gone to the newspaper offices. There was a girl with them, only she ran away..."

"Who else took part in the kidnapping? Don't try to conceal anything now. There were four of you, we've got witnesses. Quickly. Who's this doctor? What's his name?"

"I tell you, I don't know! They either called him 'Boris' or 'Doctor.' He was from the same town as the journalist. I heard them say that a hundred times, when they were at the dacha."

"So they were taken from the railroad station to Sysoyev's dacha at Tsaritsyno, is that it?"

"Yes."

"In the ambulance?"

"Yes."

"What was the registration number?"

"The doctor had as many of them as you liked. He used

to make them out of plastic, so you couldn't tell the difference between them and a metal one."

"What were these experiments of his?"

"All kinds. He'd give you a little gas, and everything would be great. You'd laugh until your sides hurt. Or he'd give you an injection. Then you'd tell him everything you knew. You'd wake up an hour later unable to remember anything you'd said. Or . . ."

"What did he do to Belkin?" I repeated impatiently.

"He wiped out his memory," Akeyev said. "He did the same thing to Sultan, too, only *he* escaped."

"What do you mean, 'wiped out his memory'?"

"Just what I say," said Akeyev. "By injecting them with something. I heard him swear to the boss that in three weeks the journalist wouldn't remember a thing, either about the coffin or about the dacha. He used to inject morphine three times a day into them, and some other drugs too. I don't know what drugs."

Svetlov and I exchanged glances. Fifteen days had passed since Belkin had been abducted. The achievements of Soviet medicine have become well known from the accounts of open trials involving dissidents and those held *in camera*. A lot of secret research has also been conducted in psychiatric laboratories belonging to the military. I have no special knowledge about this myself, but I have heard one or two things from the forensic experts I know. These days doctors have huge numbers of psychotropic drugs at their disposal, and although they are most frequently employed in KGB investigations, what is there to stop somebody using them for their own purposes? If we couldn't find Belkin by tomorrow or the next day, then we ran the risk of finding him with his memory totally erased. That would be a great present for Brezhnev's press corps on the day he was due to meet Carter in Vienna!

"OK," Svetlov said, going up to Akeyev. "What else do you know about this doctor? You'd better start remembering, and fast! What does he look like?"

"He's fairly young, a little on the fat side. He's got black hair and brown eyes, and wears a signet ring on his right hand. That's all I can tell you."

"Who else knows him?"

"Sysoyev, my boss."

"I realize that, but he's out of the country. Who else? Herman Dolgo-Saburov?"

"He's out of town, too."

Svetlov grinned. He'd caught Akeyev. "So you know Dolgo-Saburov?"

"Also through my boss. He works for him too, bringing opium north and taking morphine down south. Only he won't tell you a thing about the doctor, never in a thousand years."

"Why is that?"

"He's madly in love with the doctor's sister."

"Have you seen her? Do you know her?"

"Hell yes!" he replied, his eyes darting towards Lena Smagina, who sat in silence with her eyes closed and was slowly rocking from side to side in abject terror. "She's just like that whore over there! Good for nothing but screwing and hanging out in bars! But she's good looking, I'll tell you. You know what they say: pure in appearance but a whore underneath! That's all there is to her! But Herman comes from aristocratic stock. Once he'd fallen for her, all he could say was—'Natasha Rostova! Natasha Rostova!' But she's as much like Tolstoy's character as I'm like Tolstoy! She's a bitch, that's all there is to it!"

"What's her name? Where does she live? Does she work?"

"No, I don't know anything except that she's called Natasha. That's all. But this slut here might know something, the two of them dragged me out to a restaurant a week ago."

I went up to Smagina, but as soon as she opened her eyes, I could see that it would be a waste of time trying to get anything out of her. Her eyes were vacant, full of despair and nothing else.

"Don't waste your time," Svetlov said, coming up to me. "Let's go. We have to deal with the nephew."

Then he nodded towards Akeyev and Smagina. "Take them to Pshenichny, boys. He'll cross-examine them."

*16:42 hours*

"Unbelievable! It's already five o'clock!" Svetlov said, as

he got into the police Mercedes waiting for us outside Sysoyev's apartment on the Embankment. The car was something of a new and unusual sight on the Moscow streets, and I hardly have to add that it was surrounded by a swarm of inquisitive boys, peering in through the windows, touching the bumpers and handles and asking the driver hundreds of questions. Svetlov shooed the most persistent of them away from the door and we climbed in. He sat back in the seat, exhausted. "I haven't eaten all day!" he complained.

"Where to?" the driver asked cautiously.

"Just go, then we'll make up our minds."

The radio telephone started to beep. It had to be the Petrovka switchboard trying to get in touch.

"That's the fourth time they've tried to reach you," the driver said, glancing down at the telephone as he started the engine.

Svetlov lifted the receiver and turned up the volume so I could listen in.

"Lieutenant-Colonel Svetlov here. Hello?"

"At last, Comrade Colonel!" came the voice of Captain Laskin, in charge of the surveillance groups tailing the "nephew".

"All right, calm down," Svetlov said. "What's up?"

"This guy's a maniac! He's distributed drugs to sixteen different places so far! Both Arbats, New and Old, the Hotels Belgrade and Ukraine, you name it! And everywhere he goes he picks up more money. I don't know, he must have at least a hundred thousand by now!"

"OK, so where is he at the moment?"

"He's stuck in an elevator, as you instructed."

"What do you mean, 'as I instructed'?"

"You told us to delay him for an hour or an hour and a half, until you were free. Well, he's been stuck in an elevator for the past sixty-five minutes with the famous singer Slichenko."

"*Who?*" Svetlov said, visibly brightening.

"It may seem funny to you, Comrade Colonel, but I've got a major public disturbance on my hands. In order to delay him in the elevator, I had to cut off the electricity for the whole block, and it's an enormous place. There's a jeweler's on the ground floor, while the rest of it is filled with academicians, diplomats, famous singers and the like. And they've been without any light for the last hour!"

"All right, I'll make sure you get a reward for inventiveness!" Svetlov said. "Hang on a little longer. I'm on my way. Where are you exactly?"

"Right outside the building, colonel. We've got an old electric repair van here, and we've cordoned off the area. I have some pneumatic drills tearing up the asphalt to make it look like we're looking for an electric cable."

"OK! Pneumatic drills, huh? And what was the nephew doing in the building?"

"He had just been with the hockey player, Zhluptov. He left the last package of morphine with him. It's already five o'clock, and he needs to go to the hairdresser's..."

"All right. Out for now. I'll be with you in five minutes."

Then Svetlov asked the operator to put him through to the Incident Room. "They're trying to get through to you themselves," she replied. Then we could hear the voice of Svetlov's assistant coming over the radio.

"Comrade Colonel! The Moscow Energy Department has really been getting on my nerves!"

"I know, I know! Tell them that we'll have the cable repaired in five minutes. And listen. Is Colonel Maryamov there?"

"Yes. He's catching a little shut-eye in the corner."

"Wake him up! Tell him to get the chief steward along to the Enchantress hair salon as fast as possible. He's waiting downstairs. I'll come after them. Any questions?"

"No, colonel! Everything's clear."

Svetlov switched off the radio and looked at me. "Well, let's go through everything one more time. We've got two choices. Either we arrest the nephew now and bring him face-to-face with Akeyev and everybody he's just distributed drugs to. Large-scale drug trafficking is punishable under Article 224 and he'll get fifteen years. Do you think he'll give away the doctor?"

"He might," I replied, not sure of the answer. We *did* have incontrovertible evidence linking him with the illegal sale and distribution of narcotics. But then there was Dolgo-

Saburov's aristocratic background. He was the direct descendant of an ancient and noble family, after all, and yet the reality of life in the Soviet Union had turned him into a railroad employee! Something like this could turn somebody like Dolgo-Saburov to crime, and it would have been a conscious decision on his part, too, without any feeling of guilt. He might not betray his accomplices. And if you added the fact that he was in love with the doctor's sister, as Akeyev had just told us, well . . . It was quite possible that you wouldn't scare him by threatening him with Article 224.

I remembered the telephone conversation I had had in Dolgo-Saburov's place with the anonymous woman. The tone had been intimate and there had been something seductive in her voice. I now had no doubt that I had been talking to Natasha and that she was the one that Belkin had fallen in love with at the airport in Baku. *Cherchez la femme!* as they say . . .

"The other possibility," Svetlov was commenting meanwhile, "is that I do the same thing with the nephew as Ozherelyev did with Smagina. I could say the CID is after the whole gang, but the one that reveals the whereabouts of Belkin will get off scot-free."

"I don't think he'd betray the others," I said. "He *is* a count, after all . . ."

"OK. Let's say he didn't take the bait and didn't provide us with Belkin's address. He might take measures to get in touch with the doctor and his sister . . ."

"But they may know what's going on already. I told you before that it was a woman who phoned Dolgo-Saburov's home. I had a few words with her, and I'm sure it was Natasha. And what she told me she will have told her brother, you know."

"So what? Dolgo-Saburov doesn't know that! That's why he may try to warn them!"

"All right," I said. "Do it your way. After all, what do we have to lose?"

We were careening down the Novy Arbat. In the distance we could see the "electricity repair team" of Captain Laskin and his group standing outside the "Agate" jeweler's. Meanwhile, a couple of real repair workers, called out by Laskin, were breaking up the asphalt with their pneumatic drills.

We arrived. Svetlov ordered them to finish the "repair work" and went off to the hair salon to meet the chief steward. When Irakly Golub arrived a couple of minutes later, accompanied by Maryamov, Svetlov ordered Laskin to start the elevator again. Everything was ready for the "nephew's" reception. The agents disguised as electricians and road repair men were hanging out outside the building, while Svetlov and Irakly Golub were walking up and down outside the Enchantress hair salon. I was sitting in Captain Laskin's car, waiting to see what would happen.

Finally, Herman Dolgo-Saburov walked out of the entrance, accompanied by the famous gypsy singer, Nikolay Slichenko. They bid a friendly farewell to each other and then walked quickly towards their respective cars. I could understand why Slichenko would be in a hurry to get to his Volga, but why would Dolgo-Saburov be rushing to his Zhiguli if all he had to do was reach the hairdresser's across the street? Perhaps he needed something? No, there he was, sitting down in the driver's seat and slamming the door. A cloud of exhaust fumes came out of the back of the car and he roared off at top speed.

I looked at Laskin anxiously. Frowning deeply, he tried to move his repair van into the stream of traffic, but because nobody knew that it was a police vehicle, the other cars wouldn't let us out, as if on purpose. As we passed, some of the "repair men" jumped into the van through the open door. I grabbed the microphone of the radio telephone, and called Svetlov.

"Marat, Shamrayev here! Something's wrong! He's driving past the hair salon. I can still see him, but he'll disappear soon!"

"He's not going to disappear anywhere!" Laskin said and flipped the switch on some kind of instrument—the van was equipped with all kinds of things, none of it having anything to do with electrical repairs of the ordinary kind. It had *every*thing to do, though, with periscopic vision and long-distance monitoring of conversations between suspects. The instrument Laskin had switched on immediately began to beep, and a point of light began to flicker and move on the screen of a portable direction-finder.

"He won't disappear anywhere," Laskin repeated. "There's a homing device underneath the car and a microphone inside. He's been carrying them around since this morning. We managed to put them on at the hump-yards. Now I bet he'll begin driving all over Moscow again..."

The flickering light on the screen did a sudden U-turn to the right. "He's turned onto the Dragomilov Embankment next to the Hotel Ukraine," said Captain Laskin, as he sped up. Traveling alongside us I could see a black, unmarked Volga carrying Marat Svetlov. He looked gloomy.

Dolgo-Saburov's car had stopped at a red light, and we came to a halt about five cars behind him. Svetlov quickly moved to our repair van.

"Where's he going now?" he asked Laskin in a disgruntled voice.

"Should I get out and ask him?" Laskin asked with a grin.

"A whole day's work turns out to be a total waste of time!" grumbled Svetlov for both of us. "We set up the chief steward for him, we have one of his women waiting for him at the beauty salon, and what does he do...? Hey, let's go! Step on it!"

As the light changed to green, Dolgo-Saburov's car was off, heading towards the Kiev railroad station and doing far more than the official speed limit. We kept behind him at the same distance. Nobody said a word.

"Why can't I hear him?" Svetlov asked at last. "Doesn't he even cough occasionally?"

"Well, he has some English-language tapes that he switches on, whenever he goes anywhere," Laskin said. "It drives you nuts, listening to them all day. Switch it, Sasha," he said to one of the technicians who was sitting somewhere in the back of the van. We could immediately hear a metallic voice pronouncing English-language drills and then giving their Russian translation. "He spends the whole day traveling around Moscow," said Laskin, "and listens to nothing else... *I have been, she has been* ... See, even *I've* managed to pick it up!"

Laskin suddenly brought the van to a halt. Dolgo-Saburov had stopped a little ahead, beneath the clock at the Kiev station, and the shapely figure of a woman dressed in a light summer raincoat slipped into the car. I looked up at the sky. It looked like rain. What with running all over the place, you don't notice petty details like the weather. The English lesson was turned off. We heard the sound of a quick kiss, followed by a voice I had heard before.

"Huh, you're really on time, aren't you? I've been waiting forty minutes. I didn't know what to think. Couldn't you at least call?"

The car moved off and turned right, in the direction of the Lenin Hills. We listened to the rest of the conversation with increasing interest, while the technician made sure that every word was being recorded.

"I couldn't call you or anything!" Dolgo-Saburov said. "I spent a whole hour stuck in an elevator on the Arbat. But at least I had Slichenko to talk to. That was something!"

"Who?"

"Slichenko, you know, the singer. Anyway, enough of that. What do you have to report?"

"I couldn't find out anything else. Katya came off her shift this morning. Still, you've got one thing to thank me for. When I phoned you this morning, I almost fell into a trap. The cops were already there, waiting. 'Come on, you prick,' I said. 'Are you still asleep?' It was you I had in mind, of course..."

Svetlov looked at me and grinned. There aren't many women who can swear and get away with it. Usually only the most beautiful can pull it off, and not all of them possess the art. Here was one of those cases, however...

"Well, what could they have on me?" Dolgo-Saburov said. "There were no drugs left there by then. Morphine, opium—I'd removed everything, and they missed it all the first time, anyway! I didn't kill my aunt, either. So I'm clean. The old man is a real prick, though! Why did he have to choke her to death? She would have given me everything herself. All I had to do was ask."

"But he was only trying to frighten her..."

"Frighten her? I can imagine what his 'frightening' is

like! Never mind! She lived her life . . . It's a pity, though; it's because of her that we're in this jam now with the police sniffing around everywhere."

"Why do you say that? Nobody's panicking. It's only the boxer and the old man they're looking for. The old man is a long way off, and it'll be some time before they find the boxer. He's sitting in the apartment guarding an empty safe and never goes outside. Even Lena he only lets come to see him every three days at prearranged times."

"Listen, you're talking as if it's the most ordinary thing in the world," Dolgo-Saburov replied. "But do you realize that we're driving through Moscow now for the last time?"

"So what? I couldn't give two shits. I know every inch of the place anyway, and we've got the world in front of us!"

"But I love Moscow. If it wasn't for this Soviet government—may they rot in hell!—I wouldn't leave the place in a million years."

"Not even with me?"

"Just wait, Natasha. As soon as you get your cut in the West, you'll want to get away from me as fast as you can."

"Idiot! I love you! Don't get scared, count! I really do. Everything's going to turn out just fine." She must have been smiling, and then we could hear the sound of another kiss. "And what a life it's going to be, darling!"

"You know, I wouldn't be too sure about that!"

"Why are you being so horrible today?"

"You'd be horrible, too, if you'd had to spend an hour stuck in an elevator on a day like this! That cost me five thousand roubles, you know! I had no time to go to the hair salon."

"So that's what's eating you! You didn't get to see the 'enchantress'! Well, you only have to say the word. We can always drive back there."

"I can't. Boris told us we had to arrive no later than seven o'clock, or else we'd miss the plane. You haven't even brought a suitcase with you."

"Boris has all my things already. How much did you collect today?"

"Ninety-two thousand. To hell with it! We have enough for the flight out, anyway!"

"Let me look at the telegram."

"Don't be crazy! I managed to eat it this morning, while the wagon was being searched."

When I heard this, I could feel my cheeks turning red, although Svetlov didn't even glance in my direction. I had been searching for the aunt's jewels, after all, so what was the point in looking in his mouth?

"But can't you at least remember what it said?" Natasha asked, to my extreme relief and satisfaction.

*"Dowry costs 200, wedding in a week. Fly out with money urgently. Dad,"* Dolgo-Saburov said. "OK?"

"Yes," Natasha replied. "It means that for two hundred he's managed to bribe the commander at the frontier post or somebody at the aerodrome. We'll be on our way in a week's time, but meanwhile he needs the money urgently."

"He's got a hundred already. I managed to collect ninety today, and Boris has another fifty. So we've got enough for the journey out, and the rest of it is no good to us, since we'll need hard currency after that. How much did Sysoyev have in the safe?"

"Didn't the old man tell you, or are you just checking?"

"How the hell should I know what you do? You may have all agreed to pocket some of my share, for all I know!"

"You're impossible! I love you, you idiot, can't you see? Boris and the old man might have come to some private arrangement when they opened the safe, but can you really imagine Boris doing so behind my back?"

"Well, I've learned to expect anything from your brother . . ."

"You'll get a black eye in a minute, count!" Natasha said in a serious voice. "Boris is a genius! Can you imagine anybody else getting us out of that mess with that stupid coffin of yours? Do you know what Sysoyev told Boris under hypnosis at the time?"

"I know. I heard all about it. Only nobody else was there, so maybe Boris invented it all. Maybe Sysoyev was never under hypnosis at all."

"In that case, smart guy, how did he discover the combination to the safe?"

"I don't know..." Dolgo-Saburov said slowly. "OK, let's assume that he did drag that out of him under hypnosis. There's no guarantee that he didn't simply invent the rest of it to drag the rest of us into the affair—you, me and the old man."

"OK. You can get out now, if you like! Right now! We'll arrive at Boris's place, you get your cut, and that's it."

"No, now that you're all about to make off with Sysoyev's diamonds, they're bound to nail me. So I'm going to see this one through with the rest of you—to the very end. It's just that it's like what you see in the movies—fleeing across the border with a bunch of diamonds..."

"Shut up! In films, people who try to escape across the border always get caught. That's because the censorship won't have it any other way. A director told me all about it once. Otherwise the movie won't get a public showing."

"Did you go to bed with him?"

"With who?"

"This director of yours."

"Oh, God! What's that got to do with anything, count? Just remember this. Whether you like Moscow or not, whether you want to go abroad with me or not, we can't stay here any longer, any of us—and it's your fault, not ours. It's all because of that stupid idea of yours about the coffin!"

"Why was it stupid?" Dolgo-Saburov asked, flaring up suddenly. "In the end it was thanks to the coffin that we came across Belkin with those frontier passes of his. If it weren't for them, the old man wouldn't be on the border waiting already. It's an ill wind..."

Svetlov seemed to be taking in every word, and so was I. We were both sitting glued to the speaker, afraid to miss a single word, intonation, or nuance. This was better than any cross-examination, and we only wished that it could go on longer. Suddenly we heard the woman's voice say, "Don't go so fast! Look at that rain!"

She was right. A veritable June cloudburst was thundering down on the streets of southwest Moscow, right where Dolgo-Saburov's Zhiguli and our unmarked police Volgas and "repair van" were headed.

"Don't worry, countess," Dolgo-Saburov said. "We're all going to come out of this alive."

"Right," Natasha said with a laugh. "We ought to kiss my brother's feet. Sysoyev's boys were ready to bump us all off, thanks to your conspiracy with the coffin."

"They're bastards, all of them!" Dolgo-Saburov said. "They're able to get narcotics across the border, *and* hold Swiss bank accounts *and* use government money to make official trips abroad! Brezhnev's son even managed to hire a yacht and go elephant hunting in Africa! Oh well! It doesn't matter. We'll meet them all soon enough. Sysoyev, Balayan and the rest will undoubtedly travel abroad again some time. I'd give any number of diamonds to get them when they do! They'll get what they deserve, those fucking 'servants of the Soviet people'! I'll beat the living shit out of them!"

"I don't think you've understood," said the woman's voice slowly. She was obviously taking a long drag on a cigarette. "Boris has a completely different idea. If somebody like Sysoyev or Balayan comes to the West on official business, we'll be able to find out where they are from the newspapers. Then we can kidnap them, like Belkin, and force them to reveal the numbers of their Swiss bank accounts. They won't even be able to report it to the police. If they did, they wouldn't be able to return to the Soviet Union. It's a pity that we won't have time to get Sysoyev in Geneva, while he's there at the moment..."

"Not bad!" Svetlov said, with a whistle. "The movies have nothing on this crowd! This is definitely a useful tape," he added, nodding in the direction of the recorder.

Suddenly we heard the sound of Dolgo-Saburov's tape recorder being switched on. Here came the English lessons again. They weren't on for long this time, though. We could soon hear Natasha saying, "What's that?"

"It's English," came the reply. "I'm learning."

"God, you scared me!" Natasha said. "I didn't know whose voice it was. Listen, darling, I'll teach you English and French, don't worry. *Je veux traverser la frontière* ... Don't you have any music?"

"What did you say?" Dolgo-Saburov asked. He'd just

turned on some jazz, but not very loudly, and we could still catch what he was saying. In fact, with the jazz playing softly in the background, the whole conversation sounded more like a movie soundtrack than ever!

"I said: *Je veux traverser la frontière! Honte à vous, monsieur le comte!* I know French and English, Boris knows English, and even the old man, a convict, a professional crook, knows Azerbaidzhani! But you . . . What about all your nannies and governesses?"

"But that's the point," came the reply. "My governesses first got bumped off in 1917 and then they had a second crack at them in '37—before I was even born!"

"*À propos, mon chéri,* at least Soviet power has given me something. Without it I could only have been a nanny to your children, but now I have the chance of becoming a real countess."

Now that they had begun to talk about less important things, we were able to think about something else and analyze the information. So, the four of them—Dr. Boris (we did not know his last name, but in Belkin's manuscript he figures as Ziyalov), his sister Natasha, the old man (alias the Chief, or Semyon Gridasov) and Herman Dolgo-Saburov—each had a place in the gang that was selling drugs on the black market. The head of the gang was Viktor Sysoyev, who was also the head of the Chief Pharmaceutical Authority. Above him was somebody else called Balayan, and the involvement of even higher-placed officials couldn't be ruled out. Sysoyev seemed to look after the money. The scale of their drug-trafficking organization was enormous, as were the sums of money involved. These were converted either into jewels or hard currency, which was then, somehow or other, transferred abroad. We would have to pass this information on to Malenina and the KGB, of course—it was really their department. Meanwhile, my characters seemed to have had a little something going on the side. Unknown to their bosses, they had tried to move a coffin filled with drugs from Central Asia to Baku with a chance to make a million roubles from the deal. The reward was certainly worth the risk. The bosses didn't look kindly on such private enterprise, though: in that, Natasha was absolutely correct. So was Dolgo-Saburov. If he stayed in the USSR and was arrested, they would finish him off, no matter what camp he was sent to. "Traitors", informers or people who simply know too much are all treated the same way sooner or later. The Main Directorate of Corrective Labor Institutions is always receiving short messages such as, "Prisoner so-and-so died while felling trees through the misuse of mechanical equipment," or words to that effect.

So, I thought, if they really had found out from Sysoyev, while he was under hypnosis, that the big bosses had decided to liquidate them, then there was no hope for them inside the Soviet Union. In that case, we'd have to give special thought to the future of Akeyev. Whether we arrested the whole gang, or whether we wouldn't be allowed to touch the people right at the top and they would be given special treatment once again, we would have to fix Akeyev up in a special camp for high party workers. At least he'd have a quiet life there. Two such camps had been set up ten years ago. Although it isn't customary to talk about them, they do exist. After all, there has to be someplace you can lock up erring party workers, city council presidents and secretaries, militia chiefs, prosecutors and so on, when their misdemeanors become so obvious to the public that the CPSU Central Committee itself sanctions their arrest. To put them in ordinary prison camps would be tantamount to condemning them to death, because the other prisoners would finish them off before long. So it is that the privileged caste in our country even has its own privileged camps and prisons...

As far as Dolgo-Saburov and company were concerned, their part in the gang's activities seemed more or less clear. Dolgo-Saburov was one of the people who transported the drugs around the country. Gridasov organized a market for selling the merchandise in Baku. And Akeyev was the person used by Sysoyev to keep an eye on the criminal proceeds and on the drugs themselves as they were stolen from the pharmaceutical warehouses or brought up from the south. At the same time, he had involved his mistress, Lena Smagina, in the drug dealing, just as Dolgo-Saburov had involved Zoya, the woman from the Enchantress beauty salon.

As far as the doctor and his sister were concerned, though, we still had to work out their part in the whole affair. What was certain was that the frontier passes, which Belkin had so lightheartedly neglected to return to the Chief Border Police Authority in Tashkent, had fallen into their hands, probably in Baku, when they had disappeared from the airport carrying his identity papers. By the way, it was interesting that Belkin hadn't mentioned the disappearance of the frontier passes in his manuscript. Nice guy! But when their scheme to import extra opium in a coffin literally fell apart and the gang leaders had decided to deal with the problem their own way, then those border passes of Belkin's came in pretty handy. That was when they came up with the idea of stealing the diamonds belonging to the whole gang from the safe and escaping abroad with them. With this in mind, they lured Akeyev out of the apartment for a couple of hours and got him to go to the Prague restaurant. Meanwhile, they cleaned out the safe. One thief stealing from another! Aside from that—you might as well make hay while the sun shines!—Gridasov smothered the nephew's aunt to death in order to lay hands on the last (or rather, next-to-last) diamonds belonging to the Dolgo-Saburov family. After this, Gridasov flew to Uzbekistan where he made use of Belkin's passes to get to the airport at Charshanga. He'd probably altered the surname. The important thing was to have the pass itself, duly signed by the commander of the Border Regiment, Central Asia Military Region. For two hundred thousand roubles he'd also managed to bribe the chief officer at the frontier post or one of the helicopter pilots.

Maybe he'd bribed them all. After all, two hundred thou is a lot of money. The telegram reached Dolgo-Saburov while he was traveling on his train from Tashkent to Moscow. He could have gotten it at any of the stations *en route*. And that was why he had spent all day running around Moscow, putting together a hundred thousand roubles. He'd sold all the stocks of drugs that he had, and had probably wanted to get some more from the pharmaceutical warehouse to make more cash by the end of the day. He'd managed to collect ninety thousand, the doctor had forty thousand more, and he was supposed to arrive at his place no later than seven that evening, so as to fly to Gridasov in Central Asia. They wouldn't be traveling anywhere now, of course. When a detective is pitting his wits against those of a criminal, the most important thing is to keep a step ahead of your opponent. Over the last four days, apart from a few details, we'd gotten practically all we needed to know about this criminal gang, and in some respects we had more information than they did. For example, they didn't know anything about Akeyev's arrest yet, or that he had confessed everything. And they didn't realize that we were following Dolgo-Saburov's every step or that we were tailing him at that very moment. Through him we could finally get to this "genius" doctor who was trying to erase Belkin's memory.

Of course, we'd made a fair number of mistakes ourselves during the investigation, and we'd wasted a large amount of time with those stupid searches of Dolgo-Saburov's apartment and rail wagon. I could have kicked myself for missing the drugs concealed in the honeycombs, and the way we'd slipped up over the telegram that the old man had managed to send Dolgo-Saburov was inexcusable. The whole business with Irakly Golub had been a waste of time, too, and there were other things. Still, nothing ventured, nothing gained! And to make up for it we had some of Belkin's kidnappers in front of us. We could see them and hear what they were saying. We were following them at about half a mile's distance. We didn't want to get any closer in case they grew alarmed. And there they were leading us to their hideout. Soon we'd know the one thing we still didn't know—whether Belkin was alive, and, if so, where and in what condition. Still, don't be in too much of a hurry, Chief Prosecutor, you'll get them all in good time . . .

The rain was easing up as we sped down Sevastopol Prospect towards the outskirts of Moscow and the Outer Ring Road. Dolgo-Saburov and Natasha were seated comfortably in their car, listening to some cool jazz and making plans for their future life together in France. I soon realized that what they were most afraid of was not the actual crossing of the border, but what might happen to them during their first day in Afghanistan. They could easily get robbed, and, according to Natasha, the only thing that would save them was the fact that Gridasov and Boris had a knowledge of Azerbaidzhani, which for all intents and purposes was the same as Turkish. Even Natasha knew a little. She and her brother had grown up in Baku, after all.

"Well, that's not the only thing," Dolgo-Saburov said. "Look! I've got this nine-cylinder automatic with me, and that's no toy!"

"And what about me?" Natasha immediately exclaimed.

"You don't need one. The old man's got a Kalashnikov and Boris has a Tokaryov revolver, so we'll protect you somehow or other."

Svetlov looked at Captain Laskin and then at me. Frowning, he grabbed the radio telephone and said to the two police Volgas that were following us, "Attention! All men are to put on bullet-proof jackets and to have their weapons ready. There may be some shooting."

"Maybe we should wait until they start making love, Comrade Colonel," came a voice from one of the cars.

"I'll let you know when I want to hear a joke!" Svetlov replied.

Then he contacted the chief duty officer at Petrovka Operations. "Colonel Serebryannikov, I am in pursuit of two armed criminals. I am about to drive out of Moscow on the Kaluga Highway. It's not clear yet when and where we will arrest the gang. I'm on their tail right now, letting them lead us to their hideout. There may be gunfire during the actual arrest. Please have an ambulance sent immediately."

"Do you need more men?" asked the colonel, who was one of the old guard at CID headquarters.

"No, thank you. We'll manage. There are eight of us and only two of them. We should be able to do it."

"All the same, it would be better if you could avoid using firearms."

"I know."

"I'll have a helicopter flying overhead, just in case."

"There's no point, colonel. It may scare them."

"It'll be one belonging to the Transport Police. They've been circling over the Ring Road for years. Drivers are used to them."

"All right, only tell the pilot not to fly low, unless I give the order."

"Keep in direct contact from now on. Report back every minute."

The operation was nearing its climax, and I could imagine the scene at Operations. All those who had nothing else to do would be standing around the main radio console, listening to what was going on. Meanwhile, an ambulance was almost certainly on its way from the nearest hospital and a helicopter manned by armed CID men would presently take off from Domodedovo airport. Svetlov was now supposed to report on the progress of the operation every sixty seconds. The four men sitting at the back of the "repair van" had already donned their bullet-proof jackets and had released the safety catches on their revolvers. One of them offered a couple of jackets to Svetlov and me, and without saying a word, we put them on.

It was all very businesslike, one might almost say routine—even though the next few minutes might see all of us blasted into the next world or, at the very least, into the emergency room at the Sklifosovsky hospital. And in the background all the time we could hear cheerful jazz music coming from Dolgo-Saburov's blue Zhiguli sedan, which we could see traveling way ahead of us down the Kaluga Highway. I looked at my watch. It was twenty after six. I could hear the voice of Captain Serebryannikov saying, "Marat, an ambulance is on its way to you from the nearest hospital. It should be at your disposal in three or four minutes. The helicopter will arrive in about one minute. I have radio contact with both of them. Report on your situation."

"Everything is normal at the moment, Comrade Colonel. I am continuing to follow the suspects. We are now approaching the Ring Road, and the suspects are about to pass the State Automobile Inspection post at the exit to the city."

But Svetlov's tone of voice suddenly changed. "Fuck! What the hell's he doing?"

"What's wrong, Marat?" Serebryannikov asked anxiously.

"A fucking militiaman has stopped the suspects' car!" Svetlov shouted. "Colonel, call the Transport Police and tell them to stop him! Put the brakes on, Laskin!"

Laskin signaled to the drivers of the two following Volgas, and we all pulled over to the side of the road. Ahead of us something was happening that no one could have foreseen. The militiaman had been standing by the side of the road, waving Dolgo-Saburov's car down with his baton. Now he idly walked over to the Zhiguli and the usual policeman–driver exchange began.

"You were speeding, comrade."

"Oh no I wasn't, captain," Dolgo-Saburov replied, trying to sound innocent.

"Give him the three roubles," Natasha whispered.

"Look at this," said the captain, showing him the speed-trap. "You were doing thirty-three miles an hour and the speed limit is thirty. Are you going to pay the fine, or do I have to write a summons?"

"I'll pay now," Dolgo-Saburov said, without hesitating.

"Give him a ten-rouble note," Natasha whispered again.

"I will, I will, don't worry," Dolgo-Saburov said, just as softly. "Here you are, Comrade Captain."

"Let me see your papers," said the officer.

"Surely there's no need for that, captain. We're in a hurry, we really are! Here's a ten. There's no need to bother with a receipt, and I don't want the change."

"I want to see your papers—now," the captain said more harshly.

"Fuck it!" Svetlov shouted, hammering his fist against the car seat. "For Christ's sake, take the bribe, you son of a bitch! Take the bribe!"

Then he grabbed the microphone and shouted, "Colonel! What the hell is this traffic cop doing? Get someone to order him to take the bribe and let the Zhiguli go!"

"They're calling him now," Colonel Serebryannikov replied. "We'll get it fixed."

"Like hell! If they were calling him, he would have heard by now!"

"Come on!" the officer said. "I can hear my phone ringing. Or don't you have any papers?"

"What do you mean, captain? Of course I do! Here they are. It's just that we're in a hurry. I wish you'd taken the ten roubles."

"We'll take the money, all in good time, Comrade er . . . What's your name? Hmm . . . Dolgo-Saburov. That's interesting. Herman Veniaminovich Dolgo-Saburov. Another officer will be along in a moment. I'd like you to go with him to headquarters. They want to have a word with you ... OK, I'm coming, I'm coming," he said, in the direction of the telephone. "As for you," he said to Dolgo-Saburov, "drive off the road and pull up in front of the booth, as quickly as you can."

"All right ... !"

We saw the Zhiguli slowly move off the road to where the captain had directed. He, meanwhile, was heading towards his booth.

"That's it then," Natasha said. "We're caught."

"Don't worry," Dolgo-Saburov replied. "Don't look back. I can see him in the mirror."

"What are you going to do? Go to headquarters? He didn't say that by accident, you know ..."

"I'm not going anywhere," he said. "Don't worry."

Everybody's eyes were now fixed on the movements of the militiaman, ours from a distance, Dolgo-Saburov's from up close. There was nothing we could do. This over-efficient traffic cop had obviously remembered the signal that went out that morning about keeping an eye open for Dolgo-Saburov. It was an unusual name which must have stuck in his memory. As for the rest of the message, however—that the suspect was not to be apprehended, but merely have his whereabouts reported to CID Operations—it had completely evaporated during the course of a long and busy working day. It had been swallowed up in the routine mass of orders and instructions that a militiaman has to deal with. Who was there to complain to? The matter was in the hands of God—and Dolgo-Saburov. The moment the captain reached his booth and his back was turned to the Zhiguli, Dolgo-Saburov drove off as quickly and as quietly as he could. But the officer must have heard something, because he turned around and shouted something in the direction of the disappearing car. In another second or two, he would have had time to answer the telephone and then let Dolgo-Saburov go, after extracting the relevant fine. In that case, things would have turned out differently for everybody, but there we were ...

"Ha ha, you son of a bitch! You won't get anything on

us!" Dolgo-Saburov shouted exultantly, as his car flew down the highway at top speed. The militia officer immediately jumped on his motorcycle and took off in pursuit.

"Goddammit!" Svetlov said, enraged. "The whole operation's fucked!" He ordered Laskin to follow Dolgo-Saburov and the militiaman.

"Svetlov, give us a report on what's happening," a voice said over the radio. "The traffic inspection post isn't replying!"

"What is there to tell you?" Svetlov said angrily. "It's all fucked up! That idiot cop has left his post and gone after the suspects on his bike. They are armed and may take a shot at him any second. The whole operation's been a waste of time. We'll have to reveal our presence so the criminals know it's useless to shoot. Where's that helicopter of yours?"

"It should be almost with you. Give me your bearings and a description of the suspects' car."

"We're on the Kaluga Highway, south of the Ring Road. In front of us is a dark-blue Zhiguli sedan. Then there's the motorcycle, then our repair van, and finally two black Volgas. Only tell the men in the helicopter not to take aim at the driver and his passenger. We need them alive!"

"OK. Can you see the chopper yet?"

Approaching at low altitude from the south we could see a MIL-6 helicopter heading towards us. "Yes."

Meanwhile, the gap between the Zhiguli and the motorcycle was closing. From Dolgo-Saburov's car we could hear the sound of a verbal struggle.

"Don't shoot him!"

"Don't interfere!" Dolgo-Saburov said grimly.

"Don't shoot, Herman!"

"Don't interfere, I said! Keep your hands away!"

Laskin had his foot firmly on the accelerator, and we were doing well over 85 m.p.h. as Svetlov switched on the siren. The two police Volgas had supercharged engines, so they had already overtaken us and drawn up next to the motorcycle. The captain looked around him in amazement. He probably realized that he had an important customer on his hands, so he redoubled his efforts and increased his speed.

Dolgo-Saburov's car had reached a speed of 90 m.p.h. The other cars on the highway kept out of the way of the chase. Our vehicles came closer and closer together, while the helicopter flew overhead to help, if need be.

Suddenly, we heard Dolgo-Saburov speaking again. "Turn off that fucking jazz, for Christ's sake!"

The music suddenly stopped and we could hear Natasha's voice. "Look! Look how many there are! Don't shoot, you fool!"

Suddenly we heard a shot. The noise of Dolgo-Saburov firing came over the radio. But he missed his target. He was simply shooting over the shoulder at random, simultaneously keeping one hand on the steering wheel and his foot on the accelerator. Natasha was in hysterics.

"Herman, Herman! What are you doing? We'll be killed! Stop!"

"Shut up, you slut!"

"Herman! I'm begging you! Darling, please! Look, there's a helicopter above us too. We're surrounded . . . Stop!!"

"Like hell I will! Did you sleep with Balayan? I bet you did! And with Sysoyev? And with Vekilov in Baku! You'd go to bed with those pigs to save your brother! It's too late now! We're going to die, the two of us!"

Between us, the Volgas and the motorcycle, we had Dolgo-Saburov's car hemmed in, with the chopper thundering along just over our heads. Over the radio Svetlov kept shouting, "Don't shoot! Don't shoot!" The Zhiguli suddenly lurched sharply to the left and was heading towards a dump truck coming along on the opposite side of the highway. By some miracle the terrified truck driver managed to avoid a head-on collision at the last moment. The truck careened off the road and turned over on its side. The helicopter immediately flew ahead, one of the CID men in it using a loudspeaker to halt all traffic on the highway. We could hear Natasha's heart-rending scream of terror as Dolgo-Saburov drove full speed into the next vehicle coming along the road, a cement-mixer crawling slowly along in the outer lane.

We were traveling at such a speed ourselves that we shot right past the place where the accident happened, but Laskin slammed on the brakes and we swung back in a U-turn.

The cement-mixer was leaning to its side and under its wheels we could see all that was left of the Zhiguli and its two passengers—part of the back section, which had squashed on impact, and a heap of twisted metal, bits of body and human intestine. There was blood everywhere. A few drops of gasoline were dripping onto the asphalt from the wreckage of the engine.

The helicopter landed a few yards away, and the CID men who had been flying in it ran towards us. Inquisitive drivers and passengers, halted by the accident, were running up from all sides. Some ways off the ambulance had arrived and the medical orderlies were busying themselves with the driver of the overturned dump truck. The terrified young driver of the cement-mixer was slowly picking his way out of his cab. When he saw the mish-mash of mangled bodies and metal under his truck, he rushed to the side of the road to be sick.

The militia captain had tried to do an about-turn but had driven his bike into a ditch. He got off the ground, switched off his engine and slowly limped towards us. He was as white as a sheet, and his lips looked gray without a trace of blood in them. As he looked at the remains of the Zhiguli he couldn't help saying, "What a bastard!"

"You're a fool, captain," Svetlov said quietly.

Then he turned to Laskin and myself. "There's nothing else for us to do here. Let's go. We must arrest the people who bought drugs off him today, and as quickly as possible. One of them may know who the doctor is. Am I right?" he asked, addressing himself to me.

I nodded in agreement. I wanted to get away as quickly as possible anyway. I've seen enough things in my time. I've been in any number of morgues, and visiting the scenes of fires, accidents and catastrophes in general is part of my job. All the same, to hear two people talking to each other one minute—about their love, their jealousy, their plans for the future—and to see a shapeless mass of twisted metal and mangled human remains the next . . . I can hear the girl's final, despairing scream ringing in my ears to this day.

*20:42 hours*
Major Ozherelyev would be waiting for us in the Incident

Room, but I left for there alone. Svetlov, Laskin and the others went directly to the Arbat and all the other addresses which Dolgo-Saburov had visited during the day to sell drugs. There were at least seventeen people for them to arrest, including Zoya the Enchantress, and if any one of them were to confess right away and start naming names, there would be even more dealers to nab. If they had known Dolgo-Saburov, it was difficult to believe they wouldn't also know this "Dr." Boris, and at least be able to tell us his surname, where he lived, where he worked.

It had been quite a day! It had started at five in the morning with the search of Dolgo-Saburov's sleeping car. Then I had visited Anti-Fraud Squad headquarters, and searched Dolgo-Saburov's apartment for the second time. After that there had been the whole business with the arrest of Akeyev and his mistress, Lena Smagina. And just when we thought that we were on the point of arresting the doctor and discovering the actual whereabouts of Belkin, everything had gone wrong. Dolgo-Saburov had killed himself and Natasha. Where did that leave us? We were going to have to start all over again, beginning with the cross-examination of Dolgo-Saburov's former customers in the hope of building a verbal picture of the doctor. Then we'd need to show the resulting identikit picture around every hospital and clinic in Moscow and the surrounding region. He was twenty-seven years old (the same as Belkin) and trained as either a psychiatrist, a psychotherapist or an anesthetist. It was enough to go on, but not if you needed to find your suspect within the next twenty-four hours!

And one day was practically all we had at our disposal— two days at the most.

Dolgo-Saburov had said to Natasha that Boris had warned them not to arrive later than seven o'clock or they'd miss the plane. He would hardly fly off now without the other two. But on the other hand, if he had anybody else like "Katyukha" to tip him off, then he'd find out about the car accident by either tomorrow or the next day. In that case, he wouldn't show up at any of the airports in Moscow. He'd fly to Central Asia, from Kiev, Leningrad, Rostov, Perm or somewhere like that—and just try to find him then! All the same, while Svetlov was on his way back from the scene of the accident, he had used the radio telephone to contact the airport police at Vnukovo, Domodedovo and Bykovo. He had asked them to check on all flights to Central Asia and had given them as much information about our Dr. Boris as he could, while also mentioning that the good doctor would most probably be traveling under an assumed name.

Arresting Dolgo-Saburov's drug contacts and placing a check on flights to Central Asia was all well and good, but *...we were running out of time*! We couldn't wait for the mountain to travel to Muhammad. We had to come up with a new approach. But what?

I arrived at the Incident Room feeling irritable and depressed by what I had just witnessed on the Kaluga Highway. Ozherelyev and Malenina were waiting for me. Malenina seemed elated. The first day of her search at the pharmaceutical warehouses had revealed that ten percent of the morphine ampoules, awaiting release in cases to various military and civilian hospitals, were missing. One of the warehousemen had already confessed that ampoules were removed and the cases repacked at the stores themselves. She had been looking for me during the past hour to tell me of her success. Pshenichny had let her know that we had arrested Akeyev, and she couldn't wait any longer. She wanted to immediately cross-examine the boxer concerning dealings arranged by his boss, the director of the Chief Pharmaceutical Authority.

Meanwhile, Major Ozherelyev, having just returned from searching Sysoyev's dacha, was able to tell us the following:

"The dacha was empty, Comrade Shamrayev. Empty of people, that is. It was full of clothes, Persian carpets and expensive furniture. There was a stereo record player, a color television, a cassette tape recorder and piles of records and tapes. The refrigerator was full to overflowing, and there was enough booze in the cocktail cabinet to keep a party going for days. To judge from the amount of dirty laundry left in the kitchen, they must have held a party for about twenty people before the owner left. There was lipstick on the glasses, and all the sheets in the bedroom showed signs of a wild orgy. I've had all the glasses and crockery sent away to be tested for fingerprints, of course. Meanwhile, I found the hiding place in the garage, the one mentioned by Akeyev, but it was empty. There were two mattresses in the garage as well, and I would guess that they had been slept on by Belkin and Rybakov. I found some rope, too. It looks as if they were tied up. The garage is made of brick and is some distance from the dacha itself. You could hold someone prisoner there for a month and nobody would know. All you'd have to do would be to stuff something in his mouth to stop him from screaming. But the most interesting discovery was this cassette. We spent more than three hours searching the place, and had the tape recorder going the whole time. It was a shame not to listen to such good equipment, you know . . . When we suddenly found this. Listen to it yourself."

Ozherelyev inserted the cassette into a portable tape recorder and turned it on, while Pshenichny, Malenina, myself and Baklanov (he had finished his own case and had been hanging around waiting for me to turn up) listened to the energetic voice of a young man:

". . . sixteen glaciologists plus workers. Any of them can go down into Charshanga or Dzharkurgan. Why shouldn't they? There's nobody to stop them. The frontier zone is like anywhere else. People live there, and there's a market and there's stores. The only thing is you need a pass to get into the area in the first place."

"Is the aerodrome very far?" asked the voice of another man.

"No, it's right in Charshanga itself. The street comes to an end, and the aerodrome starts. It's just an ordinary airfield with poppies growing around . . ."

"Is it protected in any way? Are there any guards?"

"Not really. It is an agricultural airfield, after all. There's an old man on crutches who hangs around. He's from the collective farm. And the Border Regiment has one solider on duty there. There are planes all over the place, and somebody can always hop off over the border. In theory, at any rate."

"And in practice?"

"Well, that's not so easy. You'd need to know the password. There are electronic detection devices all along the border. Before you knew where you were, they'd send up a ground-to-air missile, and that'd be the end of you!"

"But do the pilots know the passwords?"

"Well, the military pilots do, of course."

"And how far away is the military airfield?"

"It's very close. About two miles. Though I've never been to it myself..."

"You say that there are electronic detectors all along the border. Where do the men who operate them and the missiles go when they're off duty?"

"What do you mean? There's nowhere for them *to* go. There's a cinema and the occasional dance, but nothing else."

"How about the officers?"

"It's the same for them. Oh, I see. You want to skip abroad and you're wondering how to do it! Well, it's quite simple. There are plenty of Koreans living near the border with Afghanistan. There are whole state farms run by them, producing practically nothing except opium poppies. But then you know that yourself, I suppose. After all, you brought a coffin filled with the stuff back to Baku! These Koreans are always popping over the border into Afghanistan, taking their opium with them. And the border guards shut their eyes to it. I got blind drunk with the chief officer at the frontier post one night, and he told me all about it. The Koreans flog their opium in Afghanistan for hard currency. Then they bring the money home and get it converted into roubles. That way everybody makes a profit—the state, and the drug smugglers. They've got their own weapons and everything! I could have written a fantastic article about it, only it would never have gotten past the censorship. That's about it. Crossing the frontier is a piece of cake! All you need is to slit your eyes like the Koreans! Ha-ha-ha!" The speaker couldn't help laughing at his own joke. But his laughter seemed overdone somehow, overexcited like the rest of his conversation.

"And what's the name of this officer?"

"Major Ryskulov. Only don't think that you'll be able

to bribe *him*! He's amazing! He can toss a coin in the air and shoot a hole right through it with his revolver. He gave me one of their sheepdogs as a present, but what was I going to do with a dog? I spend all my time flying around the country. Do you think I could have another little injection? I can feel the high already beginning to go . . ."

Ozherelyev stopped the cassette recorder.

"Unfortunately, that's all there is, Igor Iosifovich," he said. "We turned the place upside down to see if there wasn't some more of it somewhere, but there wasn't. Akeyev has identified the voices as those of Belkin and of the doctor they call Boris."

A few hours earlier, I thought, and this cassette would have been really useful. Now it could tell us practically nothing that we didn't know already. In fact, we knew a good deal more. We knew that Gridasov had already entered the frontier zone, for example, and that he had succeeded in bribing somebody for two hundred thousand roubles— possibly some of the helicopter pilots, possibly some of the border guards and perhaps even Major Ryskulov. Belkin's voice had sounded spontaneous and relaxed, if a little overexcited. But even that wasn't of any great interest now. The tape was old. It must have been made before May 26, the day Rybakov was murdered, because after that the criminals had quit the dacha, taking Belkin with them. But where was he now and what had happened to him? Was he alive? Did he have any memory left? The one thing that Ozherelyev's tape proved was that Boris, the leader of the ring, knew how to loosen somebody's tongue through hypnosis or drugs, or perhaps a combination of the two. After all, Belkin was hardly likely to have told him all that about the border if he'd been in his right mind, just as Sysoyev would scarcely have told the doctor the combination of his own safe of his own free will.

I wondered whether there was any news from Baku. (There wasn't.) Then I stopped by the buffet to eat some sausages and yogurt and made my way to the Petrovka's cell-block to cross-examine Akeyev. Malenina insisted on coming with me.

*Secret*

### TRANSCRIPT OF THE INTERROGATION
### OF SUSPECT AKEYEV

June 7 1979
Moscow

I, V. M. Akeyev, have been informed that I am held on suspicion of kidnapping Citizens V. B. Belkin and Yu. A. Rybakov, of murdering Citizen Yu. A. Rybakov and of acquiring and selling narcotic substances without special permission.

(Signed) V. Akeyev

INVESTIGATOR'S QUESTION: You are being shown three photographs. Tell me whether you recognize any of these men?

ANSWER: I recognize the man in photograph number two. It's Vadim Belkin. He was the one we kidnapped at the Kursk railroad station.

Q: Are you sure?

A: Yes.

Q: Now look at these other four photographs. Do you recognize any of the people?

A: Yes. Number seven is the Old Man, and number nine is Herman Dolgo-Saburov.

Q: I am now going to show you some ordinary snapshots. Do you recognize anybody in them? And where do you think these photos were taken?

A: I recognize Herman Dolgo-Saburov and his former mistress, Zoya, who works in the Enchantress hair salon. The photographs were taken at the very beginning of May—May 1, I think—on the Black Sea coast. Sochi. Dolgo-Saburov showed me them himself.

Q: Do you recognize anybody else in these photographs?

A: No, nobody else.

Q: What do you know about the events that took place on May 24 at the Kursk railroad station in Moscow?

Give us a detailed description of the kidnapping of Belkin and Rybakov.

A: On May 24 I was on duty at Sysoyev's dacha. I've been working for him for more than three years, since before I got sent to prison. I used to guard the drugs and valuables which he had in his possession, and sometimes I used to transport them for him. He started off by paying me twenty-five roubles a day, then this went up to fifty. He first employed me in 1976 after I had knocked out my opponent in the European boxing championship. He wanted a personal bodyguard. When I got sentenced for starting a fight in the Sokilniki beer-bar, he was very upset about it. If it hadn't been for a report in *Komsomolskaya Pravda* headlined *Boxing Champion Flies into a Rage,* he would have managed to get the whole thing hushed up and I wouldn't have been sent to prison. The Sports Committee petitioned on my behalf, too.

Q: Come back to the events of May 24, please. Why were you in Moscow and what part did you play in kidnapping Belkin? Let me remind you that your direct participation in the crime has been corroborated by the witnesses Sinitsyn and Silinya, both of whom recognized you.

A: I understand. I was sent to Moscow by the company building a new chemical plant in Kotlas. They employed me as a "fixer." I was supposed to get the ministry to provide spare parts for bulldozers, cement-mixers and other heavy equipment. As a well-known boxer, it was an easy matter for me to soft-talk the women who work in the accounting and planning departments. My former boss, Sysoyev, found out that I was in Moscow and suggested that I start working for him again. I said yes, of course, and he managed to get my trip to Moscow officially extended there and then at the Ministry of Industrial Construction. So it was all totally legal. On May 24th, as I've already said, I was on duty at Sysoyev's dacha, looking after the place and especially the drugs, which he'd removed from the warehouse and brought along in his

own car. At ten o'clock that morning he'd called from
town to tell me that two men, Herman and another
person, would be arriving soon to pick me up. I was
to get the two suitcases with the drugs out of the secret
hiding place and go along with them wherever they
went. Sure enough, an ambulance arrived, driven by
Herman Dolgo-Saburov, whom I'd known for a long
time. Traveling with him was Boris.

Q: Describe his appearance.

A: He's about medium height, kind of pampered-looking,
and even a little on the fat side. He's got a heavy,
round face with dark, penetrating eyes and black hair.
He dresses well in imported clothes, and wears a gold
signet ring.

Q: Is he Russian or Azerbaidzhani?

A: Russian.

Q: Where did you go when you left the dacha?

A: They told me that we had to go to the Kursk station
to meet the train from Baku. Someone called the Old
Man was supposed to be arriving with a hundred thousand roubles in a suitcase. We'd give him the merchandise, and he'd give us the cash. As usual, I was
supposed to do the actual handing over.

Q: What happened at the station?

A: When we arrived, I stayed in the ambulance with the
goods, while Herman and the doctor went off to meet
the Baku train. Then, according to their story, the
following happened. The money wasn't being carried
from Baku to Moscow by the Old Man himself, but
by this young guy, nicknamed Sultan, and his girl,
who knew nothing about the whole operation. But the
Old Man had traveled up by the same train, only in
a different compartment. It would have been dangerous for him to carry the loot himself since the police
were on the lookout for him across the whole country.
So, without telling Sultan, the Old Man had followed
him secretly the whole way from Baku and was going
to meet him on the platform. Then we were supposed
to exchange the goods and Sultan was to take it all
back to Baku, with the Old Man keeping an eye on

him from a distance. But when the Old Man, the doctor and Herman went to Sultan's wagon, they could see that he was being met by Belkin. Herman overheard Belkin trying to persuade Sultan to go along with him to the newspaper office and spill the beans about the drugs operation, the Old Man and everything.

Q: How did Sultan, that is Yury Rybakov, react to Belkin's suggestion?

A: I don't know, and it really didn't matter. If he'd already let the cat out of the bag to Belkin, that meant that he could do the same to somebody else. So they left Herman standing near Sultan, Belkin and the girl, while the Old Man and the doctor rushed back to the ambulance. They told me that we'd have to grab all three of them now: Sultan, his girl and the journalist. I said that we couldn't do it, not in broad daylight and with so many people around. We'd have to wait for the right moment. They reckoned we wouldn't get another chance, though, as the journalist would probably drive Sultan over to the newspaper office. And that would be the end of everything. In any case, the doctor said that he had some other things to talk over with the journalist. So he and I both put on white jackets. We had to pretend to be medical orderlies from a mental hospital, trying to pick up three inmates who had escaped. We drove right up to the taxi stand where Sultan, Belkin and the girl were waiting. Then Herman and I threw ourselves on top of Belkin and held his arms, while the Old Man and the doctor grabbed Sultan and the girl. The two men were so surprised at what was happening that they made no attempt at resisting. We simply threw them into the ambulance. But the girl bit the doctor in the arm and ran off. I wanted to go after her, but a traffic policeman appeared at that moment, and we drove away as quickly as we could. On the way the doctor changed the license plates just in case, though nobody was following us.

Q: Where did you take the two men?

A: We went to Sysoyev's dacha. I forgot to tell you that we also grabbed Sultan's suitcase with the money, and it was all there. That evening the boss arrived, and they decided what to do with Sultan and the correspondent. The boss said we had no choice. Since we'd been stupid enough to bring them to his dacha, they'd have to be bumped off. But the doctor reckoned that was nonsense. In three weeks he'd be able to erase whatever he wanted from their memories. The boss didn't like the idea. But he said he'd take the advice and let them know what he had decided at his party on Saturday.

Q: What party was this?

A: The boss always has a party before he goes abroad. On May 28 he was due to head a delegation to Geneva, so he arranged a big party for Saturday—orgy, more like. The doctor brought some nurses along from his hospital.

Q: Which hospital?

A: I don't know. I wish I did!

Q: All right. Who was present at this "orgy"?

A: The boss, Dr. Boris, the Old Man and five guests of Sysoyev's. I didn't know them.

Q: Describe them.

A: I didn't see them myself. I was in the garage guarding Belkin and Sultan. But the Old Man was at the party. He told me that two of the guests were from Baku. They'd come for the diamonds they'd been promised as a pay-off for hushing up the incident with the coffin. So at the beginning of the party Sysoyev and the doctor came into the garage, got the diamonds out of the hiding place and put them in the document case that they had ready for the two Azerbaidzhanis. Meanwhile, the boss was swearing away at the doctor, while Boris was begging Sysoyev not to be in such a hurry to hand over the diamonds. He reckoned that he might be able to persuade them to take the money instead. So they went out with the document case. They took the suitcase with the two hundred thousand roubles with them too, just in case. Then the Old Man told me what a good time everybody was having across the way. The party was going very well. The doctor hadn't just brought a few nurses with him, he'd brought some laughing gas as well. You know, the kind people are given when they're having an operation or in labor. When they'd had enough brandy, the doctor tried out the gas and they had an orgy, group sex. The Azerbaidzhanis had never seen anything like it before! Then, at about ten o'clock, the two visitors left with the money instead of the diamonds. They had to get to the airport to catch the last flight to Baku.

Meanwhile the boss was having a really good time with two of the nurses. The doctor arranged a hypnosis session with the others trying to guess each other's thoughts and telling things about themselves that they would never have revealed in normal circumstances. I was able to see some of that for myself, because the Old Man had come to relieve me by this time. When I walked into the dacha, the nurses were sitting there stark naked, smoking hash and telling the others things I've never heard in my life before. By this time the boss was completely drunk and he wanted to unburden himself too. But the doctor took him into a separate room in case something slipped out that wasn't for the nurses' ears. Sysoyev was very grateful to the doctor for saving the diamonds and palming the two Azerbaidzhanis off with paper money. About eleven, the doctor drove off with three of the nurses, leaving another two to spend the night with the boss. The three of them went off to the summer house, completely naked, while I started to clean up the mess in the dacha. I could hear them singing some pretty bawdy songs through the window. Then they all started making love together. Then the boss insisted on showing them the diamonds and taking the two of them out for a joyride in the car. The nurses were very young, probably not more than eighteen years old. But that's how Sysoyev likes them. He's fifty-seven himself. All three of them turned up at the garage, Sysoyev carrying the document case with the diamonds and wanting to drive off in the car. But the Old Man tried to persuade him not to. Sysoyev hit him in the face and opened the garage doors himself, leaving the document case lying on the hood of the Volga. Then Sultan somehow untied the rope and jumped up out of the pit.

Q: So Belkin and Rybakov were tied up in a pit. What kind of a pit was it?

A: An inspection pit. Just for repairs, you know, so that you can get to see the underneath of the car. The two of them were lying there bound and gagged. Usually they were pretty quiet, though, because the doctor used to calm them down with an injection.

Q: What sort of injection?

A: He used various powerful drugs. So I don't understand how Sultan managed to untie the rope and jump up out of the pit. Perhaps because the doctor hadn't given him an injection that night. Either he'd forgotten, or he'd been too busy at the party. Anyway, by the end of the evening he looked pretty irritable and depressed . . .

Q: When did he become "irritable and depressed", as you put it—before the hypnotism session with Sysoyev, or after?

A: After. Why do you ask?

Q: What form did this irritability take?

A: After Sysoyev had had his heart-to-heart talk, the doctor rushed out of the room into the kitchen and swigged down half a tumbler of brandy in one go. I told him that we ought to make the boss get dressed now, but he started to swear at me and him.

Q: Please return to your description of how Rybakov managed to escape.

A: When the boss opened the garage and had the argument with the Old Man, Sultan suddenly jumped out of the pit and ran off into the bushes. The Old Man went after him, but how was he going to catch somebody like Sultan? Then the boss noticed that the boy had grabbed the document case which had been lying on the Volga. I started the car and drove off in pursuit, with the Old Man sitting beside me. It was midnight now and the boy had nowhere else to run to, except the railroad station. He managed to take a short cut there, though—past the Tsaritsyno Ponds and the ruins of Catherine the Great's palace. We had to drive the long way around so he reached the station before we did. There was an old night watchman there. We gave him a tip, and he told us that the boy had climbed into a freight train carrying new Zhiguli cars. The train had just begun to move out of the station towards Moscow. We jumped on it ourselves, and began to run up and down the cars, looking for Sultan. I headed towards the back of the train, while the Old Man took the front. But I couldn't find anything, and I was just about to walk back when I suddenly saw the two of them fighting in the front car. I started running towards them. The train happened to be crossing a bridge over the Moscow River at that point, and I was afraid the two of them might fall into the river. But by the time I got there, the train had crossed the bridge and the Old Man had smashed Sultan on the head and hurled him off the car. About a mile or so down the line the train stopped at the signals. The two of us were able to slip off and make our way back up the track to look for the document case with the diamonds. We walked back as far as Tsaritsyno station, but found nothing, except for Sultan's corpse. The Old Man had a good look at it to make sure that he was really dead and checked through all his pockets. Then we left the body where it was lying. We thought about hiding it or dragging it back to our car. But that was parked a couple of miles away and it would have been dangerous to do so. We decided it was better to leave it where it was. Let people think that he had fallen off the train. At least a hundred trains go by that spot every night, after all.

Q: Tell me when and where Belkin was taken after being at the dacha.

A: He was taken away the same day, or actually the next morning. Sysoyev went nuts when the Old Man and

I arrived without Sultan and without the document case. He was already dressed, and there were no nurses left by then. I don't know where they went. Maybe they went home by train. The point is that he was now in the dacha by himself, and he blamed the Old Man for the whole business. The Old Man reckoned that the boss was to blame for it himself. It was really stupid of him to have opened the garage and left the diamonds on top of the hood of the car. Anyway, they really yelled at each other. In the end, the boss said he had no time to deal with it now, but as soon as he got back from his foreign trip he'd settle everything with the Old Man and the doctor. Meanwhile, the money and valuables still at the dacha—including everybody's share—were to be taken back to his Moscow apartment as quickly as possible. The dacha would be vacated. So he called the doctor and told him to come over as quickly as he could to pick up the Old Man and the correspondent. He wasn't bothered about where they were taken. Then we emptied the secret hiding place in the garage of everything, including the iron box of diamonds and a couple of sacks of money—one full of dollars, the other roubles. We placed everything in the trunk of the Volga, and the boss ordered me not to take my eyes off it for a second. An hour later the doctor arrived. He and the Old Man put the correspondent in a car and drove off. Sysoyev and I locked up the dacha, and then we left, too.

Q: Where did you go?

A: To the boss's place in Moscow, where you arrested me today.

Q: Did you see the doctor and the Old Man again?

A: No.

Q: Why did you agree to go to a restaurant with the doctor's sister and your girlfriend, if Sysoyev had ordered you to stay in his apartment and guard the safe containing the valuables?

A: Because I was fed up with sitting around. It was like being in prison again, or even worse. At least you've got some people to talk to in the camp, but there I was completely on my own without even a stoolie to talk to. Apart from that, I wasn't afraid of leaving the apartment for two or three hours. The whole building is occupied by high government officials, so who's going to rob it? In any case, you'd have to know the combination of the safe. There's no other way of opening it. So I'm telling you again that Sysoyev took the diamonds himself and has gone abroad with them. Mark my words, he won't come back. Meanwhile, he left me behind guarding an empty safe so the rest of the gang wouldn't smell a rat.

Q: Did this doctor visit the dacha when Sysoyev wasn't there, to interrogate Belkin?

A: Yes, the doctor came calling every other day after we'd kidnapped Belkin and Sultan. He used to inject them with drugs and they'd sing all day, from dawn to dusk.

Q: What do you mean "sing"?

A: I'm sorry. I mean that they'd tell him everything he wanted to know. There are special injections to make people do it, but I've forgotten what it's called. Inhibition, or something...

Q: [MAJOR MALENINA]: Amytal-caffeine disinhibition?

A: Yes, that's it, I think.

Q: Were you present at any of the conversations or interrogations?

A: No, I wasn't. The doctor wouldn't allow anybody else to attend. He'd record everything on cassette and then let the Old Man listen to a few extracts. They wanted to find out what Sultan had blabbed to Belkin, and what Belkin had told other people or written for his newspaper.

Q: How do you know that this was what they were trying to find out?

A: They told me so themselves.

Q: Did the doctor's sister, Natasha, have a sexual relationship with your boss, Sysoyev?

A: I can't say for sure, although the boss did once tell me that he had slept with her. That was why he got her brother a residence permit in Moscow.

Q: Who is Balayan?

A: Balayan is the USSR Deputy Minister of Health.

Q: What connection does he have with the criminal actions of Sysoyev and others? How is he connected with the theft and illegal sale of narcotics?

A: I can't answer these questions.

Q: You can't answer them, or you don't want to?

A: I know that I have the right to refuse to give evidence. For this reason I refuse to answer that question.

Q: During your last meeting with your mistress Smagina at Sysoyev's apartment, a few minutes before your arrest, you were heard to tell her that your boss had connections with some extremely influential people, if not with government ministers and members of the CPSU Central Committee. Whom did you have in mind?

A: I refuse to answer that question, too!

Q: Can you tell us why you refuse to answer these particular questions?

A: Because if I were to name names, your hair would stand on end, and I'd be dead before I reached camp.

Q: After your trial it would be possible to send you to a special camp for former government and party officials. Ordinary criminals wouldn't be able to get you there.

A: That may be, but the former government and party officials sure could! No, I've already told you more than I should—out of spite, because Sysoyev left me guarding an empty safe. I can't understand why you don't let the KGB in on it. They could catch him while he's in the West. Please have this request of mine entered in the report.

Q: Very well, that will be done. Can you tell us whether Balayan had a sexual relationship with the doctor's sister?

A: I can't answer that question, either. I simply don't know.

Q: Did Natasha visit Sysoyev's dacha while Belkin and Rybakov were there?

A: No.

Q: [MAJOR MALENINA]: How long has the theft of drugs at the Central Pharmaceutical warehouse been going on?

A: I've been working for my boss for three years, and I know that we've been receiving drugs from the warehouse during all that time. What used to happen before I started working for him, I don't know.

The duty guard officer suddenly looked in at the door. "Comrade Investigator, you're wanted on the phone at the Incident Room."

We had to interrupt the interrogation. Besides, it was nearly 10:45 p.m. and you're not allowed to prolong the cross-examination of suspects and prisoners beyond eleven. Malenina and I left the prison block and walked across the dark inner courtyard. She headed for the exit and I walked towards the Incident Room.

I could see the tiny red pinpoints of cigarettes as I walked past the smoking room, and I could hear a voice saying, "They were screwing for an hour and twenty minutes with the whole CID listening over the radio. Then Shcholokov walks in, the Interior Minister . . ."

I grinned and thought to myself, So that's how legends are created! Then I entered the Operations Section.

The corridor on the first floor was full of people. More than forty people were sitting or standing around waiting to enter the cross-examination rooms, like patients at a dental clinic. I asked the guard what was going on. It turned out that these were the drug dealers arrested in connection with the Dolgo-Saburov affair. They had been brought in from all over downtown Moscow.

I walked up to the Incident Room on the second floor. An exhausted Colonel Serebryannikov nodded towards the telephone receiver lying on a table next to his desk.

"Some woman has been trying to reach you. She says it's urgent."

"Who is she?"

"Someone from *Komsomolskaya Pravda*. She won't give her name."

I picked up the receiver.

"Hello. Shamrayev here."

"Igor Iosifovich?"

"Yes."

"Good evening. Sorry to disturb you. This is Inna, the typist from *Komsomolskaya Pravda*. Do you remember?"

"Of course I do. Has something happened?"

"I've got some important news about Vadim."

"I'm listening."

"I can't tell you on the phone. You've got to come here, so I can talk to you in private. Can you come right away? Or else he'll have to fly back."

"Do I have to come on my own?"

"Well, I'm not sure," she replied hesitantly. "I'll ask. Who do you want to come with?"

"Some friends of mine."

There was a moment's silence. She had obviously placed her hand over the mouthpiece so I could hear nothing of what was being said at her end of the line. Then I heard her voice again.

"Igor Iosifovich, he'd rather talk to you by yourself. But if you insist . . ."

"No, of course not. I was simply checking to make sure you weren't being threatened."

"Oh, no, certainly not! I can trust him. It's just that he's afraid . . . I can't tell you over the phone. Please, come—now! It's important."

"I'm on my way. What's your address again?"

"No. 17, 12 Parkovaya Street, Apartment 73, and in case you need it, the phone number is . . ."

I left the number with Colonel Serebryannikov and told him I would be there for about a half-hour. Then I went downstairs to my car. As I was walking down the corridor on the first floor, I suddenly stopped. Svetlov was addressing the assembled company of drug dealers in the following highly original manner:

"Today each of you received a consignment of drugs from Herman Dolgo-Saburov. That is why you have been detained and you will be charged under Article 224 of the Criminal Code. However, we are not allowed to question you after 11 p.m. It is now 10:56. That is to say, in three or four minutes you will all be taken to cells in the Petrovka prison-block and the cross-examinations will continue tomorrow. However, we need to get certain information now, urgently. We are looking for a dangerous criminal, and anybody who helps us catch him will be able to leave here very quickly with no charges brought. This criminal is a friend of Dolgo-Saburov's called Boris. He is a doctor, twenty-seven years of age, who arrived in Moscow from Baku a couple of years ago and has been working since then either as a psychiatrist, or as a psychotherapist, or as an anesthetist. I give you my word as an officer that anybody who can tell me his present whereabouts, or at least give me his surname and place of work, will be able to leave here a free man. I'll even get a squad car to take him back to where he lives."

Yes, that sounds like Svetlov! He's not allowed to cross-examine prisoners after eleven o'clock, but doing a deal with them is an entirely different matter. There was no time for us to stand on ceremony, of course. The week the Chief Prosecutor had given us was ticking away, and there was still no sign of Belkin.

Svetlov waited for an answer, but none of the suspects said a word. Some of them shrugged their shoulders, or exchanged glances, while others did nothing and simply kept staring gloomily at their feet.

"All right," said Svetlov. "Let's do it another way, just in case somebody knows something but is afraid of telling me in front of the others. Each of you will have one chance to go from his cell to the latrines. On the way there, you can let the guard know and he will summon the duty investigator, Comrade Pshenichny, and tell him. And don't forget: it's a good offer. We really need to find this doctor. Anybody who can truly help us will have much to be grateful for, I promise you. That's all. Guards, take them away."

The guards started to lead the prisoners away to the prison-block where Malenina and I had just been questioning Akeyev. Svetlov sat down on a chair in the corridor and said, "OK, that's it! My last ounce of energy! I need someone to take me to my cot, or I'll go to sleep right here."

"There is something else you could do," I said. "You can come along with me to visit one of Vadim Belkin's female acquaintances. She has some news for us."

Svetlov gave me a questioning look, but I didn't try to explain.

"Get up," I said. "Let's go. You can catch forty winks in the car."

*The same day—Thursday, 23:37 hours*
Inna's other guest turned out to be Rady Sverdlov, grandson of our country's first president and the *Komsomolka's* special correspondent in Azerbaidzhan. On the table there was a bottle of export vodka, a few snacks and the familiar bottle of *Chornye Glaza*. God, had three days really gone by since the Monday evening when I first read Belkin's story at Inna's apartment? The other item on the table was a second copy of Belkin's famous manuscript. It turned out that Inna had made two copies. The top copy she had given to me, the carbon to Sverdlov.

This lovestruck lass had been carrying out her own, private investigation, it turned out. She had persuaded Granov, the chief administrator at *Komsomolskaya Pravda*, to have Rady Sverdlov summoned from Baku to Moscow. When he'd arrived, she'd given him a copy of Belkin's diary to read. This portly, thirty-five-year-old descendant of our first president downed half a glass of vodka to give himself courage, and told me the following story in confidence and with great vehemence.

"Listen, Igor Iosifovich, I tell you this as one half-Jew to another, it's a real mafia we're dealing with. They're everywhere . . . ! *Of course* Vadim was arrested and kept in the detention cell at Baku. And *of course* everything written in this manuscript is the truth. In fact, Belkin has left some parts out! And he did stay at my place—I was lying to you when I spoke to you on the phone before. Why did I lie? I'll tell you! On May 22 Vadim flew to Moscow, and five days later, on Sunday, I was suddenly invited to call on Vekilov at MVD headquarters. Do you know who he is? He's the same blue-eyed son of a bitch who interviewed Belkin. He also happens to be chief personal assistant to the Azerbaidzhani Minister of Internal Affairs. You wouldn't believe the things he gets up to! My grandfather certainly helped to give us a stick to beat ourselves with! Anyway, Vekilov invites me to visit him at his office and he says to me, as openly as I'm talking to you now, 'Rady Moise-yevich, do you want to carry on leading a quiet, enjoyable life in Azerbaidzhan?' Well, what am I supposed to reply? 'No, I don't?' I say yes, of course. Everybody likes to have a good life, don't they? 'In that case,' he says, 'remember one thing: Vadim Belkin did not stay at your place a week ago.' 'What do you mean,' I say, 'he didn't stay at my place? He even dictated an article over the phone to Moscow from my place!' 'Well,' he says, 'nobody else knows that. He could have dictated it over the phone from anywhere. The main thing, and I tell you this for your own good,' he says, 'is that you didn't see or hear from him while he was in Baku, nor do you know what he was doing here. OK?' Then he looks at me with those pale blue eyes of his. What a bastard! He was just trying to scare me, of course. But if they find out that I've been sitting here with you, telling you all this, it's certain death. They'll throw me down the sewers, get me killed in a car, put poison in my food— anything. So I beg you, please . . ."

"But you haven't told me anything yet. Let's get down to brass tacks."

"I know. And maybe I won't be able to tell you anything of use. But all the same I want to reach an agreement with you. Everything that you are about to hear from me, you didn't hear, OK? I'll never corroborate this evidence any-where, understand? Do we have a bargain?"

"All right," I said, unenthusiastically. "Agreed."

"What you really want to do is find out where Belkin is *now*," he said. "Am I right?"

I said nothing in reply, but he obviously wanted verbal confirmation. "Am I right?" he repeated.

"Yes, you're right," I said.

"And the only people who could have kidnapped him are the man called Ziyalov and his sister. Am I right again?"

"What makes you think that?"

"Because Belkin was looking for them all over Baku, and even went to look for them in Moscow. And not because he was in love with Ziyalov's sister. That's baloney. He falls in love with women all the time."

At this point he looked over at the woman. "I'm sorry, Inna," he said, "but he's a playboy. There's no getting around it." Then he turned back to me.

"You see, they stole his border pass! He didn't write that in his diary. In fact he says specifically that all his papers were returned. But he told me that they had stolen the pass allowing him to enter the border zone. And he was afraid they'd use it. They *were* criminals, you know! But he didn't want to tell the police. If he did that, he'd be in a lot of hot water, and he couldn't travel to Vienna with Brezhnev. So that's why he was running all over Baku, searching for Ziyalov, you know..."

"But the man's name isn't Ziyalov," I said.

"That's the whole point! Belkin couldn't remember his surname! He even paid a special visit to the Pioneers' Palace to find his old teacher in the Geographical Society..."

"What's the Pioneers' Palace got to do with it?" I asked in surprise. "He and Ziyalov were at school together."

"That's what he says in the manuscript!" exclaimed Sverdlov. "In the *manuscript*! But you remember yourself how he said at the very beginning that he had decided to mix fact and fiction. I thought that you would probably be looking for Ziyalov among Belkin's old school friends. You have, haven't you? In fact you still are? Am I right?"

"Yes," I replied.

"Ha!" he exclaimed triumphantly. "They were never even in the same *school*, let alone the same class! But they *were* both members of the Geographical Society at the Pioneers' Palace. It was a very famous society in those days. It used to win all the prizes at the competitions that brought young geographers together from around the country. And the reason was that it was led by a really remarkable man. Or that's what Belkin told me, at any rate. And he paid a special visit to Kyurdamir to find out Ziyalov's real name and his address. The old man still corresponds with half his ex-pupils..."

"Did he find out?" I asked.

"I don't know. I really don't. I think he did, but I had already left Baku by that time. He went to Kyurdamir the day before he flew back to Moscow, and I had to be in Lenkoran that day, taking photographs for an article about cotton growers. Vadim mentions it in his diary."

"And what makes you think that he found out where Ziyalov lives?"

"Take a look at this," Sverdlov said, placing a torn sheet from a notebook on the table in front of me. I recognized Belkin's bold handwriting. "Old man!" it said. "Everything's turning out fantastically. I'll get them. Thanks for everything. Vadim."

"I found this note at my place when I got back from Lenkoran," Sverdlov said.

I looked at my watch.

"Rady, what time are you flying back?"

"Please don't come on my flight!" he said beseechingly. "It'll seem obvious enough as it is. I fly to Moscow and back, and then an investigator turns up after me."

"Listen, Rady Moiseyevich. If you took the decision to pass important information on to us, then you must have realized that I would have to use it. Why else did you ask to see me?"

"Because I read *this*!" he said, thumping Belkin's manuscript with his fist. "He calls me Kotovsky in the diary, and at least he writes about me with affection. I'm supposed to have been like a mother to him, and a doctor. How can I let those Baku sons of bitches do whatever they like to him? They're filthy crooks! But we let them do whatever they want! If only my grandfather would rise up from his grave, he'd show them what's what!"

He was suddenly interrupted by the telephone. Inna answered and passed the receiver over to me. "It's for you, Igor Iosifovich!"

It was Colonel Serebryannikov. "Igor, do you have access to a radio of some kind?"

"What for?" I said uncomprehendingly.

"Can you get 'Voice of America'?"

I looked around the room. There was a radio, of course.

"What happened?" I said to Serebryannikov.

"You listen to 'Voice of America'. They'll be repeating their news summary in ten minutes. And get Svetlov to listen too. He'll also find it interesting. See you later." With that the colonel hung up.

Svetlov was asleep in the car, but with Inna's and Sverdlov's permission, I brought him upstairs and we all sat down to listen to the Washington announcer's familiar voice.

"This is Vladimir Martin with the final summary of the news. According to a Reuters report, a large number of drug traffickers were arrested in Moscow today at the hotels Ukraine, Metropole and Peking, at the Zhiguli beer-bar in the Arbat and in a number of other public places throughout the capital. The agency also reports that one of the traffickers was involved in an accident on the Kaluga Highway, south of Moscow, with the result that two people were killed. As we know from data provided by UNESCO, the Soviet Union occupies third place in the world narcotics league, with only Turkey and Pakistan producing more. At the same time, huge consignments of opium are exported illegally from the USSR to the West. According to Western correspondents in Moscow, this action on the part of the police proves how widespread drug addiction is within the Soviet Union, especially among young people. There was news from Madrid today concerning . . ."

We didn't bother to listen to the latest news from Madrid. We turned off the radio.

"So there you are," Svetlov said in a puzzled voice. "We're famous."

"It's incredible how quickly they find things out!" Sverdlov said. "That's real workers for you!"

I looked at my watch. It was ten after twelve. Friday had arrived.

"What time does the plane leave for Baku?" I asked Sverdlov again.

"2:40," he replied.

I had already filled Svetlov in on the details of my conversation with Sverdlov. "The best thing for me and you to do," he said, "is to leave Moscow right now, before everything hits the fan. And then to fly back tomorrow night and find Belkin. They won't can us then."

But at that moment the telephone rang again.

"No, we've left it too late," Svetlov said.

"Perhaps we shouldn't answer," Inna suggested.

"Pointless," Svetlov replied. "There's a radio telephone in the car down there, so they'll get us whatever we do."

I lifted the receiver. "Hello?"

"Igor?" said the voice of Serebryannikov.

"Yes."

"You're to appear at the Chief Prosecutor's office at nine o'clock in the morning. He's just called me himself."

"But I have to fly to Baku in an hour."

"That's your business. I was just instructed to tell you. You're to appear before Rudenko, and Svetlov is to see Shcholokov—both at nine o'clock. Sleep well, Igor!"

I immediately passed the message to Svetlov. "If there's any trouble," I said, "blame it all on me. I am in charge, after all."

"Fuck them all!" he roared. "Don't any of these ministers ever go to sleep, or do they spend all their time listening to 'Voice of America'?"

"We have to get in touch with your men in Baku," I said. "They have to give up checking Belkin's school and start checking the Pioneers' Palace. They have to find out who was in charge of this Geographical Society."

Then I turned to Sverdlov.

"What was his name? Can you remember?"

"No. I had no reason to remember. It was a long, funny name. Jewish, I think."

"Well, it'll be easy enough to find out at the palace itself," I added.

"Listen to me," Svetlov said pensively. "I don't think we ought to send my men there. Let them keep sniffing around Belkin's old school. Vekilov knows damn well what they're up to, but as long as they're on the wrong track, he's leaving them alone. We've got to do this quietly. Igor, either you or I have to go to Baku incognito. Rady Moiseyevich will have to stay in Moscow for the time being. I'm sorry, Comrade Sverdlov, but if you go back to Baku now and Vekilov summons you to his office again, I think you'll crack and tell him about our little meeting today." Then he turned back to me. "Could you get the chief editor of *Komsomolka* to delay him here in Moscow?"

"I'll do it myself," Sverdlov said. "Only I'll have to cancel my booking pretty quickly. Flight registration begins in an hour."

"We can do that over the phone," I said. Then I took a clean sheet of paper and drafted a telegram to send to Svetlov's boys in Baku.

### TELEGRAM

To Comrades Rogozin and Shmuglov
Hotel Azerbaidzhan, Baku


CONTINUE SEARCH FOR BELKIN'S FORMER CLASSMATES STOP LATEST DESCRIPTION OF SUSPECT AS FOLLOWS STOP AZERBAIDZHANI AGE 27 MEDIUM HEIGHT BLACK HAIR DARK EYES BOTANY ENTHUSIAST AT SCHOOL STOP REPORT PROGRESS DAILY STOP SHAMRAYEV

*Friday, June 8, 09:22 hours*
  *Secret*
To USSR Chief Public Prosecutor
Full State Juridical Counselor
Comrade R. A. Rudenko


### SPECIAL DISPATCH

At 18:42 hours on June 7 1979, at a point twenty-five miles south of the city center on the Kaluga Highway, a collision took place between a GAZ-62 cement-mixer and a Zhiguli sedan. As a result of the crash two people died: the driver of the Zhiguli, Citizen Herman Dolgo-Saburov, and an unidentified passenger traveling in the same car.

The incident occurred because the said Zhiguli sedan was being pursued by a group of CID operatives under the command of USSR Special Investigator Comrade I. I. Shamrayev. Because of the unusual nature of the case, I consider it my duty to inform you personally of the circumstances surrounding the incident.

At 18:15 hours at State Automobile Inspection Post No. 7 on the Kaluga Highway, the officer on duty, Captain P. R. Sergeyev, stopped the driver of the Zhiguli sedan registration no. MKTs-22-57, Herman Dolgo-Saburov, for exceeding the speed limit. Because the Moscow CID had circulated all transport police with instructions to seek and detain the said Dolgo-Saburov, Captain Sergeyev decided to take him to Automobile Inspection headquarters. However, the suspect did not do as he was ordered and drove off in his car. Captain Sergeyev then gave chase. At the same time Comrade Shamrayev's team, consisting of three vehicles and a CID helicopter, also joined in the pursuit. In his attempt to escape, the suspect drove at maximum speed, crossed into the left hand lane and collided with a cement-mixer going in the opposite direction.

As a result of the crash, the bodies of Dolgo-Saburov and his passenger were mutilated beyond recognition, and it has been impossible to identify the woman passenger from her facial features. The trunk of the Zhiguli was found to contain a cardboard box filled with banknotes to the sum of approximately 92,000 roubles. This money has been impounded by Comrade Shamrayev and his team.

In my opinion, the actions of my subordinate, Captain P. R. Sergeyev, were in no way the cause of the victims' demise. The car crash was the fault of Investigator I. Shamrayev who, instead of arresting this dangerous criminal at the appropriate time, engaged in passive surveillance of his movements resulting in the traffic accident.

Head of State Automobile Inspection
Moscow City Executive Committee
Major-General N. Nozdryakov

June 7 1979

"And that's just for starters," said the Chief Prosecutor, as he proceeded to move documents across the desk. "Read these."

*Top Secret*
*By Special Field Post*


To USSR Chief Public Prosecutor
Comrade R. A. Rudenko
Copy to Chief of CPSU Central Committee
Ideological Section
Comrade N. Savinkin (for information)


On June 7 1979, your subordinate, Special Investigator
Comrade I. I. Shamrayev, carried out a series of arrests,
as a result of which thirty-seven management staff at a
number of hotels and trading enterprises in downtown
Moscow were apprehended.

Comrade Shamrayev's action was not cleared in advance with the Committee of State Security, and as a
result three KGB agents were among those arrested. This
has had serious repercussions on our undercover work,
since for the past three years these agents had been gradually infiltrating an illegal drug-trafficking network. This
was expected to facilitate KGB operations for the great
influx of foreign tourists into Moscow during the Olympic Games to be held in the summer of 1980.

I request therefore that agents A. I. Gorokhov, P. O.
Zhitomirskaya and M. R. Ginzburg be released as quickly
as possible.

At the same time I have to inform you that the un-
concealed nature of Comrade Shamrayev's actions, caused
by his failure to liaise in advance with the organs of state
security, has led to his operation becoming widely known
in the capital. It has also caused an unhealthy reaction
on the part of the Western news media, particularly un-
desirable on the eve of Comrade Brezhnev's meeting with
President Carter in Vienna.

I ask you to take firm measures to ensure that such
dislocations in our work do not recur in future.

KGB First Deputy Chairman<br>General S. Tsvigun

June 8 1979

*Secret, Urgent*
*By Special Party Messenger*

To CPSU Central Committee Member
Comrade R. Rudenko

HANDWRITTEN NOTE

Dear Roman Andreyevich,

Listened to "Voice of America" last night. What the hell is going on? Why does America find out about your operations before the First Secretary of the Moscow Party Committee?

You remember what was agreed: no noisy operations in Moscow before the Olympics! And what happens? The city is full of rumors again, just as it was at the time of the Ionesyan murders.

Put a stop to this case immediately and calm things down. Let me know the names of the persons responsible so that they can be subjected to disciplinary action by the party.

First Secretary CPSU Moscow Committee
V. Grishin

June 8 1979

As I was reading these documents, I felt sorry I hadn't taken Svetlov's advice and flown to Baku that night. I knew what we were in for: "Explain your actions," "How could you allow people to get killed?", and so on. It wasn't surprising either. After all, two people killed in a road accident, the "Voice of America" chiming, and three KGB agents arrested by accident was hardly bad going! I prepared to weather the storm. I expected to get a strong reprimand from the party at the very least. And who knows? I might even get taken off the case.

But the Chief Public Prosecutor said nothing. He sat there in Stalin's old chair with his eyes closed, his head tipped slightly to one side with the folds of his chin protruding slightly over the collar of his marshal's uniform. I was waiting for him to open his whitish eyelids and for the fireworks to begin, but then . . . I suddenly realized that he was asleep. Sound asleep. He was breathing evenly with the slightest hint of a snore. His puffy hands were resting on his paunch. So much for the unsleeping eye of the Chief Public Prosecutor, I thought. I didn't know what to do next. Why didn't the telephone ring, or something?

I sat there quietly, waiting for him to wake up. Tsvigun's letter and Grishin's note were burning a hole in my hand. All General Nozdryakov was doing was protecting his own man, of course, but the other two were after my neck. And when the First Deputy Chairman of the KGB and the First Secretary of the Moscow Party Committee are gunning for you and the only thing your immediate superior can do is sit, asleep in Stalin's old chair, what could happen next?

Then he opened his eyes and started to speak, as if he hadn't been asleep at all.

"Have you read them all?"

"Yes."

"Where is Belkin?"

"We haven't found him yet, Roman Andreyevich."

"When will you have him?"

"We might have found him today. I was supposed to fly to Baku for a half a day last night, but . . ."

"I held you up, is that it?"

"More or less."

"Tell me this. Couldn't you get hold of Belkin with a little less commotion and fewer corpses?"

"Dolgo-Saburov took his own life, you know that. Everything's recorded on tape."

"Look, there's no need for all that," he said with a gentle wave of the hand. "He doesn't matter. One cheap crook, so what? It's just that you need to work differently. Use more caution. I did warn you. You made one slip, and there they are, Grishin and Tsvigun, screaming for your blood. And a copy to Savinkin! All they want to do is crush our department—any pretext will do. And you've just provided them with one. You realize that, don't you?"

"Well . . ." I mumbled.

"You have. Just take my word for it," he said dogmatically. "A car chase, mass arrests, KGB agents picked up— you're a regular Superman. Meanwhile, I have to get up at six in the morning to visit Savinkin at his dacha, to make sure that I get to him before all of them do," he said, pointing towards the letters from Tsvigun, Grishin and Nozdryakov. "What will you all do when I die or retire? Andropov or Shcholokov will tear you to pieces before six months have passed. Well, never mind. You might as well tell me what you've got, now that you're here, or else you'll do something else that's stupid."

"Well, basically it amounts to this. Belkin was kidnapped by a group of drug traffickers who are part of a much larger organization. The top bosses decided to get the smaller fry for launching out on their own..."

"What do you mean by a 'much larger organization'?" Rudenko asked, interrupting me angrily.

"I mean what I say, Roman Andreyevich. There's a well-organized mafia running this drug show throughout the whole country. Opium poppies are being cultivated in Central Asia, the Caucasus and the area around Stavropol, partly for the state and partly for the black market. Large quantities of morphine are being stolen from pharmaceutical warehouses. One of the leaders is Viktor Sysoyev, who is also director of the Chief Pharmaceutical Authority. He's away on business in Geneva right now. From him the trail leads upwards towards the Deputy Health Minister, Balayan, and outwards towards the Azerbaidzhani Minister of the Interior. And there are others."

Rudenko shook his head sadly. "And this is all recorded in the case file?"

"Yes."

"It's terrible, you know, this Jewish way you have of making these wide inferences!"

"What does parentage have to do with it, Roman Andreyevich?"

"Oh, I don't mean that literally! You may be half-Jewish, but the other half of you is Russian, I know that very well. And you're a good investigator. But you do have this habit of rummaging around in very embarrassing places. So what happened to Belkin?"

"He was captured by the same four that Sysoyev threatened to punish for organizing their own drug deals on the side. They were concealing part of the consignment from the rest of the gang and selling it themselves."

"I see," Rudenko said with a grin. "A black market within a black market! That's something new. What else?"

"According to information recovered indirectly from Belkin himself, they have managed to penetrate the border zone and are preparing to flee abroad, by helicopter or plane, from Charshanga in Uzbekistan."

The Prosecutor frowned. "Does the KGB know about this?"

"Not yet, Roman Andreyevich. I only found out last night myself..."

"For Christ's sake! We've got to tell them right away. Or were you thinking of catching them on the border yourself?" For the first time the Prosecutor looked genuinely furious.

"Well, only one of the criminals has reached the border so far," I said. "He's waiting for his three accomplices to join him. Two of them are dead already, and the third... The third one I'm looking for myself. That's why I was going to fly to Baku. He knows where Belkin is."

"I see," the Prosecutor said, striking his fist on the top of his desk. "We must inform the KGB immediately!"

He pressed the button to summon his secretary, and Vera Petelina appeared at the door almost immediately, notebook in hand.

"Write this down, Vera Vasilyevna," the Prosecutor ordered. "'Secret, urgent, to General Tsvigun, KGB. According to information in the hands of USSR Special Investigator Shamrayev, some criminals are about to attempt an illegal crossing of the Soviet–Afghanistan border by helicopter or plane from the airfield at Charshanga in Uzbekistan. At the same time, I have to inform you that the following are implicated in illegal drug-trafficking: Viktor Sysoyev, head of the Chief Pharmaceutical Authority, and Edward Balayan, USSR Deputy Minister of Health. Signed: Roman Rudenko.'"

Then he turned to me and said, "Can you let those three KGB agents go?"

"Yes," I replied. About half an hour earlier Pshenichny had told me that none of those arrested claimed to know the doctor, and he had handed them all over to Malenina for further interrogation.

"Add this to the letter, Vera Vasilyevna," he said. "'In accordance with your request the three KGB agents will be released today.' That's all. Have it sent by special messenger, no delay."

Petelina left the room and then he said to me, "That's that! Now they can come to us for information, and not the other way around. When does your plane leave for Baku?"

"I'm going on the regular flight at 12:40," I replied, looking at my watch. It was already 10:07, and I still had to book my flight, get money from the accounts office and leave instructions for Svetlov and Pshenichny.

"All right," he said. "Don't waste any time. And *please* find Belkin by Monday. I beg you. Otherwise you and I are really going to get it from the Central Committee, and I'll have my grand-niece to deal with, too! Understand?"

"Of course, Roman Andreyevich."

"OK. Now tell me this. Do you have the impression that yesterday's car crash might not have been an accident?"

"What do you mean?" I said in surprise.

"Well, I'm not certain, but . . . From what I've gathered, you sent instructions that Dolgo-Saburov wasn't to be detained at noon—12:10 to be exact. But six hours later that transport policeman still didn't know about it. Doesn't that strike you as odd?"

"But who would have wanted it to happen, Roman Andreyevich?" I suddenly felt quite disoriented.

"I've already told you. Shcholokov, for example. And Andropov, too. They want to mess up the operation. Of course, they couldn't have calculated in advance that an accident would happen, but all the same: they do whatever they can to throw a monkey wrench in the works. Nozdryakov doesn't mention that the Automobile Inspection ever received instructions about Dolgo-Saburov after all. I must tell you again to be very careful. You're going to need all your Jewish cunning. Does anybody know that you're going to Baku?"

"Only Svetlov and two employees of *Komsomolskaya Pravda.*"

"Keep it like that. Goodbye. Oh, and one more thing. I don't think it's worth getting our accounts office to organize your trip to Baku right now. Just to be on the safe side. You can never keep a secret anywhere. Settle with them when you come back. Meanwhile, I'll sign your travel papers. OK?"

He looked me in the eye, and those eyes of his expressed more than his words. The Chief Public Prosecutor knew that he had to find ways of acting without their knowledge. Here was a man who had survived Stalin, Malenkov, and Khrushchev. He used all his time, brains and energy trying to outsmart the snares and intrigues of his rivals and enemies.

"But what do I use for money, Roman Andreyevich?" I asked.

"Why don't you borrow some from somebody? I'd lend you some myself, but I don't have any on me right now. The wife's got it all, in the savings bank, you know."

Of course, why should the Chief Public Prosecutor, a marshal and member of the CPSU Central Committee, carry money about on his person? I doubt if he even knows what it looks like!

Without waiting for the elevator, I ran up the stairs to my office. Everybody looked at me as I ran by, some with curiosity, others in silence, as if they had just seen a corpse, and others with a scarcely veiled look of triumph. They had all listened in to the "Voice of America" last night, of course, and they had all heard about the letters from Tsvigun and Grishin. They obviously thought my days in the department were numbered. For all I knew, they were right. After all, I hadn't found Belkin.

Baklanov appeared out of his office and gave me a questioning glance. "Still alive?" he said.

"So far," I muttered. "Can you lend me a couple of hundred?"

I quickly opened my office and went inside. The telephone was ringing.

"Hello," I said.

"Mister Shamrayev?" said a cheerful voice with an obviously non-Russian accent. "This is the *New York Times* correspondent. I'd like to interview you in connection with yesterday's operation. Could we meet in some restaurant, one of your choice?"

Saying nothing, I put down the receiver and went next door to borrow money from Baklanov for my trip to Baku.

*17:50 hours, Baku time*
*The same day, Friday, June 8*
Chingiz Adigezalov, the Director of the Pioneers' Palace in Baku, studied my travel documents and my Prosecutor's Office identity card very thoroughly. I could see that he wasn't so much reading and rereading them as pondering how to deal with me. I'd appeared in Baku like a bolt from the blue on this beautiful June day. Though it was getting quite late, the sun was still beating down on the buildings outside his office. There was a strong smell of oleanders coming from the public garden next door, and away over the roofs of the houses I could see the calm, translucent green of the Caspian. Adigezalov was about to entertain some Komsomol leaders from Azerbaidzhan, Georgia and Armenia. The table in his office was covered with shashlyks, grapes, wine and cognac. The Festival of Friendship between Caucasian Pioneer organizations was in the process of being officially opened in the palace assembly hall. Then, at the most inconvenient moment, this special investigator turns up from Moscow!

"But couldn't it wait until Monday?"

"No, I'm afraid not," I replied.

"You see, my chief personnel officer has gone home already..."

"Well, you'll just have to ask him or her to come back to work. Either phone or send a car. I'm here on the express instructions of the Party Central Committee, you know."

"I can see that from your papers," he replied. This is what Rudenko had written:

Igor Iosifovich Shamrayev, Special Investigator at the USSR Public Prosecutor's Office, has been sent to the Azerbaidzhani SSR on extremely urgent government business, in connection with which all party, government and other administrative organs are to afford him whatever help and assistance he may require.

"All right," Adigezalov sighed. He had obviously decided that it would be best to get rid of me as quickly as possible. "Let's go. I'll open her room myself. Maybe I can find what you're after."

We walked out of his office and down an old, impressive-looking marble staircase (the Pioneers' Palace had been built by a pre-revolutionary oil tycoon). On the ground floor we entered what looked like a tiny storeroom. We could hear children's voices coming from the assembly hall, amplified by microphones and punctuated by thunderous applause.

"It's strange," Adigezalov said. "Two weeks ago we were visited by a journalist from Moscow who was also asking about the geography teacher. He said that he wanted to pay him a visit in order to write an article about him. And now you turn up from the Public Prosecutor's Office. He must be either a great man, or a great criminal!"

We entered the storeroom, which turned out to be a cross between an archive and a personnel office. The shelves along the wall were filled with piles of children's exercise books, photo albums, sketch pads, posters, diagrams, photomontages and broadsheets. There were maps, globes, card indexes and boxes containing letters from all over the world. Each box had the name of the countries of origin written on the side: Cuba, Poland, Brazil, Algeria, Lebanon, France.

Adigezalov produced a faded photo-display from one of the boxes. More than a dozen group photographs of former Pioneers were mounted on it in a circle, and right in the middle was a picture of a smiling man of about fifty. Above it were written the words, "To our dear Lev Arkadyevich Rozentsveig on his fiftieth birthday—April 5 1958."

"Rozentsveig," Adigezalov said with apparent difficulty. "No, I'll never be able to pronounce it. What strange names some people have, it's incredible! Well, that's your man, and these are all his pupils. The journalist from Moscow is among them somewhere. He showed me himself."

"And where is Rozentsveig now?"

"Working at a forest school near Kyurdamir."

"Where exactly is the school?"

"You can be driven there. You've got a car, of course?

Just tell the driver that you want the 'Communard' Collective Farm, and he'll take you right there. It's an enormous place. Everybody knows it."

"So I'm to go to the forest school on the 'Communard' Collective Farm near Kyurdamir," I said repeating his directions. "How long will it take to get there?"

"Well, you'll do it in about three hours by car. What kind of car do you have? A Volga?"

I ignored him. "Why did Rozentsveig leave Baku for some collective farm school out in the sticks?"

"It happened before my time," he said, raising his hands defensively. "But I can tell you why. Can you really imagine anybody working in the Central Pioneers' Palace with a name like his?"

I left the building with the sound of fanfares and applause ringing in my ears. I turned around and saw Adigezalov standing at his window and looking after me in astonishment. There was no car waiting for me at the entrance. He just couldn't understand why a special investigator on urgent government business should be walking down the road on his own two feet. I could see from his expression that he didn't approve. But there was nothing I could do to oblige either him or myself. By coming here straight from the airport, I'd already found Rozentsveig's address. Of course, all I needed to do was lift a receiver and dial the Azerbaidzhani Prosecutor's office, the head of the Baku Militia or Central Committee headquarters in the town, and I'd have a Volga placed at my disposal immediately, and a helicopter or motor-launch. All I had to do was ask. But would they be able to get me to Rozentsveig?

I went up to a passerby and said, "Excuse me, but can you tell me where the bus station is?"

*23:00 hours, Baku time*
I will leave it for writers such as Vadim Belkin and his like to describe the "charms" of the road between Baku and Kyurdamir. I'll say only that the crush for tickets which he described at Baku airport has nothing on the scene that greeted me at the Baku bus station. The people were the same, however—unshaven for the most part, with huge

moustaches and dressed in those enormous Caucasian caps.
There they were, storming the mud-bespattered buses as
soon as they appeared. It reminded me of the people I'd
seen rushing the trains in 1945 when I was little. Now, as
then, most of them carried huge sacks with them, or ramshackle suitcases. But now, instead of belongings, their
baggage was filled with bread, rice, tea, sugar, butter, buckwheat and other supplies which you can get in big cities
these days, but practically nowhere else. It was like any
crowded scene at the railroad stations in Moscow, except
that this Caucasian crowd was more chaotic and boisterous
than anything in Moscow.

The only way I could get a bus to Kyurdamir was by
showing my Prosecutor's Office identity card. Otherwise I
might not have gotten anything at all. There were no ticket
offices. The only thing to do was try your luck in the crush
with the crowd of Azerbaidzhanis. After three unsuccessful
attempts I realized that I was up against a barely concealed
display of national solidarity and that not a single Russian-
looking passenger had gotten on the last three buses. I found
the manager of the bus station and placed my identity papers
silently before him. A minute later he obsequiously guided
me towards a bus which he placed at my disposal, and I
was off. I realized that I had to uncover my incognito again,
but what choice did I have?

Meanwhile, the bus station manager phoned his counter-
part in Kyurdamir to warn him that a USSR special investigator was on the way. When I arrived at 10:30 p.m.,
Captain Gasan-zade, head of the Kyurdamir Militia, and a
local party official, Comrade Bagirov, were all waiting for
me. They looked anxious and confused, obviously not
knowing what to do with me. I turned down their offer of
dinner or a room in a hotel. All I wanted was a car to take
me to the "Communard" Collective Farm. I got one immediately. The police officer volunteered to accompany me,
but I said "no" very firmly, and went off immediately with
only the driver for company—a young Azerbaidzhani with
gleaming white teeth. What his boss's parting words to him
were, I don't know, as I don't speak the language. But the
driver did try to strike up a conversation as we drove through

the night. I was determined not to play into the Baku Militia's hands on this occasion, though, even though I had more or less already abandoned my anonymity. I said nothing in reply.

When we arrived, the driver handed me over to the chairman of the farm, a fifty-year-old man by the name of Rizazade. He had obviously just been woken up by a phone call from Kyurdamir announcing my visit, and he still looked shell-shocked. Around us lay the silent Azerbaidzhani village, all in darkness now that most of its inhabitants were asleep.

"What's happened?" asked the farm chairman. "Why are you here?" Obviously the arrival of a special investigator from Moscow late at night was no laughing matter if you were the boss of a huge wine-growing collective buried somewhere deep in the mountains, and a boss who had something to hide.

"I'll tell you everything in the morning," I said. "Only right now I'm very tired, and I want to get some sleep. Can you find me somewhere to lie down?"

"Don't offend us, comrade. Of course we can!" Rizazade replied. Now that he saw a way of obliging his uninvited Moscow guest, he moved into action. "We've got a whole building set aside for visitors. It's a wonderful place! I'll get you something to eat! Where are your things?"

"I left them in Baku, at the baggage office. And I don't want anything to eat. All I want to do is sleep."

"*Please*, comrade. How can we send you to bed without giving you anything to eat?"

"I'll tell you what. I'll eat a good breakfast in the morning. OK?" I said this with particular emphasis to make him realize that he could show me as much hospitality as he wanted in the morning. He saw what I was getting at, of course, and breathed a sigh of relief. He would be able to get off by giving me a bribe, a first-class breakfast or something along those lines. He suddenly became much more cheerful and led me off to the farm guest-house, not forgetting to give me a lengthy description of the collective's achievements as he did so—how they always exceeded their plan, and what sort of wine and brandy did I like?

The guest-house was really a lavish place, set in a beautiful garden and fitted throughout with Finnish furniture. My room contained a refrigerator filled with local wine, cognac and vodka, while the table was loaded with fresh fruit and vegetables. I could have sat down to dinner or breakfast on the spot!

But I made it clear I was tired. I collapsed in an armchair and began to take off my shoes.

"That's all, my friend, thank you very much," I said. "I'll take a shower and then I'll hit the sack. We can talk tomorrow."

"At what time?" he asked impatiently.

"Oh, I don't know. Let's say nine o'clock, or ten . . ."

"All right. Are you quite sure you don't need anything else? Should I send a woman along to fix things up?"

"No, I don't need any woman. I just want to sleep, I'm very tired. Good night."

He finally went away. Twenty minutes or so later, I turned out the lights and went outside onto the steps. I was surrounded by darkness. I could see the Milky Way above me, looking extraordinarily immense and close. The village was asleep. The only thing breaking the silence was the occasional sound of young people's laughter from a little ways off. I walked down the steps into the garden and headed in the direction of the laughter.

Half a dozen young people were sitting in the courtyard of another building, drinking tea out of slender, molded glasses and listening to a "Voice of America" broadcast in Turkish. When I appeared, the radio was turned off, but a pack of Moscow cigarettes which I had with me was soon being passed around the circle. Then they offered me a glass of tea, which I didn't refuse. They soon started to describe the sights of the collective farm, and within ten minutes or so I had discovered the whereabouts of the forest school. "Can you see that light over there in the hills? That's their campfire. They'll be singing songs around it until midnight at least."

After finishing my tea and saying good night, I went back to the guest-house. But instead of going in, I stepped out in the direction of the hills, heading for the light which

I could see flickering feebly in the darkness.

It was 11:17 p.m. The light seemed very close. Just a few hundred yards up the hill and you'd be able to touch it ... But it wasn't like that at all, as my thumping heart and my light Moscow shoes bore witness.

Tired, dirty, with scratches on my arms, a thorn in my hand, and one pants leg torn by a bush, I finally reached the glowing embers of the campfire at five minutes before midnight. I found my way there in the end by following the direction of the singing.

Lev Arkadyevich was a lively, cheerful, youthful-looking man with a shock of black hair. He looked no older than he had been twenty years earlier in the photograph I had seen. Tall and wiry, with a face burned by the sun and wind, he was dressed in a T-shirt, sports pants and sneakers. He was sitting around the fire in this forest glade, surrounded by his pupils, all singing folksongs. When I arrived, everybody stopped. The school itself consisted of a cookhouse and a dozen or so large tents pitched some way from the center of the collective farm itself. We were up in the hills, and if you looked around, you seemed to be surrounded by nothing but an ocean of blackness.

About twenty minutes later, when the others had gone to bed, Rozentsveig and I had a chat. As a result, I finally found out the real name of the notorious "Ziyalov"—it was Boris Khotulyov. He was thirty-two years old and, as we already know, had once been a member of Rozentsveig's Geographical Society at the Baku Pioneers' Palace. He had won many prizes at various national competitions for budding young chemists and had gone on to graduate from the Baku Medical Institute. He then had done research in psychotherapy at a medical institute in Moscow, and was now a consultant at Psychiatric Hospital No. 5 at the settlement of Stolbovaya in the Moscow Region.

Rozentsveig really did seem to know everything about his former pupils, so it had been well worth the trouble of finding him. I felt like a cook who has spent four days baking a cake and who is finally ready to take it out of the oven and open the lid. And because the cake was ready and wouldn't stand another minute's baking, I wanted to get

back to Moscow right away and run over to Stolbovaya. If
the Chief Prosecutor hadn't delayed me that morning, that's
what I would have done. I would have been in the Stolbovaya psychiatric hospital at this very moment. It made
me very angry to think that I had lost a whole day, but even
angrier to realize that I had to lose more time now. There
was nothing I could do about it. Rozentsveig told me that
the last bus from Kyurdamir to Baku had already left and
that there wouldn't be another one until morning. There
wasn't any other traffic at night either, not even taxis, because people around there were afraid of being stopped and
robbed.

So I spent the rest of the night talking with him. We were
surrounded by sleeping children — forty-five of them from
hospitals all over the republic. When Rozentsveig had been
made "redundant" at the Pioneers' Palace, he had had the
idea of setting up a boarding school for children with respiratory diseases. He wanted to improve their health with
gymnastic exercises in the morning and long walks in the
sun during the afternoon. The details of his life have no
connection with this story, of course, and I found myself
wondering all the time where Khotulyov was at this moment.
Was he still waiting for his sister and Dolgo-Saburov to
appear, or had he listened to "Voice of America" and realized
the two of them had died in the accident? If he had, he
would already be making his escape. But where would he
be running to? The Old Man at Charshanga? In that case,
he'd find that particular escape route already closed . . .

I asked Rozentsveig how he felt about living in Azerbaidzhan and whether he held a grudge about being made
"redundant."

"You know, it's the same everywhere," he said. "It's the
same people, wherever you look — whether you're talking
about this collective farm, the district committee in Kyurdamir, Baku, or even Moscow. But I've risen above all that
now. I live in the mountains, surrounded by fresh air. And
I've got forty-five children, and I teach them all to breathe
the fresh air too. I've been surrounded by children all my
life, you know, and that helps."

"But then one of them turns into a Khotulyov."

"And another into a Belkin. And another turns into you. Khotulyov came to me when he was fifteen years old. His character was already formed by then. Some of my work doesn't turn out right. I'm willing to admit it. But you asked me how I felt about this blackness that surrounds me, all the graft and brutality. I feel sorry for them, you know. I look down at them from up here, and I feel sorry for them. I have fresh air to breathe, while they, well . . ."

*Saturday, June 9, 05:00 hours, Baku time*

Just before five o'clock, as dawn was beginning to appear, Rozentsveig showed me the way down to the farm village. Everybody was still asleep. It wasn't far, and we got there in seven minutes. It had taken me nearly an hour to find my way up the hill in the darkness the night before.

But I didn't go into the village. I sent Rozentsveig back the way he had come, and sat on a rock by the side of the road. After twenty minutes or so, my patience was rewarded. A truck carrying cabbages came heading down the mountain road towards Kyurdamir. I managed to wave him down, and within a quarter of an hour I was at the bus station in Kyurdamir. Distances seemed a lot less than they had been the night before.

The bus station was empty, if you could even call it a station. It consisted of nothing but a closed wooden hut, a battered concrete shelter and a couple of ramshackle benches. It was only 5:40 a.m., so there were no passengers or buses. I sat down on one of the seats. There was nothing to do but wait for the first bus or taxi that could take me to Baku, and the next flight to Moscow.

A minute later a police Volga pulled up to where I was sitting. The rear door was opened by the Kyurdamir militia captain that I had met the previous night.

"Are you going to Baku, Comrade Investigator?" he asked obligingly. "Good morning. Jump in. We'll take you there."

Apart from him and the driver, there was one other person in the car, sitting at the front. He was a thick-set, broad-shouldered Azerbaidzhani, dressed in civilian clothes. He looked more like an athlete or a wrestler than anything else. I couldn't help but be reminded of Akeyev. He had the same heavy, muscular appearance.

Captain Gasan-zade remained in the back seat. Without getting out, he had opened the car door and was looking at me expectantly with a smile on his face. "There are no busses today, Comrade Investigator. We've had a landslide in the mountains, and I've had to halt all traffic."

This was an outright lie, of course, and his laughing eyes made no attempt to conceal it. I was alone in a strange Azerbaidzhani village, and there in front of me were the people who ran the place—the local police chief and his henchmen (unless the man in civvies turned out to be one of the bosses himself). There was nobody else around, so I was naturally in their power. If they were to put a bullet in my head right there, not so much as a dog would be around to bark about it.

I smiled, got up from my bench and got into the Volga next to Captain Gasan-zade. The "wrestler" then got out and came and sat next to me at the back. Now I was completely hemmed in by the two of them. The car moved off and we began to descend from the heights of Kyurdamir to the lowlands of Baku.

Meanwhile I said nothing but just waited. Of course, they could have bumped me off and thrown my body into some chasm on the way, so that even the most experienced CID sleuths couldn't find it. The special investigator might have gone anywhere, after all. Who saw him? He didn't even tell anybody that he was making the trip. Yes, he did apparently visit the "Communard" Collective Farm, then he walked off into the mountains during the night, obviously got lost and, well . . .

But what would be the sense in killing me? After all, Moscow had initiated the investigation. They'd merely send another investigator—Baklanov, perhaps.

"Listen, my friend," Captain Gasan-zade said. "We're men of the world, so let's talk frankly to each other, man to man. I realize that you're on a case and are just doing what you're told. And you've been doing a pretty good job, too, I think! I heard about that Moscow operation of yours on the radio. Whoever did that, I thought, has got to be a pretty smart worker! Then last night somebody asks me:

who's this Shamrayev fellow who's turned up? From the Moscow Prosecutor's Office? That's the one they were talking about on 'Voice of America'. Glad to meet you! Amazing how many crooks you managed to pick up in Moscow that day! But I'd like to know something. Have you come to us about the same case?"

I said nothing.

"You see," he went on, "it's like this. In Moscow you're in charge. You can arrest whoever you like. It's up to you—they've got it coming to them for the most part. But we've got our own republic, you know. What do you have to come poking around here for? Who are you trying to get?"

I still made no reply. Meanwhile, the car was zigzagging its way down the mountain road. Every minute or two we came to a hair-raising bend with deep valleys yawning beneath us. We hadn't come across any other traffic. The man sitting on the other side of me suddenly coughed into his fist and addressed me in perfect Russian, without any trace of an accent. "Igor Iosifovich, we know that you're investigating Khotulyov, Sysoyev and Balayan. What set the whole ball rolling was that coffin business at Baku airport, and now things have gone as far as Balayan. And it's led *you* to our republic. But we're not going to let you harm our country, you see. You're *our* guest now. You can see that perfectly well yourself. If you don't accept what we have to propose, you'll never leave here alive. But if you accept, then everything will be all right—for you and for us. OK. This is what we've got to offer."

He leaned over the back of the seat and lifted up a small suitcase. It was fairly heavy, and he plumped it down on his lap. He undid the locks and opened it. It contained a large number of neatly arranged piles of banknotes. "There's a hundred thousand here," he said, "and it's all yours—as long as you agree not to touch anybody in Azerbaidzhan, and to remove all documents relating to our republic from the case file. Deal?"

I still said nothing. I had no choice, of course. I had to do as they said, but I still kept quiet.

"Stop the car," he said to the driver.

We stopped by the side of the road—or on the edge of

an enormous ravine, to be more exact.

"It's up to you, Igor Iosifovich. Either you take the money, or . . . We haven't any choice in the matter I'm afraid. It's our job. We're acting on government instructions, too," he added with a smile. "Either you put us in jail, or we kill you. But there is another way out." He stared at me with those tranquil, dark-brown eyes of his.

I took hold of the suitcase, closed the lid and clicked the locks shut. "OK, let's go," I said to the driver.

"Now you're talking!" Captain Gasan-zade said. "I knew you'd accept. Praise be to Allah! It would be a crime to kill somebody like you! Let's drop off somewhere for a drink and something to eat."

The "wrestler" looked at me, too, waiting for an answer.

"No," I said, "I've got no time for that on this trip. When is the next flight to Moscow?"

"Nine-twenty this morning, local time."

"Will you take me to the airport?"

"Of course we will!" Captain Gasan-zade replied. "What a question!" He really did seem pleased that he hadn't had to kill me.


*The same day, after 08:00 hours*

They drove me directly to the airport, avoiding Baku itself. On the way there we stopped just once, in Lokbatan, for the "wrestler" to make a call from a telephone booth. He was probably calling his boss to tell him I'd "accepted."

At the airport they helped me buy a ticket for the next flight, wished me a happy journey and wondered, with a smile, whether I might lose the suitcase and would I like a bodyguard? I assured them that suitcases like this never get lost and that there was certainly no need for anybody to protect me. The "wrestler" gave me the keys to the case, and in his presence I locked it and put the key away in a purse. I placed the purse in the inside pocket of my jacket.

Then they left. There was still twenty minutes to go before check-in time for the Moscow flight. I didn't like the fact that they'd gone away without accompanying me to the plane. There was something strange about that. I entered the waiting room and sat down on one of the seats.

Then I pretended to fiddle with the keys in the lock, as if I intended to start opening the case in front of everyone. I suddenly realized that I had walked into a trap. Two tipsy passengers had followed me into the waiting room. I noticed how they sobered up immediately and looked at me in alarm as soon as they thought I was going to open the case. I smiled inwardly, stuffed the key back into my pocket and went up to them. They started pretending to be drunk again, embracing each other and mumbling incoherently, but I went right up to them and said rudely,

"I want you out of this airport in sixty seconds!"

"Why?" said one of them in astonishment.

"The orders have been changed. There's no need for you to protect me. The operation is off."

"What? You mean nobody's coming?" the other one said.

"That's exactly what I mean. I said the operation is off, that's all. You can go."

I was bluffing, of course, but in cases like these a good offense is the best defense. They shrugged and went back to the departure hall in confusion. I had a few minutes left to me before they phoned their bosses and realized what was going on. I watched them disappear in the direction of the airport militia office and then ran over to the baggage lockers. A handful of passengers dozed nearby, but none of them paid any attention to me. All the same, I went down one of the rows of lockers as far as I could, found an open locker (No. 54), and then, with my back turned to the room, opened the suitcase and quickly emptied all the money inside. After that I placed the suitcase on the ground, dialed 675185 on the lock of the door (this was the number of my plane ticket) and slammed the door shut. I walked out of the waiting room as quickly as I could. Everything seemed peaceful. I spent a few seconds considering what to do next and then crossed the departure hall to the buffet on the other side. I bought a bottle of *kefir* and a slice of cheesecake and stood near the window consuming them and waiting for events to develop.

And develop they did—fast. Suddenly policemen were running out of the militia post in all directions—probably all that were there. Then my two luckless sleuths appeared and, to their total astonishment, found me calmly munching cake and drinking *kefir* in the buffet. One stood there staring at me, while the other ran back to the militia office to tell them I was still there and hadn't run away.

A few minutes later registration for Flight 247 to Moscow was announced over the loudspeaker. The militia's eyes were on me all the time now, as I walked over to the check-in desk and stood in line. The scene was exemplary. The police made all the passengers line up straight, while the Aeroflot staff were courteous and polite, just like in the movies. I realized that the stars in this performance were myself and my "heavy" suitcase. When I reached the head of the line, the girl stamped my ticket and I placed the case on the scale. Suddenly cameras clicked and bulbs flashed from all directions. Somebody's heavy arm held my hand against the suitcase. Ahead of me, behind the check-in desk, I noticed a young face with blue eyes and guessed that this must be Vekilov, the Azerbaidzhani Interior Minister's personal assistant, the one who had questioned Belkin and tried to frighten Sverdlov, and possibly even one of the visitors from Baku who had called at Sysoyev's dacha for the diamonds and gone away with a suitcase full of paper money. Who knows, I might have been carrying the same suitcase . . .

"Bring the witnesses here!" he ordered, and two airport workers suddenly appeared at his side. They had obviously been warned in advance of what was going to happen.

"Comrade Shamrayev," he said. "We have reason to suspect that you are carrying money in that suitcase which you have accepted as a bribe. Will you open it, please?"

"Go ahead and open it yourself," I said calmly, without taking my hand away from the case. I was pressing it down as hard as I could, so that the airport scale wouldn't give the game away.

Vekilov's plan was simple. He thought he had me red-handed. I would be at his mercy, and would agree to anything. And if I were to prove obstinate, then he had incontrovertible evidence—photographs showing Shamrayev and a suitcase full of money. He would have them immediately sent to Rudenko and the Central Committee, the compro-

mised investigator would be taken off the case and the results
of his investigation wouldn't be worth a plugged kopeck.
He had me dead to rights—or so he thought.

I produced the key and placed it on the counter in front
of Vekilov, letting go of the suitcase as I did so.

"Please, go ahead and open it," I said.

He didn't notice how the needle on the scales suddenly
slipped back to around two pounds. He took the key and
handed it over to one of his assistants. "Open it," he ordered.

As soon as his assistant removed the suitcase from the
scales, Vekilov's face registered alarm. The case was obviously too light. But the MVD photographers continued to
click away, and we were surrounded by a mob of curious
passengers. Vekilov's assistant opened up a perfectly empty
suitcase.

I picked up my ticket from the counter and walked over
to the departure gate.

*The same day, on board the TU-104, after 11:00 hours*
After Voronezh we finally made contact with air traffic
control at Vnukovo, outside Moscow. I had made my way
to the cockpit and was listening to the captain, Oleg Chubar,
talk over the radio.

"Vnukovo, this is flight No. 2546 here. I have a special
investigator from the USSR Chief Prosecutor's Office on
board. He has an urgent message for CID headquarters on
the Petrovka. Can you take it? Over."

I stood behind the pilot's seat and waited. As soon as
we had left the runway at Baku, I had shown the stewardess
my identity papers and she took me right up to the cockpit.
But it turned out that the plane could only contact ground
control city by city, and that we wouldn't be able to get
through to Moscow until we had passed Voronezh.

Chubar turned to face me and said, "What number do
you want at the Petrovka?"

"The duty officer," I replied. He relayed this information
to Vnukovo.

"Get up and let the investigator sit down for a while,"
he said to his co-pilot.

"There's no need," I replied, but it was too late. The co-pilot had already left his seat and was offering me his headset. I put it on and could immediately hear the voice of the Moscow traffic controller.

"Vnukovo here. We have the Petrovka on the line. Go ahead, please. Over."

Chubar nodded to me, and I proceeded to dictate the following message: "To Lieutenant-Colonel Svetlov. Urgent. Dr. Boris Khotulyov, aged thirty-two, place of work—Stolbovaya psychiatric hospital No. 5. Signed Shamrayev. You got that? Over."

"Understood," came the reply. "I'll transmit it to the Petrovka now. You can listen in. 'To Lieutenant-Colonel Svetlov. Urgent. Dr. Boris Khotulyov, aged thirty-two, place of work...' Hey!" He suddenly stopped talking. He was silent for a few seconds, and then said to me, "Comrade Shamrayev. I have an urgent message for you from the Petrovka. I'll repeat it sentence by sentence as it is given to me by the duty officer. 'Investigation team under the command of Lieutenant-Colonel Svetlov left for the settlement of Stolbovaya at 11:05 a.m. We expect a report on their progress at any moment. Duty Officer, Moscow, Colonel Glazarin.' Is that clear? Over."

I looked at my watch. It was 11:25. That meant that twenty-five minutes ago Svetlov had also learned the whereabouts of the doctor.

To Investigation Team Leader
Special Investigator
Comrade I. I. Shamrayev

### REPORT

Following your instructions to check the personnel at psychiatric hospitals and clinics in Moscow and the surrounding district, with a view to discovering the identity of the doctor known as Boris, wanted in connection with the kidnapping of Citizens Belkin and Rybakov, the investigation team visited the following medical establishments over the period June 7–8 1979:

Psychiatric clinics Nos. 1–21
Psychiatric hospitals Nos. 1–12

The questioning of medical staff and the examination of personnel office records at the above institutions yielded no positive results. However, during my questioning of patients regularly attending clinic No. 21 in the Oktyabrsky district of the city, I found one patient, A. B. Pekarsky, who identified the identikit picture as that of a doctor who had once treated him. The doctor's name was Boris Yuryevich Khotulyov, who is now in charge of Department 4 at MVD Special Psychiatric Hospital No. 5, near the settlement of Stolbovaya in the Moscow region. This was where, six months ago, the patient, A. B. Pekarsky, underwent a three-month period of treatment at the request of the courts.

Acting USSR Special Investigator
V. Pshenichny

Moscow, June 9 1979

I didn't get to read this report until some time later, in Moscow, of course. Meanwhile, I said to the air traffic controller at Vnukovo, "Understood. Thank you very much. Please ask Colonel Glazarin to send a car to pick me up at the airport. Over and out."

*Stolbovaya settlement, just after noon*

EXTRACT FROM THE REGISTER OF PATIENTS
ADMITTED TO DEPARTMENT 4, MVD SPECIAL
PSYCHIATRIC HOSPITAL NO. 5

May 27 1979. Patient Ilya Nikolayevich ZAITSEV admitted. Aged 27, no permanent occupation. Reason for treatment: decision of Moscow Health Department Forensic Medical Commission No. 3. Preliminary diagnosis: manic-depressive psychosis. Patient placed in secure cell No. 16 for violent lunatics.

Duty Nurse I. O. Kravtsova

URGENT, BY SPECIAL MESSENGER

To the Doctor in Charge
MVD Special Hospital No. 5
Comrade Zh. F. Galinskaya

We are sending you today Citizen I. N. ZAITSEV, declared uncontrollable by Moscow Health Department Forensic Medical Commission No. 3. He is to be subjected to compulsory chemotherapy. The court authorization is appended to this letter.

Secretary to the Cheryomushki District People's Court
N. Khotulyova
May 27 1979

*Secret*

### DECISION OF MOSCOW HEALTH DEPARTMENT
### FORENSIC MEDICAL COMMISSION NO. 9

On May 28 1979, the commission, consisting of Dr. B. Yu. Khotulyov (Chairman), and psychiatric consultants Dr. E. R. Rayenko and Dr. S. T. Lunts, examined the patient Ilya Nikolayevich ZAITSEV, admitted for compulsory chemotherapy on the instructions of the Cheryomushki District People's Court.

The patient is accused of malicious hooliganism under Article 206, Section 2, of the RSFSR Criminal Code. He is accused of publicly burning his identity papers on Kuznetsky Bridge Street while under the influence of drugs. He is further accused of harassing passersby by shouting anti-Soviet slogans and through the use of abusive language. He pretends to be a well-known journalist and a member of the CPSU Central Committee Press Corps.

As a result of our examination, we have established that the patient is in a condition of psychomotor excitation. He displays emotional instability and his mood is explosive. He is unable to adjust to his surroundings and is beyond normal human contact. His psychosis manifests itself in aggressive behavior and an obsessive belief that he is supposed to travel abroad as part of a delegation from the CPSU Central Committee. He is given to changing his surname periodically. "Belkin", "Orlov", "Volkov", etc., are among the names by which he has referred to himself.

Diagnosis: The patient I. N. Zaitsev is suffering from

manic-depressive psychosis and is not responsible for his own actions.

Treatment prescribed: The patient should be subjected to compulsory chemotherapy for a period of not less than three months. 0.25 gr. Aminazine to be injected intravenously daily.

Commission Chairman B. Khotulyov
Members E. Rayenko
S. Lunts

May 28 1979

That was it. Two forged documents, concocted by a brother and sister, were enough to lock away one of the country's best-known journalists (not to mention Brezhnev's favorite) in an MVD Special Hospital (read: prison). It takes just a couple of fictitious documents (the so-called authorization received from the People's Court was never found), and somebody can be thrown behind bars, and not even under his or her own name. He is placed in a concrete cell with soundproofed walls and an impressive number of beefy medical orderlies to look after him, strait-jacket, wet sheets and a needle full of the tranquilizer aminazine never beyond their reach. And if it hadn't been a question of telling Brezhnev about the disappearance of Belkin on the eve of his trip to Vienna, if Suslov, Churbanov and Shcholokov hadn't become mixed up in it together with a special investigator and the best detectives in the Moscow CID, then three months later this particular "patient" would have left the hospital either with partial amnesia or as a candidate for the local crematorium. I found myself wondering how many others like Belkin can be found in so-called "special hospitals" in Moscow, Tula, Saratov, Novorossiysk or wherever, and how much aminazine, barbamil, haloperidol, sanapax, frenolon, largactil and other tranquilizers or stimulants are being pumped into completely innocent people . . .

Belkin was asleep, but his rest was far from that of a normal human being. It was more like a temporary reprieve in the life of a tortured animal. Who could have imagined that a man who only three weeks before had gone har-

pooning in the Caspian, climbing and collecting edelweiss
in the Pamirs, falling for the next pretty woman to come
along, and finally trying to uncover a major drug ring all
by himself—who could have imagined that this young,
talented, energetic journalist would now be lying on a bunk
in a cell with concrete floor and walls, showing no reaction
to the voices of others and only occasionally staring into
empty space with clouded eyes, as completely devoid of
understanding as a newborn calf.

"He's been throwing himself against the wall and demanding aminazine all the time," Svetlov said. "I thought
he'd smash his head in. They had to give him an injection—
half a dose. What will happen to him after this I can't
imagine."

"Where's the head doctor?" I asked.

"She's yelling a blue streak down in her office, waiting
for you to turn up."

"And where are Lunts and Rayenko?"

"They're in the consulting room discussing what's to be
done next. I told them that I wouldn't let them out of the
hospital until Belkin returned to normal. He's turned into
an addict, you know, demanding a fresh injection every
couple of hours or so."

"What happened to Khotulyov?"

Svetlov spread his hands helplessly. "He disappeared yesterday morning. He probably went to join the Old Man in
Uzbekistan. I would have flown there myself, only I had
to talk to Tsvigun at KGB headquarters yesterday. This is
between ourselves. He more or less told me that the KGB
itself sends drugs out of the country. This is one of its most
lucrative sources of foreign currency. Also, if they want to
supply one of these 'Red Brigades' or whatever with American dollars, it's easier for them to hand over a case of
opium. The 'Voice of America' was right in saying we
occupy third place in the world drug league—and that doesn't
include the deals they don't know about! Anyway, Tsvigun
and Tsinyov deal personally with anybody who breaks this
particular state monopoly. Tsvigun takes care of those inside
the country, Tsinyov of those outside. He told me that Khotulyov and Gridasov wouldn't be going anywhere. The KGB

are already lying in wait for them at Charshanga."

"What about Sysoyev?"

"He's flying back from Switzerland the day after to-morrow. Malenina is waiting for him."

"What are we going to do about Belkin?"

"I don't know. We were waiting for you to arrive."

"OK. Let's go join the doctors."

The consulting room was on the ground floor of the hospital just by the exit. We went down a long white corridor on the second floor, past long rows of freshly painted cells. Everything in this hospital reminded me of a prison, except that here everything was painted white and blue and the brawny, unshaven warders were dressed like medical orderlies in starched, white smocks. There was a checkpoint with a metal door by the staircase, and there was a similar door on the ground floor by the exit into the courtyard. The courtyard itself was surrounded by a high, barbed-wire fence and watchtowers. On the other side of the fence lay the little settlement where the medical staff lived. It was a beautiful place, lots of wooden dachas, spread around in a pine forest with summer-houses and interconnecting paths. Carved fences enclosed flower and vegetable gardens, which were grown and tended by the hospital's quieter inmates.

In fact, MVD Special Hospital No. 5 was not unlike a monastery where a ruling caste of doctors turned their patients into benign, pliant robots.

The six doctors who worked in the hospital's fourth department had control over the more violent patients, and they were all sitting in the consulting room, having been virtually arrested by Svetlov. They were under the constant protection of the MVD, which sent any number of dissidents and genuine schizophrenics and other psychotics to them for treatment. Nobody ever checked up on the activity of these medics, let alone disciplined them. Gorged on the fruit and vegetables which their patients cultivated for them, they were in control—sitting on top of the world. But they all saw now that they were on a knife-edge. Locking somebody up without the knowledge of the MVD was tantamount to turning the place into a private prison. It was an unforgivable crime, since it involved encroaching on the state's monopoly of punishment. Of course, they would do their best to defend themselves by blaming everything on Khotulyov, but I had no intention of discussing with them how Belkin had ended up there and how ostensible experts like themselves had tried to "cure" a perfectly healthy man by administering monstrous doses of aminazine.

I stared at their frightened faces and said, "Colonel Svetlov has already told you the circumstances of this case. We have three days to get this journalist back to normal. If we succeed, I can't guarantee that you'll be able to continue your work here unhindered, but I can promise you that if Belkin is in a state to travel to Vienna, this will be taken into account when your future is decided. What do you have to say?"

Nobody uttered a word. A fat woman dressed in a doctor's coat, who had a moustache and a face like a trooper, turned away from me and was looking out of the window. The rest of them—three women of varying age and two men, one an albino, aged about thirty, and the other a wiry old man with an ancient pipe—just sat there, looking down at their feet.

"Look, this isn't a kindergarten and we're not playing games," I said sharply. "What I want to know is this. Is it possible for you to cure a drug addict in two days? Get your brains moving and start remembering what you were taught at medical school. If we have to, we'll transfer him to the Sklifosovsky or Serbsky Institutes. Now, how can we bring him around? I'm waiting."

"I can't understand your tone of voice," the moustached trooper said suddenly. "How dare you address us in this manner? We are carrying out our duty here. That Khotulyov was acting illegally is another matter. I warned them a long time ago that—"

"What's your name?" I asked rudely.

"Eleonora Frantsevna Shpigel. I am secretary of the party organization here."

"I don't need you. You may go."

"What?" she shouted indignantly.

"I am waiting for you to go," I replied.

A party secretary! Even here! I hadn't expected that!

Still, it stands to reason, I guess. Eighty percent of our doctors are party members, and they need some control.

Eleonora jumped up on her fat legs, moustache bristling, face purple with anger. "You . . . you . . . you . . ."

I waited. She waddled over to the door.

"Don't think you're going to get away with this, you spineless idiot!" she shouted. With that, she slammed the door so hard that it shook some test tubes and bottles in a nearby glass cabinet.

"Now to continue," I said.

"I'd like to say something," the old man with the pipe said. "What you're asking is impossible. That is, people can get unhooked, of course, but not in such a short time. He'll need to be tied down to his bed for a month in case he tries to kill himself. You get cases like this. At the Butyrki prison a dissident called Borisov hanged himself when they stopped injecting him with aminazine. He was twenty-seven, too. Tying them up is the only way to do it. Then all you can do is wait until they pull through."

"But addicts can sometimes cure themselves?"

"It's extremely rare and usually only happens in moments of severe stress."

"Like when?"

"I don't know . . . During a war, maybe, or while giving birth. But he's not a woman."

"What's your name?"

"Lunts. I was the one who insisted on the aminazine. Khotulyov wanted to prescribe sulfozine, but that would have been even worse."

"Couldn't you have seen to it that he wasn't prescribed anything?" I couldn't help but ask.

He stared at me with an open, frank expression. "But that's why people are sent to us in the first place. We *have* to prescribe something. How was I to know that he was brought here illegally?"

"Dr. Lunts," I said, screwing up my eyes. I suddenly had an idea. "If we are dealing with a patient who has a particularly strong penchant for the opposite sex, couldn't we make use of that in some way? I know of a case in Baku, for example, where a young addict stopped injecting himself with morphine when he fell in love with a beautiful girl from Riga."

"It's not too easy to find somebody to fall in love with *here*," Lunts said wryly. "Who would you suggest? Madame Shpigel?"

Valentin Pshenichny suddenly looked in at the door.

"Igor Iosifovich, he's crazy again, shouting for an injection."

"Tell the nurse to give him some novocaine," Lunts said. "It's only a placebo, like this empty pipe of mine, but he'll get some involuntary relief from the injection itself, and then the novocaine will act as a painkiller. The lack of drugs will be giving him a terrible aching feeling in the bones."

Pshenichny disappeared and Lunts continued. "We could give him ECT I suppose, but we haven't used that since 1953. Many people can't take it."

"All right," I said. "We won't give him electrotherapy. Let's try women therapy instead."

*The same day, after 14:30 hours*

Svetlov and I were sitting in one of the hospital's summer-houses, like two veteran procurers, discussing our options. If Shakh-Rybakov had managed to go cold turkey because of Aina Silinya, then we had to find somebody who could do the same thing to Belkin. The first person who came to mind was Inna, the typist from *Komsomolskaya Pravda*. We knew that she loved Belkin and would certainly be ready to do anything for him. If this were some sentimental love story or film, then the author would reward her for her self-sacrifice and affection by letting her be the one who enters the hero's cell and brings him salvation. But we were concerned with life in the real world, and we had to be honest about what would actually happen. Belkin had left Inna ages ago. She wouldn't be able to administer any kind of amorous shock to his system, so we had to forget about her.

You may think this all sounds very cynical, but the next person we considered was Aina Silinya. I remembered very well the section in Belkin's manuscript where he described her, half-naked on the beach near Baku during the struggle with Mosol. Belkin had Shakh in a full nelson, and while

Lina (alias Aina) was desperately trying to kiss her lover, her breasts inadvertently pressed against Belkin's arms. That had made quite an impact on him, despite the dramatic circumstances of the shooting. In general, he seemed strongly attracted to minors. I remembered that nymph from Rybachy Island too ... Svetlov and I spent a long time discussing this possibility. A plus was Belkin's character, inferred from what we already knew of him. But there were many factors which argued against. In the first place, Silinya was still legally a minor, and although she was no longer a little girl, we still had no right to involve her in amorous intrigues. Apart from that, she hadn't really recovered from the death of her bridegroom-to-be, Yury Rybakov. So, sadly, we also had to abandon that possibility.

Of course, the best person of all would have been Natasha Khotulyova. It wasn't surprising that he had fallen for her the first time he saw her at Baku airport. If only she hadn't died two days before.

"Lena Smagina?" Svetlov said.

I made a wry face. Of course, Akeyev's mistress from Kotlas wasn't bad-looking, but Belkin was hardly likely to go for somebody he would consider a commonplace provincial.

"OK," said Svetlov. "The Moscow CID has the records of forty thousand prostitutes on file. As a last resort, why don't we choose a seventeen-year-old whore from one of the hard-currency bars and see if she can't do her thing?"

Then I had my brilliant idea. It was Svetlov's mention of the currency bars that did it, and the sort of people who frequented the Metropole, the National and other Intourist hotels. I stood up.

"Let's go," I said. "I think I know our woman."

Without waiting for him to catch up, I rushed to the office of Dr. Zh. F. Galinskaya, who was in charge of the whole hospital. The outraged Zhanna Fyodorovna was closeted with Eleonora Shpigel, but I took no notice of either of them. I picked up the receiver and dialed Chief Prosecutor Rudenko at his private dacha. We were allowed to do this in cases of real emergency.

"Roman Andreyevich?" I said. "This is Shamrayev. Sorry

to disturb you. We've found Belkin alive, but he's in very
bad shape."

"What's wrong with him?"

"He was locked up in a mental hospital and has been
injected with aminazine. It's not fatal, but it will take some
time to break him of the addiction."

"How much time?" he asked.

"I'll be able to tell you that in a few hours. Meanwhile,
I'd like you to tell your grand-niece that he's alive. You
told me that she was very fond of him, remember?"

There was a moment's silence at the other end of the
line, and then Rudenko coughed in slight embarrassment.
"Do you want to tell her about it yourself?"

"Yes, if you'll let me."

"Why not? Write down her number: 455–12–12. Olga
Rudenko. Got it? 455–12–12. By the way, there's one more
thing. It would be better if as few people as possible discover
where you found him and what condition he's in. Do you
follow me?"

"More or less," I said. The Prosecutor obviously wanted
me to keep Belkin's state of health a secret from the Central
Committee for the time being. We had found him: that was
the main thing. I pressed for the dial tone and started to
dial Olga Rudenko's number.

*The same day, 17:30 hours*

She arrived in her own car, a white export model Lada. I
found it difficult to recognize her, she had changed so much
during her time at Moscow University.

None of the ladies I'd encountered at the Intourist, Metropole, or the Prague Hotels were as enticing as Olga Rudenko. True, I had asked her over the phone to look as
alluring as she could, but I hadn't realized that lovesick
women could perform such *incredible* miracles. She was
like a beautiful creature from another planet, with velvety
eyes and a mass of golden hair gathered into a tight bun.
She was wearing some kind of light, diaphanous shift which
emphasized her lithe, slender form.

I met her at the hospital gate, got into her car and filled
her in as much as I could.

"Olga, I have to tell you something. He isn't responsible for his actions. He's been injected with very large doses of a certain drug. I'm afraid that you may be in for a disappointment. You look unbelievably gorgeous. I could fall in love with you myself. I'm sure that if he were in a normal condition, he'd fall for you at first sight, but . . ."

"But what? What do you mean?"

"I'm afraid that when you see him, you may change your mind and refuse to . . ."

"Igor Iosifovich," she said with a smile. "I'm sorry, but how old are you?"

"Forty-two. So what?"

"Have you known a lot of women?"

"Well, I . . ."

"I bet that you've never slept with one in a mental hospital, have you? Am I right?"

I have to admit that these young people don't beat around the bush!

"You may be right," I said, smiling in my turn.

"Well, it's my first time, too. I find it extremely interesting. Let's go. I really want to do it!" There was a mischievous expression in her laughing eyes. She obviously regarded it as a challenge. I even felt envious of Belkin at that moment.

"Besides," she went on, "making love under the influence of drugs is fantastic!"

She sounded the horn, and a watchman appeared at the checkpoint. I motioned to him to open the gates, and Olga drove into the hospital.

*Ten minutes later*

We were standing outside the door of cell No. 18, listening to Belkin screaming and roaring. One moment he was hammering on the walls with his fist, the next he was hurling the full weight of his body against the door. "Injection, injection!" he was shouting all the time.

Olga put her eye to the peephole and peered in. Belkin was charging around the cell like a wild animal. She abruptly walked away from the door and with one deft movement let her shift fall to the ground. She was nearly naked. All she had on was a pair of briefs. She wasn't even wearing a bra. The same hand moved to unpin her bun, and the golden hair tumbled onto her suntanned shoulders and firm breasts.

"Open the door," she ordered the flabbergasted medical orderly.

I pressed a button, and the automatic door moved noisily to one side. The frenzied Belkin immediately charged at us from the depths of the cell, but suddenly stopped as if frozen to the spot. For the first time his eyes appeared to betray some measure of recognition.

He backed away as Olga entered the cell like a lion-tamer about to face a wild animal.

"Shut the door," Olga commanded imperiously, her eyes fixed on Belkin. "And bring us a mattress."

Every twenty minutes or so after that they would ask us for something—food, cognac, clean sheets or cigarettes.

"A definite calming effect," mused Dr. Lunts. "Not a complete cure, to be sure, but a certain return to normality. I think you may have been right."

# Epilogue

EXTRACT FROM A TASS REPORT
On June 15 1979, Comrade L. I. Brezhnev, Secretary-General of the CPSU and Chairman of the Presidium of the Supreme Soviet, left Moscow for Vienna to meet President J. Carter. During their meeting they will be signing the Strategic Arms Limitation Agreement between the USSR and the USA (SALT–2) and will also exchange views on bilateral relations... Accompanying Comrade Brezhnev at the airport were the following: Politburo members Yu. V. Andropov, V. V. Grishin, A. P. Kirilenko, A. N. Kosygin, A. Ya. Pelshe, M. A. Suslov; Candidate members P. N. Demichov and V. V. Kuznetsov; CPSU Central Committee members B. P. Bugayev and N. A. Shcholokov; Candidate members S. K. Tsvigun and G. K. Tsinyov; Member of the CPSU Central Auditing Commission Yu. M. Churbanov ... Accompanying Comrade Brezhnev on the flight to Vienna were the chief of CPSU Ideological Section L. M. Zamyatin and a group of accredited journalists.

EXTRACT FROM INSTRUCTION NO. 156, ISSUED BY THE USSR
PUBLIC PROSECUTOR ON JUNE 15 1979
In recognition of the professionalism and drive shown by I. I. Shamrayev and V. N. Pshenichny in carrying out a government task involving the uncovering of a particularly serious criminal action in the shortest possible time, I hereby instruct that the following special preferments be made: Igor Iosifovich SHAMRAYEV to be given the rank of Senior Juridical Counselor, and Valentin Nikolayevich PSHENICHNY the rank of Junior Juridical Counselor.

EXTRACT FROM INSTRUCTION NO. 429,
ISSUED BY USSR MINISTER OF INTERNAL AFFAIRS,
GENERAL N. SHCHOLOKOV, ON JUNE 18 1979

In recognition of the professionalism, courage and resourcefulness displayed by Comrade M. A. Svetlov in carrying out a task on behalf of the government, as a member of an inter-departmental investigation team, I hereby authorize that Marat Alekseyevich SVETLOV, head of Moscow CID Second Section, Third Department, be awarded the rank of Colonel of Militia.

EXTRACT FROM INSTRUCTION NO. 336, ISSUED BY THE
MOSCOW CITY COUNCIL ON JUNE 28 1979

As a result of representations made by the USSR Public Prosecutor, the Moscow City Council will make available the following accommodation to Comrade I. I. Shamrayev, Special Investigator and Senior Juridical Counselor: a one-room apartment measuring 21.8 square meters, address— 6 Red Army Street, Apartment No. 37.

Signed: V. Promyslov
Chairman of Moscow City Council
N. Pegov
Secretary to the Council

EXTRACT FROM THE SECRET CORRESPONDENCE BETWEEN
KGB FIRST DEPUTY CHAIRMAN, S. K. TSVIGUN, AND
THE USSR PUBLIC PROSECUTOR, R. A. RUDENKO

... I have to inform you that, on June 13 1979, an attempt was made to steal a military helicopter near the town of Charshanga in Uzbekistan. In the gun battle which followed, the following wanted citizens were killed: Boris Yurevich Khotulyov and Semyon Yakovlevich Gridasov. They were found to be in possession of foreign currency, diamonds and other valuables, together with five boxes containing narcotics. These objects to the value of 7.5 million roubles have been handed over to the USSR Finance Ministry.

EXTRACT FROM PUBLIC PROSECUTOR
RUDENKO'S INSTRUCTION TO SPECIAL INVESTIGATOR
SHAMRAYEV, DATED JUNE 17 1979

Concerning the illegal imprisonment of *Komsomolskaya Pravda* correspondent V. Belkin. In accordance with Article 211 of the RSFSR Criminal Code and the regulations concerning surveillance by the Public Prosecutor's Department, I rule that:

1. All materials relating to the arrest of V. Akeyev and thirty-three others on the charge of drug trafficking should be handed over to the MVD Anti-Fraud Squad to be incorporated into the investigation of the Chief Pharmaceutical Authority being carried out by MVD department head N. P. Malenina.
2. All materials relating to the illegal arrest of Citizen V. Belkin at Baku airport, as well as to drug trafficking in Azerbaidzhan, should be passed on to the Public Prosecutor of the Azerbaidzhan SSR, Comrade A. V. Gasanov.
3. Bearing in mind the instruction received from Comrade N. I. Savinkin, the head of the CPSU Administrative Organs Department, as well as the fact that the Deputy Minister of Health, General Balayan, is also the head of a KGB Special Department, responsible for carrying out work of extreme importance to the state, all charges against Comrade Balayan concerning abuse of power should be dropped.
4. Monies and valuables to the sum of approximately 1.5 million roubles confiscated during the course of the investigation, including the 100,000 roubles recovered from the baggage office at Baku airport, are deemed to be the property of the state and have been transferred to the account of the Ministry of Finance.
5. Criminal proceedings relating to the premeditated murder of Yury Rybakov and Olga Dolgo-Saburova should be halted in view of the death of the person accused of both murders, S. Ya. Gridasov.

EXTRACT FROM THE SECRET CORRESPONDENCE
OF KGB FIRST DEPUTY CHAIRMAN, S. K. TSVIGUN, AND
THE USSR PUBLIC PROSECUTOR, R. A. RUDENKO

As a footnote to our letter of June 14 1979, I have to inform
you that on June 10 in Geneva, V. V. Sysoyev, the head of
the USSR Health Ministry's Chief Pharmaceutical Authority, applied to the Swiss government for political asylum.
According to information received from our agents, the
reason for Sysoyev's defection was a broadcast put out by
the "Voice of America", giving details of the arrest of Sysoyev's own agents on drug trafficking charges in Moscow.
Additional information received in Moscow from Geneva
has revealed that, on June 14, V. Sysoyev died in a car
crash in circumstances which remain unexplained.

EXTRACT FROM A LETTER WRITTEN BY
R. ROMANOV, CHAIRMAN OF THE COUNCIL OF MINISTERS'
CENSORSHIP COMMITTEE, TO L. KORNESHOV, CHIEF
EDITOR OF *KOMSOMOLSKAYA PRAVDA*

Regarding the article written by your correspondent, Comrade Belkin, about the misuse of drugs by teenagers in Baku,
I have to inform you that this report cannot be published,
since *there is no drug-abuse problem in the USSR*.